PRAISE FOR

BAD HABITS

"A primal scream of a book . . . Amy Gentry is in utter control of this anaconda of a story as it twists, squeezes, and lashes out at the reader. And all the reader can do is stare helplessly back, mesmerized. In case it's not clear, I loved it."
— Laura Lippman, *New York Times* best-selling author of *Sunburn* and *Lady in the Lake*

"With deft, crisp prose and unerring wit, Amy Gentry charts a singular young woman's perilous ascent to the academic firmament — and then unravels all the secrets she had to keep to get there. By turns wicked and tender, ghastly and hilarious, *Bad Habits* is Amy Gentry's best book yet — and the most fun I've had in ages."
— Elizabeth Little, *Los Angeles Times* best-selling author of *Dear Daughter* and *Pretty as a Picture*

"Hailing Jamesian roots as it explodes into the world of academia, *Bad Habits* layers precise detail, dread, and dark desire in an addictive page-turning story. The unforgettable ending made me immediately want to read the entire book again. Do not miss this hypnotic masterpiece."
— Mindy Mejia, author of *Everything You Want Me to Be* and *Strike Me Down*

"Whip-smart and beautifully written, *Bad Habits* is one hell of an exploration of what can happen when friendship tangos with an insatiable appetite for success and control. This novel is unexpected and surprising, and has a diabolical ending I won't forget anytime soon."

—Hannah Mary McKinnon, internationally best-selling
author of *Sister Dear*

"With shades of *Special Topics in Calamity Physics,* Gillian Flynn, and Megan Abbott, this seductive novel of psychological suspense and its corkscrew-like twists and turns held me in their grip until the final, jaw-dropping reveal."

—May Cobb, author of *Big Woods* and *The Hunting Wives*

BAD HABITS

ALSO BY AMY GENTRY

Last Woman Standing

Good as Gone

BAD HABITS

AMY GENTRY

Mariner Books
Houghton Mifflin Harcourt
Boston   New York
2021

For information about permission to reproduce selections from this book, write to trade.permissions@hmhco.com or to Permissions, Houghton Mifflin Harcourt Publishing Company, 3 Park Avenue, 19th Floor, New York, New York 10016.

hmhbooks.com

Library of Congress Cataloging-in-Publication Data
Names: Gentry, Amy, author.
Title: Bad habits / Amy Gentry.
Description: Boston : Mariner Books, Houghton Mifflin Harcourt, 2021.
Identifiers: LCCN 2020034157 (print) | LCCN 2020034158 (ebook) |
ISBN 9780358408574 (trade paperback) |
ISBN 9780358126546 (hardcover) | ISBN 9780358439974 |
ISBN 9780358440871 | ISBN 9780358125051 (ebook)
Subjects: LCSH: Psychological fiction. | GSAFD: Suspense fiction.
Classification: LCC PS3607.E567 B33 2021 (print) |
LCC PS3607.E567 (ebook) | DDC 813/.6—dc23
LC record available at https://lccn.loc.gov/2020034157
LC ebook record available at https://lccn.loc.gov/2020034158

Book design by Margaret Rosewitz

Printed in the United States of America
DOC 10 9 8 7 6 5 4 3 2 1

for ln & smy & ncb

Gwen's perfect laugh reaches me from across the hotel lobby just as I step into the elevator. Through some acoustical trick of polished floors and curved walls, the unmistakable peals echo inside the elevator for a moment, a memory replayed in stereo. I turn just in time to catch a glimpse of her tossing her dark, glossy hair beneath a glinting halo of upside-down wineglasses at the hotel bar.

"Eleventh floor," I say.

The grad student I picked up at the reception, all elbow-patched corduroy and absurd woolen scarf and lips pouting suggestively around the word *Lukács,* pushes the button. I try to focus on this eager young man from Yale—or is it Harvard? Fresh off my keynote, I wasn't paying attention, but it hardly matters. The doors start to close. Once we're alone, I'll slide my hand down his chest, check his badge, and use the lanyard to yank him in close for a kiss as we rise skyward to my corner suite.

This train of thought is halted by the shuffle-and-clatter of drunk women in interview heels. A pair of assistant professors

I recognize from the reception waves for us to hold the elevator, and my grad student, playing the gentleman, leans past me for the button. As the doors reverse their course, I note with displeasure more stragglers on the way—an elderly woman with a cane, a mother dragging a small boy. Not only do these newcomers promise to make my elevator ride with Harvard substantially less interesting, but their slipshod progress across the lobby is giving me ample time to reflect on the oddity of my first impulse, which was to ignore Gwen altogether, to pretend, as I was on the point of doing a moment ago, that I didn't see her, didn't know her, haven't spent half a lifetime trying to be her.

But I have seen her, and I can't unsee her now.

I dip into my pocket for the hotel key in its soft paper sleeve and hand it to my Ivy League companion. "Wait for me in my room," I command, without listening for an answer. From ten paces away, the women are already squint-and-scanning our badges. In another moment one of them will recognize me from my talk and buttonhole me with the words, "Your book changed my entire way of thinking about *X*," a conversation sure to segue into a full-blown explanation of *her* book, *Discourses on Y,* and a request that I read and endorse it. Without a backward glance, I step out of the elevator and into the lobby, calculating the odds that I could lose my starfucker to a bigger star in the time it takes him to get to the eleventh floor. These two women certainly don't look important but, then, I absolutely refuse to squint.

By now the lobby is filling up, and Gwen is temporarily obscured by clusters of conference attendees deep in probing conversations about Heidegger that might lead to screwing later on. I've sighted Gwen around so many corners over the years that for a moment I let myself think I am mistaken, experimenting with the mixture of relief and sadness this would bring. But the closer I get, the more certain I am that the woman perched at the bar, bare legs crossed at the knee, one hand pushing back her hair as if to listen more attentively to the handsome older man toward whom she is radiating her special brand of vanilla-cashmere calm, is Gwendolyn Whitney.

My best friend.

When she sees me, Gwen's eyes widen and her mouth opens, and I nervously anticipate some outburst of emotion, something to bridge the ten-year gap since we saw each other last. But that's not Gwen's way. Instead, she lays her thin white hands on the bar, closes her eyes for a moment as if pained, and steps down from the bar chair, losing a few inches of height in the process. Whispering a word to her conversation partner, she walks around the back of his chair, and by the time I reach her, she's settled her mouth into a smile tinged with just a hint of sadness — an acknowledgment that we have not, despite our best intentions, kept up.

"Gwen."

She notices my name badge. *"Claire?"*

"I go by my middle name now."

"It suits you." She opens her arms. "So good to see you."

I enter into the obligatory hug and find myself briefly enveloped in her subtle perfume. I back away quickly and the scent dies.

"Of course, I should have known you'd be here." She indicates the sign in the lobby. "How's the conference going so far?"

"Good. I just gave a keynote." She looks a bit too surprised, so I add quickly, "There are several. It wasn't the opening or closing address." More of an audition, really, for the Very

Important University with whom I am interviewing first thing in the morning. One more reason I really ought to hurry up to the room and conclude my business with Harvard on the early side.

"Still," she says, nodding appreciatively.

"Are you here long?"

She shakes her head. "Just for the night. I'm flying to Rome in the morning."

Typical of Gwen to avoid the big chains and spend the night in a luxe boutique hotel. I can't help but feel a tingle of pride that our tastes have once again converged, however accidentally —the Association of Emerging Studies, for all its problems, has a reputation for style. The quaint deco exterior of this historical 1920s high-rise has been preserved, its interior made over with a ferocious sleekness. "Wish I could say the same."

"But you're happy at . . . ?" She checks my badge again, noting the name of my university and, I assume, its less-than-glamorous location. Even though Gwen and I are technically only friends in the sense of people who haven't yet deleted one another from social media, it stings a bit to know she hasn't followed my career online, knows nothing of my book and my other academic successes. However painful it is to be reminded of the tragic accident that led to Gwen leaving the Program in the middle of our first year, I have managed to keep up with her various career shifts since then—the brief stint in law school, the turn to public policy, and then various NGOs for clean drinking water, the eradication of global poverty, that sort of thing. I am momentarily struck with the fear that her more virtuous world is so far removed from academia that she doesn't realize my university is Research I, and therefore a terrific job.

"Very happy," I say, wishing I could add that if tenure review goes as it should, I'll soon be done with backwaters for good. The hiring committee chair of the Very Important University did, after all, nod twice during my lecture. I content myself with saying, "I'm up for tenure next year."

Gwen frowns. "That can't be right."

"I made good time," I say modestly.

"Still, that would mean it's already been . . . ?"

"Ten years."

She puts a slender hand to her forehead, closing her eyes briefly. Then she opens them again, and her smile returns. "Look at you. You have the life we used to dream about."

I take in the monastic luxury of her simple cream dress, suddenly self-conscious about my artsy academic getup—black leather pants and a bulky woolen cocoon of a wrap. The oxblood boots that draw compliments from the tenured elite of bicoastal universities feel clumsy and adolescent next to Gwen's pale, expensive-looking pumps.

I smile tightly. "We'll see if it lasts."

She shakes her head and waves her hand toward the tweedy crowd. "You'll get tenure. You were born for this."

But Gwen is the one who was born for it, not me. She went to better schools, had better ideas, sounded smarter in class, looked smarter, *was* smarter. She cared about all the right things and hurt no one intentionally. She was perfect. If not for certain fatal events, she'd be the one giving the keynotes, and I'd still be in her shadow.

The next moment she proves it, annihilating me with a single word.

"I've missed you, Mac."

MAC

1

I was born Mackenzie Claire Woods in Wheatsville, Illinois, a Chicago suburb with a historic downtown and an ice rink in the shopping mall. My father wanted to give me an old-fashioned name like Mary or Sarah, but my mother overruled him. She thought Mackenzie sounded unique.

A lot of other moms must have thought so, too, because five years later the whole kiddie pageant circuit was lousy with them. There were two in my "baby bunnies" ice-skating class, one in jazz-and-tap, and one in the baton-twirling camp my mom ran out of our backyard three summers running. To my mom, this only proved she'd picked a name worthy of a sequined sash.

Though they lasted only a few short years, the pageants loom large in my memory. Childhood, to me, is the acrid smell of Cover Girl base, the scalp-tingle of a French braid, the flash of my mother's diamond studs as she knelt to do my makeup, the sound of my father's hands clapping when I won the crown.

My mother trained me well, but she didn't clap. She had her hands full with my baby sister, Lily, who had recently transformed from a babbling infant to a stiff little stranger prone to violent fits. My mom sat through my competitions waiting for Lily to go off, her features drawn so taut, you'd never believe she was the Miss Decatur, Illinois, with the brilliant smile in the framed mantelpiece pictures. Except for the earrings, they looked nothing alike.

My father, on the other hand, looked just as he had in their wedding photo, the same thick brown hair rising from a decisive hairline. When I was very young, I confusedly believed he was a writer because of the awed way my mother spoke of "his" books on the bookshelf. In fact, he had only read them, not written them; forcing other people to read them was his trade. He was a high school English teacher, though he spoke as little as possible about his job and always kept a drink within arm's reach. Wherever he went, he seemed to have a wonderful time, which is another way of saying that if he wasn't going to have a wonderful time, he didn't show up. He started coming to the pageants when I started winning them.

So, I kept winning.

Until, one day when I was eight, everything changed.

The day began, as so many did back then, with baton-twirling. Mom knocked a pair of drumsticks together, five-year-old Lily clinging to her shin, while I marched through the soft grass in a phalanx of pageant hopefuls, admiring the way the sun glinted on my baton. Then I noticed my father at the kitchen window, mixing a drink.

"Mackenzie Claire!" my mom hollered. "Eyes on your baton!"

My fingers tripped, and the baton fell to the ground with a soft thump. I glanced toward the window, but my father was already drifting away.

After the lesson, my mother dragged him down to the basement to yell at him. I caught Lily's name and mine; *ten o'clock in the morning, for chrissake;* and *the least you could do.* I turned up the TV and sat by Lily on the couch, picking the scab under my T-shirt where the rickrack on my leotard left a red welt.

My father stomped up the basement stairs and into the living room, a shoebox under his arm. "Come on, princess. We're getting out of here." I knew he was talking to me. He hardly ever spoke to Lily, and never called her *princess.*

We went to the mall. After he dropped off the box at a shoe repair place, he asked me where I wanted to go next, and I pointed at the ear-piercing kiosk I wasn't allowed to visit until my tenth birthday, and he laughed.

"The world's your oyster, princess." His breath was whiskey-sweet.

When the hot spike of pain in my earlobes had dulled to a throb, we hit the food court for lunch. I pulled him toward the Hungry Panda, counting on him to forget my mother's favorite expression, "A moment on the lips, a lifetime on the hips." I was dumping soy sauce over a glistening pile of fried rice when I noticed my father staring over my shoulder.

I turned. Behind me was the carousel, a rotating gilt birthday cake I treasured from afar. Yet another thing my mother didn't allow; there was never enough time, and the flashing lights were too much for Lily. But today was a special day, a father-daughter day. A pierced ears, Hungry Panda day. I held my breath and waited for him to ask if I'd like a ride.

"This is it," he said softly. "Mall Chinese and a fucking calliope."

My hopes ebbed. "What's a *cull-lie-pee?*"

He blinked at me, his eyes still far away. "Calliope. Queen of the Nine Muses. Her son Orpheus brought Eurydice back from hell but lost her when he looked back. Careless fellow, Orpheus."

I couldn't help feeling this was some kind of test. I looked around. "Are they . . . here?"

He laughed abruptly. "It's also a kind of pipe organ. But that one's a synthesizer. Fake, like everything else."

Although I had only taken a few bites of my lunch, he was clearly ready to go. He braced his palms against the table edge to scoot out his chair, but then he paused, leaning forward until I could see the little red spot in the corner of his left eye. "Listen, princess. You don't belong here any more than I do. We were made for better things. Remember that."

I did remember, because after he dropped me back off at home that day, we never heard from him again. He never even picked up his shoes.

With my father gone, the pageants had to stop. There was no money for them, much less for ice-skating, voice lessons, jazz-and-tap. It was only a matter of time before everything worth having, from cable TV to name-brand macaroni and cheese, disappeared from our house. My parents' wedding photo vanished, too, along with all other pictures of my father.

And then my name was gone.

"I have to go back to work. I'll be taking classes at night," my mother said, putting her hands on my shoulders. "I need you to be a brave girl, Mac."

Mac. As if she didn't have time to say the whole thing. It stung like a slap.

But if the pageant world was over for good, at least its vague militarism had prepared me well for the role of *brave girl.* I attacked my new duties with zeal. Lily entered kindergarten, and every morning we marched to the bus stop together, her hot, clenched fist in my hand. After school I met her at the door of her special class and ushered her safely through the gauntlet of kids who only stopped shrieking, it seemed, to point and stare. At home, I'd make a snack and play with her wispy brown curls while we watched TV. On nights when my mom had class, I lay beside her in the dark and sang songs from commercials until she fell asleep.

Sometimes, I burned with a helpless hatred of the things that made her, and therefore us, different. Other people's emotions affected Lily like rasps drawn over her skin, and the rocking and hand-flapping she used to comfort herself drew stares in public. Her long silences and refusal to make eye contact disquieted strangers. Then, too, her tantrums had grown more intense since our father left, and harder to predict; sometimes when we walked together to the bus, she would come to a full stop, tilt her head back, and wail, while kids hung out of the bus windows yelling obscenities. I had to stop holding her in my lap after she accidentally split my lip with her elbow during a commercial she didn't like. We couldn't eat out, even when the budget allowed; the one time my mom took us to Bob Evans, to celebrate her nursing job, Lily's napkin fell off her lap and the ensuing chaos meant we had to leave before the appetizers arrived.

At school, Lily's survival was my survival. By fifth grade, I was an expert at protecting her, taking out hall passes to check on her at recess, skipping my own recess to patrol her lunch. I'd tackle any kid in any grade who called her a name, flailing my fists until I ran out of fight or a teacher split us up. Once I threatened to throw one of her bullies into the river that ran through downtown Wheatsville—a glorified creek, really, but I'd seen a mob movie while my mom was at work one night and thought it sounded cool. I was suspended for "violent behavior," and the school counselor recommended therapy.

My mother was furious. She threw my conduct sheet down on the table and said, "Can't you just hold it together a few more years, Mac?"

But in the end, she was the one who fell apart.

When I was eleven, my mother disappeared for a week.

Since the car was gone, too, I assumed she had left for good. Strange that it had never occurred to me that she could leave, since my father had done it. But, three years later, that tragedy seemed unavoidable, even a little romantic. Besides, he had left us with her; she had left us with no one.

I didn't panic. Lily would be able to tell if I panicked, and then someone would find out we were alone in the house. I didn't know what would happen next, but I knew it would be bad. That our mother might be hurt, even dead, was a thought I didn't allow, because it would make no difference to our current situation. I dropped it down a well so deep, even I couldn't see the bottom, and I turned off my feelings like turning off a tap. It was strangely easy to do, so easy I barely noticed I was doing it. Every morning, I got Lily up and took her to school and dropped her off at class, and every evening I threw a frozen pizza in the oven for dinner like nothing was wrong. I even learned how to run the dishwasher.

On the fifth day, we ran out of frozen pizzas. I went into my mom's room, which I'd been avoiding, to look for cash.

I started with the curio boxes that crowded her dresser, a collection of crystal shells, porcelain hearts, and beveled, brass-seamed mirror boxes, all covered in dust and grime from neglect. I'd long ago exhausted my curiosity about them, but now I opened them all one by one, just in case, and peered inside. Next, I searched the dresser, from the top drawer with its stretched-out bras the color of graying skin to the bottom, where an emerald-green bathing suit I recognized from my mom's old pageant pictures lay folded neatly under heaps of faded bikinis with rotting straps. I unfolded it, and out dropped a fuzzy black box with my mom's diamond studs nestled inside. She'd stopped wearing them around the time my father left.

I put the diamonds in my ears and watched them twinkle like little stars. Then I took them off and put them in my pocket. It wasn't like she needed them now.

On the seventh day, Lily refused to take her bath. She allowed herself to be undressed while the water ran, but when I cut the faucet off, she stood shivering next to the tub, feet cemented to the mat.

"Lily, it's bath time," I said, keeping my voice deliberately neutral. "Get in."

"No."

Things could always get worse. What would happen if kids started smelling her on the bus? Eventually a teacher would notice and tell someone in charge, and we'd be taken away.

"Lily, you have to. *Please.*" Tears prickled in my eyes. I blinked angrily at them, knowing they'd only make things harder. I could almost feel Lily shudder as one escaped and raced toward my chin.

Her jaw set. "I don't want to."

I tried to make myself breathe deeply. *Lily is my sister,* I reminded myself, and then, *Lily's survival is my survival.* "What's wrong?"

"Mom does bath."

Breathe. "I do bath now."

"Mom does bath."

"Mom isn't here right now." I said it as gently as I could.

She stared obstinately at the door. "Mom does—"

"When I was eight, I did my *own* bath," I snapped, the compulsion to cry suddenly shoved aside by a feeling like a balloon swelling in my chest, about to burst. It was rage, the same rage I had vented on the playground in kicks and punches at the kids who made fun of Lily, now directed at Lily herself. Rage at her immovable flesh, her insurmountable will, her blamelessness. Rage at the dwindling pile of pennies in the change dish and the rubbery ground meat I'd microwaved for dinner in a frozen block, its cold center bleeding all over the plate, and finally, rage at the thought of what would happen if Lily refused to bathe tomorrow and tomorrow and tomorrow. Some part of me watched from a distance while inside me the balloon grew bigger and bigger, pushing against my rib cage until I thought it would crack.

Powerless to stop myself, too exhausted to try, I took a step forward and put out my hand with no plan for what came next.

Just then I heard the front door open and shut.

"Mom does bath," Lily said, smug.

The woman who appeared at the bathroom door barely looked like our mother. Her week of absence had turned her the color of bruises, purple around the eyes and yellowish everywhere else. The skin sagged around her scrawny elbows and too-prominent collarbone as if she wore someone else's castoffs. She stared at us unseeing for a moment. Then she began to sob, and the bag of bones rattled to life. I drew back as she threw her arms around Lily, who politely ignored her tears.

When Mom released her, Lily stepped into the bathtub

without a word. I watched numbly as they began to perform the evening ritual of bath time, thinking only that it was over. There would be no more raw meat for dinner. Although it was only eight o'clock, I went to bed and fell asleep instantly.

Sometime later that night, I awoke to the sound of my mom on the phone in the next room. I listened for as long as I could keep my eyes open.

"I tried to stop on my own, I swear, but the pain was so bad. I thought, I'll just take enough to get through work every day and I'll get it somewhere else, anywhere but the clinic . . . I don't even know what that guy gave me, Karen. I swear, I didn't know how long I was gone." Odd, dry sobs, like a record skipping. "I need help. I'm drowning, I'm drowning, I'm drowning . . ."

The words went on and on, and then I was asleep again, no longer in bed, but back in the bathroom with Lily, trying to get her into the tub, stuck in the moment right before my mom came in. This time, I shoved Lily as hard as I could. Her eyes went wide and she fell backward, her head hitting the porcelain with a crack. Then she was underwater, not in the bathtub, but in the river, her hair waving all around. Beneath her, in the murky green depths, a forest of dead men planted in concrete reached up their arms.

The clinic didn't press charges for the stolen opioids, but my mom's job was gone for good, her license suspended. The court ordered outpatient rehab, a caseworker for home visits, physical therapy, pain management classes. *Everything's mandated but an income,* she cracked sourly. *How're you supposed to get that.*

A girl on the bus whose mom worked at the same clinic said all nurses have aching backs, but they don't all become drug addicts. Every day for weeks, she hung over the back of the seat in front of me and told me about the cancer patients who had died in pain because my mom shorted their IV bags. I just stared out the window.

I could hardly bear to be in the same room with my mother now. She ate ferociously but gained no weight, and she'd picked up smoking again, which made the house smell and Lily cough. Her breath reeked so badly, I wondered if the drugs were still sitting in her stomach, sending poisonous gases up her throat. *A moment on the lips, a lifetime on the hips.*

Her new plan was to homeschool Lily. A friend had told her she could apply for aid from the state if she was Lily's full-time caregiver. "Public school isn't serving her needs," she recited. "Anyway, it's only temporary. I'll get a job in home health as soon as I get my license back."

The moment she said the word *temporary,* I knew it wasn't. Lily was her project now, and my mom never did my hair again. Neither of us could forget that I had taken her place for a week. In fact, I had been too brave.

I had longed for independence from Lily, but the reality was awful. I missed her horribly. The thick shell I'd grown protecting her was not so easy to dismantle, and school was achingly lonely and purposeless. My classmates quickly forgot why they weren't supposed to sit next to me on the bus, but the aura of disgrace hung around me like a fog, mingling with the stink of poverty. All my clothes came from church basements and garage sales now, and I outgrew them far too quickly. My mom cast evil glances at my lengthening limbs, interpreting my lurch into puberty as an act of rebellion. She guarded my sister so jealously that I had to sneak into Lily's room at night to sing her to sleep with the song from her favorite movie, *Spirit: Stallion of the Cimarron.*

One night, Lily interrupted the opening bars. "When are you going away, Mac?"

"I'm not going anywhere," I said gravely. I had just turned thirteen. My options were limited.

"Dad went away. Mom went away."

I still had nightmares about that week, though it had happened over a year ago. I answered carefully. "Mom was only gone a couple of days."

"Dad went away. Mom went away," she repeated matter-of-factly. "You'll go away. And you won't come back."

"I won't go away, Lily."

I could feel her evaluating the truth of the statement, processing it the way she processed everything, by running it through her body. The napkin on the floor of the Bob Evans, the screaming at the school bus.

"Okay, then," I amended. "If I go away, I'll come back for you."

This seemed to satisfy her.

After a moment, she said, "Do you know the difference between horses and ponies? Ponies are less than fourteen hands tall. Fourteen-point-two for English. A hand is four inches."

"Oh."

"And ponies have different *conformations.*"

"I promise I'll come back, Lily."

She sighed under the blanket. "Conformation means they have different bones. They look like horses, but they are an entirely different breed."

"Lily—"

"They can survive on a lot less grass."

We breathed quietly together in the darkened bedroom.

"I know," I whispered, choosing to hear, *Don't worry about me, I can wait.*

The day I turned fifteen, I walked to the nearest strip center and got a job at the Frogurt Palace. We'd never replaced the Pontiac my father drove away, and if I ever hoped to escape after high school, I had to start saving for a used car now.

I kept ten percent of my paycheck; the rest went to household expenses. This appeased my mother, who had less and less patience for my existence, and ensured we always had non-SNAP-eligible goods like toilet paper. My cash tips I rammed inside the smelliest shoe in the back of my closet—a needless precaution, since I was the only one who ever cleaned.

The Frogurt Palace was where I met Trace and the Kevins, a trio of red-eyed burnouts with sagging wallet chains who started coming in near the end of my shifts. I knew Trace vaguely from the bus, and Kevin Tran and Kevin Botti trailed behind him wherever he went. I let them have the frozen yogurt I cleaned out of the spigots every night, a grayish-pink slurry that tasted like strawberry toothpaste, and I wasn't their only benefactor; Quimby, the owner of the Golden Crown Video next door, kept them high and supplied for the price of listening to his weird stories. After a while, they convinced me to come along.

Quimby turned out to be a pale, puffy man in a sweaty T-shirt and eccentrically patterned chef pants who lived in the basement apartment under his store. With his baby face and unwashed hair slicked back from a balding pate, Quimby's age was impossible to determine, but I had to think the owner of a video store—even a shitty little video store that was mostly porn—had to be a lot older than us. On the rare occasion when a customer rang the bell, he'd run upstairs, exchanging his ratty bathrobe for an equally ratty blazer on the steps.

My first time smoking out at Quimby's, Trace held the bowl for me and told me to suck in. Just when I thought my lungs would burst, he released the carb, and a giant hit of smoke hammered my chest. I coughed like crazy and my eyes streamed, first with pain and then with relief as all the girls I had been —the brave girl, the tough girl, the winner, the wanter—exited the building, and I became nothing.

"Hamlet was, on reflection, not a wise name for any pet, even a golden retriever of his particular splendor."

On a winter afternoon my sophomore year, I sat on the floor with Trace and the Kevins, mightily stoned, sneaking a look at Quimby's wall of DVDs and videos. I couldn't make out the hand-scribbled labels on the spines, but they looked unsavory.

Quimby, as usual, pontificated from a beige recliner.

"However, my mother believed a young boy should never be talked out of a budding romance with Shakespeare, and so the dog's fate was sealed." He paused for dramatic effect. "The bullet that separated gorgeous breath from golden body was chalked up to a hunting accident, but I always suspected my father of pulling the trigger."

Trace yawned. Kevin Tran rubbed his shaven head; Kevin Botti took a hit.

Quimby's voice jabbed me like a finger in the back. "Want to watch one, Jennifer?" It was the first time he'd ever addressed me directly.

"Dude," said Trace, looking up from his combat boots for the first time in an hour. "Her name's Mackenzie. She's been coming here for, like, *months*."

"Of course, she has," Quimby said. "Darling Jennifer, please pick out something we'll all enjoy."

Either because I was getting paranoid, or because the recliner gave Quimby an imperial height, it felt more like a command than an invitation. Determined not to flinch, I leaned over, tipped out a videotape at random, and handed it to Quimby. All I could make out of the title was "*Madame de . . .*" —the ellipsis like a dirty wink. Kevin Botti passed me the bong, an obscure gesture of respect.

But Quimby was regarding the video with an expression of mild astonishment. "*The Earrings of Madame de . . .*" He said solemnly, "Gentlemen, there's more going on in Jennifer's scraggly little noggin than anyone knows." Then he swiveled the recliner and loaded the tape.

If it was porn, it certainly wasn't like what I had seen on the internet. It was black-and-white, with subtitles. In the beginning, a woman in an old-timey dress walked around her fancy bedroom trying to find something to sell. One by one, she touched her treasured possessions. The scene was shot from her point of view, so that in my stoned state, I could almost feel the cold slither of a diamond necklace over my palm, the tickle of fur under my fingers. A shudder of delight ran through me, pushing up on the roof of my mouth like a yawn, and suddenly I could see colors in the black-and-white. They were only the shy souls of colors, palest pink and pistachio green and robin's-egg blue, like a faint residue of reality lingering in the image. I forgot the subtitles and relaxed into pure deliciousness. The woman pawned some diamond earrings, but somehow they made their way back to her husband, and then her husband's lover, and then back to the woman again, around and around. She wrote a letter to her lover, ripped it to shreds, and threw it out of a train window, where it transformed into flurries of snow. Guns were drawn. The credits rolled. Tears streamed down my face.

I looked around. Trace and the Kevins were gone.

Quimby had been watching me for some time. "Oh, fools," he said tenderly.

Many years later, when I heard someone say the name of the film's director out loud — *Ophüls* — I felt like an idiot. But in the moment, I thought he meant the others, and blushed.

On my way out, he handed me a crumpled paper bag stuffed with videos.

"These are for you, Jennifer," he said. "When you need more, just let me know."

I dug up an old TV/VCR combo from the back of my father's closet, where it had been banished when we bought a DVD player. I dragged it into my closet and watched movies late into the night. The colors never came back, but I knew they were there, and that they were as close as I'd ever get to perfection.

And then I met Gwen.

December 29, 2021, 8:30 p.m.
SkyLoft Hotel, Los Angeles

t's Claire now," I remind her.

Gwen winces. "I'm sorry. Old habits die hard."

We look down at our very different shoes for a moment.

"So, *Claire*. Will you have a drink on me and catch up?"

"I shouldn't." Since the accident, I have been on certain medications that are strongly contraindicated for alcohol.

"Just one?" She smiles conspiratorially.

But I've already had one—a rather large glass of wine at the reception. "I have work to do tonight," I say, thinking of Harvard up in my hotel room.

"You always did work too hard." Her delicate allusion to our differences and how I so improbably overcame them seems to move her. She steps closer and touches my forearm. "Please?"

There's no word for losing a friend like Gwen. *Breakup, separation, split*—all for romantic partnerships, and all suggesting a clear end, something you don't get in a friendship unless you're one of those drink-throwers or *bitch!*-screamers in the viral videos. *Falling-out* is too final to describe the particular uncertainty, the lengthening silence. The only phrase we have for the slow, specific entropy of a dying friendship is *drifted apart*. As if you fell asleep sunbathing on floats and woke up on opposite sides of the swimming pool.

As if it didn't hurt.

Which is why, against my better judgment, against every instinct that tells me to go straight to bed and fuck my stranger and get a good night's sleep for tomorrow's interview, I nod and say, "Maybe just one."

Gwen points out a table in the corner, and we head in that direction.

"Your admirer at the bar will be disappointed." The man with the salt-and-pepper hair has been following us with his eyes. Now he pulls out his wallet and throws down a bill.

"Oh, he's not an admirer. Just killing time waiting for his lady friend," she says with a short laugh. "Besides, this always scares them off." She holds up her left hand and wiggles an engagement ring, though I could have sworn it wasn't there a moment ago, when her hands were folded on the bar.

"Congratulations." In the time-honored tradition of best friends, I take her hand to get a closer look and see a giant solitaire on a double-rowed band of tiny diamonds like teeth. Her fingers are cold and dry. I feel something like an electric shock at the contact and hold her hand a little longer so as not to jerk mine away. As a result, we are still connected at the fingertips when she climbs into her chair, and I am left with the distinct impression of having helped her into her seat. I draw my hand back and sit down. "It's stunning."

Gwen smiles her thanks, and I open my mouth to ask the next obvious question. But just then, with an alacrity I am certain he reserves for people who look like Gwen, the waiter appears. I point to a scotch located three-quarters of the way down the drink menu, at that precise inflection point that suggests both expensive tastes and a certain restraint in indulging them. "Double, neat."

It's Gwen's turn. "Make me something good?" She flashes the waiter a smile, and he scurries off to comply, leaving us alone.

"Who's the lucky guy?" I say, thankful that the interruption has kept me from betraying my rabid curiosity. "I had no idea you were even seeing someone."

She blushes. "I haven't posted anything about it online." And she names a recently exiled Brazilian director whose first film, made on a shoestring, was so universally adored that several big Hollywood names are rumored to be lined up for the second.

"Wow." My eyebrows shoot upward, though I manage not to gasp. "I can see why you're keeping that close to the vest. So, what's he like?"

"Oh, you know. Wonderful. Amazing." She laughs. "I never know how to describe people."

"He must be brilliant."

She shifts in her seat. "He's very private."

That seems like a clear enough signal to move on, but I can't help myself. "Must be hard for him being famous, then."

"He's not," she protests.

The waiter arrives with the drinks and we are spared the argument. He tosses a pair of thick white napkins on the table and sets down my tumbler of scotch and Gwen's slender highball, something cloudy with a twist.

"Cheers." She raises her glass. We click rims and take a sip.

While I'm still savoring the warm shudder of scotch going down, Gwen asks, "How are your mom and Lily?"

I grimace and exhale ninety-five-proof through my teeth. "They're great, thanks for asking."

"Did you see them at Christmas?"

"My mom knows not to expect me, with the conference," I say a little stiffly.

"Having a big annual conference smack between Christmas and New Year's must be awful."

"It really is," I lie.

"It's like a naked bid for loyalty." She wrinkles her nose.

I take another sip. I know all about naked bids for loyalty. My mom's first relapse happened just after I drove away to college for the first time. I wound up living at home and commuting. Further relapses always coincided with some important opportunity; my application to the Program was very nearly derailed by one of them.

Gwen breaks the silence with a laugh.

"I'm sorry I'm having so much trouble with your name. My mom used to have a patient named Claire. She always had her panic attacks at dinnertime for some reason. The phone would ring right as we were sitting down, and it would be Claire hiding in a bathroom stall at some charity banquet, and my mom would have to talk her down." She pauses and takes a sip, looking thoughtful. "I hope she's doing okay."

"Your mom?"

She laughs, startled. "Her patient. Mom and Dad are fine."

Of course, they are. What do a physics professor emeritus and a psychoanalyst with family money have to worry about? "They must be delighted about the engagement."

She's been fiddling with her napkin, and now she crumples it abruptly. "Gallant died last year."

"Oh no! I'm so sorry."

"Well, he was twenty-two years old. A ripe old age for a cat."

As Gwen launches into the details, I find myself drifting

back to the nights I spent in the Whitneys' guest room with their big black-and-white cat curled up beside me. The alcohol has softened my defenses against the uncomfortable realization that despite my success, there's some part of me that still longs for Gwen's house in Wheatsville, where Gwen herself lived only a couple of years. A few words are enough to conjure it all back: the breakfast nook and formal dining room they actually used, the modern rug in the always-neat living room, Gwen slumped on the white sofa looking like a Pre-Raphaelite painting, the TV screen light flickering over her face instead of stained-glass lozenges.

At the same time, there is another part of me that is becoming increasingly aware that all this inane chatter about cats is taking the place of something Gwen very much doesn't want to talk about, and that I very much do.

Without bothering to wait for a natural pause, I ask, "When's the wedding?"

Gwen flushes, and then I do, too. I'm not invited. We haven't *drifted apart*. Gwen doesn't want me in her world.

I never belonged there in the first place. But she's the one who invited me in.

GWEN

2

Gwendolyn Whitney showed up on the bus in the middle of sophomore year, soft ivory beret setting off her long, dark hair, belted camel coat standing out in the sea of ski jackets and buffalo plaid.

Beside me in the seat, Trace cracked a dirty joke. I turned away, leaned my knit cap against the window, and watched my breath fuzz over the outside world.

An hour later, there she was again, sitting a few rows ahead of me in homeroom. "Gwendolyn Whitney?" the teacher said, solving the mystery of how the two of us happened to wind up in the same classroom: Whitney, Woods.

If it weren't for that shared initial, I might never have known Gwen's name. Her new Prius was already on order from the dealer, an apology from her parents for moving her away from Manhattan in the middle of the school year; once she turned sixteen and got her license, she'd never set foot on a bus again. Everything would have been different if her name hadn't been Whitney, if mine hadn't been Woods.

It seemed my father had left me something, after all.

. . .

Two weeks later, Gwen spotted *La Règle du jeu* in my unzipped backpack during homeroom.

"*Rules of the Game,*" she said. It took me a moment to recognize the English title. "Is that Renoir?" She leaned over for a closer look, and the ends of her dark, shiny hair brushed my forearm.

"Uh, yeah," I said.

"Why did you bring it to school? Is it for a class?"

Nothing I did was for a class. "I'm returning it today," I said uncomfortably.

"Is it good?"

The question stumped me. Quimby had never asked my opinion on the movies he lent me, and it had never occurred to me that I could have one. The films I liked best — subtitled, black-and-white, thronged with women in opulent gowns and men who wore pistols — were clearly not made for me. Watching them late at night in my closet already felt like a transgression.

But the girl kept looking at me with her unblinking dark brown eyes, and I felt myself blush.

"Um, yeah." I racked my brain for something else to say. "It's really good."

"What is it about?"

Another challenging question. I'd been high as a kite when I watched it after my shift last night, and the black-and-white figures in their warm ocher wash had often looked interchangeable. Anyway, I didn't watch Quimby's movies for the plots. I watched them to get lost in their strange, luxurious foreignness, to get a glimpse of that shimmer of something more I'd seen the first time. But I was afraid if I didn't answer the question, or an-

swered it wrong, Gwen would stop talking to me. And I wanted
her to keep talking to me. She shimmered, too.

"There are these people," I tried. "And they're all in this
house together, and they're having affairs." My face burned.
With a burst of inspiration, I remembered something that had
seemed important: "And they go hunting."

Pathetic.

"Do you think I could borrow it?"

So quickly and naturally had she moved from wanting to asking that her hand was already reaching for it. It wasn't a greedy
gesture; there was something generous in it, even, a default
assumption that giving was as easy for everyone as it must be
for her.

I slapped my hand down instinctively, crushing the flap over
the video. "The guy who gave it to me probably wouldn't like me
lending it out."

She frowned, and I instantly regretted it. For a second she
had thought we were the same. What I really wanted was to
watch the film with her—she was so clearly its rightful audience—but I couldn't invite her over. I pictured Gwen in her
pristine coat walking through the kitchen, past countertops
littered with Dollar Tree bags and unwashed dishes, and then
pausing to examine the pictures on the living room mantel—
toddler-me in a tiara, Mom's pageant photos, my father cut out
of the family shots—while Lily's TV chefs yammered in the
background.

Worst of all, I thought of my mother sizing Gwen up, taking in her ivory beret. Asking me, with a sarcastic smile, how
we'd met.

Gwen was looking at me carefully. "What if you came over

after school and we watched it at my house? We ride the same bus, right?"

Later, I marveled at her tact, the way she'd clocked my expression and corrected course. At the time, I felt only a rush of pleasure that she'd remembered me from the bus. "Sure," I said, already thinking of an excuse for Trace and the Kevins. "I'll see you after school."

The bell rang. Gwen said *au revoir,* with a shade of irony. I decided to sign up for French.

I never went back to Quimby's. His copy of *La Règle du jeu* lay on the floor until I accidentally kicked it under the bed.

These days, I watched movies with Gwen on her flat-screen TV. We rented them by mail from a film society in Chicago, and what we couldn't rent, Gwen found online and bought.

In February she turned sixteen, and after that we drove the Prius into the city almost every weekend for repertory screenings. Gwen was still too nervous to drive alone—she'd taken driver's ed by correspondence, and what with one Dr. Whitney working overtime at the particle accelerator lab and the other always on the phone with her Manhattan patients, the practice hours had been fudged. Gwen's anxiety about driving worked in my favor, inuring her parents to my constant presence in their house. My mom certainly didn't object to seeing less of me.

When Gwen started picking me up for school in the morning, my attendance record improved. We'd go back to her house after school and do homework in her room until it was time for my shift, and then she'd drop me off at the Frogurt Palace. Now that I had a ride everywhere, new vistas of time opened up. My floundering GPA slowly began to right itself.

Gwen never talked about missing her friends in New York,

where she had attended a famous prep school for girls. "Everyone knew everyone there," she said when I pressed her for details. "Imagine being in the same classes together since first grade. It was really boring."

I knew that New York couldn't possibly be more boring than Wheatsville. But even if the suburbs were not as novel to her as she pretended, Gwen clearly liked having her own personal tour guide to Wheatsville's low-rent charms. When we weren't watching movies, we hit the pancake house for bowl-shaped Dutch babies filled with powdered sugar and lemon slices, or the kitschy-quaint gift shops along the Riverwalk for hand-pressed stationery, or the grocery store for a picnic of fruit and fancy chocolates—Gwen always managing, discreetly, to pay. At night we strolled aimlessly around the Riverwalk, kicking pebbles into the oily water, or hopped the wall at the public library to roam the sculpture garden. And all the while, wherever we went, we talked and talked about life, art, boys, the movies we watched together, and the books from my father's old bookshelf I'd started plowing through in an effort to catch up to Gwen's vast and seemingly innate knowledge.

Now that I wasn't high all the time, I'd started waking up earlier, before Mom and Lily got up. The house was so quiet and peaceful that I found myself able to finish my homework every morning before Gwen came to get me. In the shelter of my thoughts, I sometimes pretended I was just doing a little extra studying before heading to my private school on the Upper East Side, where I'd known the girls so long they bored me to tears.

Over the summer, Gwen and I holed up in her basement viewing room and lived together in the films of Godard and Truffaut and Varda, Pasolini and Visconti and Fellini. By fall, a shared fantasy language had begun to infect our reality. After

Blow-Up, we mimed a tennis match in Millennium Park; inspired by *Daisies,* we bought black-and-white dresses from Goodwill and practiced drawing thick rings of eyeliner around our eyes to match its reckless heroines, Marie I and Marie II. Even though I was taller, it went without saying that she was Marie I.

"We even look the same," she said, snapping a photo of us as the Maries with the retro Polaroid she got for her seventeenth birthday.

We looked nothing alike, but I wasn't going to be the one to say it.

"I'm pretty sure the missing Corn Queen from three counties over is buried under this log."

We were picnicking in the forest preserve late in the afternoon spring of senior year. The seventeen-year cicadas were out, screeching their heads off.

"I do hear those local pageants get very competitive," Gwen said, kicking her heel on the underside of the trunk. "Do you think the runner-up hired a hitman, or was it an amateur job?"

"It was probably a satanic cult. Those were very big when I was in pageants. These woods were supposed to be swarming with D&D-crazed teens who needed little blond beauty queens to chop up for their rituals."

Gwen looked around appreciatively, taking in the slant of light through the twisted tree trunks. "To be fair, this is where I'd go."

I nodded. "There was also a wandering meth lab that roamed from grove to grove in an old ice-cream truck, luring junkies with its haunting jingle." I took a bite of bread and spoke around it as I chewed. "And, of course, sex traffickers."

"It's a wonder your mother let you out of the house."

I snorted. "There were probably more pervs by the yard in that kiddie pageant culture than in a federal prison."

Gwen unwrapped her chocolate bar. "I got flashed on the subway when I was nine. It's a rite of passage in New York. When he caught my eye, he lifted his newspaper and I could see it, like, lying in his lap." She wrinkled her nose in disgust. "That's one thing I'm not looking forward to about—" She stopped herself abruptly.

"You were going to say 'going back.'"

Her face flushed an ugly red.

"You got into Columbia."

She was silent for a second, and when she looked up her face was white. "Mac, I'm a legacy."

"It's okay." It was absurd to feel disappointed. Sure, I'd managed to drag my GPA out of the gutter, and my standardized test scores were the same as Gwen's. But it wasn't like *my* dad had been a professor there. "At least I got a full ride to Urbana College." I chucked a hard elbow of bread into the trees and grabbed an apple with a fake smile. "Just imagine, Urbana College! A whole thirty minutes away."

Gwen had been studying her chocolate bar wrapper, but now she looked up. "It's actually a good school."

"I didn't notice you applying." She looked like she'd been struck. I forced my voice to soften. "Anyway. Congratulations. I'm glad one of us is going somewhere."

"Thanks." It was barely audible.

I pictured the Columbia brochure. Velveteen quads nestled in thriving metropolis. Then I took a deep breath and picked up a paring knife to cut the bruises out of my apple. "Can I visit?"

"Whenever you want," she said eagerly. "You can even stay at my parents' place—they have plenty of room."

"They're moving back, too?"

"Well, with me in New York, there's no reason—"

"Right." I dug the blade in. No reason for anyone to stay here a second longer than they had to.

"What I mean is, my dad's job at the lab finished up last year. They've been staying for me. I wanted to finish high school here."

There was a pause while I took it in. I cut a slice off my apple and tried to think of something to say.

"Anyway, undergrad doesn't matter," she went on smoothly. "It's what you do next that counts. After graduation you can get an apartment with me in New York and become a filmmaker."

"What will you do?"

"I don't know, publishing or something." She shrugged. "Maybe grad school. It's a long way off."

Four years. It did seem long. Impossibly long.

Gwen studied my face. Then, after a moment's hesitation, she reached into her backpack and pulled out something in a frame. "This is for you."

It was the Polaroid of us from last summer, arms around each other in matching dresses, mounted on a piece of hand-made paper from the stationery store. She had written a quote along the edges of the photograph in neat, flowing script: *The eye is not a miner, not a diver, not a seeker after buried treasure. It floats us smoothly down a stream. —Virginia Woolf*

"I picked the quote because it's sort of about cameras, if you read it a certain way," she said nervously. "Is it too weird?"

I stared at the words, as measured and beautiful as ringing bells, too overwhelmed to parse their meaning. I had no objection to buried treasure, but floating smoothly sounded more like Gwen, and therefore, I decided, more like me. "It's perfect."

"You're my best friend, Mac." It was the first time either of us had said it, and it felt solemn, like a vow. "Nothing's going to change that."

To hide my expression, I take a slow sip of scotch, letting the heat melt and dissipate on the tip of my tongue. When I set my glass down, I feel completely fine about not being invited to Gwen's wedding.

"Coming up soon, then?"

"Well, it's not like it's *tomorrow*." Gwen stumbles over her words. "There's a lot of prep to do, so I'm actually heading out there now to—"

"At the villa?"

A muscle jumps in her jaw as she nods. Gwen's parents keep an apartment in Paris and a villa in Tuscany, as well as a time-share in Colorado for ski trips. It's not something she's ever enjoyed talking about, though early in our friendship I was invited to join them on several family vacations. Something always came up at home, coincidentally, just before it was time to go; some emergency with my mom, with Lily. A naked bid for loyalty.

"Andreas is on a shoot in Rome, so I'm joining him first for a little while. Then I'll go out and help my parents get the villa ready."

Wedding prep in Tuscany. A shoot in Rome. The alcohol is hitting my unaccustomed system hard. I wonder if Andreas came from money, like Gwen, or if he merely appreciates hers. Filmmaking is an expensive hobby. "It must be amazing. Being with someone like that."

"Like what?"

"Like . . ." I search for a word. *"You."*

"Andreas and I are nothing alike," she says hurriedly, then laughs. "He's so ambitious."

I laugh a bit more explosively than I intended. Gwen, not ambitious? She was the one who first told me about the Program. I can still remember the thread of panic that ran through me when I read her postcard from Columbia, with its casual reference to Emerging Studies at Dwight Handler University as the "best interdisciplinary program in the country." *People here call it "the Program" like it's a cult,* she'd written, and I knew right then that she was applying. I'd been using Urbana College more like a weekend crash pad than an education, regularly spending the night in the dorm rooms of men I hooked up with at college parties. I taped Gwen's postcard to the dashboard of my used Nissan hatchback and vowed to become exceptional. I woke up earlier, studied later, attended summer institutes where I met professors from places like Columbia and Yale who could help get me in. And when it was time, I asked Gwen, the most powerful person I knew, for a peer recommendation letter. Gwen, with typical grace, asked me for one, too. That we both got in was nothing short of a miracle, and I attributed it almost entirely to her.

It was true that in the years after she left the Program, Gwen's do-gooder career struck me as rather quaint. *Philanthropy is the teacup Chihuahua in capitalism's designer handbag.* Bethany wrote that. Gwen is the one who told me about Bethany, too. But we've all mellowed since then. Now I derive a strange comfort from watching Gwen attain success in a field so far from my own—her work for political exiles in Haiti, her seed fund for medical NGOs. That she would downplay it now bothers me, inviting the unwelcome thought that her current career uses her parents' connections more than her intellect.

"Come on, Gwen. You were at the top of the Program. The best."

Infuriatingly, she does not contradict me. Instead, she plays with the knot of her bamboo swizzle stick. "It always meant more to you than me, my being at the 'top of the Program.' I was so afraid of disappointing you."

I gulp down the rest of my drink and gesture to the waiter for another. The forbidden mix of alcohol and medication has taken full effect now, and Gwen's outline has softened to a shining brunette nimbus, her face a landscape of shadows that leap and shrink in the flickering candlelight. When I relax my eyes, I see two distinct Gwens, side by side, a present Gwen and a past Gwen. I try to sort out which is which, but they keep switching places. I wonder if she sees two of me as well: Mac and Claire, past and present me.

It's past me who answers: "You could never disappoint me."

She takes it as a joke, or at any rate she laughs. "Oh, really? I'm quitting my job, Mac." Lit up by her lemony cocktail, she's already forgotten my name again. People born rich can always choose to forget who you are at a moment's notice. "I'm not go-

ing back to work after the wedding. I know what I want, now."
She stirs her drink.

"What is it?" I steel myself: housewife, mommy, venture cap-
italist, cult leader?

"To be happy." She looks up from her drink with shining
eyes.

It's the first time this evening I want to kill her, and the last
thing I remember before blacking out.

THE PROGRAM

3

I stared up at the dark canopy of oak leaves on the quad. Beyond them loomed the gargoyles of Dwight Handler University and, further still, softened by a haze of pollution, the factory district of our northern industrial city.

I was here. I was really here.

"The students call it 'Black Square.' After the Malevich painting, of course," said the tour guide.

The leaves weren't really black, but a black-veined auburn where the sun shone through. I could see how later in the fall, when they carpeted the ground in inky piles, the quad might live up to its nickname, but now, in early September—the grass still green on the manicured lawn, the air crisp but not yet frigid, autumn sunlight transforming the abandoned smokestacks of the coke ovens into a romantic backdrop for its gothic spires—the DHU campus looked straight out of the catalog. Students lay reading in the grass. Professors with brutalist haircuts and leather satchels clicked across the flagstones in hard-soled shoes. The bell in the clock tower clanged three times.

I drew in a deep breath. Today was the first day of the Program, and of my real life. The proof was that Gwen stood right beside me, clutching an orientation folder that looked just like mine.

That morning I'd roamed around our shared north campus walk-up in a waking dream. Everything I saw reminded me that I was living in Gwen's world now. The furniture consisted mostly of cast-offs from her parents' Manhattan residence, and a brand-new TV stood in the corner of the living room, loaded with streaming apps paid for by Gwen. Even the shelves flanking the long-disused fireplace held Gwen's books, not mine; I never bought anything I could check out of the school library. Still, I'd read all but a few—many while lounging in those same wingback chairs. They felt more like home to me than my mom's house.

When Gwen woke up, we ate breakfast together—black coffee and Bircher muesli soaked in plain yogurt overnight, with a dollop of Gwen's favorite almond butter—and pored over course titles in the catalog. *Diasporic Feminisms. Futures of Art History. Dualities of Motion and Emotion. Introduction to Econo-mimesis.* It was easy to see why it took an average of six years to complete the Program. There was more than enough knowledge here to fill six years—six lifetimes, maybe. And I would spend every minute of them not just as Gwen's best friend, but as her colleague. The layering of this fledgling professional relationship over our new intimacy as roommates had an intoxicating effect on me. For the first time, it hit me that if I worked hard enough, got my degree, and landed a tenure-track job as a university professor, I'd never have to leave Gwen's world again.

Of course, before any of that happened, there was the little matter of what I would live on. All the doctoral students had tuition waivers, but my stipend was only $9,000 a year, and first-years weren't allowed to teach. I dreaded loans. I was eligible for work-study, but I knew from Urbana College what that was like: minimum wage under fluorescent lights, dishing up nachos in the cantina for professors with warm, pitying smiles and fellow students who pretended not to know you. I needed a job that was dignified, lucrative, and within walking distance — my car had died soon after I arrived. Gwen, who'd never liked driving much, had left hers with her parents. She was used to public transportation and could, I supposed, always call a cab.

At least finding work was something I knew how to do. After spending the morning together in long lines at the registrar and student ID office, Gwen and I parted ways — Gwen for an optional meet-the-faculty lunch, me for the only four-star restaurant in the neighborhood. Nona occupied the mezzanine of a grand old university-owned apartment building called the Libertorium, and it was a far cry from the Frogurt Palace. On my way, I slipped on the diamond studs stolen from my mother's dresser long ago. I'd read somewhere that a "good diamond," however small, could lend anyone an aura of success.

The earrings worked. "We don't usually hire from the university, but you look like you can hustle." The manager, Derek, handed me an apron. "That's ten dollars, we'll take it out of your paycheck. First training shift tomorrow, ten a.m. Don't be late."

Flush with success, I met Gwen back on the quad just in time for the campus tour. Strolling the grounds with a small herd of students, we listened to the tour guide's monologue on the black leaves (the color came from high arsenic levels in the soil), founder Dwight Handler's various obsessions (theosophy, Fletcherism, model ships), and, of course, the notorious rigor of the student population at DHU. Gwen and I suppressed a giggle when the tour guide solemnly pronounced the number-one ailment treated at the student health center, after depression, to be anal fissures from prolonged studying.

The tour ended on the university seal by the front gate, just as the bell tolled four. It was time for the new student reception.

"Do you think Bethany Ladd will be there?" Gwen said doubtfully, studying the campus map. "She hasn't been at any of the events so far."

"Which one is she again?"

Gwen looked up from her map, too distracted to hide her surprise at my question. "She basically invented the Program. *Ethical Negation?*" She saw my face and tried to play it off. "Everybody says she'll get a MacArthur when the new book comes out."

"Oh, right." I went beet red and followed her without any more questions. Over the summer, I'd read as many books by Program faculty as I could find, but *Ethical Negation* had always been checked out from the Urbana College library. I should have tracked it down and bought it. How had Gwen known it was the important one? The same way she had learned about the Program in the first place. Her father's professor friends or the parties at Columbia, full of boring people who knew everything. And then there were the intangibles. Like the way she'd known to wear her jeans tucked into Hunter green wellies today, even though the weather was fine, with a V-neck cashmere sweater in a calming shade of melon. The women on the tour had shown up in a rainbow of cashmere sweaters and rain boots. Even the hipsters, with their perfectly dyed undershaves and tattoos from classic children's books, wore wellies, though perhaps they were meant to be ironic. No doubt they'd all read *Ethical Negation.* How many other gaps between my knowledge and Gwen's lay waiting to trip me up?

I fingered an earring nervously and followed her across the quad to the reception.

"—and a few more surprises!"

Department chair Margaret Moss-Jones, a tall woman in her sixties wearing loose layers the color of dirt, stood at the front of the reception room, listing the activities for tomorrow's orientation retreat.

My heart raced. The whole thing was a surprise. The day-long orientation retreat hadn't been on the schedule, and Margaret had sprung it on us with the air of someone tossing a handful of confetti. First thing tomorrow morning, we were all supposed to caravan upstate to a farmhouse "on loan from a generous faculty member" for a day of team-building exercises. The retreat would culminate in a dinner and campfire where we were supposed to mingle with professors who'd made the trip. Good clean fun, and impossible for me to attend, given my work schedule.

"Without further ado, please enjoy yourselves, but don't overdo it—you don't want to be hungover for the obstacle course!"

There was polite laughter, and the students in the wood-paneled seminar room broke into chatty groups.

"What am I going to do?" I hissed to Gwen under my breath, clenching my plastic wine cup. "I can't miss my first day of work."

"Can't you drive up after your shift?"

"My car's still broken," I reminded her.

"Does someone need a ride?"

Gwen brightened and smiled over my shoulder, and I turned to get a look. The man who'd spoken was not movie-star handsome, maybe, but he was definitely TV handsome: tall and solid, a hank of black hair dangling over thick eyebrows, nearly touching the tip of his Roman nose. In his double-breasted jacket—oddly formal for the occasion—he looked older than the rest of us and a little hardened. But when he flashed his dazzling white teeth, I saw baby fat around his chin and cheeks and thought he couldn't be *much* older.

Gwen spoke up. "Mac's, um, having an emergency root canal tomorrow morning." She was a terrible liar.

Boy Gangster winced sympathetically. "Oh no," he said, with a hint of an accent too faint to place. "Does it hurt?"

I curled my tongue in my cheek and nodded. Then I lifted my plastic cup. "This is helping."

He leaned toward me, raising his glass of red and touching its plastic rim to mine. "Here's to that. When's your appointment tomorrow?"

"Ten o'clock."

"I was planning on driving up around two."

I could find a way to get cut early. It was just a training shift. "That would be perfect."

"Meet me in front of the library—*Mac*. That's short for Mackenzie, right? Mackenzie Woods. And that must make you"—he gestured at Gwen with his glass—"Gwendolyn Whitney."

"Our fame precedes us." She sidled a little closer to me. "I haven't seen you around today."

"I just got in," he said vaguely. "Rocky." He thrust his hand out, and we each shook it in turn.

"So, what have you got tomorrow morning?" Gwen said.

Rocky raised his glass of wine meaningfully and winked. "The same thing I have every Saturday morning. Most Sundays, too." Catching sight of someone behind us, he drained the glass in one gulp and rattled it so that the last few beads of red slid back and forth along the bottom edge. "Speaking of which. If you'll excuse me." He wandered toward the bar with his empty glass.

"I wonder what his deal is." I took a tiny sip and licked my lips compulsively to ward off red wine stains. "I don't remember a 'Rocky' on the email list. I guess it's a nickname."

Gwen was still following him with her eyes. "Oh my god."

"He doesn't seem like a first-year. What do you think—third? Fourth?"

"He wasn't on the email list because he's not a student." Gwen grabbed my jacket sleeve and turned me toward the open double doors, where a woman in her fifties with a dark red bob and blunt-cut bangs was shrugging off a stiff woolen cape. In her knee-high boots with dramatic spike heels, she only came up to Rocky's shoulder, but she had the air of a much taller woman. Expertly balancing his already half-drained refill in one hand while receiving her cape with the other, he seemed to shrink into the background.

"That's Professor Pyotr Semyonovich," Gwen said in awe. "*Mr.* Bethany Ladd."

Six o'clock came early the next morning. Sheepish about my mistake and nervous about my first shift at Nona, I had left the reception early and walked home alone. Before I went to bed, I'd pulled Gwen's copy of *Ethical Negation* off the shelf and flipped through it idly. This morning I cracked it open again, determined to get through the introduction over breakfast. But I must have been groggier than usual, because after only a couple of pages, I found myself completely lost and had to start over. By the time I left for my training shift at Nona, I had managed half a chapter but had to admit to myself that I'd need to read it again. I didn't really understand it.

My trainer at Nona looked me up and down with a bored smile and showed me around the kitchen until the Saturday slam hit. Within minutes, our section filled up with boozy brunch-goers, and I forgot about everything but carting French toast out of the kitchen, refilling coffees, and tipping the contents of mimosa pitchers into champagne flutes.

When it was all over, and my trainer had thrown a couple twenties my way and left, the time was 1:30. I was supposed to be meeting Rocky in half an hour.

"Shit." I yanked at my apron strings. "I have to get out of here. Am I cut?"

Derek flashed me a sadistic smile. "Trainees do the side work. Guessing you haven't started yet?" He gestured toward the laminated sheets dangling on strings near the walk-in. "I'll need to check it before you leave. Sometimes we get a second slam. You wouldn't want to leave your coworkers hanging, would you?"

"Right." I thought of my actual cohort, the pack of grad students enjoying lunch on the farm, perhaps doing trust falls into bales of hay. I took a deep breath, checked out the laminated sheet, and started hauling racks of glasses and coffee mugs to the wait stations. I sprigged parsley and wedged lemons as sloppily as I dared, arranging the prettiest ones on top. I did the same trick with my tub of silverware, rolling the top row as tightly as cigarettes and stacking them neatly over the disastrous rolls below.

Still, it was 2:04 by the time Derek okayed me to go. I was officially late. I ran to the library, bag bouncing on my back all the way.

I slowed down when I turned the corner and spotted Rocky standing in front of the library smoking, but I was still sweating and panting when I got there.

"I'm sorry I'm late."

"I've only just arrived," Rocky said with a mysterious smile that made me wonder if he was lying. His cigarette wasn't even half-smoked, but who knew how many he'd already gone through?

"Well, thanks for waiting. I mean, thanks for giving me a ride." Everything was coming out breathless, but, then, I had a feeling any conversation with Rocky was destined to leave me a little out of breath. Despite his hints last night about a hangover, he looked bright-eyed and freshly shaven, and his dark jeans and strategically rumpled sweater made my work uniform of black pants and a white button-down seem somehow both fussy and sad.

"How was the root canal?"

I followed his glance down to an errant smear of whipped cream on my pants leg and laughed sheepishly. "I made forty bucks."

"Not bad for one tooth. I'll have to try it." Rocky grinned. "Come on, I'm parked close by. You look ready to drop."

In the car, we stayed silent for a while. I listened to Rocky's retro-punk playlist and spot-cleaned my pants with a bottle of fizzy water. But as we drove farther away from campus and out toward the suburban and exurban sprawl, he turned the music down.

"So where are you from, Mackenzie?"

"The Chicago area. People call me Mac."

"Like the computer." He twisted his mouth ruefully. "I know, I'm one to talk."

"Where'd you get your nickname?" I already felt so comfortable with him. At Urbana College, I was never the kind of student who fraternized with professors or friended them on social media, but Rocky was different. He seemed more like one of us than a professor.

"In America, nobody really likes saying foreign names." He scratched his nose. "I was born in Ukraine and came to the States for college. Everybody expected me to be really good at *fútbol* because I was an international student, but I was terrible."

"So . . . Rocky?"

"Pyotr means 'rock,' more or less. Someone thought they were very clever." He gave me a sidelong glance. "Maybe it was a comment on my passes, as well. I never asked."

"I didn't pick mine either."

"I was just happy to have an English-sounding name. When you're shy like me, every little bit helps. Besides . . ." He flashed a grin. "I look like a Rocky, don't I?"

"What you don't look is shy." I immediately regretted it. Too flirty.

But he smiled. "I hide it well with charm," he said gracefully. I noticed he played up his accent for jokes. "So, what about you? What are you interested in?"

"I'm studying—"

"I know what you're studying. I was on the admissions committee. I meant outside the Program."

I blinked. It hadn't occurred to me that anyone would want to know. "Film."

"So why study them? Why not make them?" He sounded more eastern European with every word. "The world needs good movies more than it needs academics."

"And what if the academics are good?"

"Good, bad. Doesn't make a difference," he said offhandedly. "It's all garbage."

The wind rushed out of my lungs as if I'd been punched in the stomach. "I don't believe that. I don't believe that at all."

Rocky looked sideways at me, hands tightening momentarily on the wheel. His eyebrows furrowed for a moment, and I could have sworn I saw a flicker of pity in his black eyes. Then he looked at the road again. "That's good. You'll do well here."

He turned the music back up.

The "farmhouse" was a two-story glass box set high up on a hillside surrounded by trees. From the gravel drive where Rocky parked the car behind a trail of hatchbacks and sedans, I could see straight into the large front room, an atrium with walls of glass and a dizzyingly high ceiling. The back wall, in contrast with the modernist furniture and glass walls, was weathered gray shiplap hung with giant sculptural farm machinery parts, three stories high, like the side of a barn sliced off and displayed in a museum showcase. In the open-plan kitchen, tin and cast-iron appliances were set in austere concrete blocks that seemed to rise from the concrete floor on their own. A floating staircase led up past the barn wall to a balcony perched high over the main room.

"Wow," I said as we made our way up the drive.

Rocky kept his eyes on the path ahead. "Impressive, isn't it? Bethany hired a German architecture firm for the remodel."

I was speechless. So, the farmhouse belonged to Bethany and Rocky. On the whole drive up, he hadn't even mentioned it.

"She wanted it to blend in with the surroundings," he continued. "Many of the materials were harvested from other buildings on the property."

"Other buildings?"

"It's a farm. The land was slated for development at some point, but it had been sitting there for years when Bethany bought it and restored it to its former glory. The new working farm is on the other side of the hills, over there." He waved his hand vaguely. "There are horses. It's all very American."

I gathered that Rocky didn't care much for his wife's project. Looking up at the walls that were all window, I said, "It must be hard to get work done in a place like that. With everyone looking in."

"There's plenty of privacy in the loft. I just don't like working." He laughed shortly.

"Bethany does?" I stumbled over her first name. It felt normal when discussing her with Gwen but weirdly intimate when talking to her husband.

"I assume that's what she uses it for."

Before we reached the door, Gwen emerged from the woods with two other grad students, carrying a basket and laughing. She waved. "Mac! Come join our team."

"Team?"

"We're in the middle of a scavenger hunt." Gwen held the basket aloft. "For dinner."

"That's my exit cue," Rocky said, gesturing toward the door, a splotchy metal slab set in the glass wall. "It was lovely to get to know you, Mac. Best of luck being a good academic." He leaned in very close, with a wry grin. "I hope your team wins."

"Thanks." My face burned, but he was already walking away.

Gwen thrust the basket into my hand. "I think your team was supposed to be dessert, but nobody'll care if you help us with the sides." A dozen or so ears of corn rolled and bumped around the bottom of the basket.

"They grow corn here?"

She gave me a look. "I presume it's from the Food Lion. It was hidden in a well. We have to find butter next. Come look at the clue sheet, I think Connor and Letty have almost got it."

There was a round of quick introductions. Connor Yu was tall and gangly, wearing a multicolored scarf and just a few too many coordinated layers to be straight; Letty McMillan's pixie cut made the tiny redhead look even tinier. Letty glanced up from the paper and frowned, pushing her green-rimmed glasses up her nose. "This part is a reference to *The Anatomy of Melancholy*."

"Letty's a medievalist," Connor said. "She knows her Latin."

Gwen flashed me a look of pride. "Show it to Mac, she's really good at spotting patterns."

As I leaned over the page of clues, a warmth spread through my chest. It was almost four, and the sunlight had the emphatic strength it gets just before the slant becomes noticeable. I was finally in the right place, at the right time, surrounded by the right people, after a lifetime of having always been a little wrong.

By the time we made it back to the glass house on the hill, the spaghetti crew was already chopping garlic while a giant pot of water came to a boil on the big black stove. Team Salad stood rinsing greens over the antique double-basin sink. The only team we had beaten back to the house was dessert, presumably still roving the grounds in search of apples and frozen pie crusts, and I felt slightly guilty for having abandoned them. But nobody seemed to be keeping score. A small group of professors chatted on the white sectional sofa under the floating staircase, their thumbs squeaking across stemless wineglasses like a tiny orchestra of mice. I dumped the basket of corn on the kitchen island, a brick kiln topped with a huge square of teak, and Letty, Connor, Gwen, and I started shucking.

The kitchen seemed to get louder and tinier as the evening wore on, the glass walls going opaque with steam between us and the darkening night. Tiny Letty was shucking corn opposite me, and I found my gaze drifting over her head toward the knot of professors conversing just beyond her. A pair of nearly identical white men in their mid-forties with rectangular glasses and tight-fitting sweaters (specialties: economimesis and future shock) waved their hands at each other in animated discussion. Rocky (virtual museum studies) chatted with Margaret (diasporic feminisms or the feminist diaspora, I'd seen it both ways). Alone in the corner, an ancient, white-haired Shakespearean fidgeted.

"Where do you think she is?" Connor hissed into my ear.

I pulled back, startled. "Who?"

"*You know who.* Bethany Ladd. Do you think she donated her house just so she wouldn't have to come? Like a Faustian bargain? After all, she's the reason most of us are even here."

I glanced at Gwen, who was the reason I was here. She was tugging husks off corncobs on the opposite corner of the kitchen island. I shrugged. "Maybe she's busy."

"Drinking the blood of virgins, you mean?"

"If that's what she drinks, it's no wonder she's not hanging around here." I was rewarded with a chuckle.

"Who's going to sleep with whom?" Connor whispered. *"Point your corn."*

I let the tip of my corncob drift more or less at random to the right, where it settled on Arjun, broad-shouldered and square-jawed, currently whipping vinegar and oil together with screeching fork tines.

"So far, I approve." Connor pretended to be absorbed in the strands of silk clinging to his cob. "And . . . ?"

Morgan, a swanlike hipster with a waterfall of blue hair.

Connor squinted. "Darwinian. I like it."

"Your turn."

Connor flattened a thin strip of green corn husk on the counter, placing one fingertip right in the center. Then he rotated it like the hand of a clock until the frayed end pointed diagonally across the table at Gwen.

I gasped, giggled nervously. "And . . . ?"

Keeping his pointer finger firmly in place, Connor scooched the compass needle counterclockwise.

"Little Miss Latin?" Anything seemed possible in this world.

"Not Letty, dummy."

I looked past Letty and flushed so hard it felt like opening an oven door. There was a pause.

"Come on, he's hot, right? You drove up with him—don't tell me you didn't notice."

I shucked furiously. "I didn't know professors were in the game."

"Everyone's in the game, hon," he said with a grim laugh. "Even me."

A few minutes and a lot of kitchen bustle later, we perched on barstools balancing loaded plates on our knees. A knife clinked insistently against a glass, and a flutter of earth tones drifted toward the center of the room. Margaret Moss-Jones, flushed with wine, stood in the center of the white fur rug, backlit by antique lanterns hanging from the high ceiling. The professors fell silent around her.

"As department chair, it is my gracious duty every year to welcome a new group of scholars to the Program. Every year, in every market, graduates from this Program continue to fill tenure-track positions in emerging studies departments at top-tier Research I universities. That is because we do not tolerate anything less than the best from our students. Not all are well-suited for the level of academic rigor they will find here. On average, by the end of the first year, thirty percent—four of you, rounding up—will drop out of the Program. If you wish to avoid this fate, you would do well to find allies among your colleagues." She waved her glass vaguely. "And that includes faculty. You're graduate students, not undergrads. We are your colleagues now. And now, without further ado—"

A blast of cool air in the kitchen announced a late arrival. I whirled, expecting Bethany Ladd, but it was Tess, the only black first-year in the Program, and Soo-jeong, a Korean international student. Each carried a shopping bag with "Minty's Bakery" printed on the side.

"Team Dessert," Connor murmured.

Margaret looked flustered, as if she had just remembered their existence. "Tess and Soo-jeong! I hope you don't mind us starting without you. You'll want to get started chopping apples for that pie."

"No need." Tess set her bag on the counter and pulled out a bakery box. "Sorry it took so long. It was kind of a hike driving all the way into town and back."

"You were supposed to—"

"Use our resources. That's what I did." Tess smiled. "Minty's is where I got my wedding cake. They make the best apple pie in town, and I know the owners, so I get a mean discount." She put up one hand, as if staving off objections. "Trust me, it's for the best. I don't bake."

Soo-jeong said, "Me neither." She had evidently been eating a slice in the car.

Tess poured herself a glass of wine and sat down next to the Shakespearean.

"Well," Margaret said, her expression unreadable. "Looks like dinner is served."

After dinner Lorraine, the department secretary, crouched over the fire pit with lighter fluid for an hour, while the smokers — students and professors now freely intermingling — leaned together tipsily under the awning. I wandered a little apart from the group, admiring the house, until Gwen appeared at my elbow. She bumped me with her shoulder, and I bumped her back. We drifted down the path that wrapped around the rear of the house, and for a moment it felt like we were strolling the Riverwalk again, arm in arm on a coffee-buzzed night, under stars like icy flowers.

Gwen broke the silence first. "So, what do you think of all this?"

I thought it was a place where gracelessness could not survive, where ugliness would be redeemed by the study of ugliness, and where those who studied it would be lit from within by fires of intellect and passion.

"It's okay," I said carefully.

She raised an eyebrow. "Feels more like summer camp than grad school to me."

I shrugged. I'd never been to summer camp.

"Scavenger hunts and bonfires are fun, I guess, but I'm here to learn. I want to be talking to the professors about ideas. Not doing trust falls into their arms."

So, there had been a trust fall. I quashed the impulse to reply with a winking Connor-ism about it. Earlier, I'd seen Rocky reach out from the smokers' circle to tap drunkenly at the shoulder of Gwen's pea coat as she walked by, and they'd had a long conversation. She'd even accepted a cigarette, as she sometimes did after a few drinks. "Weren't you talking ideas with Rocky back there?"

She looked amused. "Poor Rocky. He really does look like a raccoon, doesn't he? With those big circles around his eyes. I was trying to pick up some clues from him about working with Bethany."

I'd had him all to myself for an hour in the car, and the thought hadn't even occurred to me. "I tried to register for her class, but the website wouldn't let me."

"He said you have to submit an essay. Like an audition."

"A personal essay?"

"An *impersonal* essay." She scrunched up her forehead. "I tried to get Rocky to tell me what that means, but he wasn't very cooperative."

"He doesn't seem to like talking about her very much."

"I guess not." Gwen grabbed my forearm. "Just promise me you'll at least try to get into her class."

"Of course."

Gwen slipped her fingers into the crook of my elbow, and we walked like that for a while, the sounds from the house growing quieter behind us as we continued down the trail. "I'm so glad you're here, Mac," she said in a low voice, and I realized she was a little drunk. "It would be awful without you."

I imagined an alternate universe in which I hadn't gotten into the Program. I probably would have stayed in Wheatsville forever. "I'm glad I'm here, too." Gwen's presence didn't seem to be in question.

A burst of drunken singing came from the direction of the bonfire, which had evidently roared to life at last. We turned and walked back around the hill, following the trail of sparks vaulting skyward like fast-dying stars.

4

For the next three days, I labored over my impersonal essay. I saw it as a chance to redeem myself for my ignorance about Bethany and prove, to myself more than anyone, that I belonged.

The topic stymied me, though. What was an impersonal essay? How could I articulate why I deserved to be in the class without referring to myself? I picked up *Ethical Negation* again, hoping for guidance, and found only Bethany's repeated assertion that there could be no ethical selfhood, only the negation of selfhood.

Finally, at 1 a.m. the night before the deadline, I began writing.

I was born Mackenzie Claire Woods in Wheatsville, Illinois, a suburb of Chicago with a historic downtown and an ice rink in the shopping mall ...

I wrote about the pageants, how I won them and why I stopped. It was both simple and cathartic to tell the story of a girl who had so thoroughly disappeared. As I wrote it, I felt myself wondering what happened to the Little Miss Sweetness Upper Midwest Division in the pictures, the way you wonder about someone who moved away abruptly, before you ever learned her last name. Probably she'd grown up poised and graceful in a modest house with enough money and a father who'd stayed. Maybe she'd studied broadcast journalism in college and then quit the local news to become a housewife. Wherever she was, I imagined she was very happy. She'd never lost.

I attached a few pageant photos and sent the whole thing to the email address Gwen had given me for submissions.

I got an email response within twenty-four hours. I was in.

I saw at once which seat belonged to Bethany Ladd. At the head of the seminar table, a black tote bag hung from an empty chair. In front of it next to a mug of tea sat a single cruller, untouched.

The students who had already arrived clustered around the opposite end of the table, leaving as much space as possible between them and the cruller. I set my stuff down next to Gwen —she had also gotten in, of course—and joined them in silent waiting.

The clock ticked. The seats around the table filled. I felt pleasantly surprised when Connor came in, so late that he was forced to take one of the seats next to the Bethany-shaped absence at the head of the table. Five minutes passed, then ten, as we waited for someone to fill the final chair.

Bethany strode through the doorway eleven minutes late carrying a stack of thick, stapled syllabi, dark red wedges of hair swinging forward past her cheeks like twin ax blades. She saw the cruller and dropped the papers with a thump, glancing around the table at us sharply. "No one has eaten the pastry."

Silence.

"I brought this for you." She didn't seem to be addressing

anyone in particular. "I don't eat pastries." She slid the cruller to Connor, who stared at it. "Go on," she urged.

Connor tentatively picked it up and took a bite.

Bethany sighed as if at a loss for what to do next and took her seat. The room held its collective breath as her eyes traveled around the seminar table, brows invisible behind the red wall of her bangs.

"First, some housekeeping. The course schedule is incorrect. This class meets on Mondays and *Fridays,* not Wednesdays."

My face reddened. I worked Friday lunches.

She went on. "If you come here on Wednesday, you will have to teach yourself. Which might be for the best." Nervous chuckles from around the table. "You, with the pastry."

Connor, still struggling with the dry cruller, coughed. Pastry flakes flew out of his mouth onto his fist.

"Why don't you begin. Who are you?"

He swallowed strenuously. "Connor Yu."

There was a pause. "And?"

"I'm a first-year."

"And?"

He grinned hugely and spread his hands apologetically. "I'm just happy to be here."

A few students laughed, but the next student spoke up quickly. "Jordan Ash, ret-con dynamics and the sedentary sublime."

As students around the table continued to rattle off their increasingly baffling subjects of study ("Tim Barrett, seance theory"; "Evie Haglund, instantiation"), I wrestled internally with my schedule, trying to make it work. Derek had said I needed to hold down at least three shifts a week if I wanted to stay on the schedule. I didn't have the seniority for dinner shifts, and I had classes the rest of the week. Fridays were nonnegotiable if I wanted to keep my job.

I was sitting nearest the door. While all eyes were on a second-year studying dermatillomania in eighteenth-century Dublin, I quietly picked up my bag and left.

I didn't have time to mourn Bethany's class for long. I didn't have time for anything.

The readings for my other classes—Diasporic Feminisms (Margaret Moss-Jones), The Futures of Art History (Rocky), and Economimesis (Grady Herschel)—added up to almost a thousand pages a week, and I found them nearly impenetrable. The courses I had taken at Urbana College had prepared me for the idea of reading difficult theory, but not the actuality. I often lost track of who had assigned which article, because typically I had only the vaguest concept of the subject matter. I printed them out at ten cents a page, made notes, underlined important passages with red pen, and left them lying in dog-eared heaps around my bed every night just before falling asleep. Having quickly run out of binder clips, I kept them separate by stacking them at right angles to each other, a complicated game of Jenga that always ended when an accidental kick sent them sliding across the floor.

My weekends went to Nona. Some Fridays, I'd fold up a few pages of an article and shove them into my apron to read in the wait station between slams. But between slams there was always silverware to roll, ice to haul, and side work to finish so I could leave the moment I got cut. After an iced tea spill left several pages of Deleuze sopping wet and unreadable—though, hardly more so than before—I gave up the practice. Anyway, I couldn't risk getting caught. I had used up my goodwill with

Derek when he caught on to my trick of always swapping for first cut so I could go home and study.

"I'm going to be frank with you, Mac," he said, bushy eyebrows wrinkling his bald head. "This is why we don't usually hire students. You'll never make bank here cutting out early. And if you're not interested in making bank, I'm not interested in you."

"I'm interested in making bank," I assured him.

In fact, I was desperate. Fixing the car had dropped my bank account down into the danger zone where a single mistake could set off a cascade of overdraft fees. I turned tables as quickly as I could and upsold furiously, but Derek was right. If I wanted to make real money, I had to start staying out my shifts. I was too tired after work to concentrate, anyway.

To compensate, I began to wake up earlier and earlier during the week, trying to trick a few more minutes out of my brain when it was at its clearest. The gym opened early, so I started my days reading on an elliptical and then headed to the library to reread the bits I hadn't understood the first time. On a good day, the reading left me buzzing with questions, but I quickly learned not to ask them in class. Classes weren't for asking questions. They were smartness competitions, chances to attract the attention of the professor and earn a reputation among fellow students. Often, I left more confused than I'd gone in, my notebook full of copied-down phrases to regurgitate next time the subject came up in class. My willpower for the day all used up, I'd start walking toward the library and wind up in a student pub called the Parlor, where Gwen and Connor and I sat at a table pretending to read until we got too tipsy to pretend.

Gwen's study habits were a mystery to me. Graceful mornings of the kind we had shared during orientation lasted through

the first week, and then vanished once classes were fully underway. Except for Rocky's class, which we shared, we had opposite
schedules. I left before she woke up in the mornings, and although we saw each other every day, we were hardly ever alone.
When we went out with Connor, we spoke more to him than to
each other, performing our friendship as a duet of good-natured
needling. Even as we let fly jokes that were occasionally a bit
too barbed—as when I informed Connor how recently Gwen
had lost her virginity, and he guffawed so loudly she had to let
on how irritated she was or risk him blurting it out to the whole
bar—I told myself I was enjoying the new lack of exclusivity in
our friendship. It felt like a natural maturation, something like
the way long-married couples circulate at parties, so connected
that they can risk a mild flirtation with someone else. We were
having our fun side by side, and with Connor there was no danger of either of us pairing off and leaving the other in the cold.

And it was cold. The oaks had lost all but the most tenacious
of their leaves, temporarily painting the quad a darker shade of
eggplant than I had anticipated. But it didn't stay black for long.
On Halloween, a freak snowstorm dumped two inches on the
oily city streets, heralding a long and bitter winter. Coal dust
from the coke ovens, invisible at other times, left odd powdery
shadows on the blank sheets of white snow until the parade of
boots stirred it into a gray sludge. The red, salted brick of the
sidewalks slashed across the gray-scale quads like long, coagu-
lated wounds, giving the campus roughly the same color scheme
as my printouts marked in red pen. I had a recurring dream
that I was trudging through campus only to find myself wading
through some article, the words sticking to me like mud after
a thaw. I'd wake up with my heart racing and read for hours in
the middle of the night. As the weeks dragged by, the full weight

of exhaustion came down on me like a hammer, and even my mornings grew foggy. I found myself lapsing into unintentional naps in the library.

On Friday of the sixth week, I jerked awake from one of my library naps to the sound of someone saying, "What did I do wrong?"

I opened my eyes.

Bethany Ladd sat across the table from me.

Bethany looked younger up close, her eyes as round and childish as doll eyes, with pupils of startling purple-flecked hazel. She wore no makeup, and next to the fierce auburn of her immaculately straightened bob, her pale skin had a translucent cast. The curtain of bangs, formidably solid from a distance, had caught on her eyebrows and split, revealing a glimpse of worried forehead.

"What did I do, Mac?" she repeated, a little impatiently. "You walked out of my class. Did I say something that offended you?" Her voice, like her face, was unexpectedly girlish and imploring.

I rubbed my eyes. "What are you doing here?"

"Rocky told me you come here every morning." I struggled to remember when I'd told Rocky about my schedule, but she went on. "I know it's a hard class, but I can't help it if I think it's a good one."

"I—I didn't think you would notice."

"Of course, I noticed. I don't get that many kiddie pageant alums in my class, you know." She heaved a sigh as if the thought caused her considerable pain and folded her hands in front of her on the table, bracing herself, perhaps, for further disappointment. "I'm here to ask you to consider re-enrolling. The class needs you. It's not a strong group."

This woke me up. I opened my mouth and closed it, racking my brain to think what I could possibly have done to earn this compliment. To the best of my knowledge, I had never uttered so much as a word in Bethany's presence. I thought of Connor and Gwen and Jordan the ret-con specialist. *Not a strong group.*

She waited for my answer.

"I'm sorry, I should have explained. I have a conflict on Fridays. When you announced the schedule change, I knew it wasn't going to work, and I didn't want to waste anyone's time."

"What could you possibly have on Fridays? Nobody schedules class on Fridays." Her eyes narrowed in disbelief. "I had to apply for special permission to do it myself. You wouldn't believe how long that took to approve. Hence the mistake in the catalog."

I weighed the pros and cons of revealing my illicit off-campus job to Bethany. She didn't seem like the squealing type, but, then again, telling her wouldn't help. What good would it do to spill my problems now?

She noticed my hesitation.

"It's work-study, isn't it? I've seen your aid package—you can't be surviving on that. No wonder you're so tired." Her voice dipped into a maternal register, but only for a moment. "Still, aren't they supposed to let you schedule around classes? File for a new assignment. I'll write a note to the work-study office and say Fridays are off-limits."

She was already moving to pull out her laptop, as if she intended to write the email this instant. I had to do something to stop her.

"It's not work-study. I wait tables at Nona, and I can't take Fridays off. My manager already hates me." I said it all in a rush.

"I really wanted to take your class, and I could have if it was at the original time, but it isn't, so I can't."

"Well, actually it was the registrar that had the wrong information—"

"I'd re-enroll if I could, but I can't." I sped up my words, seized by a strange foreboding that she could somehow make me. "I'd get fired. I really can't get fired."

Noticing my distress, Bethany became distressed herself. "Ah, no, no, no, little beauty queen," she said. "We don't want to get you fired. And we won't. We won't do that at all."

I nodded mutely, relieved and a little embarrassed.

"So, what we'll do instead . . ." She paused between words, tracing the wood grain in the table while she thought it out. "What we'll do instead is—listen, when *can* you meet? When have you got a couple of extra hours?"

I contemplated my reading schedule with horror. I was already worn down to the threads. Where would I fit in the hundreds of pages of readings Connor and Gwen complained about having to lug around for Bethany's class?

"Listen, I know you're busy. The first-years always have a meltdown over the reading. You know you're not supposed to do it all, don't you?" She cocked an eyebrow at me. "You don't know that. I can see by your face that you're trying to do it all. That's admirable, but stupid. Nobody expects you to do all the reading. Most of the first-years have figured that out by now. You're a little slow, aren't you?"

Her tone was cordial, but I winced at the about-face from compliment to insult.

"Come on. What are you doing that's inessential? Probably going to the pub, right? That's what all the first-years do. You can skip it once a week. Come to my office hours. How is

Wednesday afternoon? Good? Wednesday afternoon at three.
Oh, that's right, you're in Margaret's class, aren't you? How boring. What a slap in the face to me. Well, come to my office at
four, then, after you've done your diasporas and feminisms and
things, and we'll talk."

"Talk?"

"Independent study. Ethical negation." And just like that,
her face clamped shut, as if the conversation had driven her beyond her capacity to tolerate petty irritations. Before I could
process what had just happened, she was on her feet, severe and
stiff in her woolen cape as she had been in class, black tote bag
dangling from her shoulder. "I'll see you in my office, Wednesday, four p.m. sharp. I'll file the paperwork to make it official.
And, Mac?"

"Yes?"

"You're welcome."

She turned and stalked off, boot heels clicking. After she'd
gone, the library was silent again except for the whir of desktop
computers and the occasional librarian's yawn.

The Bethany who invited me into her office when I knocked
that Wednesday at 4 p.m. was neither girlish nor gruff, but so
close to ordinary I could almost believe I'd imagined the exchange Friday morning.

Except that I hadn't, because here I was.

"Mac, come on in. I'm so glad you remembered." As if it had
been a casual invitation, mentioned in passing.

Bethany's office was a bright white box, the bookshelves lin-
ing one wall nearly empty, with only a few objects scattered here
and there. They were ordinary objects—a stapler, a bud vase
—but somehow they all looked slightly larger than normal, so

that, like the rustic tools hanging in the farmhouse, their objecthood made an impression. In any other setting, I wouldn't have wondered whether the tape dispenser on the second shelf was a functional tape dispenser or a Tape Dispenser, the piece of pottery a mug or some sort of ironic commentary on the platonic ideal of a Mug.

Bethany, wearing a black sweater and leather pants tucked into her knee-high boots, sat in a rolling chair behind her desk. Her window was choked with ivy, gray and skeletal, and a gargoyle with a skullcap of snow jutted at an odd angle outside. A mug of tea steamed on the desk in front of her, and as she spoke she dunked the bag rhythmically, a comfortingly ordinary motion.

"Close it behind you, will you? Not all the way." I obediently cracked the door. "Now come have a seat."

The only place to sit was a love seat arranged at a ninety-degree angle to her desk, a woven throw folded and draped over one arm, so that it looked a bit like the therapy couch I'd seen in Gwen's mom's office. I wondered if anyone ever used the throw, if they asked before draping it over them, and if they folded it afterward or left it for her to fold.

"I haven't read *Ethical Negation*," I blurted, as if I'd been in the interrogation chair for hours.

"Don't bother," she said lightly. She turned her chair, which, in the style of everything else in the office, was an ordinary desk chair but also a Chair. "I'm working on something that will render it completely obsolete: *radical* negation. As a matter of fact, I was hoping the class would help me think it through, but I've plied them with readings, to no avail. As I said, it's not a strong class."

It had never before occurred to me that professors assigned

readings based on their own needs, not their students'. I paused to grapple with this disorienting thought.

"Not to say they're not smart!" she went on. "They're extremely intelligent. All my students are. Well, most of them. All except one, really."

My mind spun out trying to remember every face in the room and guess which one she was talking about. Could it be me? Did I even count as her student yet? But before I could figure it out, she was on to the next thing.

"Your friend with the hair—you know, what's her name, Gwen. She's the smartest student I've ever taught."

"Gwen's smart," I parroted numbly, recognizing something that made sense at last, even though it made my heart sink a little.

"Brilliant," Bethany agreed. "But not strong. Not like you, Beauty Queen. None of them are strong. I can feel the strength coming off you in waves, and that's what I want for the book. I don't want smart. I want strong."

"Oh."

She didn't want smart. She wanted me.

"You're smart, too, BQ," she said with a little laugh. Still recovering from her last remark, it took me a moment to understand the acronym: BQ, for Beauty Queen. "I wouldn't have pushed so hard for your acceptance into the Program if you weren't. Oh, yes, I was on the admissions committee, and I fought for you. It was a very contentious application, with a lot of opposition."

"Uh, thank you." The whiplash of compliments and insults had left me so confused, I could think of nothing else to say.

"Mac, do you know what the Joyner is?"

"Sure," I said, retreating to easy falsehood. Six weeks of

classes with people who already knew everything had replaced my instinct to ask for explanations of what I didn't know with an automatic nod to show that I did, accompanied by a thoughtful expression, as if I were puzzling over which bit of knowledge about the thing I knew nothing about would be most relevant to the current discussion.

Bethany turned briefly to lift the tea bag out of her tea. As she spoke, she squeezed it against the inside of her mug with her bare fingers. "So, you already know that the Joyner is the most prestigious and highly funded fellowship offered in the Program, or indeed the field—a unicorn of a fellowship, a Sumatran rhinoceros of a fellowship, funded by an eccentric alumnus with an enthusiasm for the humanities? And you know that it allows one exceptionally ambitious student from DHU to conduct up to two years of dissertation research at any partner European university, while living on a stipend most find ample, even luxurious? And that it is as close to a guarantee of a tenure-track Research I job as you are likely to find in this fallen world?"

Europe . . . ample funding . . . a tenure-track job. *Escape.* I forgot my white lie for the moment and let my eyes go wide at the prospect.

She dropped the used tea bag into a little dish evidently kept on her desk for that purpose. It was an actual mesh pouch with drawstrings. I could not imagine how much a whole box of tea like that would cost. "And I suppose you know that it's only given out every third year, and that this is a Joyner year?"

I nodded quickly, wishing we could drop the fiction of my prior knowledge.

"Then you surely also know that one of my students always gets the Joyner."

It seemed she wouldn't go on until I nodded again. I got it over with.

She shook her fingers lightly, and half a dozen tiny tea droplets flew into the air and evaporated instantly, as if they'd been dismissed.

She leaned forward.

"Well, let me tell you something *I* know. Every year, I know which of my students is going to get the Joyner. My students don't know, but they know *I* know. I have never been wrong about who was the best fit. Not once." She tented her fingers in front of her. "Some might say I have a knack for choosing the right horse."

The energy in the room seemed to hiss and pop, the air around Bethany growing wavy with heat, as if she were a radiator just turned on. Under her intense gaze, my chagrin melted into a shaky kind of excitement.

"Would you like to go to Venice, Mac?" she said softly. "Would you like to study in Brussels? Oxford? Edinburgh, perhaps? The University of Lyon is one of our most sought-after partner programs, due to the city's great beauty." She touched her lips in a gesture I recognized from long years of watching my mother, and I knew Bethany had once been a smoker.

I spoke slowly. "I wouldn't be going there for the beauty. If I went there."

She looked at me from under half-lowered lids, her hazel eyes shifting subtly. "The fellowship application is due at the end of the semester. You're going to have to work very, very hard." Before I could respond, she said, "Starting *now*. Get out your notebook."

I hardly knew what happened for the rest of our meeting, though I took copious notes on the words that spilled from

Bethany's mouth and curled around me like smoke. Later I went back to look at my notes. I had accidentally taken them in red pen, and the page looked as if I had opened a vein over it. I recognized the word *negation,* underlined several times, and there was a series of bullet points that appeared, on closer inspection, to be a list of birds—tern, wren, crow, finch. The rest I couldn't make out.

It was all very confusing, as everything Bethany said was confusing. But leaving her office, I felt the architecture of dreams taking shape around me and growing solid under my feet. I had been chosen. And she whom Bethany chose, I gathered, did not go unchosen by others for long.

I pulled out my phone to text Connor, and my stomach dropped. I had missed seventeen calls from my mother over the past hour. My voice-mail box was full. My mom never texted, but there was one from Gwen: *Your mom is calling me every ten minutes to ask if you're home yet, PLEASE call her.*

I didn't bother listening to the messages. My mom had a million reasons for calling, but they all added up to two little words with the power to stop my life's forward motion as implacably as brakes stopping a high-speed train. I headed to the apartment to call her back in private. The damp air turned to a freezing drizzle, and I walked faster and faster, the two words pounding in my head to the rhythm of my steps:

Come home. Come home. Come home.

5

Damp, miserable, I crouched on my bed with the phone in my hand.

"Did you hear me, Mac? I said I need you to come home for a while."

"I heard you, Mom. I——" I tried to say, *I can't come home right now. I'm sorry. It's not a good time.* But, as always happened in my nightmares about this moment, my throat closed up. It was useless. "What's wrong?"

"'What's wrong?'" she mimicked. "Some people's lives. What do you think is wrong? It's Lily."

My heart leapt into my throat. "Is she okay?"

"What a question." Her voice went momentarily quiet, as if she had pulled away from the receiver. After a crackle of packaging in the background, she was back, working her words around a bite of something. "Well, she has me to look after her, that's something."

"Mom." I knew she was settling in, drawing this out on purpose to make me worry, but I couldn't help it. Against my will, I started flipping through worst-case scenarios: Lily sick in the hospital. Lily hit by a car. Lily *pregnant*. "Mom, just tell me what happened."

"It's her checks. They've stopped coming."

"Her disability checks?" I had filled out the paperwork when Lily turned eighteen, found the specialist to testify that she would never be able to support herself, while my mother had cried in the background, repeating, "She's coming along. She'll get her GED." Lily, who had nothing invested in denial, had gone along with the process without complaint. "Have you tried calling?"

"Yes, I've tried calling!" she snapped. "You think you're easier to get hold of than the Social Security office? Their wait time is only an hour. Getting you takes all day."

"What did they say?"

"She doesn't qualify anymore."

"Of course, she qualifies." Something occurred to me, and I closed my eyes, breathed in deeply through my nostrils. "Mom, you've been taking her to the doctor, right? For her regular appointments?"

There was a pause just long enough for my mom to prepare her defense, and in that pause, I could see instantly what had happened: thanks to her sloppiness with doctor's visits and paperwork, we'd missed a continuing disability review. Then came the onslaught.

"You try getting her out of the house, Mackenzie Claire. I'd like to see you feed her breakfast and get her dressed and presentable, all while singing the song she likes and keeping her favorite T-shirt in sight and the *Morning Show* has to be on, Lily is my morning girl."

I felt something in me strain almost to the snapping point as

I remembered the countless times I had done all that while my mom lay incapacitated in bed.

But she wasn't finished. "And then if you manage everything just right and you get her in the car with her headphones on and she sees something—could be anything, a fire hydrant that's the wrong color—well, you know what happens. Last time she screamed herself sick. She actually vomited. And we missed that expensive appointment, which I still had to pay for, mind you, because I was cleaning her off in the ladies' room." She wheezed indignantly. "You think that's where her checks should go every month? To some therapist who can't even get off her lazy ass to help in the bathroom? Not to food and gas and electric, and the cable bill for all the TV channels she has to have, or she'll go nuts? *Is that what you think?*"

She had worked herself up into a righteous fury, the tremor in her voice gone, her eyes with their Percocet glow nearly burning me through the phone.

"She has to keep up medical treatment," I managed, but it came out less than a whisper, like something you're trying to say in a dream.

"She weighs thirty pounds more than me, Mackenzie. I can't force her into the car." Her voice was quivering again, shaking itself free of its anger, diving back into self-pity. "She hurts me, Mac. It's not her fault—she doesn't know what she's doing. Last week she threw a tantrum and gave me two black eyes. I had to wear sunglasses to the bank."

I pulled the phone away from my face and covered the receiver, forcing the sobs out hard, like vomit. If I tried to hold them in, it would show in my voice, and she'd pounce on my weakness. Lily was never malicious, but the fact that she couldn't be blamed for the damage she did made the house feel, at times, like a prison. I tried not to think about my mom having needs of her own, perhaps even aspirations—those baton-twirling lessons, the home-sewn costumes . . . But no. When she had chosen pills over us, she'd forfeited her right to personhood in my eyes.

That thought led horribly, inevitably, to the next. Had she missed the appointments because she was using again? Or, worse, was the eligibility problem some elaborate ruse to cover up the fact that she was stealing the checks herself?

I shoved it down. Lily was her life. Even at her lowest, in the doldrums of addiction, Mom had never stolen from Lily. She'd sold everything there was to sell—thank god, I thought for the millionth time, I had taken those earrings—but she'd always broken down and confessed what was happening to me before it got that far.

Still. I thought of the logic of her past relapses. I was the furthest from her I'd ever been, and the closest to escaping for good.

"Mackenzie? Are you coming home, baby?"

She only called me "baby" when it was working. I had to think. I had to clear my head. Vaguely, in the back of my mind, I could see Oxford—Brussels—Lyon. I had been chosen.

"If it's too hard to get Lily out, I'll find someone to come to the house," I managed. "We'll resubmit the paperwork—*I'll* resubmit it. And they'll see that her diagnosis is the same, and they'll send the checks again."

There was a long silence. "That's not what the lady said on the phone," she said, suddenly sullen. "I didn't write it down. I've been so tired lately. It's hard to concentrate when you're worried about the grocery money."

"I think if we get her examined, this will clear up."

"And what am I supposed to do in the meantime? While you're in school reading books and drinking with your snobby friends?" As always, her instinct for where to strike was jarringly accurate. In stabbing out blindly at the two things that seemed most luxurious to her, the most outrageously wasteful, she had boiled down what I thought of as a complicated and important lifestyle to the essentials. Reading and drinking.

"I can transfer six hundred now, and more after the weekend." So much for rent. I'd have to pick up extra shifts at the restaurant, somehow. "Will that get you through the next couple of weeks?"

"You won't come home?" She tried the wheedling voice one more time, halfheartedly, as if she already knew she'd lost the fish on the hook.

"If I come home, I'll lose my job," I said flatly. "If I stay, I can send you money. Which do you want?"

I held my breath.

"If you send it fast enough, we can manage," she sniffed. "Me and Lily do all right on our own. Don't we, Lily?"

I froze. She was in the room. In another minute Mom would put her on the phone. Lily hated the phone. "I've got to go, Mom, but I'll call you really soon to let you know about a doctor. And I'll send you that money today."

I hung up without giving her a chance to say *I love you*. For some reason that part always hurt the most.

It was only when I'd sat down to empty my checking account into hers that I remembered her line about wearing sunglasses to the bank. I'd switched her to an online-only bank years ago to make transfers like this cheaper and easier. She didn't go to the bank; didn't even *have* a brick-and-mortar bank. I shrugged wearily.

The front door opened and shut, and Gwen walked in, knocking softly on my open door.

"Is everything okay?" I could tell from her too-perfectly enunciated consonants she was fighting a three-drink slur. "What was your mom calling about?"

"Oh, it's just some stuff about Lily. Not a big deal."

"Anything I can do?" The tender inquiries of someone who could rest easy in the knowledge that they could do nothing, and therefore would be asked for nothing. "If you want to talk, or something."

Or something. I briefly imagined myself asking Gwen to float me next month's rent, then rejected it. She would say yes, and then where would we be? I had never officially borrowed money from Gwen. She had always covered me at restaurants and bars and pretended not to notice that I got her back much less often than I should. But these were luxuries, and it was understood that Gwen wanted to indulge in them herself without guilt, which meant helping me enjoy them as well. To pay for something real, something necessary, even urgent—to keep me alive for a month—that would change our relationship irrevocably, I knew. The way it had changed my mother's and my relationship the first time I floated her for a month. Breaking out of normal hierarchies of care created a sense of outrage in both the giver and the receiver that, in my experience, could not be repaired. It was Gwen's privilege to remain ignorant of the cost of such unnatural transactions, and I would do anything to keep her from finding out. Better to get a second job on top of Nona. Better to drop out of grad school altogether.

"I've already taken care of it," I said lightly.

"Great," she said, relaxing. "Because Connor's having a party on Saturday and you are very much invited. He said if you bring a thermos of buttery nipples, he may just forgive you for quitting the trivia team."

I could feel the threat of imbalance between us evaporating as Gwen's words made me into an ordinary student once more, not a charity case. "Thanks for the tip," I said with a smile.

Saturday night, Gwen and I arrived at Connor's at 10 p.m. on the dot, but the party was already well underway. Connor and his roommate, a first-year he referred to drily as Aggressively Bland Matt (the other Matt had a tattoo), had decorated for the party by clearing out the glass-front bookshelves and stuffing them with wads of dollar-store Christmas lights. Bowls of chips and trays of tequila shots, garnished with limes and little dishes of salt, dotted every available surface. TVs and laptops throughout the apartment played half a dozen different musicals just loudly enough to compete with the party music, creating an entertaining cacophony.

Gwen pointed at Little Orphan Annie tap-dancing in the fireplace. "I'm assuming this whole thing was Connor's idea."

As if summoned, Connor appeared in the hallway, a head taller than everybody around him. I raised the thermos for him to see.

"Buttery nipples!" Connor shouted, stretching his arms over the heads of his classmates, his exuberance drowning out both TLC on the stereo and "It's a Hard Knock Life" on the television. "At last!" He broke out of the crowded hallway and wrapped his arms around me, and I could tell he was already three sheets to the wind.

"I can't say no to you."

I pressed the thermos into his hands, and he pretended to cradle it in his arms like a baby.

"Where have you been all week? They registered trivia teams for the playoffs, and you missed it. The pot is three hundred dollars. We're all going to be rich!"

I made a face. "I thought I was forgiven if I brought candy-flavored booze?"

"I had to beg Aggressively Bland Matt to take your place. I'm too sad to forgive you." He sighed, then brightened. "But luckily I'm also *druuuunnnk!*" He shimmied away down the hall to the chorus of "Waterfalls," holding the thermos-baby over his head and spanking it while he sang, "'Please stick to the rivers and the streams that you're used to . . .'"

I wondered why he hadn't said hi to Gwen, and then I turned around and saw that she was gone. Alone, unmoored, I looked around for someone to talk to. I noticed Tess standing in a circle of people in the living room and approached tentatively, lingering on the outskirts while Aggressively Bland Matt held forth.

"There's not a single third-year here, man," he was complaining to someone I didn't recognize.

"I guess they're all studying for quals. I heard people get weird around quals."

"At least Bird came, didn't you, Birdsy?"

"You can always count on the Bird."

Even I knew who the Bird was. He was an eighth-year in the Program who had taken a year of medical leave halfway through his dissertation and hadn't turned in a chapter since. People whispered that he had spent that year in a mental institution, but he looked much healthier than his dissertating peers. I saw them from time to time in the library, pale and slack-jawed.

Bird's dark olive skin, on the other hand, was ruddy from sitting in the sun on the quad, surrounded by first- and second-years, and he came to all the parties.

Trying to catch Tess's eye, I edged closer. But it was Bird, a little shorter than me, balding on top, with a ponytail and little round glasses, who acknowledged me first.

"You're Bethany's new student, aren't you?"

The conversation circle instantly widened to include me, Matt and the others melting back deferentially at the magical name. In spite of my relief, I felt strangely exposed. I hadn't told anyone about my independent study with Bethany yet and wasn't sure I wanted them to know. "I'm Mac," I said.

"Prometheus Birdling III, renowned shipbuilder. Pleased to meet you." I laughed uncertainly at the fake introduction, and he eyed me. "You're very much her type."

"What is that supposed to mean?"

"She likes the prickly ones," he said solemnly. "Listen, I'm very happy for you! She's going to get us all jobs, you know. Upon graduation, every last one of us will receive a Research I job, forty acres, and a mule." He winked.

"Birdsy, be nice!" Matt shouted, giving him a thump on the upper arm.

"What I mean is, go get 'em, champ," Bird said with a penitent air. "Go, fight, win! Just don't forget the winning part." He pushed his glasses up on his nose and wandered off.

Matt shrugged. "Don't mind Birdsy, he's cracked."

Blue-haired Morgan appeared, filling the gap in the circle where the Bird had been. "I'm going across the street for more ice. Anything else I can grab while I'm out?"

"I better go with you," Matt said. "You know what they told us about the neighborhood."

"What did they tell us?" Tess, who had been silent up until now, asked. "I grew up here, so I'd be interested to know."

Matt looked at her, his mouth open to speak, and then shut it.

Morgan's hand went to her neck, half covering the pinkish-red stain that had appeared between her clavicles. "I think Matt was just saying, you know, no one should be walking around alone at night."

But Matt, who had clearly been sampling the shots, refused to be helped. "The tour guide told us DHU students have gotten beat up by locals for, like, gang initiation rites."

"'Gang initiation rites'? Please." Tess's voice was pleasant, her intonation almost musical, as if it was all a joke to her. But her smile looked painted on, and she held her body unnaturally still.

Morgan's neck had gone a solid brick-red. "I'm sure Matt didn't mean—"

"Yes, I did." Matt crossed his arms defensively. "That's not racist; it's factual. Come on!" He turned to Morgan, who shrank away. Next he appealed to Arjun, his gym buddy. "If anything, it's *statistical* racism. Like when insurance companies have different rates based on your likelihood of getting shot."

Arjun looked at him skeptically. "Dude, it's still racist though."

"No more so than affirmative action. Right?" He turned to Tess, who drew back with an audible hiss. "I mean without affirmative action, you wouldn't—"

"I have an idea," I said loudly. "Matt, shut up and go get some ice. And take your time."

"Gladly." Matt bowed chivalrously to Morgan, then to Tess.

"Don't get mugged," Tess called cheerfully after him. Then she turned to me. "I hope he gets mugged."

"It would be richly deserved. Statistically speaking," I noted.

Arjun, who'd been standing nearby, said, "I'm going to find Bird and smoke some dro." As he walked away, he clapped Tess on the back in an ambiguous gesture of solidarity. Morgan followed him, her eyes on the floor.

"Sorry about that," I said to Tess.

"Oh, please. I can have that fight in my sleep." She smiled sarcastically. "But thanks for cutting it short. It's way too early in the semester to lose my cool over fucking affirmative action."

Face-to-face with Tess, I felt suddenly at a loss. I had been impressed by the way she blew off the scavenger hunt at the orientation retreat—not to mention the fact that her contribution to the group meal had been the tastiest by far. It wasn't until you saw Tess that you realized what a person who wasn't desperate to please looked like and noticed that it definitely wasn't you.

"Well, what do we do now?" she said, bored.

I pointed to the little trays of tequila. "I think we're supposed to be taking shots."

"Not me. I'm too old for shots. To the kitchen."

We pushed our way down the hallway, past *Seven Brides for Seven Brothers,* and entered the narrow galley kitchen just as the last beer vanished from the fridge.

"Looks like gin and tonic's our only option," Tess said, staring into the sink full of open bottles, mostly empty, and a deflated plastic bag. "No ice."

"Pour."

Tess filled a couple of red Solo cups while I fetched limes

from the nearest tequila platter. Then we stepped into the doorway of one of the bedrooms to get out of the press, each leaning on one side of the doorframe.

"So, you're really from around here?"

"I've lived here my whole life, except for five or six years working in TV." I raised my eyebrows, and she smiled. "Mostly producing. I wanted to be a showrunner. Anyway, I'm glad to be back home, and I'm not in a hurry to leave again."

"You'll have to for an academic job, though, right?" It was a given in our profession that even the best of the best had to go where the jobs were.

"Maybe DHU will be ready to expand their Af Am Department by then."

"That's ambitious."

"Speaking of ambition, is it true?" She made air quotes. "Are you 'Bethany's new student'?"

I already trusted Tess more than Bird. "I'm doing an independent study with her once a week. But that's pretty much all there is to it."

She whistled and raised her eyebrows. "That's enough. Half of these assholes would promise their firstborns for an independent study with Bethany Ladd."

"What about you?"

She was silent for a moment, then shook her head. "Mm-mm. That is not for me."

"Like the shots?"

"You laugh," she said, then stopped herself. Then she leaned forward. "Does she text you?"

This was certainly not what I had been expecting to hear. "Who? Bethany?" I laughed at the thought.

"Yeah."

I saw that she was serious. "No."

"She texts me. She must have gotten my number from the office. I didn't sign up for her seminar because there was a conflict with the only Af Am class—which Margaret Moss-Jones is teaching, by the way, since Rhonda Oakes left. Now that there's not a single black professor in the department, I guess they figure anyone in ethnic jewelry will do." She made a face. "Anyway, next thing I know Bethany Ladd is texting me, like, *Why aren't you taking my class, I need you in my class.* Blah, blah, blah. Then she offered me an independent study."

I felt my throat contract a little. "You didn't take it."

She was silent again for a moment, and then repeated: "That is not for me."

"Why not?"

"Mac, when you're the only one in the room who looks like you and someone comes after you like, 'You're smart, you're strong, you're the best one here' . . ." I found myself flushing at how dismissively she threw out the words that had seduced me so completely. "I've seen it in studio meetings. It's your cue to start wondering: What is it they want from you *really*?"

"It sounds like she just wanted to work with you." The conversation had rattled me. *Why*, a small, petty voice inside me asked, *hadn't Bethany texted me?*

Tess squinted at me briefly, then shook her head. "Maybe you're right," she said in a desultory kind of way, like she was checking a conversational box. "I just like to keep it professional, you know? We're not teenage besties. This is my career, not a prom date. Don't try to make me feel special. Special is not always good."

Connor bounded up and leaned on my arm. "Have you seen Gwen? I saw her way down the hall, and now she's nowhere."

"I'll help you look." I turned back to Tess. During our conversation, a fresh batch of students had arrived, and the party
had gotten louder. "Hey, look, I'm sorry if I— I mean, you
should trust your instincts."

"Yeah, I should," she said coolly. "And you should do the
same. Unless you want to end up like Fried Chicken over there."
She gestured to Bird, who was stumbling in from the balcony,
bringing a gust of pot smoke and a group of revelers with him.

"I'll take it under advisement."

I started to walk away, but Connor nudged me and pointed
back to Tess. I turned and saw her mouthing something I
couldn't hear over a swell of laughter in the newly crowded
kitchen. I pointed to my ear, and Tess shoved her way through
the weedy-smelling bodies and grabbed my sleeve, leaning close
and speaking loud enough to make my eardrums throb: "Bird
was a Joyner Fellow."

She released my sleeve and disappeared into the crowd.

6

Sunday morning, I awoke with a splitting headache three hours after my alarm. No time to read. I had only an hour to get to my first double shift at Nona.

The double was a desperate measure. I had only two weeks to make back the month's rent, and who knew when my mom would call again to say she'd run out of grocery money? Dinner shifts were typically doled out by seniority, but with wheedling I had cracked a Sunday night on top of my normal Sunday brunch. Derek had smirked and told me anyone who survived a Sunday double could consider themselves that much closer to a Saturday night. At last I was showing some hustle.

As I forced myself to eat a handful of dry granola to settle my stomach, I ran over the events of the night before. The long, unsuccessful search for Gwen had kept me at the party later than I'd intended to stay and left me far drunker. Connor and I had made our way through the apartment, swigging sickly-sweet buttery nipples straight from the thermos, until the search devolved into a farce. We found increasingly silly hiding places to check, throwing cabinets open, peering under beds, and collapsing into giggles on the floor. I remembered with a lurch of my stomach that I had even taken a puff of Bird's pot on the back balcony. I had a vague memory of Connor holding the empty thermos upside down over the railing, shaking out the last drops, and then opening his hand. A moment later I heard the thermos crack on the sidewalk below, followed by the grating, limping sound of it rolling to a rest in the grass. I wasn't sure when I had finally collapsed into bed, but it wasn't before 4 a.m.

The coffee helped with the headache, and I packed my work apron with single-dose packets of Advil for later. By the time I got to work, I'd rallied, and the adrenaline kick of an early slam finished waking me up. For a time, I fanned strawberries atop dimensional French toast stacks, drizzled hot syrup from a flagon we kept on Sterno, and poured endless pitchers of bitter melon mimosas like I was made for it.

Then, just a few hours into my shift, I cratered. It happened so quickly, I almost dropped the thermal coffeepot at a customer's table—mid-refill, it had begun to weigh several tons more than it should. I finished the pour and stepped back for a second as a wave of dizziness crashed over me. Then I found my way to the wait station, grabbed an ice cube from the chest with my bare hands, and rubbed it on my forehead and temples.

Derek poked his head around the corner. "I just sat you a four-top."

"Right now? Is there any way you could give it to someone else, please?"

He just looked at me. "Aren't you doing a double today? We're not even halfway to first cut yet, girl."

"I just need a minute."

He paused. "I'll get their waters." Sloshing ice into four glasses where they stood prepped on trays, he palmed three waters in his left hand and picked up the fourth with his right. Just before heading out of the wait station, he looked back at me one more time. "And a drink order."

"Thanks." I ran to the bathroom, puked up half a thermos's worth of buttery nipples and everything I'd eaten that morning, and felt instantly better. Dampening a rough paper towel, I sponged the sweat off my face and inhaled the clean, dry scent of the expensive lavender soap they kept in the bathrooms. It always smelled like money to me.

The slam eased off, but the customers kept coming in a steady trickle, and no one got cut. It was 4:30 when Derek finally let us all go at once and said he'd cover the floor himself until the evening waitstaff—i.e., me—arrived. I sank gratefully into a chair at the bar to roll silver and eat. I couldn't resist ordering a burger, though it was too expensive even with the employee discount. I was starving.

After what seemed like only a few minutes, Derek came over, wearing a curious expression. "A table has requested you," he said, arching an eyebrow. "Two-top."

"I'm not on until five."

"I have terrible news for you." He swiveled his hairy wrist around and pulled back the cuff to reveal his watch. "It's five fifteen."

It wasn't possible. I looked at the silverware tub in front of me, only half-full. I hadn't finished rolling. I hadn't finished my burger. I hadn't even finished my checkout for the day shift. What had I been doing for forty-five minutes?

"Can't you just start them for me?"

"And disappoint your guests?" He pointed around the corner. "Go get 'em."

Tying on my apron again, I felt the Advil packets jabbing my leg, ripped one open, and popped a few. Derek had said it was a two-top. Gwen and Connor were the only people who knew I'd be working tonight. I tried to think of something suitably grumpy to say as I walked over. Of course, Gwen, after disappearing last night, would come up with the brilliant idea of coming to visit me at work. What did she care about dropping a few hundred dollars on a meal just to say hello? It was nothing to her. And of course Connor, having spent the day sleeping off a buttery nipple hangover, would want to come along. He'd be simply famished. They both would.

I turned the corner and almost stopped dead in my tracks. Bethany and Rocky sat in the middle of my section, Bethany's auburn hair stark against the sea of white starched tablecloths, Rocky's collared shirt stretched taut between hunched shoulders. Bethany put up her hand like a second grader and actually waved, as if I could possibly miss them in the nearly empty restaurant.

"Mac! What a surprise," Bethany said as I came closer. She did not, of course, look surprised at all. Just as she'd known where to find me in the library, she'd somehow known I'd be working here today. Rocky barely looked up, acknowledging my presence with a half-wave. He looked miserable.

"Do you guys come here often?" I asked politely.

"Not as often as you'd think, considering we live in the building," Bethany said.

I almost gasped, but stopped myself in time and said instead, "It must be a great place to live."

"We like it," she replied cordially. "Anyway, when you mentioned working here the other day—Pyotr, Mac has an off-campus job, but we won't tell anyone, will we?—it reminded me this place exists. So, we wandered down for an early dinner tonight. I was sure you said you worked lunches. You see I remember specifically, because of the Friday class. What a delightful surprise it was to spot you at the bar."

"I don't usually work nights," I was forced to explain. "This is my first."

"Well, we're easy customers, aren't we?" She appealed to Rocky without for one moment diverting her saucer eyes from mine. "What's good?"

"I don't usually eat here," I said, breaking a cardinal rule of waiting tables: never confess ignorance of the menu. "The only thing I've tried is the burger, because it's the cheapest." *Why mince words,* I thought. *Bethany likes the prickly ones.* I was feeling prickly. "But the steak au poivre and the gigot d'agneau are the two most expensive entrées, so I would assume they are both very nice."

"Perfect," Bethany said without batting an eyelash. "He'll have the steak and I'll have the lamb. House salads first. And with the meal, whatever wine pairings the chef recommends." She folded the menu and handed it to me. "There. I said we were easy."

Rocky looked up at last, handed me the menu, and said, "I'll take a scotch and soda before the meal. As soon as humanly possible."

I knew how soon he meant and made it myself, since the bartender wasn't on yet. When I set it down, he parted his lips in a bilious smile. "Hair of the dog," he said, and took a sip.

"Do you know, dear, that Mac is my new student?" Bethany

said brightly. "She's meeting me once a week for independent study. Just like you and Gwen."

Just like you and Gwen.

So, Gwen had been hiding something, too—one-on-one meetings with Rocky. I felt a pang of betrayal, accompanied by something akin to relief. Now I didn't have to feel so guilty about my own secret. Nor did I have to envy Gwen hers. My time in the Program may not have taught me much else, but I knew the faculty pecking order. Rocky wasn't a full professor, only an associate. He was respected in his field but hardly a name.

His face turned a peculiar shade of bluish white. He chuckled, then shook his head, then chuckled again. Was it learning about Bethany and me that bothered him, or the fact that I'd learned about Gwen and him?

"Bethany, you do know how to pick them," he said. "I gave Mac a ride up to the farmhouse for the retreat. She's a hard worker and a true believer." He took a long swig of his scotch and soda. "To tell the truth, I'm wishing I'd gotten there first."

"Gwen's wonderful," Bethany purred, as if they were complimenting one another's children. She turned to me. "And I forgot the two of you were such close friends!"

"We're roommates."

"So are Rocky and I," Bethany said pleasantly. "Listen, we have to have you both over for dinner. Sort of a double date."

"Beth." Rocky put down his drink.

"I insist. Rocky, they wrote statements of support for each other's applications! They've known each other since *childhood*." She turned back to me. "You'll tell Gwen all about it? And, Mac, we owe you dinner anyway, for crashing in on your work like this. Interrupting your burger."

Rocky, having drained his drink, looked rosy once again.

"Okay, Mac, what do you say? If it's no, my wife will never forgive me."

"Of course. It's a kind offer."

"Good girl," he said. "Another of these, while you're at it."

After the double, the walk home felt endless. By the time I
crawled up the stairs to our apartment and slumped through
the door, my body felt like it had been hit by a truck. There
were so many different types of pain. My head was a cannonball,
the space between my shoulder blades a tight, burning band; my
hips ached like a rusty gate, and my lower back felt as if someone extraordinarily heavy were sitting on it, kicking their heels
into my hamstrings. I had to get to bed.

But first, I turned my apron over and dumped its contents
onto the bed. I'd been too wiped out to count my tips after
checkout, a state I hadn't even known existed. I stared blankly
at the loose pile of bills, then separated it mechanically into
stacks of twenties, tens, fives, and ones. I counted the stacks.

That couldn't be right.

I closed my eyes, took a deep breath, opened them. I counted
again.

Eight hundred and eighty-four dollars.

I'd made almost nine hundred dollars in a single shift—well,
two shifts back-to-back, about twelve hours total. Still. Nine
hundred dollars was my share of the rent. I'd made rent in a
single day. The Sunday double was the answer to my prayers. If I
could pull a double every week, I'd be making twice as much as
I needed to live on—at least. I could send half my money home
and still put enough in the bank to build up a cushion for emergencies. I could buy one of those cashmere sweaters or a pair of
designer jeans from the "denim bar" Connor had told me about

on the north side of town. I could throw away my flimsy boots, which were so obviously plastic, and replace them with riding boots of thick, horsey leather. I could treat Gwen for once. The possibilities were endless.

I folded the stack with the singles on the outside and stuck it in the back of my top drawer, next to the Friday and Saturday rolls. It made them look pitifully small, like burgers from a fast-food joint after you've eaten one at a place like Nona.

On a strange impulse, I pulled out the Sunday stack again, still folded in half, and opened my mouth wide. Keeping my lips curled back, I shut my eyes and closed my teeth delicately around the outermost bills. The smell of cash, distinct and indescribable, paper and ink and millions of dirty fingerprints, filled my nostrils; its acrid breath stung the back of my throat. I slowly closed my jaw, feeling the delicious, springy give of the paper between my teeth, until the bills were fully compressed into a solid mass of pure possibility.

There was a knock at the door, and I leaned forward, dropping the mess of rapidly unfolding bills back into the drawer and slamming it shut so fast, I almost smashed my finger.

"Hey," Gwen said. She was leaning on my doorframe, eyes barely open, in her flannel pajamas and robe.

"You're still up?"

"I wanted to say hi before you went to bed." She smiled sleepily. "I feel like I haven't seen you in forever."

"I had to work a double today."

"Yeah, I know. You work all the time." She yawned. "I don't know how you do it. You must be exhausted."

"I had a hangover. It sucked."

"Connor told me you guys were looking for me."

"Yeah. Where were you?"

"Was it around midnight?" She fiddled with the drawstring of her pajama pants. "I ran out for more liquor around then. Maybe we just missed each other."

"I guess we must've."

"So, how'd it go today?"

"Pretty good. I made bank." I flashed mentally through all of today's milestones—the puking, the rolling of silver, Bethany. At least they'd left me a fifty-dollar tip. "So, um, is Rocky, like, one of your advisers now?"

"Oh." Gwen frowned slowly, as if trying to remember what I could be referring to. "Yeah. He wants to work with me. He liked my paper for Futures—you know, the one I showed you? He thinks it could be part of a larger project. Of course, he wants my focus to be on his virtual museum stuff, and I'm not really sure that's what I want to work on, so . . ." She trailed off.

"So?"

"So, I'm not sure," she repeated. "Why?"

"Oh, it's just the weirdest thing. I waited on him and Bethany tonight, of all people." It came back to me, and I almost laughed. "She invited me to dinner."

"Why?" Gwen said.

A hot surge of acid scorched the back of my throat. "You mean, because I'm not anyone important? Don't worry, you're invited, too. I guess we're a package deal."

Her eyes snapped open, as if she were awake for the first time. "No, come on, Mac, no. I just mean— You know that's not what I meant."

"It is weird, though, right? I'm not even in her class." This would have been the time to tell Gwen I had met with Bethany, and I had intended to, but something perverse in me rose up and blocked it. Maybe I was hurt that she hadn't told me about Rocky. I wondered what their meetings were like, whether Rocky wore his flirtatious grin when they were alone. "I guess they just felt sorry for me because I was *serving* them."

"I don't think anyone feels—"

"Just like you feel sorry for me, don't you?" It came out like a cough, the thought I'd shoved down plenty of times pushed to the surface somehow by the private sessions with Bethany, the money in the drawer. "For my mom and Lily and my deadbeat dad."

"I don't feel sorry for you, Mac," Gwen said. "You feel sorry enough for yourself." She swiveled and walked away. I could hear her sock feet padding down the hall over the creaky boards and back into her bedroom. A door closed, and there was a squeak of bedsprings followed by silence.

In the new quiet, I noticed a few twenties had fluttered to the floor when I slammed my dresser shut. I stooped to pick them up, opened my top drawer, and started straightening the chaotic heap of bills again.

One of the singles had teeth marks. I buried it in the center of the stack.

The formal invitation came the next day.

> From: Bethany Ladd <bladd@mail.dhu.edu>
> Subject: Dinner!
> To: Gwendolyn Whitney <gwhitney@dhu.edu>,
> Mackenzie Woods <mwoods@dhu.edu>
> cc: Pyotr Semyonovich
> <psemyonovich@mail.dhu.edu>

November 14, 2011, at 2:15 a.m.

Dearest Gwen and Mac,

Please join Rocky and me for dinner on Saturday, Nov. 26, at 8 p.m. I assume neither of you
are going home for the holiday, none of the first-
years do. Consider it an enlightened alternative
to Thanksgiving dinner. Mac knows the building.
Perhaps you don't know that it was named the
Libertorium in honor of the freedmen who built
it—the height of hypocrisy, much like Thanksgiving itself. Rocky prefers to call it the Liber-
tine-ium. We're in #1914. Please don't bring anything, Rocky is a wonderful cook and we have all
the wine we want or need.
Cheers,
Bethany

I saw the email first thing in the morning and decided not to
respond until Gwen and I had talked things over and I'd come
clean about the class with Bethany. But before I got a chance, I
saw her reply-all on our behalf:

From: Gwendolyn Whitney
<gwhitney@dhu.edu>
Subject: Re: Dinner!
To: Bethany Ladd <bladd@mail.dhu.edu>,
Mackenzie Woods <mwoods@dhu.edu>
cc: Pyotr Semyonovich
<psemyonovich@mail.dhu.edu>
November 14, 2011, at 10:11 a.m.

Dear Bethany,

    We're delighted to accept. Thanks so much for
the invitation! See you in class.

All best,

Gwen

So that was that. I replied, "Looking forward to it!" and got
on with my week. Now that I was back on track in the mornings, things were starting to feel much less dire than they had
the week before. Against all odds, my independent study with
Bethany had not, so far, added to my workload. The second
meeting came and went without any assigned readings. She lec-
tured, and I took notes. The only trouble was, I had no real idea
what the class was about.

"Radical negation is not the logical extension of ethical negation. In fact, it is the *negation* of ethical negation, which we
must use radical negational dialectics to see."

I nodded, as if I had figured this out ages ago and was happy
to hear it confirmed.

"Where the Hegelian dialectic rolls forward through history,
from thesis to antithesis to synthesis, lurching along—"

Like a broken thermos, I thought hazily.

"—the dialectics of radical negation obliterate thesis entirely. Instead of working for a permanent revolution, imagine
playing at an ephemeral anti-revolution." She leaned back in her
chair and folded her hands in her lap. "Questions?"

I could never think of any. Bethany in lecture mode was
passionate and funny and engaging, and her words had a
forcefulness that disabled me, somehow. Sitting so close
to her in the cramped office, I found myself nodding to the
rhythm of her arguments instead of listening to them, watch-

ing the play of sunlight through the ivy as it dappled her cheek. Occasionally a stray beam fell directly into her mouth, lighting it from the inside so that her words seemed to glow. If I felt too close to understand them, I was also too close to mistake their meaning; instead, I simply lived with them in the tiny room, accepting their truth as I accepted that of the carefully chosen objects on the shelves. It all seemed so real in the moment. But when I looked back at my notes later and tried to re-create the ideas from her lectures, I was embarrassed to find that I couldn't make heads or tails of them. No matter how fast I wrote, how hard I tried to copy down her tortuous sentences word for word, so as not to miss her frequent reversals—which were, I was given to believe, very much the point—without her vivid presence, the tangled sentences seemed—I knew they weren't, but they *seemed*—like nonsense.

When it was over, I found Bird waiting on the bench in the hall outside. He registered my dazzled expression and nodded sagely.

"Hot tip." He held up his phone. "Record it."

"What?"

"Trust me. I've been doing it for years."

I recalled just how long Bird had been in the Program and paused to decide if that made his advice more valuable or less. "She won't mind?"

"Oh, don't tell her!" He looked shocked. "Don't ever do that."

"Why not?"

Just then Bethany's voice called, "Come in." Bird tapped a button on his phone and pocketed it with a wry grin as he opened the door.

When I got back to the apartment, I tried one more time

to read Bethany's book. Then I downloaded a recording app. It certainly couldn't hurt.

Without a hangover, my second Sunday double went far more smoothly. The shifts weren't as busy, but at the end of them I still had enough money folded up in my sock drawer to launch me into the week ahead feeling safe and secure. I moved another $600 to my mom's bank account without waiting for her to ask and had the satisfaction of seeing no further calls or texts from her.

The following Wednesday, I hovered outside Bethany's office, debating internally whether to take Bird's advice. I had begun to get a feel for Bethany's personality, and even flattered myself that I was beginning to see through her intimidating facade. I remembered how haughty and spastic she'd been on the first day of class and deduced that standing in front of a classroom full of students was difficult for her. Years with Lily had taught me something about hypersensitivity to stimuli. Maybe Bethany was something of an empath, and those knee-high boots, that woolen cape—even her haircut, with its block-ade of bangs—were the armor that protected her from a world that worked on her like a raw, exposed nerve. Or perhaps it was simpler than that, and her grand, sinister motive for offering independent studies to Tess and me had been that she was shy. She was at her most relaxed and expansive in our one-on-one sessions, but even in her office, the intensity that sometimes vibrated between us could vanish with no warning and the doors to her inner world slam shut. To keep them open, I had to make her feel secure.

At the same time, I also had to learn from her. The underlying purpose of the independent study, she had all but told me on our first meeting, was to develop a project for the Joyner application that was due at the end of the semester. My proposal was supposed to grow out of these sessions, informed and inspired by her theory of radical negation—which, as she often told me, I was helping her to work out, though I had no idea how. Since she had given me no assignments or even readings so far, I assumed my final grade would be based on my Joyner proposal. And so far, I had nothing.

I opened the app, pressed record, slipped my phone into my bag, and walked in.

The session proceeded as usual, and I soon relaxed and forgot about the phone. Then, midway through one of her long, tortuous sentences, Bethany interrupted herself to say, "Mac."

It took me a moment to realize she required a response, it was such a rare circumstance. I laid down my pen and looked up.

"There's something different about you today."

I went red. Did the recording app screen glow through the fabric of my bag? "I'm sorry."

"No, no, it's good. What is it, your hair?"

I raised a hand reflexively to my shoulders and remembered that I'd tied my hair back. "I don't usually wear it this way."

"Oh, I know. Your earrings! Those are really quite beautiful. I suppose with your hair back, I can see them."

I fingered the diamond studs, which I had taken to wearing on Wednesdays for good luck. "My mom gave them to me. They were an engagement present from my father." I warmed to my theme. "He has wonderful taste."

"Indeed. They're so subtle." She leaned forward, rising halfway out of her chair and reaching her hand toward my face so fluidly, I didn't even flinch when I felt her cold, dry fingers on my earlobes. She drew closer to inspect the studs, her dark red hair filling my vision, and I breathed in her caustic, floral scent. In a low voice a few inches from my ear, she said, "They make you sparkle, little star."

Then it was over, and she was sitting back in her slightly oversize office chair, several feet away. "I hope you wear them Saturday," she said, as if she had confidence that I would do the right thing. Then she returned to her lecture.

I hadn't planned to buy something new, but after my Saturday shift, with hours to kill before the dinner, I was seized with the urge to go shopping.

For the first time, I drove to the north side of town, far from the smokestacks by DHU. Here, the ancient brownstones had been renovated into single-family dwellings instead of six-flats, and the central boulevard was lined with boutiques and cafés under twinkle lights. Even the sidewalks were beautiful: mellow red brick in a zigzag pattern, immaculately shoveled. Strolling past shop-window displays of lizard handbags and statement necklaces, I felt palpably lifted by my unusually high bank account balance, as if little wads of cash were strapped to my feet. I bypassed the preppy cashmere scarves and sweaters in colorful stripes, whose quality seemed suddenly both obvious and commonplace—Bethany would never wear something like *that* —and soon settled on a black ballet-neck dress in a heavy, expensive knit. Not too dressy, not too plain. *Subtle*.

On my way to the car, I passed a shop window displaying an exhilarating pair of stack-heeled riding boots in rich caramel leather. Emboldened by my easy success, telling myself I was only looking, I went in and tried them on. They cost twice as much as the dress; they would take the number in my bank account almost down to the double digits. But I had another

Sunday double tomorrow. I took them to the counter in sock feet and paid for them before I could change my mind.

All the way home, I felt like I had gotten away with something. So, this was what it was like, spending money. You wanted a thing, and you didn't have to ask for it, or wait for it to go on sale, or talk yourself out of it. There was no sneaking, no stealing, no looking the other way while someone else paid. You just handed the money over, and you could have anything you wanted.

When I walked into the apartment, Gwen was sitting on the couch waiting for me. Her face was pinched and pale, and she hugged her arms tightly at the elbows.

She stood immediately. "Mac, I'm so sorry."

Full of love for my new clothes, I hugged her.

"I'm sorry, too," I said, as Gwen wiped a few stray tears from her cheeks. "I shouldn't have been such a bitch about this dinner."

"No—you were right. I shouldn't have acted like it was weird that Bethany invited you." She sighed and shook her head a little, laughing at herself in disbelief. "It's going to sound awful, but maybe I was—a little jealous?"

I took a deep breath. "Gwen, I've been doing an independent study with Bethany. It's on Wednesdays. That's why I stopped coming to trivia." I waited for the expression of surprise, but it didn't come.

"I know. I mean, I didn't know the details. But I knew it had to be something like that. I got wind of it the night of the party."

I rolled my eyes. "That Bird guy probably spread it around."

"This place is so gossipy."

"It's like being back in middle school."

"I know."

There was a brief pause, and I remembered that Gwen had gone to a private middle school in Manhattan, while I spent those years sitting alone on the bus in jeans two inches too short for me.

"Anyway," she continued, "I've been kind of working on Bethany to be my adviser—you know, trying to talk a lot in class, going to office hours, that kind of thing—hoping she'd offer to work with me. And she hasn't. So, when I asked why she invited you—I was kind of fishing for information. I should have just asked."

I shook my head. "No, I should have told you. It was on the tip of my tongue, and then I got mad and clammed up."

"I don't blame you." She took a deep breath. "Mac, I know something must be going on back home. Is it Lily?"

Unbidden, my mom's voice came into my head—*some people's lives*—but I ignored it.

"It's just a money problem," I said, amazed at how completely the Sunday doubles had changed my perspective on such things. "Lily's doing fine." Relief at saying the words out loud flooded through me.

"Thank god," Gwen said, tears coming to her eyes again. "I've been so worried. I'm sorry for that shitty thing I said about feeling sorry for yourself. I just—sometimes I don't know how to handle your feelings. They're so intense."

The tension draining out of the air made me feel light-headed, and I let myself collapse onto the sofa, leaning my head on the back. Gwen sat next to me, perched on the edge, her elbows on her knees, her chin in her hands.

"I missed you, Gwen."

"Me too."

There was another long pause, and something occurred to me. "Gwen, don't be offended by this, but— Is that why you've been meeting with Rocky? To get closer to Bethany?"

I stared up at the ceiling to avoid looking at her, and she answered in a muffled voice, as if she had her hands over her face. "It's embarrassing, but yeah. I thought, I don't know, maybe he could sort of put in a good word?"

"Well, maybe he has. She invited both of us tonight."

Gwen turned to me and grabbed my elbow. "This is going to be insane, right?"

"Absolutely bonkers." Suddenly we were back in the forest preserve clearing, surrounded by a half-eaten picnic lunch, joking about meth labs and Corn Queens. I pointed at the bags in the hall. "I even bought new clothes. That's how nervous I am."

"Bring it to my room, we can get ready together."

"Solidarity!" I shouted.

"On this weird night."

"It's going to be so weird."

"Well, Mackenzie." Gwen imitated Bethany's classroom hauteur, adding a posh British accent. "You *doooo* want a top-tier job, don't you? *Research I?*"

"Bethany dear, there's more to life than academics," I rasped as Rocky, brandishing an imaginary glass in the air. "What about *drinking*? Allow me to refill that glass for you, Gwendolyn, sweetheart!"

"Oh, Pyotr, stop pinching the girls' bottoms or you'll never get tenure!"

We rolled on the sofa, shrieking with laughter.

7

It was chilly walking through the early darkness to the Libertorium in our dresses, and we were silent most of the way. The swish of my flared skirt against my new boots made the familiar path strange. Gwen had applied my makeup, and I could still feel the slow, cold sweep of the triangle sponge over my cheeks and the precise feathery strokes of the eye liner, see the fireworks behind my closed lids as she smudged my eye shadow with her little finger. When I opened my eyes and looked in the mirror, I saw a serene and beautiful woman staring back at me where I was used to seeing a flushed, anxious, overgrown adolescent. Gwen pulled my hair up into a bun, and the earrings looked, for the first time, as if they really belonged.

In the elevator, I very nearly pushed the button for Nona by mistake. As we whooshed past the mezzanine, I tried to forget that in twelve hours I'd be back here again, wearing work pants and an apron. We emerged into a white-walled hallway, my first time to see the residential part of the building, and followed it all the way to the end.

I turned to Gwen.

"Here we go," she whispered with a tight smile. She rang the doorbell.

I couldn't quite place what was strange about the sound of approaching footsteps on the other side of the door until it opened, and Bethany stood in the doorway, barefoot.

"Come in, come in! Oh, you're all dressed up, and here I am looking like a pajama party." She gestured at her oversize red sweater and jeans, which, compared to Gwen's and my dresses, looked both comfortable and enviably covered-up.

The apartment we stepped into with conspicuously clacking heels was not the icy modernist loft I had been anticipating, but rather a warm, inviting aerie, the rooms painted odd shades that complemented one another perfectly, salmon and teal and buff under white birthday-cake moldings. Photographs and brightly colored miscellany hung on the walls, and neat rows of books sandwiched between antique bronzes and fertility gods lined the mantel and windowsills and every other amenable surface, giving the apartment a comfortably cluttered look. The lights were low and ambient, emanating softly from lamps. On the dining room table, real candles flickered in tall brass candlesticks.

A beam of brightness spilled out from the navy-walled kitchen, where overhead lights were presumably indispensable, and Rocky appeared in the kitchen doorway. He, at least, was dressed to his normal level of dapperness.

"Girls! Let me pour you some wine!" I stifled a grin and forced myself not to make eye contact with Gwen as he plied us with pleasantries.

Behind me, Bethany was taking Gwen's coat and exclaiming

over her dress. I kept walking and passed the threshold into the kitchen, where Rocky hovered over a fleet of wineglasses in various shapes and sizes. "Bethany hates stemware, but I insist on using it for parties. It's good luck if it breaks."

Tiny china plates littered the countertop, each heaped with a different jewel-like substance. I gestured toward them. "These are so beautiful."

"Zakuski!" he said, beaming. "This is what we eat before the meal in Ukraine. These are cauliflowers, red peppers, and beets—I pickled them all myself. Here we have cold potatoes and sardines in oil. Deviled eggs. Cabbage dumplings. And here is salmon roe, trout roe, and, best of all, the beluga, a special treat for me." Describing the food had brought Rocky's accent to the surface. He slid a glass of white across the island toward me, sloshing it ever so slightly, and gestured toward the other glasses. "White before dinner, so as not to ruin the taste buds. We'll have champagne with the caviar—Bethany prefers it to vodka, though it's less authentic. Red with the meal. A digestif afterward."

"Are you trying to kill us?" I laughed.

"If I wanted that, I'd insist on the vodka," he said with a wink. Then he slapped his forehead. "Where are my manners? The kitchen is hot. Allow me to take your coat."

Without waiting for my assent, Rocky stepped around me and curled his fingers under the lapels of my jacket from behind, lifting it gracefully off my shoulders. His knuckles traced a path along my bare collarbone and caught on the neck of my dress lightly, in a way that could have been accidental or not. I shivered.

"You are still cold?" His voice sounded closer to my ear than I expected.

"No, I'm all right." I stepped forward and picked up the wineglass, feeling Rocky's eyes slide along my torso, from shoulder to waistline.

"You look very beautiful tonight," he said.

But when I turned around, he was already on his way to the hall with my coat. Bethany and Gwen appeared in the doorway.

"Mac, pour us some white," Bethany commanded, and I obeyed as unquestioningly as if I were taking orders on a brunch shift. "So, Gwen, remind me who you studied with at Columbia?"

Gwen thanked me as she took her wineglass, and then obediently began listing her undergraduate professors. I held out the other glass to Bethany, who turned without seeing it and led Gwen into the living room, still exclaiming over old colleagues. Unsure what to do, I followed them with Bethany's wineglass in one hand and my own in the other.

Rocky stood politely in front of his armchair while Bethany and Gwen settled onto the sofa. I placed Bethany's wine on the coffee table in front of her just as she heaved a sigh and said, "You must miss New York terribly. And, I suppose, the *real* Ivy League."

I took the only open seat on the other side of the coffee table from Rocky, but, seeing that Gwen and Bethany were still deep in a conversation that excluded me, he crossed over and pulled up a hard-backed chair at my elbow.

"So, how has the independent study with Bethany been going?" He leaned forward confidentially, putting, I thought, scare quotes around the words *independent study*. "Is she . . ." He paused to search for the word. "Enlightening?"

"I don't think she would call it that," I said truthfully. "But I do love the class. It's pushing me, intellectually. It's making me think in different ways than I ever have before."

"Hmm," he said, a menacing twinkle in his eye. "Not like my class."

"No, I didn't mean that! I love Futures. It's just—you know, you can go so much deeper one-on-one."

"Mine is an introductory-level course." He bared white teeth under his smooth, flared lips. "There is much more to be done with the topic, for those who choose to go on with it." In the background, I could hear Bethany chattering on, something about having to fire her research assistant after so many years, what a shame, and then it was back to New York again, the subways, the food, Gwen's inaudible responses drawing enthusiastic agreement from Bethany: *I know, I know!*"

"I know," I echoed. Then, perhaps goaded by all this New York talk and starting to feel the wine, I found myself saying, "I might do something with virtual museums and film. Or something."

"Really?" Rocky looked at once flattered and amused.

"Maybe. I'm still deciding."

He leaned forward and put a hand lightly on my knee. "If you want to talk more about it, I'm always available. You know, this year, I intend to support one student application for the Joyner."

The conversation on the sofa ceased abruptly. Bethany leaned forward and picked up her wineglass from the coffee table as if seeing it for the first time. She took a long sip while Rocky withdrew his hand from my knee casually but not quickly.

"Don't listen to him, my dear. Rocky is always trying to nab the Joyner for one of his students, but he hasn't done it yet. It's cute, really."

"It only takes the right student," he said, lifting his wineglass and saluting her with a swig. "What's cute is Bethany thinking it's her, and not her students, who win the fellowship. It's admirable, I suppose, how she accepts the heavy burden of responsibility."

"I haven't heard any complaints."

"Bethany's policy is take all the praise, and none of the blame," Rocky said to Gwen and me.

"Blame me all you want, darling, no one's stopping you. But don't try to poach my students from under my nose. Mac's too smart for you."

"That's patently clear," he said, flashing me a dazzling smile. "Here's to Mac." He raised his glass and took another sip, nearly emptying it.

Gwen held up her glass, which was more than half-empty. She was already a little tipsy, and I guessed, with a flash of sympathy, that she'd been sipping nervously while Bethany talked. "To Mac," she said. "My best friend."

Bethany nodded, making eye contact with me for the first time. "Mac the Beauty Queen. Long may she reign." They drank.

I raised my glass. "If we're toasting me, we have to toast Gwen. Without her, I wouldn't even be here." The wine was going to my head, too. "Here's to Gwen!"

"To Gwen!" Bethany raised her glass.

"I must refill for this!" shouted Rocky. "You deserve more than a drop for a toast."

He came back with a freshly opened bottle and made the rounds, splashing everyone full before saying, "To Gwen! The future of the futures of art history!" and swallowing half his new glass in one gulp.

Next, Rocky insisted on toasting Bethany and himself, both

separately and together, and then after that, in rapid succession, roommates, students, and colleagues. When he arrived at the department chair, Bethany cut him off, laughing. "Must we?"

"Then it's zakuski time at last! Up, up, everyone to the table."

The dining room table was a massive oak slab set with woven place mats, flanked with rough wooden benches and high-backed chairs upholstered in shockingly bright floral silk. Rocky disappeared into the kitchen and came out with armloads of the tiny plates, which he carried and placed on the table with a waiter's practiced ease. Next came towel-lined baskets that turned out to contain warm, soft buckwheat pancakes the size of my palm—Rocky called them blini—and dishes of sour cream and chives. The last thing he brought out was the bottle of chilled champagne with four flutes.

"We've already used up all our subjects for toasts, so I suggest you merely drink this as quickly as you can," he said. "Everyone dig in."

The zakuski were messy but delicious, the pickles dripping brine all over the place mats, the cold yellow potatoes weeping oil. I'd never tried caviar before, had even scraped the orange blobs of salmon roe off of supermarket sushi, but that was clearly not an option tonight. At Rocky's suggestion, I covered a warm pancake with melting sour cream and dropped a dollop of the black caviar on top. It looked so much like a pile of tiny seed beads that I half expected them to scatter and roll off my plate onto the floor.

"More, much more," Rocky urged—he sat at my left at the foot of the table, Bethany at the head, Gwen directly across from me—and I complied. When I bit into my caviar-heaped pancake and felt the cool, briny beads burst on my tongue, tears came to my eyes. "Now the champagne," he said. I took a swig

while some of the caviar was still in my mouth and felt its dry
sweetness meet and mingle with the swirls of saline. After that
I ate countless blini heaped with caviar, neglecting the dishes of
red and gold roe in favor of the expensive black beluga. Rocky
seemed pleased.

Everyone else seemed pleased, too, both with themselves
and, for the moment, with each other. Having passed over a
bump early in the evening, it was as if we were all silently turning to each other again and again, congratulating one another
on having jointly spun this warm buzzy cocoon of food and wine
and laughter. Bethany acted amused by Rocky's antics and af-
fectionate toward Gwen and me; Gwen, I thought, had seldom
looked happier.

"We are almost ready for the main dish!" Rocky said. "Who
is hungry?"

I was amazed to find that I was, but Gwen demurred.

"That is because we have had no vodka."

"Pyotr Semyonovich," Bethany said. "Absolutely not."

"Vodka makes room in the stomach," Rocky explained as
Gwen pursed her lips.

"That's Ukrainian nonsense with no basis in fact." Bethany
turned to Gwen earnestly. "They also think you get a cold from
being out in the rain."

"Nevertheless, it is true!" Rocky protested.

"I'll try it." I held up my empty glass.

"Good girl! This is a very sensible student of yours, Bethany. I can see why you like her." He went into the kitchen
again, shouting over his shoulder, "One shot! You will see how
much more hungry you are after one shot. Or, if not one, then
two."

· · ·

Half an hour later, Gwen, Rocky, and I were all roaring drunk.

Bethany, perhaps accustomed to this turn of events, had accepted her shot, but when we all tipped ours back, sending the fire straight down our throats, she only sipped off the top of hers and set it back on the table. Every time Rocky sang another song, yelled another saying in Ukrainian, and insisted we take another shot, she nursed her vodka, watching us wryly.

It really did make me feel hungrier. I put down a few more blini between shots, and when Rocky brought a platter of beef tenderloin and roasted vegetables from the kitchen, I attacked it with a fresh appetite. Rocky tipped cabernet into our forgotten wineglasses, and for a moment there was a lull in the laughter and talking as, remembering ourselves before this more serious course, we set about cutting up the beef and eating it in the politest way our drunken hands could manage. I sipped cautiously at the red, aware that the table was already slanting, and was relieved when its dusty warmth seemed to steady me.

In the temporary calm, through which the genteel dinner party music was audible for the first time in over an hour, I looked up from my plate at the three faces around me and was seized with a feeling that was both new and old. It came on me as suddenly as a stomach cramp: Bethany and Rocky, Gwen and me.

We were not a family. Gwen was not my sister. Rocky and Bethany were not our parents. Nevertheless, sitting around the table, I felt for the first time how professors could be like family, how they could, in fact, make Gwen and me into something closer to sisters than we could ever be on our own. They taught us. They mentored us. They fed us, mind and body; they protected us from catastrophe; they prepared us for the world ahead. When we were burdened with impossible tasks and surrounded with words as impenetrable as swarms of bees, they made the Program survivable. We loved them, in a way. We couldn't help it. They were all we had.

I felt tears rising and then, with a hiccup, the mellow beef. I caught myself in time. Excusing myself, I rose from my bench and walked crookedly down the hall to the bathroom. Once inside, the rose wallpaper and brighter lights woke me up a little. I flicked cold water on my face with my fingers and patted my flushed neck with a wet hand. The sentimental nausea dwindled. I looked at the mirror, trying to convince myself that I was marginally sober, and rejoiced to find that if I concentrated I could stop my reflection from tilting.

I went to the bathroom and flushed the toilet, then washed my hands, dried them, and went out into the hall. I felt steadier on my way back to the table, stable enough to look up rather than at my feet.

Which is how, just before crossing the threshold, I came to meet Bethany's eyes at a distance of some twenty feet. She was standing just inside the door to the kitchen opposite me and, like me, she had halted just before stepping into the dining room. Her eyes were perfectly steady and calm, but wide, in their doll-like, eloquent way. Without moving her head, she lowered her eyes slightly toward the table and raised them back to mine, challenging me to look.

I followed her gaze downward and saw that Rocky had Gwen's hand between his on the table and was massaging it, saying something very soft and low. From where I stood, I could see Gwen's face. She stared into his eyes with a vodka-addled expression that knocked the breath out of my lungs.

Bethany melted silently back into the kitchen, and as if I were her mirror, I reeled backward into the hall, my only thought to get out of there before they saw me watching. One of my heels caught on the runner, and I tripped and fell to my knees with a bang. When I looked up, Rocky stood over me, cracking jokes as he gallantly helped me to my feet. The conversation restarted with a rush as if a radio had been turned back on. By the time the four of us had settled back around the table in our respective spots, we were all laughing louder than ever, Gwen loudest of all, flushed and defiant over her empty wineglass. Everything looked the same. Nothing was the same.

It wasn't just a pass. Even a very drunk Gwen would have shown some confusion, perhaps even revulsion, if it had been the first time he'd touched her. Instead, I had seen something on her face I had never seen there before, in all our time as best friends. It was a combination of anxiety, tenderness, and raw, unbridled lust.

They had already slept together.

What's more, Bethany knew. Had known. The whole time we were seated around that table, laughing and drinking and gorging on zakuski, I had been the only one who'd been in the dark.

Dinner had a long snout, but a short tail. I had seen what I'd been meant to see.

Somehow or other, the beef was disposed of, a desultory offer of fruit rejected, and dessert wine poured in lieu of actual dessert. The party never quite made it to the living room, where we'd been headed; instead, we gulped our tiny glasses of tokaji in the entry hall. Only Bethany seemed capable of understanding, much less orchestrating, the part of the evening that had to happen next, herding us away from the living room and toward the coat closet. Gwen was weaving on her feet like a boxer about to go down, and Rocky looked only slightly better. The shock I had experienced, and the rush of adrenaline that went with it, had given me the presence of mind to stop drinking afterward. As a result, I was just sober enough to see that Gwen was in no shape to answer questions, but still drunk enough that I wouldn't be able to resist asking them.

Perhaps to stall that inevitable moment, I stopped by the bathroom once more, slouching onto the toilet seat and letting go with a sigh of relief that this evening would soon be over. The chorus of mumbles from the entryway, amplified in curious ways by the wood floor, was accompanied by the unmistakable sound of coat zippers. It was a comfortingly final sound. Whatever happened next, we had all survived dinner.

While I was washing my hands, I heard Bethany's voice ring out unexpectedly loud and clear: "Be a dear and walk Gwen home. Mac and I have some things to talk over."

I tried to open the door without drying my hands, slipped on the doorknob, toweled them off quickly, and burst out, all the while hearing Rocky's slurred objections and Bethany's overruling statements. But I was too late. By the time I made it to the entryway, Rocky and Gwen were gone, and Bethany was locking the door behind them.

She turned, her hands still on the doorknob, and leaned her back against the door. Then she broke into a wide, slow smile. "Well," she said. "Finally."

"Why did you send them off—?" I almost said "together," but I couldn't quite bring it out.

"To get Gwen home safely, of course. You've heard the neighborhood is dangerous, I think."

"How thoughtful of you. But I think I could have managed Gwen myself."

"Yes, you've been doing a bang-up job of it so far." She left her position by the door and walked over to the sofa, where she curled up like a cat, folding her legs and tucking her bare feet under her thighs.

"What do you mean?" I made my voice icy to cover a tremble.

"You saw them."

"I saw—" I closed my eyes for a moment, forcing myself to see it again. "Nothing really. Hands touching. It could have been an accident."

"Don't play stupid, Mac. You know as well as I do that whatever's between them didn't start tonight."

"I don't know that."

"Well, I do." She smiled smugly.

"Then why—for god's sake, why haven't you said something? And why invite us over here? Is this your idea of a fun evening?"

She stretched her arms up above her head, the bat wings of her cowl-neck sweater tugging at the hem. "I didn't say anything because I was waiting to see whether she'd tell you herself. You are best friends, after all." She dropped her arms back down. "And I invited you to dinner to give her a reason to tell."

"Why would you want that?"

"Because, Mac," she said coolly. "If she'd told you, that would have proven it was just a harmless little crush, a freshman fling —for both of them. Rocky's a big boy, but he's still a boy. He does this all the time." She looked at me pointedly. "That can't come as a shock to you, can it?"

I blushed, remembering Rocky's fingers on my neck, his hand on my knee. To clear my head, I said, "Don't you . . . mind?"

"When I was coming up, we all slept with our professors. It was a rite of passage, an apprenticeship of sorts. Mitch Betelman, my sweet old adviser, used to marry a new student about as often as he had his regalia dry-cleaned. Nobody raised an eye-brow unless it was an undergrad—and even then, it could be managed. With a proper waiting period and a certain amount of decorum." She laughed drily. "Things are different now. Except they're not different at all."

"You knew that when you married Rocky?"

For the first time, she looked truly startled by something I'd said. "My dear, he was my student at Penn."

My head was spinning, disconnected thoughts whirling through it. A rite of passage, like getting flashed on the sub-way in New York. Was this ethical negation in practice? A ques-tion at last, but this wasn't office hours. I put my hand to my forehead.

"And you think Gwen . . ."

"If Gwen had confided in you, it would have been because this has all been an exciting, naughty little adventure for her. A good girl—she's practically a virgin, isn't she?—gone bad. You would have giggled about it together, and the secret would be out, and eventually it would be over on its own."

I walked over to the armchair where Rocky had been sitting at the start of the evening and, not yet ready to sit, put my hand on its back to support me. "But she didn't tell me."

"Obviously." Bethany rearranged her cowl officiously.

"What does that mean?"

"It means she's playing another game altogether. Something far more important to her. And more dangerous to me." *To us,* I had thought she was going to say, and somehow I thought that was what she meant.

I narrowed my eyes. My head was starting to hurt, even the heavily shaded lamp near Bethany was glaring. "We're not play-ing a game here. Gwen is my friend—"

"And she went behind your back to fuck someone you were fully intending to fuck yourself," she said. "Listen, don't bother denying it. I don't blame you. He's very good-looking. Why do you think I married him? It wasn't for his brains, I can tell you that. I've got all the brains I need right here." She tapped her temple. "He makes me feel young. And he's fantastic in bed."

Fantastic in bed. I thought of all the frantic fucking I'd done in college, trying to compensate for the fact that Gwen was off strolling the green lawns of the Ivy League while I was at Urbana College. It had been thoroughly adequate fucking, and I liked the orgasms. Moreover, I had chosen every encounter. I never waited for men to come to me; I went to parties, zeroed in on my best shot, and attacked, and I rarely missed. But in the Program, I had become suddenly, uncharacteristically celibate, despite being surrounded by attractive, intelligent colleagues making eyes at one another across the library carrels. What more had I wanted? Was it Rocky? He was certainly better looking than most of my peers: broad in the chest, slender in the hips, always armored in those stiff layers of suiting that made grown men so mysteriously untouchable, all you could think about was sliding a hand beneath their jackets and finding the hidden pockets. His frank stare and constant teasing made me blush. And the way he'd leapt to offer me a ride, knowing we'd be alone together in the car, had made me feel, for once, chosen.

As if anyone would choose me when Gwen was standing right there, pretty and petite with a thoroughbred sheen. I thought of Gwen staggering off alone with Rocky into the night, laughing and leaning on him all the way home, dropping the keys as she let him into our apartment. Rocky kissing Gwen hard up against the wall, dragging the shift up over her hips, hoisting her body easily up to the chair rail, and wrapping her legs around his waist so he could stumble with her down the long hallway to the bedroom. Pushing her down onto taut, smooth sheets with such a high thread count they felt like human skin.

Fantastic in bed.

As if she could read my thoughts, Bethany smirked. "I wouldn't worry about tonight," she said. "He won't be a stallion after all that vodka. They've probably passed out by now. As a matter of fact, you should really stay here tonight, to give them time to sleep it off. You wouldn't want to embarrass them in the morning."

I sank down in the armchair with my head in my hands.

"Mac, she doesn't want him. She wants the Joyner."

I looked up, stung with the suddenness of the revelation.

Bethany steepled her hands, pressing the fingertips together. "And the sooner you decide she can't have it, the better for both of us."

It was dawning on me, clearing the confused fog of grief and rage and desire I had felt at the thought of Rocky and Gwen, their limbs intertwined. "But you said your students always get the Joyner. You said Rocky's students don't stand a chance."

"Normally that's true. He doesn't have any influence with the committee. But with Gwen, he might just have a shot."

"She's that smart?"

"You're smart," Bethany said. "Gwen's perfect."

It hit me hard, and I swallowed it down like a shot of vodka —cold and burning.

"You're going to have to work hard, Mac. Harder than you've ever worked before. Your attention is still divided, and that's what's going to lose you the Joyner. Quit the job, live on rice and beans if you have to. Gwen doesn't have a job or any other distractions—just Rocky, and he'll move heaven and earth for her now. He knows he's closer with her than he's ever been. He thinks she could take him to the top."

"That's what he wants, too?"

"Poor puppy. He's tired of being treated like a spousal hire. He wants to take me down a peg. Hooking the Joyner will make him look like the next big thing." She sighed. "And I'll start to look my age."

"And what about me?" It came out before I could stop it.

"He doesn't care about you," she said. "Or Gwen, for that matter. It's just a bonus that a girl with brains like that is also such a nice piece of tail."

My head was pounding now. "I need some water."

"Of course." She stood up immediately, back in hostess mode, and hustled off toward the kitchen. "I'll get you some headache powders, too," she called over her shoulder. I heard the tap run, a drawer open with a squeal, and then she was back, holding a glass of water and a wax paper packet. "Trust me, these are as powerful as aspirin, and they work twice as fast. The secret is a tiny bit of caffeine. Just try not to taste it."

I ripped open the packet and threw the powder toward the back of my throat, where its bitterness instantly brought tears to my eyes. Then I chugged the glass of water all the way down.

"Good girl," she said, like Rocky. "Now come over here for a minute. I won't bite."

I sat at the opposite end of the sofa.

"Allow me." She pulled my right boot up onto the sofa, moved her hand around the back of my calf to find the zipper, and pulled it down. The hot leather unstuck itself from my tights, and a cool current of air rushed down my leg. It felt wonderful. She slid the boot off and looked at it for a moment before zipping it back up and setting it carefully on the floor. "What lovely boots. Now the other one, please."

The headache powders peeled a thin layer of pain away from my skull all at once and, overcome with lassitude, I obeyed. A gush of cool air hit my left leg, and the other boot was gone. I rubbed the webbed toes of one foot on the arch of the other, enjoying the delicious feeling of stocking feet. Bethany leaned back on her side of the sofa, pulled her knees up in front of her so that our toes were almost touching, and began lightly brushing the tops of my feet with her fingernails. It felt incredibly soothing. I closed my eyes and let myself sink into the pause, a sweet stillness that I knew would have to end soon. I pushed away the thought of why.

"Bethany," I said, eyes closed.

"Hmmm."

"Please tell me something. Honestly."

"Of course, Beauty Queen."

"Was I your first choice?"

There was a pause.

"I mean, would you rather it was Gwen? If none of this had happened. If Rocky hadn't—started working with her. Did you only pick me because she was already . . . ?" I trailed off.

Bethany left off playing with my toes and got down, to my surprise, on her knees on the carpet between the sofa and coffee table. She trudged up the little trench until she was even with me, looking into my eyes. "No, little star. I picked you because you're better. You have guts." She placed a hand on my stomach. "Gwen has brains and so do you. But you want it more. You reek of it."

She leaned toward me as if to inhale, paused an inch away,

and instead put her mouth over mine. Her hand slid up from my stomach to my breast.

I jerked upright. Put both feet on the floor.

She sat back on her haunches, unperturbed, tracing her index finger around my ankle. "Mac, let's enjoy this. We know their secret, and they don't know ours. That gives us power."

"I've never—" I stopped.

"Not even with Gwen? I'm surprised."

I meant with a professor. She meant with a woman. Either way, putting Gwen into the sliver of space between us felt somehow sacrilegious. "Of course, not with Gwen."

"Look at me. Look at me, Mac." She maneuvered herself around me until she was kneeling between my legs, looking up into my eyes. "Mac, you are the one I want. I don't want Gwen. I never wanted Gwen. It was always, always you." She slid her hands up my calves to my knees. Then her hands moved to the insides of my thighs; one wrapped around my hip to pull me closer while the other warmed the crotch of my tights. She leaned in close, her breasts touching mine, her hands generating a warm friction that affected me like a drug. I relaxed and tensed at the same time, pure animal. "Think of Rocky and Gwen," she breathed, the fingers of her left hand walking up toward my navel, then hooking the waistband of my tights and sliding downward. "Think of what he's doing to her right now." Her right hand slid up my back and grabbed the hair at the base of my skull just as the fingers of her left hand sent a shock of electricity through me. "Think of him inside her."

And then she was inside me, and for the first time since I could remember, my mind went blessedly, perfectly blank.

December 30, 2021, 1:27 a.m.
SkyLoft Hotel, Los Angeles

I wake up naked, straddling Harvard on my hotel bed.

This is not the first time I've come out of a blackout in the middle of sex. My medication lowers my tolerance to that of a featherweight, and on the occasions, rare these days, when I throw caution to the wind to enjoy a beer with a colleague, I often slip and fall into a pool of blackness before I even have time to feel tipsy. There have been indiscretions. When blacked out, I seem to revert to my undergraduate days of sleeping with whoever gets me into a broom closet first; or perhaps, as in my undergraduate days, it's me doing the pushing. I become pure id.

I really shouldn't drink. Either that or, and this may be the crux of the issue, I really shouldn't medicate.

Harvard grunts beneath me. I gaze down at his narrow chest, the brown wing of his bangs falling across his bulging eyes, now pink-lidded with excitement. He's just as attractive as he was in the reception, more or less, but I'm through. I lift myself off him and roll over to one side.

"Hey, wait," Harvard slurs. I see several empty mini-bottles on the nightstand, silhouetted in blue by the glowing alarm clock, a miniature city to match the empty skyline outside the window. A plummeting sensation in my stomach heralds an oncoming wave of depression. This, too, is not uncommon after a blackout.

"Claire?"

The name is unfamiliar for a moment.

"Claire?"

Still breathing heavily, Harvard shakes my arm, as if to snap me out of a trance. When I fail to respond, his brows contract. "Fine, okay. First you keep me waiting up here until I give up and crash. Then you wake me up, horny as hell, and just when it's getting good—poof!" He smacks a hand down on the mattress. "You're done."

"Don't be petulant, Harvard." The world around me feels strange, foreign. *Unheimlich,* to use the Freudian term. Hotel rooms are such horrible places. This one, thrust skyward on the tip of an art deco erection two hundred feet above the business of humans, seems to whirl around me with particular malice. "I don't think I can take it right now."

"What about what *I* can take? I have an early panel tomorrow."

Graduate students in the humanities. It's so easy to forget, when these beetle-browed, hollow-chested brutes are swanning around in their scarves and elbow patches, that beneath the tweed they're just men with feelings and an abnormal interest in sharing them. I consider the prospect of finishing him off just to get some peace and quiet, but then I catch another glimpse of the clock on his nightstand. (My nightstand, I correct myself. *My* suite, *my* bed, *my* nightstand.) One twenty-seven a.m. There goes my beauty sleep before the interview.

But looking at the time has joggled something loose in my brain, and a scene from the lost hours of my blackout flashes through.

During a true blackout, the brain records no memories, so I suppose mine are more like brownouts. But to me, that word sounds warm and nostalgic, like an old box of sepia-tinted photographs. Whereas the images that come back to me after a lost night are crystal clear, glaringly bright, and lapped all around with impenetrable black. Like stills from a movie, they appear unaccompanied by dialogue and exposition, cryptic and unsettlingly free of context. They don't feel like memories, even —more like seeing a photograph of someone who looks like me, doing something I don't remember doing. In this particular photograph, I am sobbing stupidly on the table while Gwen awkwardly pats my shoulder.

The sinking in my stomach suddenly reverses course, and I feel like I'm going to throw up. I have a sickening feeling that the me in the photograph has just confessed to something.

"Claire? *Are you even listening to me?*" Harvard taps my shoulder. "Jeez, people told me things, but I thought at least you'd be fun."

Ignoring him, I hop out of bed and start hunting for my clothes in the dark. I have to hurry. I don't know exactly how much time I've lost, but if Gwen isn't already asleep, she will be soon. I have to talk to her, find out what she knows. Tomorrow will be too late.

I slap the light button by the bed, and the room leaps into life around me—not a swirling void after all, but an ordinary if rather plush hotel room outfitted with the corner-cutting luxuries of plush hotel rooms everywhere—too-hard sofa facing

wall-mounted TV, angular breakfast nook, fake orchids. Ah.
There are my pants, draped carefully over the back of a chair.
Even my id is careful about those leather pants. I pull them on.

Harvard sits up in bed. "Do you mind? Some of us need to
get sleep tonight."

"I suggest you get some, then." I can't find my top. I round
the corner and check the bathroom. Nothing. "I'm sure your
room is much more restful."

He glares at me and leans back on his pillow, arms folded and
shoulders squared as if to anchor him to the headboard.

I find my boots in the closet and pull them on, leaving the
laces untied for the moment. Stomping around a hotel room
in boots and leather pants and a bra makes me feel powerful,
which, in turn, makes me feel generous.

"Fine. You don't have to leave yet. I'll be out for a little while.
Charge some porn to the room if you want. Just try to be gone
by the time I get back, okay? Remember, you've got that early
panel."

One more visual sweep of the room reveals my T-shirt and
wool wrap tangled up on the floor under the bed. When I stoop
to pick them up, I notice a room key lying on the floor, just
the bare plastic card without its sleeve. It must have fallen out
of my pants when I was getting undressed. I grab the card and
shove it into my back pocket.

On my way out the door, I pause and glance back at Harvard.
I can easily imagine returning in a few hours to a trashed hotel
room or, say, a thousand dollars' worth of room service.

"I'll write you a recommendation," I call over my shoulder
just before I step outside.

Out in the hall, my head clears a bit. I've got to find Gwen.
I don't know her room number, but I could call down and have

the front desk ring her. I reach for my phone and suddenly realize that, in my eagerness to get out of the hotel room, I left it
on the nightstand. I whirl around just as the door clicks shut,
locking itself behind me.

The door handle blinks red when I slide in the key.

Damn.

I try again. Red again.

It must have been Harvard's room key, not mine, that I
found on the floor—they all look alike without their sleeves. I
feel around in my other pockets. Nothing. I'm locked out with
no phone, no key, and no clue how to find Gwen.

I briefly consider knocking, but Harvard is probably already
masturbating to porn on the department's dime in there. Down
to the lobby, then. I'll get a new key and ask about Gwen's room.

The elevator is empty on the way down. I step out into the
lobby, confirm with a quick glance that Gwen has left the hotel
bar, and hurry to the front desk, where I am greeted by the
night concierge, a young man of about Harvard's age but infinitely more self-possessed.

"Good evening. What can we do for you?"

"Claire Woods. I'm in 1102. I left my key card in the room."
With a sheepish expression, I show him my ID, and he waves it
away while at the same time discreetly glancing at the picture.

"Certainly, madam." After a few deft keystrokes and some
sleight of hand behind the counter, he produces a freshly pro-
grammed card, writes "1102" on the sleeve in neat green Sharpie
numerals, and slides it across the marble countertop. "Will
there be anything else?"

"Oh, one more thing," I say, as if it's an afterthought. "Could
I get the room number for a Gwendolyn Whitney staying at the
hotel? She gave it to me earlier, but I forgot to write it down."

The concierge's expression remains frozen in polite expectation. "We were sitting over at the bar earlier, maybe you noticed?"

The concierge makes a face of exaggerated regret. "To ensure our guests' privacy, the hotel doesn't share that information. Let's just check . . ." He clicks a few keys on the computer. "Ms. Whitney's room is on 'do not disturb' and cannot be called at the moment. Would we like to leave a message for her?"

"It's a bit of an emergency," I begin, taking in the condescending shift from "you" to "we" with a hint of panic. I close my eyes for a moment and summon up my single memory from the bar, willing the context to appear around it. If only I could remember what I was crying about. But what else could it possibly be if not our shared history, Gwen's and mine? The fallout from the dinner party, culminating so horribly in the accident?

I open my eyes after a prolonged blink. The concierge hasn't moved a muscle.

"The thing is—well . . ." Inspiration strikes. "She picked up my phone by mistake. And I'm waiting for an important call. So, you see, I really need to reach her."

The concierge's smile goes stony, and he repeats his "do not disturb" script word for word, his voice half a degree chillier than last time. But before I can come up with a wheedling response, joy of joys, a new memory surfaces. This one must have taken place just a moment before or a moment after the first, because I'm still at the table, hiccupping and wiping my nose, but I'm alone. My gaze falls to something small and sparkling on the table. Refracted through my tears, it looks like a pile of shifting white sequins. I see my own hand approaching the tiny object, like the woman reaching for her jewelry in the opening scene of *The Earrings of Madame de* . . . I close my hand around it, and the memory ends.

Hardly daring to believe it, I slip one finger into my watch pocket and find the tiny circle, weighed down on one side by a large, many-faceted bump.

I interrupt the concierge.

"There's something else. She has an early flight out, and I have something of hers she'd be very upset to miss."

"Would we like to leave it at the front desk for her to—"

"I think she'd rather I return it in person. You see . . ." I reach into my pocket and hold the glittering circle up to the light. "I have her engagement ring."

Click, click, click, click.

The concierge's fingers positively fly as he dials up Gwen's room from the front desk phone. Apparently, a ring this size trumps even the "do not disturb" setting.

Gwen's room is on the second floor—a dismal view, but then I suppose she's only here for the night. Standing outside her door, I try to gather my thoughts, make a plan for finding out what we talked about in the bar—Bethany, Rocky, the accident?—without implicating myself further. Maybe it's too late. Maybe I confessed everything. If so, how did she respond? Did she forgive me?

The thought makes me wince. There's a long list of things I want out of Gwen, and forgiveness isn't on it.

Anyway, no matter how she reacted in the moment, I have my doubts as to whether she'll feel so forgiving after thinking it over on her long flight. I feel a thread of panic. Gwen has always been a terrible liar. Eventually she'll tell someone: her parents, the fiancé.

I can't allow that.

I dip my hand into my pocket for strength and feel the sharp, hard edges of what must be eight carats cutting through my nerves. I have the ring. I have the upper hand.

If Gwen *does* know—

First things first. That's what I'm here to find out.

OH, FOOLS

8

Oh, fools.

For some reason it was Quimby's voice that kept ringing through my head as I stumbled home from Bethany's the morning after the dinner party. Giving the campus a wide berth to avoid running into anyone I knew, I passed townie bars I had never seen before, so empty at this time of morning they looked haunted, and churches spilling families out onto the sidewalks. Remembering the statistical racism argument at Connor's party, I slunk past the local residents with my head down, embarrassed to be associated with a university whose long history of restrictive covenants and land grabs had kept the neighborhood in a state of artificial decline. I may have felt out of place at DHU, but I didn't belong here either. Maybe the last place I'd truly fit in had been Quimby's basement, where, invisible under baggy clothes and anesthetized by pot, I'd been safe from the disastrous wants that had led me to the Program. If only I'd stayed there.

And yet it was Quimby who had first seen me, Quimby who had singled me out. Even if it had only been a series of mistakes

—Quimby mistaking my stoned stare for curiosity, me mistaking a Max Ophüls film for porn—these mistakes had turned into prophecy. *Oh, fools,* indeed. I'd accidentally tumbled into a world I hadn't known existed, where everything was beautiful, and beauty itself was a metaphor for truth, and each brilliant surface was a door you could open if only you had the right key. I had been searching for it ever since.

Last night, yielding to the pressure of Bethany's body on mine as we lay together in her beautiful apartment surrounded by beautiful things, I had felt the door unlock and stepped momentarily over the threshold. In bed, our bodies had been transfigured into pure form and radiant purpose, just as the words she spoke at our meetings seemed to slip off their skins of ordinary sense in the lighted cave of her mouth.

This morning I still felt her burned into my skin under the itchy tights and the wool dress and coat. I remembered with amazement the mechanics of our desire, my sudden craving to take her legs over my shoulders. Sex with Bethany had come as naturally to me as my prior encounters with men and produced more or less the same sensations. If there was a qualitative difference—and there was—it would have seemed strange to reduce it to the fact that she was a woman. Forced to locate it, I'd begin with the ache in my groin when she looked at me like one of her curated objects, the tears that sprang to my eyes when she wrote her name inside me with her fingers and tongue. Fucking her had felt like fucking power itself.

But that was last night.

The reality this morning was decidedly less thrilling. I'd been bundled into my clothes and exiled from the warm, richly decorated apartment, a travel mug full of coffee the only concession to my hangover. Rocky would be coming home any minute; Bethany suggested I arrange my route through the neighborhood to avoid him. It was imperative that I avoid him. Rocky must not know. She'd met my eyes for the first time that morning, giving me a look that was like a strong hand wrapped around my jaw.

"If Rocky finds out, I will deny, disavow, and, if necessary, destroy you to protect myself," she'd said. Then she'd pressed the mug into my hands, buttoned the collar of my coat, and brushed the hair out of my eyes, like a mother sending her child off to school. "Now, take care, darling." A peck on the cheek. "I'll see you Wednesday."

So that had been it. Still sleepy, the drug of sex after so many months of abstinence still warm in my veins, I had somehow retained the buzz of belonging to Bethany until my feet hit the sidewalk outside the Libertorium and a cold gust of wind came barreling at me between the buildings, nearly knocking me down. Now I was just a grad student who had slept with her adviser after an evening of behavior that struck me, in retrospect, as both absurd and shameful. I'd felt jealous of how well Bethany and Gwen were getting along and, in response, had eaten too much, drunk too much, and flirted with Rocky outrageously. Now I wondered whether Gwen's chattiness with Bethany had been a calculated show of deference to her lover's wife; Rocky's encouragement of me a trick to throw Bethany off their trail; Bethany's seduction a ploy to alienate me from Gwen. And I'd fallen for it, all of it, so desperate was I to feel wanted.

In the moment, the scene had seemed almost scripted: Gwen and Rocky holding hands, their locked eyes alluding to a more throbbing point of contact. Now, its immediacy faded, it took on that quality of ambiguity that tantalized me in certain films. I was less certain by the minute that Gwen and Rocky had slept together before the dinner party. Even my own motives for believing it now seemed opaque. Only Bethany's reasons for putting the idea in my head were, retrospectively, crystal clear. It had been a trap.

The whole evening had been a trap.

It didn't really matter, I realized with a pang. If they hadn't gone to bed before, they certainly had now.

Anyway, there was something else by comparison with which the fitting of parts into parts—whether mine, Bethany's, Gwen's, or Rocky's—felt unimportant. Anyone could have a lapse of judgment. Even Gwen.

But Gwen going for the Joyner was something else again. She'd let me think she was wooing Rocky to get closer to Bethany, when in fact she was positioning herself to shoot to the top with only this boyish lightweight in her debtor's column. If Gwen snagged the Joyner, it would be Rocky who would benefit by association with her, not the other way around; no one would be under the mistaken belief that he had procured it for her. She would be in a league of her own. Once more, Gwen would get what I wanted most, and I would be left with the scraps.

That wasn't even the worst part. The worst was that if I knew Gwen, she didn't even really care about the Joyner. She was simply accustomed to the best, and when she saw something worth having, she opened her hand for it. People accustomed to the best didn't need to do more than that.

Over and over again, I had stepped through one doorway only to find myself stuck in yet another of power's endless waiting rooms, staring at another locked and bolted door. The Program was no exception. It wasn't just the money and prestige

that made the Joyner so vital to my long-term plans for escape.
It was the certainty of a tenure-track job at the other end, no
small promise in an academic market hit hard by the latest re-
cession. The Joyner was the shibboleth that would open the final door to a world where money wouldn't matter because I'd
finally have enough of it. I could build a new home for myself in
thoughts and ideas while furnishing the one I'd left behind with
every comfort. While I didn't for a moment doubt that Gwen
was the rightful recipient of the award — "She's perfect," Bethany had said, drily and without romance — I knew just as deeply
that I deserved it more.

"Mac!"

Paranoid at being seen, I almost ducked. By the time Tess
caught up with me, flushed and out of breath, I'd recovered.
She loosened her scarf. "I've been calling your name for half a
block."

"Sorry. I'm kind of out of it."

"Yeah." She looked me up and down, taking in the rumpled
dress. "Where are you headed?"

"Home." I said it before I could think of a better reason to
be out this early in the morning in smeared makeup and clothes
that had spent the night on the floor.

"Right." She nodded. "Do you mind if I walk with you? Don't
worry, I won't ask any questions. Strictly your business."

I nodded my thanks with a sickly smile. "What about you?"

"I'm heading home from breakfast with my ex."

"Strictly your business?"

"My business is incredibly boring." She rolled her eyes. "If I
have to hear about his band one more time."

"Are you still friends with him?"

"I have to be. He's close to my family, especially my dad. Ronald is the son he never had, and they've given up on grandkids. Correctly."

"I'm not having kids either." I realized as soon as I said it that I'd always known it was true. Too many people depended on me already, and all I could think about was getting away from them.

"Do your folks give you all kinds of shit for it, like mine?"

I imagined my mom's face if I ever told her I was pregnant, and for a moment thought it might be worth it. "No."

"Lucky you. I stay friendly with Ronald because my friends still love him and he knows more about my dad's health than anyone. But I have to be careful. As far as they're concerned, I'm crazy for leaving him. If they knew we still get together sometimes—and yeah, not just for breakfast—they'd be all over me to marry him again."

We were only a few blocks from the apartment. "Tess, can I ask you something? Why are you in the Program?"

She stiffened. "Why would you ask that?"

My face turned red. "You just seem like you have so much going on." I fumbled for words. "A family that loves you, lots of friends, a career that makes actual money. I've never had any of that."

"Well, you're not going to find it here," she said wryly. "So, I could ask you the same thing, really. What brought you to DHU?"

I couldn't say Gwen. Instead, I reached for words to describe what it was about her that made me want to follow wherever she went. A way of being that's about more than paying the bills, I wanted to say. More than money, even, or success. I just wanted

—*more*. But that wasn't something I could say to someone in the Program, not even Tess.

I shrugged and repeated what I'd heard others in the Program say, always tongue in cheek. "Paid to read, summers off."

"Huh." She didn't sound skeptical, just underwhelmed.

"Now you."

"The life of the mind," she said simply. "I thought that's why we were all here."

Hearing the phrase without scare quotes opened up a little wound of longing in me. It was what I would have said myself only a few short months ago. That I couldn't imagine saying it now was a mark of how fearful I had become. "What does that even mean?"

"It means freedom to think. Freedom to follow an idea all the way, as far as it can go, without worrying that somebody won't like it and you'll be out of a job. In Los Angeles, it's always about money. How much can you raise, what do the investors think, who's in a position to green-light you or pull the plug?" She frowned. "It's not getting told 'no' that kills you. That I can handle. It's the projects you stop asking for because your instincts tell you the money's not there. And then one day you wake up and realize you can't even *imagine* something unless you can smell money in it first. You feel the smartest parts of your brain dying for lack of oxygen. Out here"—Tess swept her arm, taking in the stores along the street—"the oxygen follows the money, and there's never enough of that to go around. But in there"—she pointed toward campus—"the oxygen flows toward the best ideas." She inhaled deeply. "I want to breathe that air for a while."

Ideas. Everyone else had them, it seemed. I used to have

them, too, back when they didn't matter. Why, when I thought of the life of the mind now, was it Bethany's apartment I saw, with its artfully arranged antiques and expensive rugs, instead of my project? It was because I had no project. So far, I was my only project.

Then again, something in me resisted Tess's idealism. I looked down at my new riding boots, now lightly scuffed from two long walks and splashed with mud I'd need to scrub away the moment I got home, before the road salt ate away the finish. "The life of the mind is expensive."

She looked at me like I was an idiot.

"Freedom's always expensive. Where've you been?"

And then it hit me. I froze on the sidewalk, seized with panic. "No" was all I could say. "No, no, no."

"Mac?"

I fumbled for my phone and saw with a dropping stomach that it had died overnight. "What time is it?"

Tess looked at her phone. "Ten forty-five."

"I have to go. Right now."

As Tess waved goodbye, I unlocked the building door and raced up to the apartment, taking two stairs at a time all the way up. Yesterday's shopping trip, making up with Gwen, the crazy dinner and its impossible but very real aftermath, the hungover morning, and, finally, meeting Tess on my walk of shame —it had pushed the most important thing completely out of my mind.

The Sunday double.

I'd been in the building, for god's sake. I'd walked all the way home.

When my phone charged, I saw one new text:

This is Derek. Pursuant to Nona's employment policy as stated in the

employee manual, your ass is fired. Your shifts have been covered. Have
a nice weekend.

I lay flat on my back, staring up at the ceiling, unemployed.

The Nona job was just a security blanket, I told myself. The
other students did without jobs, or had part-time gigs research-
ing for professors. That was the kind of job a grad student was
supposed to have, the kind that built relationships and went on
the CV, even if in practice it was only fetching library books.
That was how this was supposed to work.

And yet. And yet. Nona had been so concrete. Putting plates
on tables wasn't glamorous; customers sneered or snapped or,
most often, ignored me, treating me like an automaton who existed to refill water glasses and fetch extra sides of squash blos-
som hollandaise for their farm-to-table egg benedicts. Nor was
it an important job, in any sense of the word. I was a mere con-
veyor belt for the creations of a chef so far above my station, he
would barely talk to me except to snarl when I was forced to ask
him for a corrected order. The meals I laid before people were
superfluous and bad for them, excrescences of obscene wealth
they'd later, I imagined, pay handsomely to melt off their torsos
at the gym. I had no romantic notions about Nona, except for
one: I worked, I hustled, I moved as fast as I could, and at the
end of each shift, I measured my success by the size of the bulge
of cash in my apron. The work was hard but the reward immediate and gloriously tangible.

Whereas the work I did in the Program had to be *believed*
in. It couldn't be felt or seen except in fevered bursts of comprehension that faded just as quickly as they'd come. It was like
a city that only existed when you closed your eyes, or like one
of Rocky's virtual museums. When I read an article, let's say

Derrida's "Economimesis" or Sablev's "The Eternal Modern," I would, after an initial terrifying period of disorientation, begin to pick up the rhythm of the words and sentences, and then a sentence here or there would make sense, and then suddenly the brick and mortar of the argument would feel as steady under my feet as the tiled floor at Nona, and infinitely more beautiful. For a moment I would be dancing within the imaginary grid of ideas. And then I would look up from the article, and it would all vanish.

I must have fallen asleep at some point, because the ceiling had turned into a round table at Nona, one of the large six-tops in my section. But it was also a seminar table, and Bethany was there with Rocky and Gwen and Connor and Tess and, for some reason, Quimby. They were all waiting for me to serve them waters that were also a paper I had to write that would explain everything. But Derek had just triple-sat me, and I had orders to put in and mimosas to pour, and out of the corner of my eye I could see a particularly insistent two-top waving their arms to get my attention, hear them shouting for me, louder and louder.

Mom and Lily.

I woke up to my ringing phone and reached for it, in my dream state half believing it was Derek calling to tell me it had all been a mistake. Then I saw the screen and was instantly awake. I took a breath and scrambled up to a seating position before pressing talk.

"Hi, Mom." It came out a croak.

"That doctor came to the house yesterday. You didn't tell me it was a woman."

"Oh," I said, rubbing my eyes. "Yeah. She's a woman."

"Well, you could have told me that. When she showed up at

the door, I thought she was a nurse. Once we cleared that up, though, things went well. She was very competent." She didn't say *for a woman,* but I heard it in her voice. Working for the handsome Dr. Donnelly had left her with a permanent prejudice against female doctors that I found grotesque considering the circumstances of her own termination.

"How did Lily do?"

"Lily was an angel. She was perfect, just perfect. She let the doctor do all these tests—blocks and rings, baby stuff, then reading and math. You should have seen the music test! Lily did so well."

"How well?" I asked, suddenly nervous. "What did the doctor say?"

"Diagnosis exactly the same," my mother said proudly, as if it had all been her doing. "I signed the papers and she said she'd submit them from her office." I'd checked this in advance, since I knew my mother could not be trusted to file the paperwork. "But, Mackenzie, honey, that lady is pricey. I barely had enough in my account to cover the co-pay. Lily and I are going to need more money while we wait for the appeal."

"Co-pay?" That didn't sound right. I had checked and double-checked the insurance coverage for home visits. "There shouldn't have been a co-pay. How much was it?"

"Six hundred and fifty dollars."

"Mom, that doesn't sound like a co-pay. That sounds like the full cost."

"Well, you're the one who said we needed a home visit."

"You did, but . . . there must have been some kind of mistake. Why didn't you call me before you paid? I could have talked to her!" I heard my voice go frantic and knew this was the wrong tack, but I couldn't help it. Six hundred and fifty dollars! Most of what I'd sent her after my last—and now, as it turned out, final—double shift. Gone in one morning.

"Mackenzie Claire," she said, icy. "I called you plenty. It went straight to voice mail, so I figured you were out at some frat party or something."

"They don't have fraternities here," I said with a surge of childish defensiveness, pricked an instant later with the thought of what I'd really been doing last night.

"Anyway, it wasn't an emergency. If it had been, I would have tried Gwen. I don't enjoy parading our money problems around that one, I can tell you. But at least she picks up. Anyway, we had plenty enough to cover it in my account, and a full pantry too. Thank God I went shopping Thursday." Her self-congratulatory tone sickened me, as if she had already forgotten the source of the "plenty enough" in her bank account, as if buying food were a special task she should be rewarded for rather than the bare minimum of what it took to sustain life. "But we'll need something for the next couple of weeks until the appeal goes through."

"It shouldn't take that long." I flashed on my empty bank account. "If they file the paperwork Monday—"

"The doctor said it'll take at least two weeks, probably more like a month. We're going to need money before that."

We're going to need money. Always "we," never "me." The dark thoughts had already returned. The constant barrage of insults, the comments to make me feel guilty . . . It all felt so familiar. She wasn't slurring her speech, but then again, each time had taught her how to hide it more thoroughly. I'd been through enough emergencies with my mother to sense something off about this one.

Fury choked me. The fact that I even had to wonder whether my mom was cashing my sister's disability checks for drugs and then asking me for money to cover the bills would always hold me back. But, of course, yesterday this would have been only a minor crisis. I had slipped up, just this once, and it turned out to be once too often.

I rubbed my temples, tried to calm down. The first thing to do when I got off the phone was call the doctor to verify her story. I should call the Social Security office, too. In the meantime, I had to hold her off for a while.

"Can you get it somewhere else? Things are a little tight right now."

"Where else am I supposed to get it? An ATM?" she sniped. "Mackenzie. You know I can't work."

"I know you can't get a—" I stopped myself and took a deep breath. "I know you have to take care of Lily."

"Someone has to."

Someone had to. All my arguments, all my defenses, broke down against that truth.

"So, we need money until her disability starts up again. Period. The end." Her tone was snappish but careful. Always careful. I was her cash cow, and she didn't want to spook me. I could hear the next words before she said them. "Or I could go back to work, and you could come home and take care of your sister for a while."

There it was, the two-word threat. *Come home.*

"I — No, Mom, I told you, I can't. Not right now." My heart was beating violently, the tears starting. The trips I couldn't go on, the classes I couldn't take. The catastrophes that had always coincided perfectly with some opportunity I couldn't seize because I had to take care of things for a few weeks or months while my mom got her shit together. Not this time. I had to finish the Joyner application. After that, I'd go home for Christmas, I swore to whatever god was listening, even though with any luck the problem with the disability payments would be all cleared up by then and they wouldn't need me. "I—I told you why."

"So, you can hang out with people who'd rather go to school than grow up and make a living?"

"Come on, Mom. I told you about my job." I nearly gagged on the word. *Don't think about it.*

"Your job that makes so much money, but not enough for us."

"I had to buy some expensive textbooks this week," I said, inspired by a distant memory of her bitching about how much her nursing textbooks had cost. "I'm sorry. I'm working this weekend and I'll send you something soon. I promise. Just— give me a week."

There was a long pause. "Well, we can make it another week, but that's it. And, Mackenzie—"

"What?" The thought of having to raise enough money in the next week to cover a month's worth of expenses for my mother, Lily, and myself sawed at my nerves.

"Thank you," she said, her tone softer. "I know it isn't easy for you to be in two places at once. I know you're working hard. I can tell you're stressed out from your voice."

Congratulations, I thought bitterly. *You're a mind reader.*

"I just wanted you to know, we do appreciate it, Lily and me. We love you. And we're rooting for you."

Where I'd always been able to hang up on her martyr's sigh, I found her gratitude unendurably painful. I had none to give her in return. "I love you, too," I forced myself to say.

"Just give me a call when the transfer goes through," she said in the same tone.

"Right," I said, visions of what it would take for that to happen going through my head. "Give Lily a hug for me."

"She misses you."

I hung up. A muscle in my arm spasmed, but I managed to keep myself from throwing the phone.

I stared down at the toes of my caramel leather riding boots, already faintly discolored around the edges because I'd forgotten to rub them with oil. These fucking boots had swallowed the last hours of my income. They were the expensive textbooks I had bought with the last fat roll of cash I would have at my disposal for the foreseeable future. Possibly ever.

Savagely, I yanked at the brass zipper on the left boot, pulled it off, and hurled it as hard as I could across the room. It hit the wall with a satisfying clunk. The other zipper snagged on my tights an inch above the ankle. After wrestling with it for a moment, I lost patience and forced the boot off, not caring if I broke the zipper or stretched the beautiful caramel leather. It came away with a ripping sound, taking a chunk of my tights with it. I aimed poorly this time and hit my dresser, which thumped the wall as it rocked back and forth, sending yet another stack of interleaved articles sliding to the floor.

From down the hall, I heard the creak of bedsprings. Gwen was presumably sleeping off a hangover. I wasn't ready to face her yet.

I had to collect myself. I had to think of a plan.

The boots lay slumped against the wall as if they'd been shot by a firing squad. Panic over my rashness washed over me. Gingerly, I picked them up and examined them. The right zipper was still stuck, but luckily the teeth weren't bent, just clamped tightly around a fold of black fabric. I wiggled the little brass beetle of the carriage back and forth, easing the shred of tights gently out from between the teeth, millimeter by millimeter. Perhaps three minutes later, there was a satisfying click as the last thread snapped out, and the zipper slid smoothly. I let out a sigh of relief.

The concentration required for the task had calmed me down, and an idea came to me. I hunted for the small bottle of oil I had purchased with the boots, mulling over something I'd heard Bethany tell Gwen early last night, before everything had gone sideways. *So many years, what a shame.* Inhaling the buttery texture and rich, wild smell of leather, I was suddenly glad I had blown the cash on boots before knowing that cash was about to become scarce. I rubbed an oily Kleenex into the boots, paying special attention to the salt-lightened patches where the uppers met the soles, as I called and left messages for the doctor and the Social Security Administration.

I had a plan. But freedom was expensive. I'd have to look the part.

I couldn't get out of the apartment without seeing Gwen. I showered and dressed as quickly as I could, zipping up the freshly oiled boots over my jeans, but it was afternoon by the time I was rooting around in the fridge for snacks to throw in my bag, and then there she was, looking absolutely awful, her pale skin yellowed like old ivory around her eyes and mouth.

"Hey, I thought I heard you." She made a sour face. "I was in the bathroom, throwing up."

"Oh god, I'm sorry." I watched her closely.

"I drank way too much last night. It was just so"—she glanced quickly at me, then brushed her hand through her greasy hair and looked down—"awkward."

"You thought so, too, huh?" I said, with a hint of sarcasm.

"I should never have had all that vodka."

"Rocky was very insistent."

She didn't flinch when I said his name. "He was really drunk walking me home last night. Singing and—he said some things, too. About his marriage to Bethany. He started crying at one point."

"What, it's that bad?"

"He was crying because he loves her, Mac. He worships her."

I suppressed a snort.

"It was really sad. Pathetic, really." She squinted, as if remembering slowly. "He's never been able to live up to her. You know he was her student at Penn, right?"

I shook my head, though of course Bethany had said so last night. It was eerie, as if our conversations—and who knew what else—had mirrored each other.

"That must be a tough dynamic," she continued thoughtfully. "Knowing he owes her everything."

The conversation was sinking me further and further into a fog. What did Gwen expect me to believe had happened last night? What did she even remember? Was it possible she was making all this up to distract me, throw me off the scent? I cut to the chase. "So, did you two talk all night, or what?"

"Oh god no. The minute I got inside, I passed out." She didn't say he left, not explicitly, and I was too embarrassed to ask. She looked embarrassed, too. "Mac, I've never done so much drinking in my life. I mean, I drank at Columbia, but not like this. I'm going to slow down. I feel like I'm losing control."

Everything turned upside down again. Gwen was always in control. "I drank too much, too. I missed my shift at Nona today and they fired me."

"Oh no!"

I shrugged it off.

"What time did you get home?"

"Around one." I watched Gwen to see if she was watching me. "You must have just gone to bed when I got in."

There was a long pause. If, by some chance, she really had gone to bed alone, she'd have no reason to doubt me. If, on the other hand, she was lying, she would know I was lying, too. I waited for her either to accuse me and implicate herself, or double down on the lie.

But she just looked at me curiously. "Why didn't you leave with us, anyway? My memories from the end of the night are kind of hazy."

"Oh, that," I said. "Bethany wanted to talk to me alone. It didn't take very long."

"Why alone?"

"I think she didn't want to hurt your feelings." I looked down at my boots. "I'm going to be her new research assistant."

9

When I got to her office Wednesday, Bethany was typing an email. I hovered at the door, queasy with anticipation.

"Come in." I left the door cracked an inch, as usual, and sat down. She typed for a few more minutes, finished with a flourish, and swiveled to face me. "Now. Let's talk about your Joyner application. Who are you listing as your other recommenders?"

I was taken aback. So that was how we were playing it. No preliminaries; strictly business. I composed myself and struggled to answer. The question shouldn't have blindsided me. Of course, I would need three recommenders. Like wishes and celebrity deaths, recommendations always came in threes.

"Rocky is out, for obvious reasons," she said drily. "Who else are you taking classes from? It's Margaret, isn't it?" She made a face, as she always did when she said Margaret's name.

"Yes, and I'm in Grady Herschel's class on economimesis."

"Hmmm." She thumped the heavy antique bracelet on her wrist against the desktop. "Grady's good. He'll be the next chair. You're doing well in his class?"

"As far as I know." Grady didn't seem either to like or dislike me, but I talked in class a moderate amount, getting my comments in early and limiting myself to narrow observations indisputably supported by the text.

"Fine. Margaret's going to be a little trickier—she loses her best students to me, and I send my worst to her—though she might say it's the other way around. But we may have had a little luck thrown our way there."

"Luck?"

"Soo-jeong dropped out."

"Oh?" I said, confused. I hadn't spoken to Soo-jeong much since the retreat—she didn't come to parties—but I had noticed her eyes looked a little red in class from time to time. I'd assumed she was just studying hard, like me. "What happened?"

Bethany waved away my question. "International students never last long," she said, rather callously. "Anyway, she was Margaret's research assistant. Margaret's looking for someone to work ten or fifteen hours a week, digging through archives, that kind of thing. You're welcome."

I sat, stunned and deflated. I had been working myself up for the ask all week. With my mom waiting on the money, converting my unpaid relationship with Bethany into a paid one had taken priority even over the Joyner in my mind. Every time I tried to work on the application, I felt a surge of nausea and had to stop to reassure myself that after what had happened between us, Bethany would have to give me the job.

"Oh, I know it's mindless work. Margaret has an archive fixation. That's why she has a hard time finding research assistants. But that's also why it's perfect for you. You spend all your time at the library anyway. I've already sent her an email recommending you for the position, with a note about your personal circumstances. And once she's come to depend on you, a letter will be—"

"Personal circumstances," I repeated slowly.

"I shared some of the details from your essay," she replied. "Mac, it's okay to admit you need money. Especially now that you've quit your job at the restaurant."

"How—?" But I knew how she knew. The same way she knew where I studied, when I worked, and everything else about me. She knew because Gwen knew. What Gwen knew, Rocky knew; and what Rocky knew, Bethany knew. If I ever wanted proof of a direct pipeline, this was it.

"I wish I could be the one to help you out, really I do. But I've already hired a new research assistant." She looked at me pointedly. "I'm sure you agree we already spend plenty of time together. I would hate for you to tire of me."

I took a deep breath. "You already hired a research assistant."

"Why, yes. I believe you know him, he's in your year. Connor?" I nodded dumbly.

"He's wonderful in my class. I felt so dismal about that seminar at first, but Connor really brings it to life. He is consistently a bright spot in my day. That's the kind of positive energy I need to surround myself with. It takes so much out of me, working on a new book. Oh!" There was a noise from her computer, and she turned toward the monitor. "Look, Margaret has already responded. She says you can start tomorrow. You're cc'd on this thread, of course. So is Lorraine. She should have the work-study papers ready to pick up in the department by this afternoon."

There was nothing to say. "Thank you."

"The job pays twelve dollars an hour. Not bad for sitting in the library."

"I said, thank you."

She shot me a look. "Don't act so glum, Mac. You wouldn't have wanted me for your boss. I'm very temperamental. Anyway, Margaret's the department chair. This is a good relationship to cultivate. We bend the rules for those who help us out of a jam. And I happen to know she has a lot of trouble with her printer." She laughed easily at her own joke. "But seriously. You could do more than one person a favor, working for Margaret. It can be useful, having access to those files."

So, I would be a spy, as well as a drudge. Terrific. "Maybe I'd better report to her immediately." I reached for my bag, barely able to contain my anger.

Bethany seemed disconcerted, though it was hard to tell whether it was sincere or part of the performance. I had the absurd feeling I was being punished, though for what, I couldn't imagine. "Don't go, Mac. We've barely gotten started. I know you're disappointed, but you'll see. I was only trying to help."

This was her way of helping. After Saturday night.

I stood and started to walk out. Then I stopped, turned, and squared my shoulders. "You want to help?"

She rose out of her rolling chair. "Please. Tell me what I can do."

"I need six hundred dollars. I can pay it back after my first paycheck. But I need it now."

"Ah." She stood stock-still on her high-heeled boots. Her voice when she spoke next was dry as a bone. "You were hoping for an advance."

"I didn't quit my job at Nona, Bethany. I got fired because

I overslept Sunday morning and missed my shift. I can't think what could have caused that, can you? I'm always so punctual."

There was a breathless silence.

"I needed that job, Bethany. Because of *personal circumstances*."

She studied my face, her jaw locked tight.

"So, you can see how six hundred dollars would really help me out."

Blackmail had not been my plan when I walked into Bethany's office. But being sloughed off on Margaret had filled me with righteous rage. Bethany was trying to get rid of me, get rid of the evidence of her wrongdoing. She had slept with me in violation of department policy, Title IX, marriage vows, and common decency. The recorder app was on right now. With just a little more evidence, I could sue her, or at least get her in serious trouble.

But I wasn't ready for that. Was I?

Bethany sighed with slumped shoulders, looking drained and defeated. "Of course, Mac," she said softly. "I understand. I'm just happy you came to me." She reached for her black leather satchel and scrounged clumsily in the inner flap, finally pulling out her wallet. "I have two hundred on me. Will this do for now? I can go by an ATM and give you the rest tomorrow."

I took the stack of twenties she handed me, feeling a twinge of uncertainty at the touch of the crisp, recently withdrawn bills, so different from the overhandled money I was used to getting in tips. Suddenly I felt weaker. I didn't want to meet her eyes, in case she was looking at me with pity. "Thank you."

"How about I take you out somewhere tonight?" she said in the same quiet tone. "We can meet for dinner and I'll give you the rest."

"Tomorrow's fine. Just leave it in my mail folder."

"All right. Whatever you say. But don't forget to ask Grady and Margaret for those letters. And, Mac—"

"What?"

"Why don't you bring in a draft of your statement of purpose next week. I'll be so interested to see your project."

I pocketed the bills without answering and walked out. Bethany knew I had no project. We both knew I needed her to come up with one and tell me exactly how to describe it for the Joyner committee. Her parting words weren't even a challenge —she knew I couldn't rise to the occasion.

They were an invitation. She wanted to see me again, and soon.

I walked over to the chair's office for the paperwork.

Lorraine was typing at her desk in the reception area outside Margaret's office. The door was cracked open, and I thought I heard Tess's voice inside.

"Oh, Mac, Margaret mentioned you might stop by." Lorraine reached for a stack of papers on the corner of her desk. "This is the work-study packet. Fill in your information and hand it off to the folks downstairs . . ."

From inside Margaret's office, I heard a raised voice. It was Tess saying, "What do you mean, anonymous?"

Lorraine cleared her throat. "She'll give you the payroll form, and once you fill that out, you'll drop off a copy here and walk the original down to payroll in the admin building, along with your W-9 and direct deposit form."

Tess again: "—implying what I think you're implying? Because if you are—" The voices grew louder, Margaret and Tess talking over one another.

"Make two copies of the completed paperwork for department payroll, get Ann to stamp them, and then drop one stamped copy back here . . ."

A chair scraped backward. A hand slammed down on a desk.

Lorraine got up quickly and shut Margaret's door. Then she sat back down at her desk, her smile wilted. "And then it's just a matter of running one last copy over to the division office for their files — and you're all set."

I took the papers, still looking at the door.

Lorraine glared protectively. "I'll tell Margaret you dropped by."

Through the closed door, Margaret's voice boomed: "I will not be spoken to like this!"

I caught Lorraine's expression and hurried out. Tess could take care of herself, I thought uncertainly.

My first step should have been to initiate the daunting payroll procedure, but between the mysterious altercation in Margaret's office and Bethany's loan burning a hole in my pocket, I couldn't stand to be in this building another second. If I hurried, there was enough time to make it to the Parlor, where Connor and Gwen and the rest of the team would be gearing up for Trivia Night. I needed a break from professors.

I had never seen a professor in the Parlor, a campus bar as dark as if its walls were painted black instead of grimed over and ballpoint-graffitied to near-blackness. The air was humid with the sweat of students who'd stopped in to say hi and then quickly become too inebriated to leave, and stale with their beer-breathed laughter. The single pool table was an island of green surrounded by mountains of shadow; a few antiquated arcade consoles flickered from the room's murky perimeter. Everything smelled like Velveeta and Wonder Bread fried in margarine, the approximation of grilled cheese the Parlor served on paper plates for a dollar apiece to avoid charges of deliberately contributing to liver damage in the student population. Other than this sandwich, the only thing the Parlor served was beer—no hard liquor and no wine. It was a carb palace where students collectively packed on pounds against the cold and huddled together to hide from advisers, library fines, and the massive debt they were accruing in pursuit of misery.

If the Parlor reminded me a little too much of the strip-mall bars back home, there was something reassuringly gothic about its location. Mabie Hall was one of the oldest buildings on campus. Its high turret was occupied by a physics professor who had invented something nuclear in the '60s and been rewarded with the entire tower for his office, where he lived out his remaining years, it was said, smoking cigars and masturbating the guilt away. It was a building that seemed to endorse this kind of behavior among hardworking academics, and thus a natural home for the Parlor.

Tonight Connor's too-brilliant ascot bloomed in the middle of it like a flower in a dung heap, a vivid splash of color visible from all the way across the pub. *Bright spot,* indeed. I had come to the bar hurt by what seemed like a betrayal—he had, after all, snagged the job I wanted—but found my pique melting away almost immediately. When he spotted me approaching the booth, he lifted his face toward the faux Tiffany hanging light, pressed his long hands together in front of his nose, and said fervently, "Hallelujah. There is a God."

This was an even warmer reception than I had expected, but looking around the booth I could see why. The trivia team was missing a member; the booth held Letty, Morgan, and Aggressively Bland Matt, but Gwen was nowhere to be seen. "We were desperate," Connor said. "I thought I was going to have to ask the Bird." He gestured toward the bar, where the balding eighth-year was nursing a beer, uncharacteristically alone. "And since he hit on Morgan rather obnoxiously at my party, he is not high on my list."

"Where's Gwen?" I said, waving at the others as I scooted in next to Connor on the bench.

"It seems like that's all we ever say to each other these days," Connor said sadly. "I miss you, Mac."

"Is it my sparkling personality or my swanlike grace?"

"It's that you don't care what people say about you," he said seriously.

"Why, what do they say?" I said, to cover my confusion. If there was anyone who cared what people thought, it was me. All I did, every moment, was try to figure out which Mac they wanted to see so I could supply them with a reasonable facsimile.

He tapped his fingertips together and waggled his eyebrows. "That you're ruthless."

"You've got to be kidding." I thought of how Gwen had lied to my face about Rocky, and Bethany's plot against them both. It seemed to me that I was surrounded by people who had grown up playing a game—say, pool, I thought, looking over at the table—and I had just picked up the cue for the very first time and was chalking the tip when they turned out the lights and declared we would all be playing in the dark. "Who says that? What does that even mean?"

"That you'll stop at nothing to get what you want, I suppose."

"And what do I want?"

"I wish I knew, sweetie," he said, giving my hand a squeeze. "I would give it to you in a heartbeat."

I bumped his shoulder with mine. "I missed you, too."

Just then a microphone screeched. "Welcome to Trivia Night finals," said the announcer over the PA. "Shit, I spilled my beer."

"Another round before they start?" I said. Connor and Matt raised their glasses. "I'll get a pitcher." I rose and felt Bethany's stiff twenties crinkle on my right hip. Ruthless. If that was really what people were saying, I could afford to spend one of the bills on the cheapest form of goodwill. I crossed the floor, which increased in stickiness as I neared the bar, and leaned forward between two empty stools.

"Hello, Beauty Queen," a voice said in my ear.

I jumped, but it was only the Bird, who had slithered into an empty chair to my right. His breath reeked of beer, like everyone's in this place, and his eyes were bloodshot in a bloated face. I shifted my elbow away from his instinctively.

"I can't say I see it," he said with a squint of his watery eyes. "But I suppose irony is its own form of beauty."

"What, did you read my essay, too?" I said. "Seems like it's making the rounds."

"I read all the essays. That was my email you sent it to. I am —was—Bethany's research assistant." He took an aggressive swallow of beer.

I vaguely remembered the unusual address. "You're Quib N. Burhan?" I said skeptically, remembering the joke name he gave me at the party the first time we met.

He straightened. "That's Q. ibn Burhan, to you. The 'Q' is for Qassim. But the people have spoken, and they prefer 'Bird.'" He chuckled unpleasantly. "Anyway, it captures my essence, don't you think? Just like Beauty Queen captures yours." He looked me up and down. "On the inside, at least." He raised his beer and coughed.

I looked anxiously at the bartender, but she appeared to be closing out a handful of tabs for a noisy party near the end of the bar. I racked my brain for something to say to Bird. Then it occurred to me that if Gwen had a project for the Joyner, she might have mentioned it in her impersonal essay. "Did you read Gwendolyn Whitney's? What was it like?"

He shrugged. "Typical ass-kissing." There was another microphone screech from the PA, and Bird said, "Look, don't feel bad about taking my spot."

"I don't," I said, thinking he meant his spot at the bar.

"Really. You look like a nice beauty queen, and I would hate for you to be all broken up about something like me being out of a job."

"Job?"

"Bethany's research assistant. The job I got in return for being such a trouper. The one assurance I had that even a mess like me could get my shit together eventually, because of" — he drew himself up to his full, admittedly not very impressive seated height — "my *promise*."

Just then the bartender finally turned around, and, desperate enough to abandon my server-honed bar manners, I waved my twenty like a flag. "There must be some mistake. I didn't take your job. I'm Margaret's research assistant, not Bethany's." The bartender made her way toward me. I hoisted myself forward with reckless disregard for the slippery patch on the bar, ordered a pitcher of the special, and sank back into my seat, relieved.

Bird, however, was frowning. "That's not right. That can't be right."

"Well, maybe not," I said with a trace of bitterness. "But it's true. She gave the job to someone else."

"Who?"

I pointed across the bar. "See the ascot?"

Bird visibly paled. "Him? *He* got the job?"

"She says he lights up the room, or something." The pitcher, thankfully, was making its way toward me. In a moment I would be free. "Honestly, Connor's my friend and he's a great guy, so no hard feelings."

"He's not even her type. *You're* her type."

"So, you've said."

Bird was obviously even drunker than I'd thought. His voice had risen to a treble, his rheumy eyes threatened to overflow, and he almost slipped off his barstool twisting around to get a better look at Connor. "But I read his essay. He has no *promise*."

"Okay." I wrapped my hands around the pitcher handle with one hand, the glass with the other. The bartender held up the twenty inquiringly, and I shook my head, *no change,* eager to escape the Bird and get back to my cozy booth. She smiled, the waving of the bill forgiven.

I started to walk away, and then I turned back for a moment.

"Hey, Bird," I said, a little nervous. "You're a Joyner Fellow, right?"

He didn't even look at me.

"Where did you study? And what was your project?"

"No promise at all," he muttered.

Cracked. I walked away, noting with irritation that the soles of my boots were now permanently stickied. Wherever I walked, the floor under me would feel dirty for the rest of the night.

• • •

I arrived home that evening, mildly tipsy and utterly elated, to find Gwen curled up on the sofa watching a rerun of *Project Runway*.

"Where were you?" I cried, forgetting that I was avoiding her. "We won! We actually won!"

Gwen smiled sleepily. "Really? Congratulations."

"It was looking bad at first," I buzzed. "Connor had pop music covered, and Aggressively Bland Matt knows sports. Morgan is a political junkie, and Letty knows a little bit about everything. But I wasn't, you know, bringing much to the table. We could have used you on 'New York, New York.' Where were you, anyway?" I didn't wait for an answer. "But then there was an Oscars category and one about horses, and—you know Lily's obsessed with horses, right? I've seen so many documentaries about them I cleaned out the category."

"Congratulations," Gwen said again. "I would have sucked at that one."

"I know!" I was almost hugging myself. After winning at trivia, I had gotten more good news: a message from Lily's doctor, confirming that the visit had happened as my mom described and apologizing for having billed the insurance incorrectly. A reimbursement check was on its way, and though I knew that could mean months, the relief was palpable. I still couldn't get through to the Social Security office, but it seemed less important now that I knew my mom was being honest about one thing, at least.

Overflowing with generosity, I pulled three twenties out of my pocket. "This is your share of the winnings, by the way."

"Keep it."

"You were there all season. You can buy me a drink sometime."

"No really, keep it. I flaked on the team," Gwen said. "You were their pinch hitter."

"That hardly seems fair." But I pocketed the money anyway, too fizzy for pride. "Thanks."

"I've been home all afternoon."

In my frictionless mood, I accepted the lie and sat down beside Gwen on the sofa. On-screen, Nina García was wrinkling her nose, and the contestants on the runway cowered. "Enjoying sobriety?"

"I got a lot of work done. I did some laundry." She made a face. "So, no."

"I got a job today. I'm Margaret's new research assistant."

"On top of Bethany?"

The phrasing amused me, but then nothing felt very serious right now. "She hired Connor instead."

"I'm sorry."

"It's okay." It was, right now at least. "Connor said she's already texted him four times in the middle of the night. Once to come over and set her coffeemaker, so it'd go off at the right time in the morning."

"Guess you dodged a bullet."

"Yeah."

We watched Michael Kors snark at someone.

"Never lost two jobs in one week before." I laughed ruefully.

"Are you going to be all right?"

"I've got the thing with Margaret," I said, hurrying us past the danger zone. "Anyway, it's probably for the best, not having an off-campus job. I feel like I've been missing out on all the fun parts of the Program—don't look at me like that, you know there are a few. I've just been working and studying and studying and working."

"It feels like you've been gone more than you've been here," Gwen agreed. "It gets kind of lonely. Maybe that's why I've been going out so much."

"Everyone's just so nice." Still glowing from the congratulatory hugs at the end of the night, I really felt that way.

She frowned. "Some of them. But I get tired of the intellectual brinkmanship, you know? Everything has to be about winning. Even Trivia Night."

"Yeah." Fleetingly, I wondered whether people were trying harder to impress Gwen than they were to impress me. The thought upset me, and I pushed it into the same box where I kept the fact that I still didn't have a Joyner project and was drunk on a Wednesday night instead of working on it. "Well, winning's nice, once in a while."

"Hey, do you want to watch a movie? I'm sick of this."

It was still early, despite the midwinter darkness outside. "Sure. What do you want to watch?"

"Something comforting."

I picked up the remote and clicked through menus. "How about Cocteau's *Beauty and the Beast*?"

"How about Disney's *Beauty and the Beast*?"

"I see the level of comfort we're after," I said. "What about a compromise: Ang Lee's *Sense and Sensibility*."

"Make it Branagh's *Much Ado* and we have a deal."

We settled in to watch the bawdy, joyful, sun-drenched film with its twinned pairs of lovers, one perfectly matched but callow and youthful, one mature and lasting, but too well-versed in each other's flaws for love to be unmixed with hate. In my expansive mood, I wondered which of the characters I'd play. Not Hero, of course. Gwen was the Hero of any story. Maybe Beatrice, older and wiser and long since disillusioned. We laughed at the comedy and made fun of Keanu's bad British accent and cried during Beatrice's speech, and by the time Hero declared, "I am a maid," solving everything, all I could think of was how good it felt to be next to Gwen again.

It was only later that night, when I woke up stone-cold sober and couldn't go back to sleep for an hour, that it occurred to me that in the play, Hero was innocent. Gwen was not. And it wasn't Beatrice I resembled, but the bastard, Don John. I was fatherless, too.

I knock on Gwen's hotel room door, and it opens more quickly than I'm expecting. Gwen hovers in the doorframe in her robe, not opening it all the way. Her hair is slightly rumpled, her face flushed, and I can see that she hasn't been asleep. I imagine her turning the room upside down, searching for the little circle of diamonds in my pocket. When she sees me, her right hand flies to her naked ring finger.

I pull the ring out of my pocket. "Looking for this?"

"Oh my god, thank you so much!" She laughs nervously, rubbing the bare finger as if it's been injured. "I looked everywhere. I was so worried I'd lost it." She stretches out her right hand toward me, a little white star of longing.

A curious impulse keeps me from handing it over right away. I hold it up by the band and turn it slowly in the light, watching the facets flash in the dull hallway. "I'm so sorry I didn't find it earlier. I overindulged at the bar."

"So did I," Gwen said quickly. "Otherwise I would never have taken it off, obviously."

"I didn't even realize I had it until a few minutes ago."

"It sometimes gets a little heavy after a long day."

"I'm just glad I didn't send these pants to get cleaned."

"Yes, me too."

Gwen looks at me, and we both look at her outstretched hand. She opens the door a fraction of an inch wider, leans a bit further forward. I can see from her eyes that she's alarmed, and wonder, for a moment, why. Then I realize, as she must have already, that I'm still holding her ring and have no intention of surrendering it anytime soon.

We stare at each other awkwardly. Her hand drops back down to her side. I have her now, and we both know it. As long as I have the ring, I can ask her anything. I open my mouth.

"Why didn't you invite me to the wedding?"

It's not at all what I intended to say, in part because I already know the answer. We're not friends anymore, not really. The accident dashed our rafts apart, permanently. But something in me must not know it, because the fear of being left behind by Gwen pokes at a cold, hard hollow at my core that seems to have existed long before our friendship, and I still cannot shake the secret belief that whatever she's doing is the best and rightest and truest thing. Living in New York, leaving New York, going to grad school, leaving grad school. Marrying a famous director. Having children or not having children. It's all perfect when Gwen does it—and all wrong when I do it. We were supposed to be more than wives and mothers, weren't we? But what does *more* look like? Me in leather pants, giving head to some Žižek wannabe after a talk? Nothing I do will ever be perfect.

Now that's something I can imagine crying about in a bar.

But I know I didn't, because Gwen's face, her guilt struggling with horror at the unbelievable gaucherie of my question, tells me that it's the first time she's heard it. Also, that it's the right question to ask.

I double down. "I know we haven't been close lately. But seeing you tonight reminded me . . ." I trail off. *We were best friends,* I almost say, but stop myself just in time. Instead, I pocket the ring again and fold my arms in front of my chest.

"I know." She sounds pained. "It all feels like such a long time ago. I wasn't expecting to relive it all tonight."

So, we did talk about the past. But which past? The one where we picnicked in the forest preserve and watched movies late into the night? Or the Program, with its long silences punctuated by disaster?

What did I tell her about the farmhouse?

Gwen is watching me closely.

I search for a way to frame the question without implicating myself. "So, that's why I wasn't invited? What we talked about earlier?"

"No! God, no. I didn't mean to imply—"

"What, then?"

She hedges. "Look, we hardly invited anyone from the States. It's not easy to get to."

"How are the other guests getting there? Charter flight?"

She looks down at her feet, and I know I've hit it on the head. "It's mostly just family."

Family. When the Whitneys invited me to spend Christmas with them in Paris, all expenses paid, my mother didn't say a word to stop me. She just relapsed. I had imagined singing carols to Lily over Skype that Christmas morning; instead I cooked ramen and bundled her into three sweaters when the heat went out.

I go straight for the jugular, while she's still upset over the charter.

"I bet dress shopping with your mom was fun. What'd you end up with—Valentino? Erdem?"

She suddenly turns fierce. "I don't owe you an explanation, Mac. You haven't been great at keeping up either, since—well, since I left." She lifts her chin. "I thought maybe you had decided I wasn't good enough for you anymore."

"That's a laugh. Admit it—you never walk away from anything unless you think *you're* too good for *it*."

She gasps, her hand flying to her throat. "How can you say that, after everything that happened?"

"After what, exactly?"

I hold my breath. If she knows, now is when she'll say it.

She goes silent. Then she seems to gather herself, reach inside for strength. She levels her gaze at my pocket. "Please just give me my ring so we can both go to bed."

"I want to talk."

"Do you really think what we need is a heart-to-heart?"

"We did when it was you asking."

She folds her arms across her chest.

I soften my tone, the vocal equivalent of the coaxing hand she placed on my arm earlier tonight. "Gwen, please. We haven't seen each other in years. I happen to run into you right before you head off to Europe to get married. It's not just the wedding. I think we both know we're not likely to see each other again, after tonight."

She sighs, but I can see her shoulders lowering, her defensive posture going slack.

"It's two a.m. Where would we even go?"

"Anywhere. Wander around the hotel, pretend it's the Riverwalk."

I give the nostalgia a few seconds to set in, and then sigh in faux resignation as I reach for my pocket.

"Wait." She hesitates, still blocking the doorway. "Hang on, I just need to get my room key."

I nod. As she turns toward her room, releasing the hotel door, I shove my foot in the crack for a moment and peer through the doorway into her hotel room.

The bedclothes haven't been turned down. She's barely been in her room at all.

She steps into the hallway and lets the door close behind her, and I see that what I thought was a robe is actually a long cardigan wrap over clothes that are flowy, but still chic. Even her loungewear outclasses me.

"You've changed," I observe.

"We both have."

"I meant your outfit." While she recovers, I add, "It looks comfortable."

She gestures dismissively. "Plainclothes."

"What, like a cop?"

She blinks and laughs, as I understand a moment too late. "*Airplane* clothes. Early flight, remember?" She yawns. "Do you want to go down to the bar again? They might still be open."

"I'm done drinking for the night."

"There's a lounge area near the elevators."

"Fine." We start to head in that direction.

Gwen yawns again, closing her eyes and covering her stretched-out mouth delicately with one hand. "How did we ever stay up so late, Mac?" Then she opens her eyes. "I mean

Claire. Sorry I keep forgetting. Claire, Claire, Claire. Clarion call. *Clair de lune.*"

"Claire's Boutique." Junky little cards with three pairs of earrings stuck through them for $5.99. In high school, I would sometimes pretend I'd dropped something and do a quick sweep of the floor underneath the racks. I always found at least one lone earring on the floor. Mismatched them to look like it was on purpose.

"Why'd you change your name, anyway? I liked Mac."

"And I liked Gwen," I say quietly.

"Friends lose touch," she says, a little desperately. "They meet again when life brings them back together—"

"Usually when one of them gets married."

She sighs. "Well, then I'd say we're right on schedule, wouldn't you? Come on. Something's on your mind. Go ahead and ask. Is it about Andreas?"

"You said he was 'deeply private'; I didn't want to pry." I tamp down my sarcasm, thankful to have found a topic we evidently didn't discuss at the bar. The main thing right now is to get her talking.

"I swear, the details aren't that interesting. We met last winter, skiing in— Ugh, you don't want to hear this." She throws me a sidelong glance. "'Skiing in Aspen with my parents.' I know how it sounds." She flashes with irritation, then immediately softens. "I'm sorry. I'm on edge. Honestly, it's this wedding. It's not really important to Andreas and me. We won't feel any different afterward."

"Then why do it?"

"Mostly for my parents."

I try, and fail, to imagine it.

"You know how they are. They don't pressure me—or at least, they don't try to. They only want the best for me. But they're just so *generous*. Too generous. I don't think it occurs to them there's anything in the world they can't give me. And it makes them so happy, I just . . . let them." Hearing herself makes her squirm, but she continues staring down at the ground, stubbornly refusing to look at me. "At first it was going to be just family. But then they started talking about how much money they're saving doing it there, and I knew it was all over. My dad decided to use the excuse to improve the grounds, and my mom had the guest quarters renovated and expanded, and suddenly everyone in the world was invited for a weeklong vacation in Tuscany."

She really sounds a little miserable as she says it, but not quite enough not to catch herself on the last part. She looks up at me. "When I say, 'everyone', I mean their friends, not mine. Hardly anyone I know is going to be there."

"Is Connor going?"

She blushes bright pink.

"Wow." Connor's not on social media, though years ago I heard he's teaching at a private school somewhere in upstate New York. In my mind, he's somewhere safe, far away from anyone who could hurt him. Including me. "I didn't know you were in touch."

"Come on, Mac, don't take it personally." She's stopped trying to correct herself on my name.

"Does he hate me?"

"His feelings were hurt pretty badly. But I think mostly he just wants to forget that part of his life. I do, too."

"You don't remind each other? How nice for you both."

"Connor was there for me during some tough times, right after I left," she snaps. "I helped him leave, too. It wasn't easy for either of us."

"You make the Program sound like an abusive relationship."

"You said it, not me."

"Don't you think that's a little hyperbolic?"

She stops cold and looks at me, and I realize we passed the lounge area long ago and walked the hallway circuit instead. We've looped back; we're nearly to her room again.

"No, I don't," she says, with an intensity I haven't felt from her before. "The Program changed you."

"I'm not the only one."

"Doing anything to get ahead—"

"Keeping secrets—"

"What you did to Connor—"

"Playing innocent one minute, and the next—"

"—ruthless."

"—shameless."

The words came out at the same time.

"'*Shameless*'? What's that supposed to mean?" she says.

We stand looking at each other. I haven't mentioned Rocky's name yet—not that I remember, anyway. I wonder whether she did, at the bar. I was alone when I saw her ring. Maybe she was in the bathroom, crying, too.

But I can't gamble on that right now. "Nothing."

She stalks toward her room, and I race after her to stop her. "All I'm saying is that you suddenly had a lot of new friends." I pivot back to the theme of Connor. "And I find it interesting that now we're all out of it, you're still the one who does."

She looks at me in disgust. "Poor Mac. Poor Research I,

tenure-track Mac. It makes you furious that I don't want any of this." Her gesture takes in the hotel, the conference, everything. "It's not enough for me to be happy for you. You want me to want it, too, so that you can feel good that you got it instead of me."

"For the last time, it's *Claire*." I allow my fury to come through in my voice. "And no, I know you'd rather be skiing in Aspen and throwing parties in your Italian castle, despite what you want everyone to think."

"And what do I want everyone to think?"

"That you hate your money. That you're ashamed of it." My eyes burn. "When as a matter of fact, you love it."

"Yes! I like having money!" She throws up her hands. "Is that what you want me to say? It makes life easier. It always has. I'm thankful for all the good things in my life. I liked that my father was there for my childhood, and that my mother was functional, and that I didn't have a sister who needed constant care. Haven't you made me pay for it? When will it ever be enough for you?"

Toward the end of this speech, her voice churns with a wild, desperate mix of anger and pity, and she starts crying. I know that if I keep pushing her, she'll spill the truth of what she knows.

Ten feet in front of us, the elevator doors start to slide open, laughter spilling out.

I catch a glimpse of our reflection in the black windows: two maudlin drunks shouting at each other after closing time. We're a mess. Twin messes. And the hotel is chock-full of my colleagues.

Our eyes meet. Gwen doesn't want to be seen in this state

any more than I do. She turns back toward the room, but then a door down the hallway opens. Raucous, last-round laughter echoes from the elevator. In a moment, we'll be surrounded.

"In here." I open the stairwell door and pull us both through it. The heavy fireproof door swings shut on the sound of partyers with an echoing, metallic crash. "If we're going to fight, let's at least do it where no one can hear us."

"I don't want to fight, Mac." Gwen chokes back her tears.

I don't want to fight either. For once in my life, I don't even want to win. I want to kill. I've felt it before, and I know the difference.

BAD HABITS

10

In the cold light of day, it seemed impossible that I had gone to the Parlor last night, wasted twenty bucks on beer, gotten drunk, and then come home and watched a movie afterward. Those were scenes from my normal life, before I'd known about Gwen and Rocky and the Joyner, before I'd slept with Bethany and lost my job and extorted money from her. Now only two things mattered: my Joyner project, and the envelope of cash that would buy me the time to keep working on it.

The money was supposed to be in my mail folder, but the Program office didn't open until 8 a.m., and it was 6 a.m. now. So, I headed to the library. Tucked away in my study carrel, my mind kept drifting back to the $400 waiting for me in my mail folder. Even the stained-glass window above my carrel reminded me of money. One of many artistic tributes to industry that dotted the campus, it depicted a couple of pickaxes crossed under a golden sun that looked like a coin.

I forced my attention back to the task at hand.

"Don't go to grad school if you don't want to write," one of my Urbana professors had warned me. I had nodded, secretly annoyed. At the time, I churned out A-level papers in one night. But now, staring at the blank page, I felt profoundly empty. Nothing came to my head. Nothing at all.

Thank god I had recorded Bethany's lecture. Maybe without her in front of me, I could finally get some clarity on what she was actually saying. I put in my earbuds and found the file, and there I was, back in her office, surrounded by her. I had intended to transcribe, but I found my mind wandering to Saturday night.

I heard a noise behind me and yanked out my earbuds, half expecting it to be her. Outside, a pigeon flapped against the stained glass. When it flew away, the silence was deafening.

Not knowing why, I opened the web browser and searched for Bethany's name. I started with her faculty bio, then moved on to blog posts and interviews, then an image search. I saw Bethany lecturing at a podium, hands sculpting the air; Bethany in a group photo at a conference; Bethany at a reception holding a wineglass. It wasn't enough. I wanted to see her shopping, brushing her teeth, crying at a movie. Being a person. I found ProfTalk.com and read hundreds of student reviews. "So cool." "Too hard." "I dream about her." "She's brilliant." "I'm obsessed with her boots." "She really cares about her students." "She's a heinous bitch." "She walked out of my presentation." "I keep wondering whether she likes me or not." "She made a girl cry in class." "Intense." "The smartest woman in the world." "Bitch." "I worship her."

I snapped my laptop shut.

Hands trembling, I pulled out my notebook and flipped through it at random, hoping to refresh myself on economimesis. Grady's paper was just as important, and I was seeing him later today. I found and read my dubious notes from early in the semester:

> Economy: resources in a society OR careful management of available resources

> Mimesis: imitation of life in a work of art (e.g., birds pecking at Zeuxis's painted grapes)

> Econo + mimesis: careful management of available resources in an imitation of life

An imitation of life. It reminded me of the Douglas Sirk film, which reminded me of what Rocky had said in the car on the way to the retreat: the world needs movies more than it needs academics. A film was an imitation of life that I could wrap my brain around. Maybe I could write my paper about a film.

While I was still puzzling over this, the campus clock tower tolled 8 a.m. Thank god. I scooped up my things and hustled out of the library. Once in the department, I hurried to the racks of folders along the mail wall and slipped my hand into my folder, fishing out a letter-sized envelope that felt satisfyingly heavy. Cash, at least, was real.

Before I could look inside to count it, Margaret came out of her office.

"Oh, Mackenzie, thank goodness you're here." I stuffed the envelope hastily into my bag. "I need you to help me with something. Lorraine's little boy is sick, and she's not coming in today. I am really beside myself."

"Oh." I had been planning to make the deposit right now, before Grady's office hours.

"Don't worry, I'll make sure you get paid for your time. I just need to get this letter printed out and walked over to the Dean's office as soon as possible."

Clearly, I had no choice; my work-study job was beginning now. I thought of the Joyner letter I needed from Margaret, took a deep breath, and sat in Lorraine's ergonomic chair, which Margaret held away from the desk expectantly.

"Now, let's see, she keeps all the passwords *there*." She pointed to a manila folder sitting neatly erect in an upright file holder to my right. I opened it and found a single sheet of legal paper with a list of passwords. "Yes, that's the one."

For the next five minutes, Margaret used me as a living keyboard and mouse to search for her file, indicating which folder she wanted me to open by pointing over my shoulder.

"Lorraine has a place for everything, I just don't know how to find it. Ah, 'Disciplinary,' that could be it." She jabbed her finger toward a folder that we could have found in ten seconds by looking at the "recently opened" tab. Moving the cursor to open it, I started at the file name: "filmore_tess."

"Yes, that's the one. If you could just open that up, print out a copy on letterhead, and bring it to me to sign. Shouldn't take a minute."

She retreated to her office while I skimmed the letter, feeling more and more nauseated.

Dear Dean Cadwallader,

It is with deep regret that I write to initiate disciplinary proceedings against Tess Filmore, a first-year student in the Emerging Studies Program. While Ms. Filmore's classwork has shown promise, her poor attendance, antisocial tendencies, and lack of initiative outside of class suggest motivational impairment. As you are well aware, the attrition rate among students of color in the Program is problematically high, and we have made it our policy to address signs of motivational impairment early on, so as to give all of our students the resources and support they need to succeed. Unfortunately, Ms. Filmore has responded to my concern with hostile and threatening behavior.

Ms. Filmore displayed antisocial tendencies as early as the First-Year Orientation Retreat, where she refused to participate in team-building exercises and influenced a student who has since left the Program to do the same. Anonymous sources report that she has repeatedly rejected offers of faculty mentorship. She has also had several absences in my class. My assistant, Lorraine Cho, witnessed Ms. Filmore's violent outburst when asked if she needed financial or emotional assistance. During this incident, I feared for my safety.

While I do not wish to be rash in stigmatizing a student, I feel it is our duty to require Ms. Filmore to seek immediate assistance from mental health services. For my safety and that of my staff, I recommend that she be required to provide an affidavit of mental competence before she is allowed to reenter the Program offices.

I hope Sheila is well, and that we are all able to have brunch again sometime soon when the weather gets a little better —

"I don't hear the printer," Margaret called from her office.

I ripped myself away from the awful letter. "There was a paper jam." I got up, shaken, and opened and shut all the printer
doors in rapid succession. Then I dropped a piece of letterhead
into the printer tray and went back to the computer. While it
printed, I pulled out my phone and snapped a quick picture of
the screen, scrolling down to capture the second page. Then I
brought the printed letter to Margaret's desk.

"Mackenzie, you're a lifesaver! Bethany said you would
be." Margaret signed the bottom of the second page, slashing
through "Dean Cadwallader" and writing "Jim" over the strike-
through. She handed it back. "If you could just run this down to
the Dean's office on your way out, I would be so grateful. And
don't forget to log this on your timesheet! Let's round this up to
an hour. Our little secret." She winked.

I closed my thumb and forefinger around the corner of the
signed letter, feeling about it as if it were something that had
come straight out of her asshole, and turned to go. Once out
of Margaret's office, I took a detour to the bathroom, where I
locked myself in a stall to read it again.

The whole thing was ridiculous. Insubordinate, for buying a
pie. The rest—motivational impairment, emotional problems
—defied comprehension. I recalled the conversation I had
overheard through the office door yesterday and almost laughed
out loud at the thought of Margaret, nearly six feet tall, quaking
in her chair from fear of Tess, who stood all of five foot two. I
remembered Tess's argument with Matt at the party, her dry
sarcasm. Tess had a coolness to her I couldn't imagine someone
like Margaret disrupting.

I held the letter, not sure what to do, longing to drop it in
the toilet and flush. I imagined it backing up the department

toilets, and Margaret, up to her ankles in bilge water, yelling for an absent Lorraine.

Racked with indecision, I slid the letter into my bag and got out my phone. The very least I could do was warn Tess. I texted, *Tess, you need to see this. Prepare yourself, it's bad.* Then I sent the snapshots of the letter.

The bathroom door opened, and I heard sturdy shoes shuffle and squeak toward the accessible stall. I could barely see Margaret's clogs through the gap in the stall. I flushed and fled.

Downstairs, I stood outside the Dean's office for a moment, the letter weighing a metric ton in my hands. To deliver it was to betray Tess. But if I delayed or destroyed the letter, there would be email follow-ups from Margaret, or perhaps they really would get brunch with Sheila sometime and discover what had gone wrong. The misdelivered letter would be traced back to me.

I needed a recommendation from Margaret. Three letters for the Joyner, and Rocky was a nonstarter. It had to be Margaret.

I walked into the Dean's office and dropped the letter in the receptionist's in-box. The Dean would never believe this pile of tripe. Tess would apologize, Margaret would back down, and the whole thing would blow over.

As I walked out of the building, my phone started vibrating with responses from Tess. A long string of invectives, some extremely creative — more or less what I'd expected. Her last text read: *When did this go out???*

I paused, then checked the tiny date on the picture of the letter. I'd been too upset to update it before printing out the letter. After some hesitation, I typed and sent: *Yesterday. So sorry.*

· · ·

Patiently, I sat in Grady's office enduring his definition of economimesis, which was exactly the same every time I asked, and which I understood no more or less than the first time I'd heard it. Grady had a well-controlled stutter that only came out rarely, when he got terribly excited; at all other times, including now, he spoke slowly and calmly, measuring his words as if in perfectly leveled teaspoons, rectangular glasses millimetering down his nose with every word.

"I was thinking about writing my paper on a film," I said, waiting half a beat after one of his sentences stopped. It was sometimes hard to tell when Grady was finished talking, since he used almost no inflection. "Something about dinner parties? I was thinking of Resnais, or maybe Buñuel."

Grady paused reflectively, as if assessing his response in advance so as not to accidentally surprise himself. "That would be appropriate," he said in four-four time by the metronome, "though not necessarily successful." He paused. Just as I was about to open my mouth, he finished. "Buñuel, I am inclined to think, more so than Resnais."

"I was thinking more of Buñuel, too." I launched into a quick reading of *The Exterminating Angel* as an economimetic structure. Whenever Grady began to purse his lips, I backpedaled or reversed course, until I'd produced a skeletal argument that appeared to satisfy him. I finished talking and waited for his opinion.

The heavy glasses had wiggled themselves down to the bridge of his nose, and he pushed them up against his brow bone before he began. "Or perhaps, after all, Resnais." He finished this pronouncement with a squint that launched the glasses once more on their infinitesimal slide. "If executed well. I'll look forward to reading it, Mackenzie."

I took his use of my name as my signal to change the subject.

"Professor Herschel," I said, waiting for him to tell me to call him by his first name, Grady. He did not. "I was wondering whether you might be willing to write a letter of support for my Joyner application."

Grady's eyebrows shot up above his frames, and the glasses actually hopped downward.

"I'm getting a letter from Bethany," I added.

Grady nodded slowly, but only once. Then he reached up and removed his glasses. Without them, he looked younger, his bare eyes blinking beneath thick eyelashes. "Of course, I'm happy to write you a letter, Mack-k-enzie," he said. "I d-didn't know you were int—" He paused, took a breath, and continued, "*inter*ested in the Joyner."

"Isn't everyone?"

"N-no." He wiped his glasses with a Kleenex he drew from a box on his desk. Then he replaced the rectangular black frames at the very apex of his nose's slope, transforming his face back into that of a cartoon robot. "The Joyner is for students who come in with a strong project and stand to benefit from a faster pace. There have been—m-missteps."

Who would benefit more from getting through the Program quickly than someone with a family to support? His answer chilled me. Despite Bethany's confidence, it felt like everywhere I went, I was haunted by subtle suggestions that I wasn't cut out for the Joyner. I squared my jaw. "It doesn't hurt to try, right?"

"Certainly," Grady agreed slowly. "This paper will give me a sense of what you're capable of. Why don't I just wait until I see it? The Joyner isn't due for another couple of weeks. Is it?"

"The last day of the semester."

"Excellent, yes. Plenty of time. Just be sure to give me a good paper to work with." He turned back toward his computer, and I could feel myself disappear in his peripheral vision. "Buñuel," he said, by way of goodbye.

"Buñuel," I responded, and left.

The envelope held, as promised, $400 in cash. I headed straight to an ATM to deposit it, along with the $180 I had left after last night and $60 of trivia winnings. Still in the kiosk, I pulled out my phone and transferred most of the total to my mom's account. It left me with no grocery money for the rest of the month, but with any luck the Social Security people would get to the appeal quickly and my payroll forms would go through and everything would sort itself out. Until then, I'd just have to start going to more department events. They were always catered.

I was about to toss the envelope when I caught sight of a note inside. *BQ: Don't be mad. Fri @ 9?* followed by an address and a room number. I pulled out the sticky note and a soft paper sleeve came with it.

The sleeve held a hotel room key.

Of course, I went. I hated myself for it. I had taken money from her less than twenty-four hours ago, and she had treated me like a servant or worse in return, and I did not have even the excuse of loving her. I did lust for her—for the thought of what she could do to me, what she could make me into, by wanting me. I supposed it was what women had felt toward powerful men for centuries, and powerful women, too, in the shadows.

That is why I went to Bethany's hotel on Friday, parking downtown and riding the elevator up to the penthouse suite. I used the key and found her reading and drinking a glass of wine in an armchair. When she saw me, she butterflied her book, put her hand around the back of my head, and, without setting down her wineglass, drew me in for a long, deep kiss.

"Lover, if you need anything, anything at all, you have only to ask." The words licked at my face like a grooming cat. "You don't ever have to do without."

I kissed her back, not for the first time, but for the first time sober. Then, without understanding why, I began to cry.

"Shhhh," she said, and started taking off my clothes.

Later, I lay on my stomach facing away from Bethany, who absently traced circles on my back with her nails.

"We need to get you a project," she said.

"Mmmm," I said without conviction, my body so flushed that the cooling of the sweat-soaked bedsheet felt pleasant. She leaned forward to kiss the spot between my shoulder blades, and I felt the tips of her hair brush my back.

"This is important, Mac," she said, close to my ear. "I can't just tell you what to work on."

"Why not?"

"Darling, be serious." She settled back. "We've got to grab some of what I saw in that essay you wrote for me. That spark, that drive. There's something there. But it's got to come from you."

I couldn't really grasp what she was saying, but I wanted her to keep moving her fingers, so I nodded.

"There are only three questions that matter in life. What do you know? What do you like? And what do you want?"

"I want the Joyner," I said promptly.

"Cross that one off the list, then," she said, unimpressed. "But you're supposed to do them in order. What do you know?"

I hiked myself up on my elbows and turned to face her. Bethany's body was smaller and leaner than mine, lightly muscled, with breasts the size of teacups and a little belly like an inverted mixing bowl. Lying down, her square jaw was softened by little blobs of migrating flesh that smoothed the path to the delta of her neck, where gravity had lapped her skin into a series of concentric curves. Compared to the men I had been with, she was so neat, so compact, yet so unpredictable, the vectors of her desire coming from every angle at once, coiled into unlikely knots to fit the limits of her body.

"What do I know." I put my hand on the dip of her waist, felt the muscle there jump and then soften again, marveled at the sharpness of the hip bone through fat. I slid the flat of my palm into the hollow under her hip, and then down further. "I know how to make you come."

"Be serious," she said again, but gradually succumbed.

Afterward, she lay on her back panting. "What do you want, Mac?" she said, in a voice close to despair.

"I already answered that one."

There was a long pause. She looked away, a strand of red hair sticking to her cheek. "What do you like, then," she said flatly.

I opened my mouth to answer, then closed it again. "I like this." I moved toward her again, but she pulled back.

"Yes, fucking is high on your list," she said impatiently. "As, I've noticed, is caviar. Are you sure you're an intellectual, darling, and not just a hedonist?"

Stung, I pulled back quickly. "I work hard."

"I know you do." It didn't sound like a compliment.

"I like . . ." I struggled for words. "Knowing things. And . . . wanting things."

"So do I, Mac. So do I." She sighed deeply.

"Well, then, you answer. What do you know? And what do you want?"

She looked into my face so intently and non-sexually that I suddenly felt as if I were sitting across from her at a conference table, fully clothed. I thought, at first, she had no intention of answering, but after a moment, she looked away.

"I know what it feels like to be under someone's thumb," she said finally. "I learned it from my first husband. I like not feeling that way anymore. And what I want is never to feel that way again." She sat up in bed and scooted to the edge, swinging her feet to the floor.

It was hard to picture. A Bethany who was powerless and weak was an entirely different Bethany than the one I knew. A woman to pity, maybe, not to—what we were doing. "Is that why you married Rocky?"

I meant why she had married someone so much younger, but she cast me a startled glance. "I suppose he did look something like a bodyguard back then, fresh from Kiev." She seemed about to say more, then shook her head. "Forget it. I told you before, it was mostly the sex." She saw my puzzled expression. "Everyone has things they want to forget, Mac. You're not the only one. Better leave Rocky out of this."

"I thought you said you had some kind of agreement. About" —I flushed—"affairs."

"About *his* affairs." She stood up. "And so we do. He has as many as he wants, as long as he doesn't leave me powerless. If he leaves me, he leaves his money, too."

"His money?"

"*The* money." She waved her hand impatiently. "Money is just an exchange rate, Mac—it doesn't belong to anyone. It's

a placeholder for things that can't be given. Never let it distract you." She was getting dressed, buttoning her red blouse
over bare breasts, and I could feel her attention slipping away
from me.

"And what about your affairs?" I said, to get it back.

"I don't have them," she said, matter-of-factly. She walked
around the bed in her blouse and underwear and sat next to me,
reaching out a hand to stroke my cheek. "Dearest Mac, I see
you fighting so hard to forget where you came from. But you
never forget. You just get used to the fact that no one around
you cares. They're too busy with their own forgetting. You remind me so much——" She stopped.

"Of Rocky?"

"Of me." She laughed drily. "And that's a dangerous thing."

Dangerous for whom, I wondered.

She got up and started pulling on her black leather pants.
Then she walked to the nightstand and picked up the menu
card by the phone. "I'm hungry. How about room service before
the kitchen closes?"

"What about the ones who already know?"

She looked back at me, receiver in hand. "What do you
mean?"

"The ones who knew you before. Who know where you
came from."

"You get rid of them." And then, into the receiver: "Two
steaks bavettes, please, rare. Beurre blanc, asparagus, and a
green salad." She looked at me. "Crêpes suzette or Sacher torte?"
When I didn't answer, she ordered one of each.

N ow what?" Gwen's voice echoes through the stairwell.

I lean over the railing and look up at the vertical landscape of concrete stairs spiraling tightly upward.

The fact that she followed me in here tells me something valuable: I have something she wants, too, and it's not just the ring. It's time to press my advantage.

"I have a crazy idea," I said. "Let's take the stairs up to the eleventh floor. I'll show you the view from my room."

Gwen cranes her neck. "Here's another idea: elevator."

"And run into some drunk colleague with a bone to pick about Rancière?" I roll my eyes. "No thanks. Come on, it'll be fun." It'll be hard. But that's the point, for both of us. I want her to remember what it was like, tackling something together.

She looks up again, wavering. Whatever she wants from me, she's not sure it's worth it.

"It's only nine floors." One last nudge: "I'm sure I'll wear out first. You're in far better shape."

"Hardly." But she takes a step up. "Fine. I have nowhere else to be at two in the morning."

"Except in bed."

"Except in bed." She sighs and takes three steps up, so that she's next to me on the same step, her hand on the opposite handrail.

Side by side, we start to ascend.

"So, what ever happened with that guy up in your room—Harvard?" She laughs. "Was he still waiting when you got back?"

Ah, another glimpse of the lost conversation at the bar. I laugh along carefully. "Oh, yeah, he was there. He drank the entire mini-fridge. Cute, though."

"Did you . . ." She trails off, either to be coy or because she's conserving her breath.

"That would be telling." I try to sound playful. "Don't worry though, he's long gone." I hope it's true by now.

"You're not seeing anyone?"

I keep planting one foot in front of the other and hoisting myself up the steps. It feels good to climb. "I see lots of people."

"But no one special?"

"I like to think they're all special in their own way." She sighs. "I just don't think it's in the cards for me, Gwen. True love."

"And in the meantime—what, you sleep with students?"

"I avoid my own." This is not, strictly speaking, true—or, at least, the policy is not one hundred percent successful. "I'm not much older than the grad students, so I have to keep the boundaries very clear. You can't depend on students to enforce them. You know that better than anyone."

"What is that supposed to mean?"

"Oh, you know. When a professor is young and good-looking and shows you a little extra attention—well, you of all people should know. I've had students misinterpret a look, a word, even a grade. And before you know it, they're throwing themselves at you. All those young, taut bodies. It's hard to resist. All you have to do is . . . encourage them. An email here. A compliment there."

Gwen blushes but stays silent.

"It's a mutually beneficial arrangement."

"So you say."

She sounds bitter, but I keep pushing. "Anyway, I don't see what the problem is. Two consenting adults, what's the harm?" I resist the urge to glance at her reaction. "Right? At least I'm not married."

"Shut up, Mac."

The strange thing is, even as I needle her, I can't tell who I'm really talking about: Rocky and Gwen, or Bethany and Mac, or Harvard and Claire, whoever she is, a phantom who seems to vanish a little more with every step. We've climbed two flights so far, and while I stop on the landing to catch my breath, Gwen keeps marching resolutely upward. I grin at her back and begin following a few steps behind. Better to trail her for a while and close the gap slowly than wear myself out catching up now. We have time.

"I'm sorry. I thought this was just girl talk. Like the old days."

"We're not girls anymore. We're thirty-two."

"How old was—"

"Don't say his name," Gwen says sharply.

"Oh, I remember. Thirty-seven." I puff out a short laugh. "You are such a hypocrite, Gwen."

"Look." She stops on the landing ahead of me, and I stop too. For once, she has the height advantage. "You've been hinting around about this all night, so let's just get it out in the open. I was in love with him."

"Is that what it was?"

"Yes, that's what it was. I'm not saying it was particularly no-ble. But that's what it was." She turns the corner and continues walking up.

"Well." I reach the landing in one long step and round the corner to catch sight of her again. "I guess that's just something I'll never understand."

"No, you probably won't."

We climb two more flights in silence. It's easier to maintain a steady pace that way. We pass the number 7 on the next door.

I break first. "Explain it to me."

"I already know what you think."

"Then I won't say anything, I'll just listen." She shakes her head, but I persist. "You weren't exactly forthcoming at the time. We weren't talking about it late into the night." I register her hesitation and take a deep breath. "Now's your chance. Tell me what happened. I won't say a word."

There's a pause. I'm betting she's never told the whole story to anyone, not even Andreas—certainly not Andreas—and that she's always wanted to. I wait, and after a while, she begins.

"It was like . . ." Still climbing, she speaks in short bursts, panting in between. "I didn't know why I was there." She glances down at me over her shoulder. "You were so certain about the Program. Everyone was, but me. That's why I drank too much. Acted like an idiot. Ignoring the fact that—I didn't want to be there." I wait for her to continue. "Rocky didn't either. He didn't feel like he belonged. Inside he was still—a kid, starving on the streets of Kiev. A frightened little kid."

Thug, more like, I think, but hold my tongue, as promised.

"He played around. Tried to get himself fired. Nothing worked. He just got away with more and more." Flagging, she uses the handrail to hoist herself up. "I really was taking that class with him to get closer to Bethany, at first. He knew it, and he would talk to me about her. That's how it started. Then he got more . . . honest. He was burned out, he wanted something different for his life, but he didn't know where to start. So, he just—repeated the pattern. Bethany slept with him. He slept with his students." She flushed. "That night at Connor's party, I ran into him at the liquor store. We took a long walk. He and Soo-jeong had just stopped—well, you know about that. She left not long after." She was silent for a moment. "He was a mess that night. He hated himself for sleeping with her."

What a creep. It takes all my effort not to say something out loud, but I can't keep myself from grunting in disgust.

"Yeah. I know. That's why we . . . didn't."

I wait for her to go on, but she goes up four more steps without finishing the sentence. "Didn't what?"

"Sleep together."

That first night. Surely she means, they didn't sleep together the first night. Rocky must have wanted to, but because of Soo-Jeong, Gwen held him off. Maybe even a second time. I think of all the nights I couldn't find Gwen: Connor's party. Bethany's dinner. Trivia night. And those are only the occasions I remember. What about when I was with Bethany at the hotel? Or the long days when I was working a double shift? There were a million opportunities.

"We wanted to. *I* wanted to." She's still climbing. Little black dots have started appearing around the edges of my field of vision, and every once in a while, I blink to clear them away. "Not trying to—romanticize it. You're right. I was stupid. I came on to him. He wouldn't."

Worse and worse. I can't believe what I'm hearing. A sad professor, too in love with Gwen to fuck her? More likely, as

Bethany had once suggested, he was too drunk to perform, and Gwen too inexperienced to know the difference. Either way, it was pathetic.

"After everything came out—later—those emails. Never been so—humiliated." She stops, huffing and puffing, a few steps shy of the tenth-floor landing. "I knew what—everyone thought. What you thought."

Think, I correct her mentally.

Bending over to massage her knees, she takes a deep, shuddering breath and exhales forcefully. Straightening, she leans on the handrail and rests her back against the wall. Her cheeks are red with exertion, and she flashes me a dopamine grin as I climb the last few steps and lean against the handrail across from her, the back of my head just touching the bottom rail of the next flight up. "Then why didn't I deny it. Right? If we weren't." She gathers the sweaty hair off her forehead, collecting the dark, glossy mass in one hand and fanning her face with the other. "Because I was embarrassed. Because the difference was academic. Because it was still cheating. And because—my plan was—" The smile flees, replaced by a sick expression. "It was going to be our first time. That night at the farmhouse."

The word *farmhouse* seems to change her whole body as it passes through her mouth. She goes limp against the wall, releases her hair, drops her hands to the rail. "So now you know everything," she says dully.

Do I? Maybe she's lying about not sleeping with Rocky, but she's not lying about being in love with him. Maybe she's still hung up on him. Maybe that's the real reason she's so reluctant to talk about her fiancé. Why did she take off her engagement ring in the bar? When I first saw her, she was talking to a man in a suit whose face I never saw clearly. Is virtuous, blameless

Gwen here to meet someone for a final fling before getting tied down to her Brazilian director?

It occurs to me for the first time that it's quite a coincidence, Gwen staying in the conference hotel the night before her flight. If she's here to meet someone, the odds are good that it's someone from the Program.

Either way, I've accomplished my aim in launching her down memory lane. She's out of breath, and I'm all caught up. I match her pace for the next flight up. I begin to pull ahead.

11

I drove away from Bethany's hotel the next morning in a buoyant mood.

I had awakened early, and by the time Bethany opened her eyes, I was already dressed and ready to kiss her goodbye. Closing the door of her hotel room behind me, I felt a lightness and calm so unlike our first time together that it was like stepping into a new skin. Almost as if I'd rectified some prior mistake. This time, I had controlled the encounter. I had chosen to go to Bethany of my own free will, sober and with eyes open. There had been no surprises. Glossing over my tears at the start of the encounter—it was natural to feel overwhelmed at the beginning of any relationship, I reasoned, let alone one with so many complicating factors—I lingered instead on our second round of lovemaking, the one I'd initiated. The sex that time had been more fun, even relaxed, and with my defenses lowered, I had been able for the first time to feel my power over Bethany. She had opened up to me afterward, become gratifyingly vulnerable. She would never have admitted it, but with Rocky wrapped up in Gwen, she needed me. If I kept my head, I could turn that to my advantage. It needn't be high drama. I could learn from her, soak up her mentorship, and move on in a couple of years, grateful for her unique role in my education. To that end, I'd even attempted something rather daring: I'd recorded the whole evening. I'd had a feeling she would go into lecture mode at some point in the night, and she had, many times over. I was pleased with myself for holding something back from her in order to get what I needed.

Of course, the audio was nine hours long and only intermittently useful. At home, I put my earbuds in and immediately blushed. Skipping *those* parts didn't work; I kept missing things I was supposed to transcribe. I would have to listen passively to the whole nine hours first, preferably while performing some mindless chore, and mark the points to go back and transcribe later.

The apartment hadn't gotten a good deep clean since we moved in—I'd been swamped with work, and Gwen, whose parents used a maid service, was an indifferent housekeeper —so I got out the cleaning supplies and went to work. The physical activity was just distracting enough, and soon I slipped into the oddly hypnotic task of eavesdropping on my own night. Wincing at my weaknesses, thrilling to moments when I'd held my own, and finding, even with the remove of the recorder, that Bethany's voice held its strange power over me.

"Stop this," Bethany said loudly in my ear. I jumped, feeling caught. The comment had been preceded by a particularly long bout of silence—we must have gone to sleep at last—and I had nearly forgotten I was listening.

"You need to stop calling," she went on coldly. "I have nothing left to discuss with you."

There was a pause. She was on the phone.

"Get hold of yourself. I don't care what you think you heard. The fact that you spent your time in Munich skulking around listening to conversations that didn't concern you rather than studying is the whole problem."

Gwen appeared at the bathroom door, and I jerked the earbuds out. She was sweating and panting, just in from a jog.

"I haven't done that for ages." She beamed. "I ran around the park, and then all the way to the campus track and around it a few times and back." She bounded toward the kitchen. "What were you listening to just now? Want to go out somewhere for lunch?"

"I can't, I'm meeting Tess." I didn't elaborate. I was itching to get back to the recording and find out more. "Then I have to work on my paper for Grady's class."

"I can't believe that guy built his entire career on one Derrida essay. What a charlatan." She opened the refrigerator and poured water from a Brita pitcher. "What's your paper going to be on?"

I forced my brain back to work mode. "*The Exterminating Angel*."

"Are you planning to rewatch it? I'll see it with you."

"Sure. How about tonight?" Watching *Much Ado About Nothing* together seemed to have unlocked something of our high school relationship, a comforting return to normalcy I hadn't realized how much I was missing. "Invite Connor over, we'll make a night of it."

She drained the water glass and refilled it one last time before closing the refrigerator. "I'd be curious to read the paper, too, if you need a pair of eyes."

"That'd be great," I said, honestly. "I can return the favor any time."

"Thanks. Maybe you can take a look at my paper for Beth-any's class. I've been working really hard to crack it." She frowned. "They say your critical faculties improve much faster than your writing skills, and the gap can feel really painful."

It was both a shock and a relief to hear Gwen admit to hav-ing trouble with a paper. If even Gwen was struggling, maybe the writer's block that had been growing worse and worse with every passing day was more common than I thought. What's more, she didn't seem particularly distressed by it, so maybe I shouldn't be worried either.

I pulled out my phone to check the time and frowned. I'd missed a call from my mom while I was cleaning. I opened my banking app quickly and checked the balance; my transfer had definitely gone through. Could she be asking for more, so soon?

My mood instantly darkened. This problem, at least, wasn't all in my head. If I had to keep funneling more and more money to my mom, I'd have to find some other source of ready cash than Bethany, or risk losing the fragile balance of power I'd fi-nally achieved with her last night. It was one thing to promise me anything when she was trying to get me into bed, but Beth-any didn't know what that meant in reality; had no idea how much my family could take and take. If my mother was relaps-ing, she could turn money into pills faster than I or anyone else could make it. Mom and Lily's needs would quickly outstrip any passing need Bethany had for me. There were relationships that could not be dissolved, no matter how much you wished they didn't exist. But love wasn't one of them. Once Bethany saw me for the bottomless pit I was, it would all be over in a heartbeat.

When it was over with Bethany, I'd lose the Joyner, and ev-erything else would go with it. I'd never find another job near campus that paid as well for as few hours as Nona—but even if I did, I already knew that trying to juggle the Program with a job like that didn't work. I had a dread of student loans. It seemed obvious to me that only someone who didn't really need them would feel confident enough in the future to take them out. Once at Urbana, when the hot water heater broke down at home, I'd tried. I'd gotten as far as reading the promissory note before walking out of the student loan office. With my mom and Lily to take care of, I knew I'd never be able to pay them back. My life was already so compromised in the present moment. I couldn't bear to put my future self in chains.

Without the Joyner, I'd have to go home.

"I can't." I turned my phone over so I couldn't see my mother's message waiting to be played.

"Oh," Gwen said. "Well, don't worry about it if you don't have time."

I had forgotten all about Gwen's paper. "I meant, I can't right now. I'm supposed to be meeting Tess at two."

"Say hi for me," said Gwen.

I ran out the door so fast I forgot to bring my earbuds. I'd have to listen to the rest of the recording later.

Well into the second hour of our late lunch, I had found, as yet, no convenient time to pass on Gwen's greeting. I'd finished my sandwich, but Tess's lay nearly untouched in its basket.

"And the nerve to suggest it's all because I'm *poor*." Tess rattled the sugar spoon in her coffee. "I get by, thanks. I scrapped it out in L.A. I think I know how to live in my own neighborhood."

"Margaret's the worst." I thought of her magnanimous glow when she told me to round up my hours. "I'd like to get Lorraine out for a drink sometime. I bet she could give us an earful."

"Give you, maybe," Tess said darkly. "Don't forget, my quote-unquote 'hostile and threatening behavior' was"—she imitated Margaret's stuffy Julia Child-esque voice—"'*witnessed by my assistant, Lorraine.*'"

"Well, I'm a witness, too, and I can testify that you didn't sound 'hostile and threatening.' You barely even sounded angry."

"You better believe I was angry," she said. "But I'm not stupid enough to show it to someone like her. I tried to tell her I already had a therapist—divorce and the film industry put me through it, you know?—but she kept interrupting me, telling me to go see the university shrinks, saying not to be proud if I needed help. I raised my voice so I could finish a sentence. And you know what they think when one of us gets loud." She finally turned her attention to her sandwich, picking it up and taking a savage bite. "Angry black woman on the rampage."

I was shocked. "No one thinks that."

"Did we read the same letter, Mac?" She pushed her coffee mug aside and folded her hands patiently in front of her. "I hate to tell you, but it's right there on the letterhead. That university seal—shovels and pickaxes. Who do you think built this university that we weren't allowed to set foot in for forty years? D. Stanley Handler was a bona fide, caliper-wielding, Reconstruction-hating, eugenics-loving racist."

"Well, yeah," I started. "But so was everybody, back then."

She gave me a sour look. "The place hasn't changed much. Last year Rhonda Oakes—you know, the *actual* Af Am prof? —got crazy-black-womaned right out of the Program. She's the whole reason I came here. And with nobody to work with, I'm looking pretty disposable now, too."

I nodded. "Okay. If you're right, that's awful. But there must be something you can do about it. You can't give up."

She looked at me for a long moment, unblinking. Then she breathed in deeply. "Nobody's giving up, Mac. I'm not sitting around waiting to be committed because some white lady thinks I'm crazy."

"Maybe if you went straight to the Dean yourself—"

"I've already made an appointment for Monday. I'm getting letters from my past professors and colleagues attesting to my work ethic, a letter from my accountant about my financial standing, and a letter from my own therapist stating that I am in good mental health. Is that good enough for you?"

I sat in silence, stunned.

"I told you I was taking care of it. I do not sleep on this stuff. Just—what gets me is that it's been going on from the start. You read that letter. They've been waiting to trip me up since day one. They don't think they have, but they have." She snorted. "'Rejected faculty mentorship.' I have a pretty good idea what that's about."

I looked at her blankly.

"Oh, I know you're tight with her. She's got you gunning for the Joyner, right?"

I blinked backward, as if she had feinted toward me or made a sudden loud noise. "Bethany?"

"I'm not asking you to quit her. Go get your prize. But Bethany offered me the Joyner, too, you know. I didn't bite, because I'm not dying to be owned body and soul. So, there's my 'motivational impairment.'"

"Look. Bethany's not always easy to work with, but she wouldn't do something like that." I thought back over Bethany's work, looking for proof of what I'd just said. "I mean, she writes about ethics. Doesn't she?"

She stared at me expectantly.

I finished, unnerved. "I just don't think she'd go out of her way to retaliate against a first-year for some perceived slight."

"I hope you're right, Mac. For your sake."

"What do you mean?"

"Oh, nothing." She looked away, then back at me, seeming to debate something internally. "Just—I've seen it before. It's an old Hollywood tradition, you might say. They call it the casting couch."

"What?"

"Sometimes it works out for the actress. Sometimes it doesn't. Either way, it's dangerous." She went back to stirring her coffee. "It's your business, of course. I just hope you're having a nice time while it lasts."

I let the coffee shop noise pulse around us as it sank in. She knew. Tess knew about Bethany and me. My heart pounded, my hands sweated, the room felt oppressively narrow. Had Tess guessed after bumping into me on the way home from Bethany's? Or worse, had she heard it from someone else? Who else knew? I told myself that Tess didn't pay attention to department gossip. But still, I closed my eyes, pinching the bridge of my nose as panic rose like gorge in my throat.

"Mac?"

"Just let me know if you need my statement for the Dean." I grabbed my coffee mug and put it in the bus tub on the way out the door.

I couldn't face the apartment right away. The thought of trying to work on my paper so soon after finding out that Tess knew about Bethany nauseated me. Instead, I wandered restlessly through the neighborhood and beyond, losing track of time, walking quickly to keep my limbs from going numb with the cold. It wasn't until dusk fell between the brownstones that I realized how late it was and started walking back. By the time I opened the door, it was well past 7 p.m., and Gwen and Connor were in the kitchen cracking each other up over the remains of a pizza. I'd forgotten all about the movie. At least it would distract me from thinking about Tess.

They giggled through the opening credits. "You guys, I have to take notes," I said. "Are you high?"

"I might be," Connor said. "A little."

"Gwen?"

"It's all him. I'm only on a runner's high, I swear."

"If I make popcorn, will it shut you guys up?"

"Yes!"

We trooped to the kitchen, where Gwen and Connor watched me heat kernels on the stove and exclaimed in delight when they started to pop. We headed back to the sofa with a bowl of the fluffy white stuff, and I got my notebook back out. True to his word, Connor, seated between Gwen and me, made no more noise, but stared at the screen transfixed, moving his hand from the popcorn bowl to his mouth and back mechanically. As the movie wore on and the dinner party guests succumbed one by one to despair at not being able to leave, eventually devolving into feral animals, Connor sank into the sofa, leaned his head against my shoulder, and went to sleep.

As the credits rolled, Gwen stood and stretched languorously. "I'm going to bed."

"So early?"

"It feels late to me. I'm dead from running." She winced theatrically mid-stretch and limped down the hall with one hand on the back of her thigh.

Connor stirred on my shoulder. "What time is it?"

"It's only nine thirty, but apparently I'm the only non-wuss."

"Haven't you ever heard of a disco nap?" He burrowed his face into my sweater and said in a muffled voice, "I'm ready. Let's party."

I moved a few inches to the right and let him slide down the back of the sofa. "Sorry. I have to start working on this paper tonight."

"Oh, come on, you have all day tomorrow. Hang out with *meeeee*."

I sat back down on the sofa in despair. "Okay, but just for a little while. I really do have to work tonight."

"Don't you like me?"

"I adore you."

"Better than work?"

He started tickling me, and I screamed. "Stop, stop!"

Connor's limbs were so long that he was somehow able to hold my arms down and tickle me at the same time, which struck me as unfair. "Connor, stop! I like you better than work, I swear!"

He froze, still pinning my arms. Our faces were very close together.

"Better than Gwen?"

I blinked. "Connor."

"Enough to . . ." He let my arms go, looked down at my mouth, and pressed his lips to mine. Then he drew back a little and waited.

"What? Of, of course I like you, Connor . . ." Then my face grew hot all over as I caught up to what had just happened. "We're friends."

"Oh."

I closed my eyes for a long moment, and when I opened them, I saw a completely different Connor in front of me.

"I didn't know . . . you liked me like that."

"Oh, don't worry about it." His tone was aggressively cheerful. "It's the Asian male thing. No one ever sees us coming."

"Wait—what do you mean?"

"Uh, white people think we're all asexual? It's cool, it's cool." It clearly wasn't.

"No! I swear it's not that. At least I hope not. I just thought—"

"Wait a minute." He had been studying my face, and now his expression changed. "You thought I was gay?"

I wanted to protest that this was a completely reasonable thing to think, under the circumstances. But what were the circumstances? When had I formed this impression? On the retreat, I realized. Based on—a pink vest? A scarf? I'd thought I couldn't blush any harder, but I was wrong. Even my eyeballs were scorching hot.

But Connor was laughing. "Fashion. I get it. Gay men hit on me all the time, it's very flattering. But I'm not. I'm really not. At least, I'm straight for you, Mac." He was sitting cross-legged on the sofa now, one leg folded up against the sofa back, looking at me earnestly. "Are you, ahem, straight for me?"

"I—" I looked down the hallway toward Gwen's room. Had she known? Was this whole night a setup? Had I, once again, been the only person out of the loop? "It's just so sudden."

"Now who sounds like a queen."

"Hey, you don't get to say that." I stood up from the sofa. "Don't tell me you haven't been playing it up for me this whole time. You knew what I thought." As soon as I said it, I remembered him hugging me at the Parlor, calling me sweetie, saying he'd give me anything. Shucking corn on the retreat: *Everyone's in the game, hon. Even me.* How stupid I'd been not to notice. "But you made me think it didn't mean anything," I argued with myself out loud. "Not that, anyway. You took advantage of me."

"Who took advantage of whom?" He arched an eyebrow. "Sorry I didn't turn out to be your hilarious queer sidekick."

"That's not fair," I said helplessly. "I thought I had a friend. A *real* friend." Even as I said it, I wondered when I had started to need more friends than just Gwen.

"You do." He leaned forward again and grabbed my hands. "I'm your real friend. I just want to be a different kind of friend. A better one."

I snatched my hands away and said, "I liked the old one." Then I saw his face. "I'm sorry, Connor. I really do love you, just not like that."

"Fair enough." He slowly unfolded his legs and took his feet off the sofa, then faced forward, hands on his knees. Looking straight ahead, he said in a flat tone, "Look, I know who it is you're hung up on. But we both know it's not going to work out with her."

My heart almost stopped. But, of course. Connor was Bethany's research assistant now, a job that included running her personal errands. What if I had left something at her house — something he'd recognize as mine — and he'd found it while he was picking up her dry cleaning or something? First Tess, and now Connor. Who else knew, and what would happen if it became public knowledge?

Meanwhile, Connor continued to sit on my living room sofa, posed as the Lincoln Memorial. "Trust me, she's not into you. Gwen's even less gay than I am."

Gwen?

A massive jolt of confusion was followed immediately by a wave of relief. He didn't know. Nobody but Tess knew, and she only had a guess. The knowledge ran through me like a tonic, straightening my spine. There seemed to be nothing left to do but get him out of the apartment as quickly as possible.

I stood up. "Connor, if you want to be friends, we can be friends. Otherwise . . ." I shrugged, trying to pretend I didn't care.

He stood, too, jerking reflexively back as his head bumped one of the fan pull chains into motion. Despite the element of slapstick, his height gave him a certain dignity. "Let's take a break for a few days and think. A *friend* break," he hurried to say, seeing my expression. "You try to get used to me being straight. I'll go pick someone up at the Parlor and make sure I really am." He put on his most melodramatic tone. "I'd hate for this all to be a tragic mistake."

I opened the door.

He put his hand on my shoulder and leaned down to peck me on the forehead. "Call me when you're over her." Then he left.

12

I stayed up late stalking Bethany online and passed out with the laptop on the bed.

The following week, every time I sat down to work, I went down a Bethany rabbit hole. At first, I thought scratching the itch might clear my head and help me get my focus back. Instead, I sank into the search results each time with a giddy relief that gave rise to new cravings. I read and reread the same interviews and blog posts and open-source encyclopedia entries, clicking fresh links, looking for a fix. I memorized her career path: graduation from CUNY and then Columbia, first job, notable collaborations, hiring at DHU, rumored short-listing for the MacArthur "Genius Grant," speculation about why her follow-up to *Ethical Negation* was taking so long. I read as many free articles as I could find online, and selections from her earlier, less famous books. *The Hasty Subject. Scant Analysis. Undoings: A Praxis.* The further I got from Friday night, the more frantically I searched.

Whatever was blocking me from understanding Bethany's operatic lectures had spread to my other coursework. I no longer had even fleeting moments of comprehension when I read, just a dull senseless ache. This was not the gap Gwen had observed between critical acumen and writing skills, but a crushing, breathless feeling that had first come over me in Bethany's presence, as if she were drawing my personhood up through a straw. Now it began to follow me everywhere, even down to the library's whale belly of an archive, where I sat flipping mechanically through age-spotted periodicals for Margaret without seeing them. When I read, I felt Bethany looking over my shoulder. When I spoke in class, I tasted her tongue in my mouth. When I tried to write, the blank screen in front of me filled up with images of what we did in the dark, and I heard her voice whispering in my ear, *Stick to what you know, Beauty Queen.*

I continued to produce nothing.

Facing her at our midweek meeting was awful. She greeted me with her usual bland chatter, unwrapping a packet of tea while she talked, but when she discovered I had done nothing for the Joyner proposal, she went dead silent, her lips pressed together so tightly they went white around the edges. She leaned back, never taking her eyes off me, and began drumming her fingernails on the arm of her chair — *rat-tat-tat-tat-tat* — as if she were waiting for something specific to happen.

"I'm sorry. I just haven't been able to think of anything."

She continued to tap her fingers, her eyes drilling into me with something like contempt.

"I — Should I just go?"

"No," she snapped, lifting her hands and dropping them dramatically in her lap. "You've already wasted enough of my time. Let's not waste yours, too. We'll finish the hour. Since you obviously can't come up with your own ideas, why don't I test you on mine? After all, I have to give you a grade for this class eventually. Let's see if you've been listening. Put away your notes."

My eyes prickled with shock, but I kept them wide open, unblinking, until the immediate threat of tears had passed. "Okay," I managed.

She began to drill me with question after question about radical negation: its roots in Heideggerian metaphysics, its critique of Hegelian dialectics, its relationship to Kantian judgment, Derridean difference, Lacanian lack, Deleuzian deterritorialization. I muddled through the first few answers, drawing painstakingly on memories of my notes, but as I paused to search for words, Bethany lost what little patience she'd started with. She began cutting me off mid-sentence with ever sharper interrogations. She hinted that I must have been lying about being able to read in French. She asked about theorists and philosophers I didn't recognize, whose names I could swear had never come up before. She demanded three examples of radical negation in the natural world, three in the world of architecture and design, and three in modern-day political struggles, sneering coldly in the pause before I answered that all of these could easily be drawn from her lectures, had I been *listening*.

I stuttered and looked down at my lap. I heard myself make one last unintelligible noise of distress before my throat closed. My mouth twisted itself into a pained grimace. I shut my eyes, begging myself not to cry. Despite my efforts, two hot, humiliating tears forced themselves out.

The chair in front of me emitted a small storm of squeaks and rattles. I kept my eyes closed and listened, detached, as Bethany crossed the room. The door clicked shut.

I thought she had left, and my tears stopped. But when I

opened my eyes, she stood in front of me with her back against the door, her expression cold but calm. She seemed to have spent the greater part of her rage.

"Mac, you have got to get serious. This is not a game."

But she had told me, the night of the dinner party, that it was. I tried to force myself to meet her gaze but felt a telltale quiver in my jaw and looked down again.

"Your friend Gwen is out there right now, somewhere, fucking my husband." She crossed the room and leaned over me, getting so close that I turned my head to one side. "And I don't like it any better than you do. Sometimes I imagine killing them both. Slowly." She grabbed my chin and pulled my face toward hers. Her eyes looked so hungry, I thought she was going to kiss me, and I went limp with relief. But instead, she squeezed harder.

"But do you think they fuck first, Mac, and strategize later? No, they do not. That's why your friend Gwen has a stellar proposal, all polished up and ready to go." My eyes watered at the pressure on my jaw. "You are my dark horse, Mac. I have placed my bets on you. And you *will* ride."

She released my chin and straightened up. Then, smoothing her hair and skirt, she strode back to the door and opened it —not all the way, just a crack. She returned to her seat.

"Now. We'll continue the exam where we left off. Just do the best you can. You're doing fine." Her voice was, if not exactly gentle, mildly encouraging.

Unbelievably, I finished reeling off examples of radical negation perfectly, if tonelessly. After she dismissed me, I went straight to the bathroom and threw up. Then I cried for half an hour.

Coming out of the bathroom, I passed Tess outside of the

Dean's office. She took one look at my freshly washed face and gave me a grim nod. *Freedom's always expensive,* she had said. Even as I nodded stiffly to acknowledge our truce, I felt the cost go up.

Gwen, Connor, Tess. I was losing my friends in the Program, one by one.

In the middle of the night, I woke up gasping. I'd never finished listening to the hotel room recording. I put in my earbuds. Bethany, suspended in time, was still on the phone.

"I'm going to hang up now," she said softly, malevolently. "And don't bother calling again. You think your life is worthless now? I'll make sure of it." That was it. No other clues.

Just silence. I stayed up the rest of the night, listening to Bethany and me sleeping. When dawn broke outside, the me in the recording woke up and kissed her goodbye.

The next day I could barely function.

I dragged myself to the department to drop off some research for Margaret and checked my mail folder on the way out. Inside was a pink carbon copy of the Midterm Exam form, signed *Bethany Ladd.*

> Student showed remarkable poise and confidence, answered questions in exhaustive detail, and demonstrated a superior overall command of the subject matter. Since no further coursework will be required in this class, I am filing her final grade now: A.

At the bottom, a Post-it note.

BQ: Fri @ 9

There was something bulky in the bottom of the folder. I reached in and pulled out an old-fashioned wrought-iron key attached to a leather key fob. I recognized the address stamped on the fob.

The farmhouse.

It was an apology, a concession, an appeal for forgiveness. But it was also, as I well knew, a command.

I slipped the key into my coat pocket. I didn't know what else to do.

Like every week in the Program, this one ended with a Friday afternoon talk from a visiting professor.

I had attended enough of these talks to know that their appeal was mostly gastronomical. The same abundantly catered spread appeared at the reception afterward every time: still-life platters of hard salami and limp prosciutto; cheese, in crumbling wedges and fanned-out slices; water biscuit cascades curving around dewy grape clusters. For the vegans, a lonely tray of cold asparagus tips and roasted portobellos. And finally, the pièce de résistance, the dessert tray: a fleet of fat strawberries decorated with tiny tuxedos and pearl-necked evening gowns of white and dark chocolate, a miniature treatise on gender performance executed in fruit. Those with the patience to outstay the crowd took home Ziplocs of leftovers and unfinished bottles of wine, a more than usually glamorous way to stretch a grocery budget that guaranteed robust attendance, at least among the poorer students.

The audience for this week's speaker, an ethnomusicologist, was even larger than usual, and Margaret has asked me to help

Lorraine set up. This was rumored to be a job talk—part of the hiring process—and job talks always brought out a festive atmosphere of knife sharpening.

Undergrads and latecomers lined the floor. Lorraine and I sat with them near the exit, so we could dart out for the platters as soon as the talk finished. The first- and second-years packed the front rows, while the faculty and more advanced grad students filled seats from the third row back. The only person from our year I didn't see was Tess, whose motivational impairment I suspected of becoming more acute by the day.

The job talk proceeded according to a formula that was by now familiar. Margaret made a few announcements and then turned the floor over to Grady, who introduced the visiting speaker in adulatory, almost fawning terms. The ethnomusicologist, nervy at the beginning of Grady's stilted preamble, soon melted at the words of praise. By the time he took his place at the lectern, he looked positively delighted with himself. I zoned out during the lecture itself, "Lord Love a Duck: Spiritualism in Late '90s Birdcall Electronica." When it reached its inevitable conclusion (inevitable, too, that it ran ten minutes over), the room erupted into applause, and the ethnomusicologist opened the floor for questions with a radiant smile.

Morgan raised her hand, obeying the unwritten rule that first-years kick off the Q and A. "This is more of a comment than a question," she began, twirling a lock of indigo hair around one finger, and the ethnomusicologist nodded encouragingly. "I've been thinking a lot about gesture and the gestural in the social field. If, as you put it, sound is a social field—" She cleared her throat. "Well, I suppose if I had a question, it would be, what is the role of gesture in your argument?"

After the ethnomusicologist had answered this question in

conscientious detail, several more students delivered their comments-disguised-as-questions, always punctuated with the dutiful interrogative: "What is the role of [*something I have recently written a paper about*] in your argument?" As the minutes allotted for questions ticked away, I began to relax, abandoning the worry that I would have to ask a question. The student Q and A was over. It was faculty feeding time.

Grady raised his hand politely, and the ethnomusicologist nodded at him.

"This was an excellent paper, a really refreshing argument," Grady doled out. The audience tensed. "I have simply never been more impressed with an invocation of Pliny the Elder. And what a masterful gloss on the history of atonality in Western opera. Bravo." He clapped, twice.

"Thank you."

Beside me, Lorraine sucked in her breath with a gentle hiss. The room was silent as those familiar with Grady's speech impediment waited for him to continue.

"I did wonder, however . . ." And here Grady raised, at great length, in carefully worked-out clauses, what seemed at first to be a minor objection. As his words plodded on relentlessly, however, the mistake seemed to grow until it contaminated nearly every aspect of the argument.

". . . And so," Grady finished.

The ethnomusicologist's smile had abandoned him. He fielded the original objection carefully. Grady continued to heckle him at a snail's pace for several minutes before cutting him off to say, "Thank you," with an air of finality. He uncrossed his legs, crossed them neatly in the other direction, and leaned back in his chair.

Half a dozen more hands shot up, all of them belonging to faculty.

"Do you really think your single example bears the weight your argument requires?"

"Surely you know this work has been done, far better, in Kleinfeldt's book."

"Was your reference to Agamben perhaps meant to be ironic?"

Near the end, Rocky chimed in with a comment so lazy it was clearly a setup, and equally clear for whom. "Perhaps this argument is less radical than it pretends to be."

"It's radically inane." Bethany didn't even bother to raise her hand. "That's the only way to describe the utter obtuseness, the almost criminal banality on display. To call a fermata a 'state of exception' is to ignore or, worse, fail to comprehend my entire body of work on sonic negation. Of course, I'm not personally offended, but you've missed quite a few important theorists in the process." She began listing names.

Out of the corner of my eye, I could see the ethnomusicologist's face slowly draining of color, but I couldn't tear my eyes away from Bethany. Petite, helmet-haired, a general in tall boots crossed delicately at the knee, she eviscerated with a casual brutality that made me feel how gentle she'd been with me at our last meeting.

"To sum up, this has all been a revolting waste of time, wouldn't you say?"

The ethnomusicologist nodded miserably, his face red and blotchy. From where I was sitting, I could barely hear him say, "Thank you, Bethany. I will certainly take your comments into consideration."

Grady stood abruptly. "Everyone, one more round of applause to thank our guest."

The ethnomusicologist cast him a ghastly look as the audience began politely clapping, rising from their chairs to make way for the reception in a kind of bored ovation.

"Not a good fit," Lorraine observed as we hustled down the hall toward the department kitchen. She maneuvered her way around the carts crammed into the narrow room, opened the refrigerator, and started pulling out trays. "Go ahead, I'm right behind you."

As we passed the door to the main office, the department phone started ringing.

"Shit," Lorraine said behind me. "It's not five yet, I need to get that. Just come back for this one."

I hustled toward the lecture room, now buzzing with loud conversation. The savage Q and A had broken the fever, and everyone—except the ethnomusicologist, of course—seemed giddy. Grady held court near the center of the room, facing a semicircle of admirers. It was evident that he was being groomed for the next department chair.

I went back for the second cart and saw Lorraine emerging from the department office, looking stricken.

"It's Bird," she said.

The news circulated through the reception slowly, at about the rate of the tuxedoed strawberries.

At first the roar of conversation continued almost unabated. I pushed through the crowd toward the wine table, where I saw Gwen and Connor. Lorraine hurried to Margaret's side, standing on tiptoe to whisper in the tall woman's ear. Margaret put her hand to her chest. Watching her from across the room, I saw rather than heard her say, "Oh dear god." As she turned to share the news with the faculty around her, I leaned over to Gwen.

"Someone from Bird's family called," I whispered. "Suicide."

"Oh my god." Gwen's mouth dropped open, and her eyes instantly glassed over with tears. Connor saw Gwen's face and stooped to hear.

"What happened?"

"Bird died," Gwen said.

"What bird?"

"*The* Bird."

"His name was actually Qassim." Aka *Prometheus Birdling III*. I closed my eyes for a moment.

Across the room, an unnatural hush had sprouted as the news spread in uneven patches. The students swarming the drink table set down their cups and hugged one another uncertainly. The faculty stood in silence, shaking their heads. Someone let out a sob. I looked and saw Arjun push his way out of the room, his hand clapped over his mouth. Rocky also left, with Gwen close behind him. As the shockwave spread toward the margins of the room, I found myself drifting toward the center, toward Bethany, with Connor. As if she had the answers.

When she saw me, she said, with a perfectly professorial expression of sorrow, "What a waste. What a brilliant mind. His work was so promising."

"I saw him last week." The shock stunned me out of my usual caution when speaking to her in public. "He was miserable. I should've—"

"These things are overdetermined," Bethany said, her face a mask. Standing nearby, Margaret nodded sagely, the two in agreement for once.

"What does that even mean?"

"It means, don't blame yourself, Mac."

"Why would it be Mac's fault?" Connor said. "I'm the one who took his job."

"These things are overdetermined," Bethany repeated firmly. "There is never any single cause."

"You don't understand." Connor was getting more and more upset, his face flushed an ugly red. "He sent me an email over the weekend." He glanced at Bethany, then back at me. The room was getting quieter, and Connor's voice rang out unnaturally loud. "He was years behind. He was on academic probation, about to miss another chapter deadline."

Bethany had grown white, except for a single spot of red at her throat. Her eyes stared dead ahead, as if made of wood. "These things——" she started. Then stopped.

"As long as Bethany needed him, he knew he'd never get kicked out," Connor said to me, as if she wasn't there. "And then I took his place. He sent me that email, and then——" He turned to Bethany. In the same stunned tone of voice, he said, "Find a new research assistant. I quit."

"Come on, let's go." I grabbed two bottles off the wine table and put my arm around Connor protectively, herding him out.

Behind us, I could hear the conversational economy of the buffet and bar already prevailing over the temporary pause. Cups drained in shock needed refilling. Plates of sweating cheese set down haphazardly needed replacing. The cocktail buzz of the reception was starting back up, animated by sorrow, yes, but also by curiosity. By the time Lorraine was wheeling the carts away, there would be rumors that the Bird had jumped off a rooftop, believing he could fly.

• • •

The texts from Bethany began flooding my phone while Connor and I walked home arm in arm, swigging from the open bottles of wine. It was just after six, and already dark.

The first text came at 6:15. *Please come tonight. I need you.*

6:20. *You'll be my new RA, of course. Already filled out the paperwork.*

9:01. *I'm waiting at the farmhouse. Where are you, BQ? Did you see my note?*

9:22. *They left together. I can't be alone tonight.*

9:43. *If you're working for me you need to come NOW*

9:44. *Are you getting these*

10:20. *Mac, please come. I need you tonight.*

10:21. *Are you still angry?*

10:23. *Hurry please darling hurry*

10:50. *I don't know what I'll do if I'm alone*

And so on. For a moment I thought of forwarding one to Tess, just to prove that Bethany was texting me at last, but Connor was crying and I was crying and I didn't have a spare hand. Perhaps I, too, suffered from motivational impairment.

Connor's apartment was dark and empty when we stumbled in from our two-bottle walk.

The wine had gone to my head, and I already knew Connor and I were going to sleep together. We were too sad not to. And that made me even sadder. Because, although he didn't know it yet, once I had used him in that way, I would never let it happen again. Friendship is a habit nurtured in restraint and broken recklessly in love. I was murdering our friendship, and when it was dead, I would have no desire to desecrate the corpse.

Knowing it would only happen once, I gave myself up to it. Of all comforts, fucking was, as Bethany had pointed out, near the top of my list. After Bethany, Connor's body felt at once tall and thin and extremely strong, and our parts, as I had suspected they would, fit together perfectly. I cared for him so much, I felt my heart break with every ragged breath. But I did not love him. At least, not that way. Not enough.

Connor fell asleep right away, holding me like a teddy bear. I held out as long as I could, but my eyes had to close sometime. Just before they did, I had the fleeting thought: Connor had said to call him when I was over Gwen. In fact, it had been Bethany. But now I really was over her. I had let her use me long enough.

When Connor came out of the bedroom, his hair sticking up like a sundial, I sat at the breakfast table staring into a cup of coffee. He wore a T-shirt and an old pair of sweatpants that were comically short on him, and his sleepy eyes registered faint dismay when he saw me.

"I was going to get up first and make omelets." He crossed the room and huddled over me in a brief, confusing hug. When he withdrew, I clutched my coffee cup more tightly and forced a smile.

"Knock yourself out."

He started pulling vegetables out of the fridge, and fifteen minutes later we were sharing one large omelet off the same plate, so that I couldn't avoid his eyes. They reminded me of home.

Stop it, Mac.

He stared at me intently for a moment as he chewed.

"So, you weren't mad at me for taking the job with Bethany?"

"I was never mad at you," I said, honestly.

"It's just—after I got that email from Bird, I started thinking maybe you were angling for it, too. Gwen says you're doing an independent study with her."

"I'm dropping it." I resolved to send her an email saying so as soon as I got back to my apartment. "She's already filed my grade, but I'll tell her to revoke it."

"That's brave." He looked down at his hands. "I know I act like nothing here matters to me, but on the inside, I'm as scared as Bird was."

"We all are. We're all just trying to get a foothold, any way we can. It's normal."

"Is it?" He paused. "Did I ever tell you I'm from New Orleans?" I shook my head. "We left after Katrina. But when you grow up in Louisiana, there's always one school field trip to the fisherman's wharf. The only thing I remember is the crab crates. They don't want the dead ones, so, to save time, they just hang the crate right over a giant cooking pot and open up one side. The live ones make a break for freedom. They crawl all over each other trying to be the first to jump into the boiling water." He shuddered. "I had nightmares about it for months."

"Who are we supposed to be in this metaphor? The dead crabs?"

Connor laughed. "Better to play dead in the crate together, than wind up alone on a plate." He shook his head. "I feel so dumb, Mac. When Bethany asked me to work for her, I thought she might be tapping me for the Joyner."

"Why wouldn't you think that?"

"Because all she really wanted was a bagman," he said miserably. "That's what Bird was. A combination therapist and lackey. He didn't need the money—he had the Joyner, and I'm pretty sure his parents were loaded. All he had to do was finish the Program, but he got all wrapped up in Bethany's world and couldn't get out."

Wrapped up in Bethany's world. The endless internet search results. The blank page. "I wonder why she fired him."

"Honestly? He sounded more than a little nuts in that email," Connor said. "He was ranting about her being part of some conspiracy. A money-laundering operation, or maybe it was real estate fraud. He wanted me to look for some papers. It all sounded so paranoid, I wouldn't have been surprised if he'd told me his apartment was bugged."

"Jesus. Could I see the email?"

"I deleted it. Obviously, if I had known he was going to— but I didn't. I just wanted it out of my life." He hung his head. "I could have helped him."

I stood up, pulled him to me, and stroked his hair. We were silent for a moment.

When I let go and sat down across from him again, his eyes were red. "I don't belong here, Mac. I don't have the stomach for it." He laughed weakly. "Anyway, it should have been obvious all along who was Bethany's favorite."

"It should have?" Despite everything, I felt a flush rise to my cheeks.

"I mean, right? You of all people would know. But now I've seen it with my own eyes."

"Seen what?"

"Her Joyner letter for Gwen," he said. "It's glowing."

While Connor was taking a shower, I went through his bag. I had to see the letter for myself. I found it in the back of a notebook for Bethany's class.

Glowing really didn't go far enough.

It was incandescent.

As I replaced the letter, I noticed the inside covers of the notebook were decorated with half-finished sketches of our classmates. I couldn't help lingering over this fragmented portrait of the Program: an eyebrow peeking over a glasses rim, a shell-like ear with a skull earring, a hand I would have recognized anywhere, even without the delicate platinum band Gwen's parents had given her for high school graduation. And there, of course, was Bethany—her mouth open, lecturing, lips arrested in that peculiar grimace between praise and admonishment. It struck me that Connor must be a little in love with her, too. What else didn't I know? Connor could draw, he was from New Orleans, he wanted the Joyner, he wanted me. I hadn't seen any of it. No one saw anyone here. We had become mere fragments.

The water in the shower turned off. I stuffed the whole notebook into my bag and left.

I wanted something to remember him by.

The air had an electric charge that felt like snow coming soon.

Leaving Connor's apartment, I spotted Tess trudging toward campus, weighed down by two canvas tote bags loaded to their limit with library books. One look at her, and I knew there would be no jokes about whose apartment I was slipping out of this time; she couldn't even see me. She stared at the ground as if determined not to take in a single extraneous piece of information.

I intercepted her on the sidewalk. "Can I help carry those?"

"I got it, thanks." Her voice was gruff, and she kept her head down, the fur-trimmed hood of her parka hiding her face. "Just dropping these off at the library."

"I could return them for you, I'm headed that way."

"I don't need anything from you. Or anyone else, for that matter." I stepped around in front of her, blocking her path, and saw that her face was red and raw from crying.

"Tess, what happened?"

She looked up, eyes flashing. "What do you think happened? I'm done."

I was stunned. "They kicked you out?"

"No. I'm quitting."

"What?"

She put her head back down and started walking again, and I was forced to step to one side or take a bag of books to the shin. "They made it so I don't have a choice. They put me on indefinite probation, Mac. That means they'll always be waiting for me to fuck up. For six years. Plus, with the restraining order, I failed all my classes on attendance policy alone. They want me to repeat this semester's coursework and provide a written apology to Margaret and the Dean and show weekly proof of psychiatric treatment from a university clinician and—a bunch more bullshit."

"That's . . . insane."

"I almost did it, too. That's the worst part. Then I heard about—you know." She jerked her chin vaguely toward campus.

I nodded. Bird.

"I thought, fuck if I'm going to wind up like that guy." Her voice had gone thick, and I looked down at my feet, giving her space. I knew she didn't want to cry in front of me. For half a block, we walked in silence.

She sniffed hard and continued. "What's really grand is that it's all in the name of *helping me succeed*. They're so eager to help, they're giving me plenty of rope to hang myself. Guess they don't want to get caught with their hands on the noose."

"Tess, you have to stay and fight this," I said. "You belong here. More than I do. More than anyone."

But even as I said it, I bit my tongue. I meant it. I really did. I remembered her speech about oxygen flowing toward the best ideas, not the most money. Unlike me, she had both—good ideas and enough money to sustain herself, not to mention an enviable support network in town. If anyone deserved to make it, it was Tess. But saying the words out loud, I heard Gwen saying them to me during orientation, and for the first time felt how distant they were from any meaningful reality. They were easy words, and hollow.

Tess's eyes reflected their hollowness back to me. "It's not my job to make you feel better about your place in the food chain, Mac. Just because you're willing to put your body on the line, doesn't mean everybody is."

I looked down, gut-punched. "That's all over."

"Good." But she looked skeptical.

We walked a little further in silence.

I tried once more. "This isn't how it's supposed to work."

"This is exactly how it's supposed to work."

We had arrived at the library. We stood in front of the looming gothic entrance, with its soot-streaked gargoyles hanging over a solid bank of energy-efficient revolving doors. The book drop, a monolith in pebbled concrete, stood to our right. Tess opened its metal maw and piled the books inside, sending each load resolutely down the chute. "I'll miss this library," she said, taking a last look at the final stack. "That's about all I'll miss."

"Tess—I'm sorry."

She slammed the book drop shut with a clang, and the books tumbled down its throat.

"Goodbye, Mac. Keep on playing the game, I guess. And if

you manage to come out on top, how you do it is strictly your business."

She walked away.

I stood for a long moment watching the steady stream of students enter and leave the library through the rotating glass doors. They stared straight ahead, drained and exhausted, or looked numbly down at cell phones. Some clutched teetering stacks of books to their chests; others dragged rolling caddies that caught on every doorsill and curb. The doors turned around them all, churning and wheezing and squealing like the slowest hamster wheel in the world.

Margaret had predicted that four of us would drop out by the end of the first year. Soo-Jeong was the first. Tess was the second. I had a feeling Connor would be the third.

There was one more open slot.

I was halfway to my apartment when my phone buzzed in my pocket. I glanced down and saw a text from Bethany: *It's over.* No surprise there. But then I spotted a missed voice mail, buried in the avalanche of ignored calls from my mother over the past two days. It was from the Social Security office. I clicked and listened to a badly garbled message:

"Returning your call . . . reason to suspect fraud . . . theft . . . caretaker not responding to repeated calls . . . your earliest possible convenience."

Fraud. Theft.

My mother.

There was no time to waste. I had to stop by the apartment to grab a few things. It would take at least four hours to drive home.

December 30, 2021, 2:40 a.m.
SkyLoft Hotel, Los Angeles

We climb the last few flights without speaking, the only sounds the tandem huffing of our breath and the rhythmic clapping of soles on steps. My throat has gone dry from taking in big gulps of air and expelling them in explosive bursts. My thighs are burning, but I keep pumping mechanically, hanging on to my slight lead.

Without Gwen, the past ten years have been entirely too easy. No doubt the general exodus from the Program after the accident, of which Gwen was a part, helped clear the path for my rise. But sometimes I miss the feeling that there's someone better than me—not just at writing and thinking, but at being and living—standing almost beside me but just a little ahead, and taking for granted that I'm better, too. It can't be said that Gwen's disappearance from my life diminished my ambition, but sometimes I think it struck the killing blow to my already weak capacity for love. You can't love other people when you hate yourself. And I never loved myself more than when I was trying to be Gwen.

"Stop!"

I pause and look back. Gwen stands below me on the eleventh-floor landing. In my single-minded trudging, I forgot I'm still a floor shy of the penthouse suite. I vow to correct that shortfall in time for next year's conference and start back down, wincing as the reverse of direction turns my thighs to sacks of wet concrete. My knees almost buckle, and I lean on the railing, massaging my aching quadriceps. "Oof. I'm going to feel that in the morning."

"It's already morning."

"That explains it."

Gwen holds the door open for me. Exiting the vertiginous stairwell feels like being released from a prison tower.

I lead Gwen down the corridor to 1102. As we approach the door, a nagging feeling that's been tickling lightly at my consciousness for some time becomes newly bothersome, like when a small piece of gravel in the toe of your boot shakes loose and slides under the soft arch. I pat my back pocket and pull out the two keys I've been carrying around—the one I got from the desk downstairs marked "1102" and the naked card I assumed belonged to Harvard. I hope he got into his room all right. Or anyway, that he's not still in mine.

I shake it off and use my key, hesitating at the threshold as I peer into the dark room beyond. A tickle of apprehension crawls up the back of my neck. Something's not right. It hasn't been right all night long.

"What is it?" Gwen asks in a hushed voice.

"Nothing." Irritated with myself, I walk in and hit the light switch. The dim glow from half a dozen lamps chases the shadows away, and I take in the whole suite at a glance. It's empty. Harvard made the bed—I note his shoddy attempt at hospital corners—and even cleaned the empty mini-bottles from the nightstand, arranging my phone and my spare room key neatly on the nightstand. A letter of recommendation goes a long way in this job market.

Gwen mistakes my silence for an invitation to comment. "What a lovely suite." Despite the careful appreciation in her voice, I can see from her reflection in the floor-length windows that she's thinking of something else. She's been alternating between earnest oversharing and wary distance all night long. For the first time, it occurs to me that these confidences are not entirely spontaneous on her part. Perhaps they're even designed to tempt me to spill my own secrets.

We'll see who breaks first.

I stroll toward the fridge. "Let's see what's left in the minibar."

"I thought we were done drinking for the night."

"That was before I scaled Mount SkyLoft. I don't know about you, but I'm thirsty."

Gwen shrugs.

I squat by the fridge and open it, peering inside. "Stoli and a Red Bull. That's what I've got. Unless you want to drink it straight."

"Red Bull, I guess."

"Suit yourself." I crack open the miniature bottle of vodka and tip half into a water glass, flicking off the protective paper bonnet. Then I turn my attention to the Red Bull, pouring the fluorescent yellow heart-attack juice into the vodka until it looks like used paint thinner. I take a minute to wash my hands thoroughly at the bar sink before fishing a few slivers of half-melted ice from the ice bucket. When I turn around with the drink in one hand, half-full bottle in the other, Gwen sits cross-legged on the floor, her back leaning against the bed. I hand the concoction to her, and she takes a whiff and shudders.

"Been a while since you've had vodka?"

She glares.

"What? You used to like it." I sit down on the floor facing her.

"I used to like a lot of things. We both did." There it is, that hint of meanness that wasn't there at the beginning of the night.

I hoist the mini-bottle. "Still do. Bottoms up."

She sips and starts coughing.

I tip the Stoli bottle back and drain it all at once, like a shot. Which is easy to do, since it's filled with water. I tipped my share of the vodka into Gwen's glass at the sink when she wasn't looking.

We sit in silence, trapped in our separate memories of the same evening.

"So, you loved him." I twiddle the empty bottle between my fingers. "Do you still?"

"I love Andreas."

I lay the empty vodka bottle on the floor between us and spin it. The bottle is too small to hold its axis on the carpet, and it spins out and rolls a few feet away, pointing at the window.

Gwen stares at it with an unreadable expression. "It would never have worked out with Rocky. Obviously."

I wait.

"But I still think about him. About us. I picture us, at Yale or Stanford. He used to say he'd be the spousal hire, that I was brilliant enough for both of us." She raises her eyes to mine, disgusted. "I'm not stupid. Imagine having to look his students in the eye during office hours, wondering which ones are curious girlfriends, there for a good look at the wife. I'd be working my ass off, while he coasted on charm. He'd always be staying up all night tippling at the bar with some venerable old Marxist, while

I rushed home to take care of the baby." She catches herself and blushes.

"You weren't . . . ?" I trail off.

"No." She's angry, but only a small part of her anger is directed at me. "I told you we never slept together. I know you don't believe me."

I do now, though. Vodka doesn't lie. And, if I'm honest with myself, neither does Gwen. Omissions, yes. But Gwen has always been a terrible liar.

"After everything happened and I left the Program, I used to wish I was—you know. That's how lost I was." She looks at her empty glass. "Got any more of this stuff?"

"I'm afraid we're dry."

She gets up off the floor and walks to the window, a wobble in her step. Leans her forehead against the glass.

"Why didn't I invite you to the wedding? I don't really know. Maybe it's just that when I think about you, I remember what I was like then, when we were in the Program together. What I did. What I became. And I'm so ashamed."

I've been waiting for this moment. But just when I should push harder, take advantage of her vulnerability, I get distracted by something on the floor under the nightstand. A piece of trash, small and white. The pebble rattles in my shoe. I placate her. "None of us were at our best in grad school."

But she refuses to be deterred. "I've spent a lot of time thinking about the people I hurt. I owe plenty of apologies. Most of all to you, Mac."

"What do you mean?" I see what it is. A paper sleeve. Probably for Harvard's room key, the one I took by mistake. "Sorry for what?"

"I got caught up in things. I—I took things from you. I saw that you wanted them. And I took them."

She means the Joyner, I think distractedly. I reach under the nightstand and slide out the empty sleeve. I flip it over and nearly do a double take at the room number written on the back. The penthouse? Maybe I underestimated Harvard.

Even more confusingly, staring at the sleeve has triggered another memory. I remember glancing down at the floor on my way into the room and seeing this sleeve, with the card in it, lying in the entry. But didn't I find the card under the bed? The ticklish feeling begins again. So Harvard dropped his key by the door, and I kicked it coming in, and the card came out of the sleeve. That makes sense. It's just odd, if he dropped it right after unlocking the door, that it would be in its sleeve like that.

I make an effort to listen to Gwen, who's still talking. "I shouldn't even have been there. You wanted it so much more than I did. You needed it. I didn't."

"I find ways of getting what I need." *There's a word for that,* I think.

"Sometimes I think what happened that night was all my fault."

She watches me intently. Expecting me to protest, perhaps? *Don't blame yourself, Gwen. You were only the spark that lit the fuse —you didn't plant the powder keg.* Or maybe it's a confession she's awaiting. Something she already knows but wants to hear me say out loud.

Maybe the whole reason she's here is to blackmail me.

In that case, we'd better be getting on with the night. With the extra shot of vodka I slipped her, Gwen's drunk enough for my purposes.

"I think we could both use some air."

She looks around. "This place isn't big enough for you?"

"I mean real air. Outside. Let's get out under the stars."

Her eyes widen in disbelief. "After all that, you want to go back downstairs?"

"Not down. Further up." I feel oddly happy, like a bird about to be let out of its cage. Gwen is staring, and I realize I'm fiddling with the paper sleeve, folding and unfolding it. I thrust it into my pocket. "To the roof."

It's so much like what we used to do in high school—an innocent flirtation with lawlessness, like breaking into the library's sculpture garden after dark. At least, that's what I'm hoping she's thinking about. "Can we really get up there?"

"I bet I can figure it out."

I find ways of getting what I need. The word for that is *ruthless*. Connor said it once, but he didn't believe it. Bethany did too, and she meant it. But it was only tonight, when Gwen said it, that I knew beyond a doubt it was true.

13

By the time I reached the outskirts of Wheatsville, the snow had stopped falling, leaving hay-prickled fields of spectral blue that stretched for miles on either side of the highway in the early twilight. Empty fields soon gave way to lone gas stations on skinny farm roads, and then to pole-lit strip malls. A one-night stand in college who happened to be an architecture student had told me modern shopping centers were made of Styrofoam, the brick and stucco facades just a thin layer of plaster that could be updated easily with the changing styles. In Wheatsville, this optimism had been misplaced. The shopping strips, innocent of cosmetic improvements in my lifetime, were now studded with vacancies under dead neon.

I drove past the old half-empty indoor mall and turned into my neighborhood, winding down the curved streets past a black pond with a thin rime of ice. There it was: split-level red brick sunk into a sloped lawn, surrounded with overgrown yew hedges. I parked on the street and went up the walk, peering through the window at Lily in her recliner, bathed in the warm glow of a cooking show. I could just see my mom banging around the kitchen, trailing smoke from the lit cigarette in her left hand. For some reason, that was the detail that got to me: that ragged slip of smoke pouring upward, splitting into strands that twined around each other like DNA.

I knocked, and my mother opened the door.

"Hi." In a split second, I scanned her for signs. Pinpoint pupils, drowsy eyelids, broken capillaries from throwing up? No, no, and none that I could see. Her lit cigarette was perched on the doorframe, level with my face. Was she off-balance? Leaning too hard?

She regarded me wryly through the veil of smoke. "To what do we owe this honor?"

"Just a visit," I said carefully. "I figured you could use help sorting out this Social Security thing."

"You think?" She stepped aside to let me in, flicking the cigarette on the stoop and waving at the smoke before she closed the door.

I walked into the living room, a sea of stained wall-to-wall carpet.

"Hey, Mac," said Lily, without looking away from the TV.

"Hey, Lily." She'd need time to get used to me being here.

So would I. I headed for my room, where I set my duffel bag on the bed and looked around. It was all still here: the crummy TV/VCR in the closet, the cigar box of cheap junk jewelry on the dresser, the shelves of sad paperbacks dredged from the library's free box. Like the Styrofoam storefronts, my room was frozen at a time when everything had seemed possible.

It was six o'clock on a Saturday afternoon, and dark as midnight. I lay down on the bed beside my duffel bag and fell into a deep, black sleep.

. . .

I woke up early, disoriented and groggy, struggling to remember where I was. Then the room settled around me with a thud. My room. The room I'd left four months ago, hoping, as I did every time, never to return.

I shivered under the covers and stared at a water stain on the ceiling. The house was in bad shape. It needed a new roof, and the window frames were leaking. My first-floor bedroom, technically the master—my mom slept across from Lily's room upstairs—had always been cold. Now it was also dank.

There were a bunch of messages from Gwen and Connor on my phone. I thought of the glowing letter and ignored them all.

The Social Security office was closed until Monday, so I had an entire day to fill. I started cleaning. As I mopped the kitchen floor, I fantasized about hiring a maid service for my mom's house. But of course, if I left the Program and stayed in Wheatsville—and where else would I go?—I had a much better chance of working for a maid service than hiring one.

I made my way into the living room, where Lily was watching a TV show about horses. A perfect time to check in.

"What are you watching, Lily?" Open-ended questions still made her uncomfortable.

"*Horses of Hope,*" she said, eyes fixed on the screen.

"I haven't heard of it. Is that a new one?"

"It depends on what you mean by new. It's on its third season. So technically, it's not new. But the *season* is new."

I nodded, noting vaguely that Lily was feeling chattier than usual as I picked up candy wrappers and clothes from the floor. The carpet hadn't been vacuumed in ages. "Do you like this season so far?" I asked tentatively. An opinion was a slightly riskier kind of question, but she clearly wanted to talk.

"Season two had better horses. But I like this one because it's close to where we live."

"Really?" I glanced at the screen. "How close?"

"Eight point two miles away," she answered readily. "Every season is at a different horse ranch, and this one is eight point two miles away."

A reality show on a horse ranch, filmed near Wheatsville. "What is the show about again?"

"Equine therapy." Her monotone sounded strained, and she started rocking a little. "For people like me."

I was dumbstruck. I had heard of equine therapy, but it always seemed exotic and remote. Why hadn't I looked into it? "And you're saying this place is close by?"

"I wouldn't be very good at it."

I tried not to sound too excited, to keep from agitating her. "Lily, do you want to try equine therapy?"

She stared ahead of her at the screen, one hand flapping distractedly against the corded armchair.

I went back to cleaning, filled with new resolve. I understood her perfectly. Lily wanted to ride horses. She wanted freedom. She couldn't wait anymore. I'd had my shot, and now it was her turn.

Vacuuming in my room, I bumped into something under the bed: *La Règle du jeu*. The first movie Gwen and I had watched together.

I threw the videotape in my bag. Time to get rid of it.

The other video stores in town had long since closed their doors, but the Golden Crown was still there. Not so the Frogurt Palace next door, which was now a pawnshop. While I was there,

I'd pawn my earrings. As long as I was shedding my illusions, might as well get some cold hard cash for them.

But first, the Golden Crown. Faced with the front door, I was seized with a sudden urge to go around back to the concrete stairs that led to the basement apartment where I'd spent so many afternoons with Trace and the Kevins, stoned to the gills. Instead, I pushed open the swinging door, flinching at the jangling doorbell, and hurried nervously past the security camera.

Behind the red Formica counter plastered with peeling comix and store policies, an open doorway led down a dark flight of stairs to Quimby's basement. The call bell clicked dully when I rang it. I picked at a corner of tape on the counter and considered leaving.

Then the basement door opened, and Quimby's pale, thinning hair appeared, followed by his familiar old rusty blazer, and then finally Quimby himself, huffing and puffing like a demon from the deep. He paused in the doorway in his chili-patterned chef pants and wheezed for a moment as he looked me up and down. At last, he rasped, in a voice like day-old coffee grounds, "Jennifer, I've been expecting you."

"You—you have?"

He shook his head and coughed. "No. It's from *The Matrix Reloaded*." I could see as he lumbered toward the counter that he was fully stoned. "Well? What, as they say, can I do you for?"

I considered asking for a hit of whatever had made the blood vessels pop in his watery blue eyes, but instead I plunked the video in its plastic case down on the counter. "Just returning this."

"Ah." He leaned forward an inch and peered down at the handwritten title. "That would be, what, five years overdue? We haven't carried VHS for a while."

"Six years, ten months. Hell of a late fee."

"Forget it. It was a dub."

"Thanks."

He held the videocassette up to his ear and rattled it like a present. "Was it everything you'd hoped for, Jennifer? Did your dreams come true? Tell me, how has life treated you?"

I felt suddenly exhausted. "I went to grad school, but I'm dropping out. I have to stick around and help my family." It was the first time I'd said the words out loud to anyone, and I only said them to Quimby because he was more like a ghost than an actual person to me. "I worked so hard. But I blew it. I lost the Joyner, and I lost my friends, and I blew it. So here I am." I summed it up, with a gesture meant to encompass the movie store, the town, my whole pathetic life.

But Quimby, who had set the tape back down on the counter, frowned. "Joyner, that crook from the savings and loan crisis?"

Trust Quimby to find a tangent. I shook my head. "It's the name of some big fellowship."

"Probably the same guy," he said amicably. He pulled a stack of DVDs from the return bin, opened a case, checked the disc, and started typing something into the ancient PC on the counter. "Want to rent something while you're here? *Viridiana*?"

"I've seen it."

"Academia is full of crooks," he continued, still typing, as if he hadn't heard me. "Metaphysical, economical. I know of what I speak."

So Quimby had gone to grad school. Of course, he had. And, of course, he'd dropped out, like me. I wondered how I had ever felt overawed by this man who deserved nothing but pity. "Film school?"

"Philosophy. My *grand amour*," he said, with supreme dignity. "Film was just a sidepiece."

"What happened?"

"Touché," he said drily. "It was all fake, as you've surely discovered. A bunch of careerists grubbing with filthy paws at the truth's petticoats. Truth herself long gone, sunbathing on a nude beach somewhere, I hope. We'll never see her."

"I guess you're better off, then."

"Infinitely." He gestured around the store. "At least these light shows know they're fake. Therein lies their beauty. No truth but in lies, my friend."

It sounded like Bethany. "You remind me of someone I know."

"Don't sweat grad school, Jennifer. There are more honest ways to make a dishonest buck." He punched the last key with a flourish. "*Viridiana* is now officially available to rent."

"Money is just a placeholder anyway," I said, quoting Bethany.

"That's bullshit." He slapped the DVD case shut and looked at me. "Everything's about money, Jennifer. Except sex, which is also usually about money. Those are the rules of the game." He dropped *La Règle du jeu* into a bin and pushed *Viridiana* across the counter at me.

"I said I've seen it."

"Watch it again. You'll get more out of it this time."

I started to reach for it, but he jabbed his finger at the list of rental policies on the counter. I dug out my driver's license and credit card and handed them over.

While he entered my information into the computer, I said, "Ever see Trace around?"

"That trench-coat avenger? You think he's in here renting videos from his old dealer?"

"What about the Kevins?"

Quimby nodded wisely. "What about them, indeed."

It seemed best not to follow up. He printed out a receipt and laid it on top of the DVD. "Due back Wednesday."

"Thanks. I'll make sure this one gets back to you on time."

"I think you will, now that I have your credit card on file."

I flinched involuntarily thinking of the balance and turned to go.

"Mac."

I stopped. It was the first time he had ever called me by my name.

"If you're looking for work, I'm always hiring."

I looked around the empty store at the dusty shelves. I'd never seen a single customer in here. It occurred to me, not for the first time, that Quimby might have his own ways of making a dishonest buck.

"No, thanks." The bell jingled as I left. I wasn't that desperate.

There was something poetic about stepping out of Quimby's place, where I'd first watched *The Earrings of Madame de . . .* , and into a pawnshop to hock my cherished diamond earrings. But the pawnbroker barely glanced at them.

"Moissanite," he said. "You didn't know? I'm not surprised. They're pretty good, better than zirconia." He pinched one between two fingers and squinted at it. "The settings are nice. I tell you what, I can give you fifty bucks for them."

I walked out, the earrings crushed deep in the pocket of my jeans.

"*Identity* theft?"

The Social Security customer service representative nodded, competent and expressionless. I had woken up late Monday morning and rushed to my appointment, and I was still waking up when the officer explained that there appeared to be assets in excess of $2 million in offshore accounts opened using Lily's Social Security number. The rep did not seem particularly fazed when I assured her that Lily lived at home, had never been to the Caymans, and did not hold assets in excess of two hundred dollars, much less two million. She merely opened one of her many file drawers and selected a packet from a hanging file.

"This is the form to report fraudulent activity on your account. Please allow up to eight weeks for processing. We also strongly urge you to report this matter to the police."

"So it wasn't her diagnosis? Or . . . anything else?" I hedged anxiously.

"No, ma'am. The problem with her eligibility was initially triggered by the account. This form will correct that mistake."

"And no one has stolen or misused her checks."

"So far, all that's been stolen is a number. It's even possible —not likely, mind you—that it could be a mistake. A data entry glitch somewhere."

"A mistake?" I repeated stupidly. It had to be. Who had $2 million and needed to steal a Social Security number to hide it?

"Watch out for any other fraudulent activity, of course, and report everything to the police."

"Will that help catch them?"

"Probably not." She sighed. "I'm going to level with you. It's extremely rare to catch an identity thief, especially one operating abroad. The solve rate is about one in seven hundred." She slid the papers across the desk to me. "Your best chance at fixing things is to file the paperwork, change all your passwords, and get on with your life."

I walked out in a state of shock. Somewhere, $2 million sat in an account with Lily's name on it. And I'd probably never know who put it there.

But I knew one thing. It sure as hell wasn't my mother.

Mom looked pleased when I came home and told her everything was straightened out, or would be soon. But when I added, tentatively, that I was probably going to be staying for a while to make sure they were okay, she just rolled her eyes and said, "Sure, Mac."

We avoided each other for the rest of the week. It was a quiet week, not without small pleasures. I watched horse TV with Lily during the days and whatever was playing at the local cineplex every night, sometimes strolling the Riverwalk afterward. When I got home, Mom would always be sitting at the kitchen table, no matter how late it was, drinking a glass of wine and smoking a cigarette. Sometimes she worked a crossword puzzle.

One night, after coming home from a particularly bad movie, I started to walk past her to my room. Then I felt the earring backs pricking at my thigh in the bottom of my pocket and turned around. She hadn't done anything wrong, after all. I was only avoiding her out of habit.

"Mom, why did Dad leave?"

She looked up and ashed her cigarette. "What kind of question is that?"

"I've just always wanted to know." After a moment's hesitation, I pulled out a chair and sat down, scooting the chair a little closer. "I remember you guys fighting a lot, and I guess I always wondered if you were fighting about Lily and me." My eyes darted to hers.

"It wasn't you girls," she said gruffly.

I sat with it for a second. "I still miss him, you know."

"That's impossible," she said, disgusted. "You don't know the first goddam thing about your father."

"Because you never talked about him!"

"What is there to say?"

"Anything. Anything at all." Mentally, I ran through the possible explanations I'd come up with over the years. "Did he hit you?"

"That would have been too much effort," she said wryly. "Some men can ruin your life without even trying."

"It's not only men."

I was thinking about Bethany, but my mom jerked her thumb toward her chest, spilling flecks of ash onto her shirt. "You may not like me, Mac, but I'm the one who stayed. That counts for something."

My temper flared. To sit there across from me, crowing about what a good mother she'd been, when I'd spent my childhood covering for her addiction and my adulthood waiting in terror for her next relapse—it was sick. I'd sat down intending to have an adult conversation with her, but when I opened my mouth, what came out was the sarcasm of a sullen teenager. "Yeah, thanks a lot."

Her hand darted out, quick, and my cheek stung.

"You damn well better thank me. It wasn't easy, raising you and Lily. If it was easy, *he* would have done it. He never worked an honest day in his life, just took and took, and then when there was nothing left, he took off. You're just like him. Coming home, cleaning the house, promising you'll stay. So noble. When really you can't wait to shake our dust off your shoes."

I stood up, trembling. It wasn't the slap. It was her words.

No drug could blunt that perfect aim. She was mean and nasty and never did anything right, but she wasn't wrong.

Wanting to hurt her back with something true, I took the earrings out of my pocket and set them on the table.

At the sight of the sparkling stones, her eyes went wide and glassed over with easy tears. "Where did you—? I thought I'd done something with them, during one of my—" Her head whipped back up, and she shot me an evil look. "You took them."

"They're fake," I said. "I guess you weren't worth the real thing."

It did seem to hurt her for a moment. But she was tougher than me. She laughed harshly. "I always wondered why he didn't bother taking them when he left." She picked up her wine and cigarette and walked out of the room. "Keep them. They're all yours."

Alone in my room, I pulled out my laptop.

I hadn't stalked Bethany online since Bird died. Now, as I reeled from the conversation with my mother, my fingers found her name on the keyboard and started typing them into the browser on autopilot, the way you reach for a comforting snack.

Then I thought of something Quimby had said and stopped myself.

Instead, I searched *Joyner Foundation* and *savings and loan*.

The first link that came up was a 2003 *New York Magazine* article titled "Will a New Foundation Save Joyner's Tarnished Legacy?" I'd spent enough time on the Joyner Foundation website to recognize philanthropist Robert Joyner's bland septuagenarian visage in the lead photo.

Quimby was right. It was the same Joyner. According to the

article, Joyner had been the primary investor in a hedge fund that collapsed in the '80s in the savings and loan scandal. Hedge funds, as the article explained, were considered peripheral to the central crisis at the time, but the main reason Joyner dodged the wave of indictments that took down Charles Keating and the like was that the hedge fund CEO, Peter Armstrong, had absconded, taking with him proof of Joyner's involvement in the scam. While Armstrong was eventually apprehended in the late '90s and sent to prison for securities fraud, Joyner walked away from multiple investor lawsuits with his billions intact. The article reported that Joyner was "ready to forget his unsavory past and start investing in the future."

After 2003 there wasn't much else on *Joyner Foundation* and *savings and loan*. The story had been briefly revived during the financial meltdown in 2008, Peter Armstrong's name showing up next to Bernie Madoff's in a few listicles about pyramid schemes, but by then Joyner's name had been dropped. A footnote to a footnote.

So. The Joyner Foundation was a wholesale attempt to clean up some rich louse's image—and what's more, it had worked. It wasn't exactly shocking. Weren't most charitable institutions high-minded tax shelters at best, cleansers for stained souls at worst? Universities, too, for that matter. I thought of the black-lunged immigrants who had toiled in Dwight Handler's coal mines to fund his university and the freedmen who had built it for rock-bottom wages only to be barred from entering its classrooms. All my life, since that stoned hallucination in Quimby's basement, I'd been trying to escape the gravitational pull of money. But the closer I got to transcendent beauty, the dingier and crueler it all looked. What a lesson to draw from *The Earrings of Madame de . . . ,* a film that was about love being bought and sold at every turn until it could no longer survive a single additional transaction. What if at the bottom of every story was a pile of cash, passing from hand to hand under circumstances as seedy as the ones in which Bethany handed me those folded twenties?

Bethany, again. No matter how I tried to get free of her, my thoughts drifted back at every turn.

And then suddenly, there she was.

The photo appeared in the middle of an article I had abandoned halfway through about the trial of Peter Armstrong, the hedge fund CEO. It was a picture from his '80s heyday: young, charismatic, wolfish, his arm thrown around a celebrity Democrat, the frame crowded with champagne-sloshing admirers. In the corner, just outside the circle of exuberant motion, nearly unrecognizable—no, fully unrecognizable, to anyone who hadn't spent as much time as I had studying her every feature —was a petite woman with a Princess Di haircut in a strappy black cocktail dress. Her heavily lined eyes stared dully at the camera over a champagne flute.

According to the caption, this was Elizabeth Armstrong, Peter's wife.

According to the nights I had spent in her arms, it was Bethany Ladd.

Elizabeth Armstrong. The name was a common one. Elizabeth Armstrongs were podiatrists, marathon runners, lawyers, mommy bloggers. Narrowing the search with Peter's name only turned up a few articles noting that she'd cooperated with prosecutors to bring him to justice when he finally turned up in Milwaukee. Nothing that I could find linked Bethany Ladd to Elizabeth Armstrong.

Nothing except the Joyner.

Bethany's ex-husband had gone to prison. Joyner, his business partner, hadn't. Suddenly, the fact that Bethany happened to get a job at Joyner's alma mater a few years before he established the most prestigious award in her field seemed more than coincidental.

It was nearly midnight, but my brain was buzzing so loudly I knew I couldn't sleep. I popped *Viridiana* into my laptop's disc drive and watched Buñuel's mocking portrait of the cruelty of human nature in its entirety. Quimby was right; I did get more out of it this time. When the credits rolled, I opened a new file and began to write. I wrote and wrote, long, tumbling sentences at first, commas and semicolons swarming like gnats on half-finished clauses. And then, after half an hour or so, whole sentences. Thoughts. *Ideas.*

I fell asleep thinking, *Bethany Ladd is a fake. Bethany Ladd is a fake. Bethany Ladd is a fake.*

I woke up late the next morning to the sound of my phone. Gwen was calling again. This time, I answered.

"Mac, thank god! I've been trying to reach you all week. Where've you been?"

I had decided last night to tell her what I'd found out about Bethany. No doubt Rocky was mixed up in whatever his wife was up to, and Gwen deserved to know. But now, with Gwen on the line, I found myself reluctant. The silence had grown so thick between us when it came to those two. She hadn't even told me about Rocky yet. I remembered Bethany saying at the dinner party that if Gwen didn't say anything, it was more than just a fling. If Rocky was implicated in something illegal, would Gwen take his side?

"I just went home for a visit," I said, stalling.

"Without telling anyone? Connor's been frantic. Me, too. Is there something wrong?"

How many times had she asked me that, and how many times had I blown her off? But then, I had always shielded Gwen from my problems. She knew about Lily, of course, and my mom's addiction issues, and that we didn't have much money. But she didn't know what those things meant, not really. And I didn't want her to. It was easy when we were communicating via emails and postcards—after all, we had only lived in the same town for a few years—to pretend that we occupied the same world. And getting into the Program together had seemed to confirm our essential sameness. I'd wanted it to make everything better. But what I had truly hoped for, when I envisioned us sipping coffee together and discussing art house films in some bohemian flat, wasn't that she'd care about my problems. It was that my problems would simply disappear, absorbed into the circle of grace and mercy that was Gwen's soft life. Maybe the distance I had felt in our friendship had been sheer disappointment. It hadn't worked.

I took a deep breath.

"Yes, there was something wrong. Maybe still is. Lily's Social Security benefits stopped for a while, and I've been sending all my money home, and finally I ran out of money and I had to go home to sort it out. I thought maybe my mom was using again and stealing her checks."

"Oh god, that's awful, Mac."

"Don't worry, she's not. At least, she definitely didn't steal the checks, and I think she's clean. But honestly with my mom, you never really know."

"You should have told me," Gwen chided.

"What would be the point? It's just my life. There's always

going to be some crisis or other back home. The fact is, I can't afford to spend six years in school. I need money—not just a loan, but a steady income—and I need it now." I tried to make the next line sound logical, normal. "I'm thinking of dropping out and getting a job."

She gasped. "Mac, you can't drop out. I can cover rent for a while if you need it."

"It's not just that."

"I can do more. You know I can afford to help. Just come back, we'll figure something out."

I blinked away tears. It was what I had always known would happen. "I—I can't accept your help, Gwen. You said you don't pity me, but you would eventually. I can't let you give me money out of pity."

"Then do it for me, damn it!" she said forcefully. "Mac, please don't leave. I really, really need you right now." She started crying, too. "Didn't it ever occur to you that I've been calling so much because *I'm* having a hard time?"

I was silent. Truthfully, it hadn't.

"I've been seeing . . . someone . . ."

This was it. I had been right to level with Gwen, because now she was going to tell me about Rocky at last, proving to me that he was only a passing phase. Once she'd gotten the secret off her chest, she would ask for help getting over him. And then I'd tell her that Bethany and Rocky were mixed up in something we didn't want any part of. Maybe I'd even tell her about my relationship with Bethany. Maybe.

Her words started tumbling out. "He's married. Don't say anything, I know. But it's been awful. You don't know what it's like: the guilt, the hiding. Sneaking around. Knowing we can never be together. And things are getting worse. There's something wrong with him, the past week. He drinks and drinks. I can't ever find him, he's not picking up his phone. And then you weren't either. So that's what's going on." She paused. "Do you hate me?"

I was speechless. She actually wasn't going to tell me it was Rocky.

But she kept going. "And now—oh, Mac, his wife knows. She offered something to me—something big—to give him up."

Bethany had offered Gwen the Joyner. That explained the letter, at least. I held my breath and then let it out very, very slowly. "Do you want to? Give him up?"

"I've missed you so much, Mac. Everything is so horrible here without you."

"Gwen, what do you want?"

She didn't answer.

"If what you want is to be with *this person,* then you need to tell him. He has to choose you."

Gwen breathed in deeply through her nostrils.

"You mean an ultimatum?"

"It's what I'd do," I said.

"I'll—I'll think about it," she said. "I'm going to see him tonight, late. But, Mac—can I see you first? Connor's wrecked. I know something happened with you two, but the memorial service for Bird is tonight and you have to come. People are coming from all over for it, someone's even flying in from LMU Munich."

"Munich?"

"One of Bird's colleagues from his Joyner years. They loved him there."

So it was Bird I had heard Bethany threatening on the phone that night. She had accused him of listening at doors in Munich. *You think your life is worthless now? I'll make sure of it.*

Bird had something on Bethany. Maybe he knew about Elizabeth Armstrong and her connection to Joyner. Whatever it was, she had threatened him if he didn't stay silent about it. And now he was dead.

I looked at the clock. "I'll come," I said. "But I'll probably be a little late."

I dropped *Viridiana* off on the way out of town. I was done watching movies about bad people.

It was time to become one.

CLAIRE

14

At 4 p.m., the sky over Dwight Handler University was already a bruised purple, pollution-stained at the hem. All the colors were wrong, the thick snowflakes showing up black against the lurid sky and then flashing yellow in the streetlights before coming to a rest on the quad in swells as pale as a fish's underbelly.

It felt like it would never be summer again.

The Aaron Handler Memorial Chapel had been on our campus tour. Just a few months ago, I'd stood on these stone steps with Gwen, gazing up at the stained-glass rose window and half listening as the tour guide informed us that Handler, a lifelong atheist, had commissioned this traditional chapel after the death of his infant son. In broad daylight, the chapel always made me feel a bit cynical. Now, hulking in the gloom amid the muted strains of its organ, it looked like the physical manifestation of Handler's fear of hell. I shuddered.

I leaned my weight gently against one of the heavy wooden doors and stepped in just as the organ let forth a burst of virtuosic arpeggios. Hovering behind a screen of open stonework in the narthex, I peered down the aisle to the altar, where a tripod flanked by flower arrangements held an enlarged photograph of a much younger and brighter-eyed Bird.

The chapel was packed. As Gwen had predicted, nearly everyone was there. I spotted Connor and Gwen in the back row, not far from where I hid, and quelled a swift pang of grief that I couldn't join them.

In a reversal of the job-talk seating arrangement, the first-years filled the back rows, while the front pews held all the professors. I tried to pick out the backs of the faculty I knew —it was important to make sure they were all here, for what I was planning. I made out Bethany's red hair, Margaret's earth tones, Grady, Dean Cadwallader, and a dozen more. The only conspicuous absence was Rocky. I noticed Gwen's head moving nervously back and forth, as if she, too, were looking for him.

The organ had stopped. As the echoes of the final sepulchral chord died on the air, Margaret ascended the platform, cleared her throat, and began.

"In the passing of Qassim ibn Burhan, known to his friends here as 'Bird,' the Program has suffered a terrible loss. Qassim was a gifted student, an illustrious teacher, a generous friend. In a moment I will invite those of you who wish to speak of him as a friend or colleague to step forward to the podium. First, however, a colleague of mine who knew Qassim and his work perhaps better than anyone: Bethany Ladd."

And, unbelievably, Margaret launched into Bethany's curriculum vitae, listing her professorial accomplishments as if she were introducing a guest speaker. "Without further ado—" she began, then caught herself, coughed, and descended wordlessly back to her seat.

When Bethany took her place at the podium, I instinctively stepped backward behind the screen, dragging my foot on the stone floor. Gwen's head whipped around, and I could see that her face was streaked with tears. She had obviously turned around hoping to see Rocky. I stayed stock-still behind the elaborate scrollwork and raised my finger to my lips, pointing at Connor and shaking my head. She gave a slow half-nod, as if too stupefied by grief to care, and turned back around.

Meanwhile, Bethany, her distant face like a coin sculpted in dead white ivory, had begun speaking. "I never clip my students' wings. I make a point of urging them to think past the very edges of their intellects, to push themselves to their limits and beyond, and to brook no opposition, not even from themselves. In that, it may be, I am mistaken." Her voice cracked and faltered. After a pause, she started again. "Qassim was working on a tremendously important piece of writing when he passed. To honor his memory, I plan to finish his work and publish it as the introduction to an anthology of new work by some of my most gifted students." Bethany put her hand to her chest, as if overcome by the power of this tribute. "There was no thinker at DHU more radically negative than Qassim. His work, though less precious than his life, may at least give us some recompense for its loss. *Unbecoming: Toward a Radical Theory of Negation,* coauthored by Qassim and myself, might help us make sense—or, rather, 'non-sense'—of this tragedy."

During Bethany's speech, the air in the chapel had thickened. A faint stirring of wordless but palpable interest seemed to rise and pool into a mild buzzing overhead, like flies in a light fixture, as students in the pews considered which of them might be included in the anthology. Even the smile on past Bird's face suddenly seemed to hint at tantalizing possibilities.

I slipped back out into the dark. I'd seen enough.

The department was unlocked but deserted, as I'd expected it to be. Even Lorraine was absent, setting up the room for the reception after the memorial service. Thankfully, someone had thought to schedule the reception in a different room from the one that had hosted the job talk where the news had first spread. I wondered if they'd gone so far as to change the catering order.

I didn't know what I was looking for in Bethany's office. Connor had only said that Bird urged him to look for some papers, not what they were or what they proved. Maybe there had been more information in the email Connor deleted, but I certainly couldn't ask him about it now.

The door to Bethany's office was unlocked. The tiny room where I had spent so many hours alone with her looked more ordinary without her in it, the objects perfectly normal. Inside the largest desk drawer, I found a broad, flat wooden box with a brass lock on one side and pulled it out with shaking hands, already looking around for something to pry it open with. But the lid swung open easily on its hinges.

Rows of little mesh pouches. Bethany's expensive tea.

My heart sank. The other drawers were equally disappointing. It was as if she kept nothing at work, nothing at all, that wasn't for display. I didn't have the password for her desktop computer, but I had a feeling she wouldn't keep anything important on the university server anyway.

But there was one person in the department who would. Someone who kept all her passwords in a folder on her secretary's desk. Margaret.

. . .

It can be useful having access to those files, Bethany had once said of Margaret. Useful and maddening. Margaret, it seemed, had never deleted or archived an email in her life. Clogged with administrative minutiae related to the chair's office, her in-box held some twenty thousand emails. The message from Bethany setting up my research assistant job a couple of weeks ago was already buried. A search for Bethany's name turned up fifty pages' worth of emails.

I skimmed through them at random, despairing. Despite the undercurrent of polite loathing, Bethany and Margaret were cordial enough in their correspondence about committee work and shared students. And anyway, Bethany would never say anything incriminating to Margaret.

Then I saw it.

> From: Bethany Ladd <bladd@mail.dhu.edu>
> Subject: Tess Filmore
> To: Margaret Moss-Jones
> <mmossjones@mail.dhu.edu>
> October 2, 2011 at 10:55 p.m.
>
>
> I returned Tess Filmore's admissions file to Lorraine today. Tess was supposed to be Rhonda Oakes's, right? We really need to stop allowing faculty involved in contract disputes to hand-pick incoming students. Don't want to rehash the Rhonda issue—you know I think she should have been promoted. But she shouldn't have been on admissions. Fair warning, if Tess ends up in

your class: based on our interactions, I doubt
she's interested in working with anyone here.
 —B

I went cold all over, then hot, reading the email. So, Tess
had been right. Bethany had poisoned the well with Margaret. I
heard myself insisting over lunch that Bethany wasn't the type
to hold a grudge against a first-year—as if that were the only
way a person like Bethany could harm a person like Tess. The
email had been dashed off in a hurry, with none of Bethany's
flourishes. She'd probably composed it soon after Tess's rejec-
tion, easing the sting by throwing the blame for it on Margaret.
Bethany seemed to consider herself an ally of Rhonda Oakes,
the professor Tess said had been "crazy-black-womaned" out of
DHU last year, but her feud with Margaret had probably played
a role in her take on "the Rhonda issue," too. Their academic
rivalry was a kind of sport, with points scored by passive-aggres-
sive emails and petty grievances. People like Tess and Rhonda
were collateral damage.

The fact that Bethany appeared to bear Tess no particular
ill will made it even worse. She probably hadn't even noticed
she was selling Tess out. I thought of the casual way she had
summed up Soo-jeong's departure: *International students never
last long.* The way she had used Connor, making him think he
had a shot at the Joyner, when in fact she just wanted his "positive energy" for her book. We were not people to them. We
were assets.

But it got worse.

As I dug further, I discovered that Margaret had been in
talks with the Dean about Tess all semester long. Soon after the

retreat, they were already bandying the idea of "gently encouraging her to seek another path." After she challenged a white student for using the N-word in Margaret's class, the infractions began to rack up. Margaret disapproved of Tess's "inappropriate" slang, "primitive" arguments, and "aggressive" facial expressions. It was all sickeningly racist. Between them, Margaret and the Dean had railroaded her out of the Program, barely even bothering to soften their ugly biases for each other's benefit.

I'd failed Tess. I hadn't believed her when it counted, hadn't defended her to Margaret, hadn't listened about Bethany. I'd delivered that letter instead of raising a stink. Wrapped up in my Bethany drama, I'd never gone to the Dean on her behalf. In a way, my silence made me just as bad as the rest of them.

I'd missed too many chances to help Tess. But at least I could still hurt the people who'd hurt her.

I made two hard copies of the Tess emails and put them in envelopes. I addressed one to Tess, the other to a reporter on the higher education beat at the *New York Times*. On my way out of the department, I metered them and dropped them in the outgoing mail.

I had spent more time than I intended to in the department and turned up nothing on Bird's conspiracy theory. The memorial service would be wrapping up in half an hour. Time was running out, and I had no leads. Should I go to Bethany's apartment next? What if Rocky was there? Where else could I go, if I didn't even know what I was looking for? Connor had been vague about the contents of Bird's email. A money-laundering operation, or was it real estate fraud?

Real estate fraud. The farmhouse.

Hadn't Rocky said something about Bethany getting the farmhouse cheap after a development deal fell through? There'd been plenty of dirty land deals in the savings and loan crisis. And the architects who'd designed the house were German. Maybe they were from Munich, and Bird had heard something during his Joyner years there.

I still had the key in my coat pocket. It would take me an hour to get there, but I had a head start on Bethany, who'd be sure to stay for the whole hourlong reception, fielding questions from students eager to get into the anthology. That gave me an hour to search the loft where Rocky had said Bethany did all her writing.

I assume that's what she uses it for, he'd said. Maybe for something else, too.

The snow slackened just as I reached the turnoff to the farm road.

The winding road to the farmhouse seemed much longer in the dark. Although the overgrown trees shielded it from the worst of the snow, the narrow ribbon of blacktop was nearly impossible to distinguish from the frozen mud on either side. I crept along until the trees receded and the blacktop became a gravel road that glowed faintly in the moonlight. Derelict structures, the remains of barns and grain towers that had been plundered to build the farmhouse, loomed like ghostly sentinels on either side of the road. Then the farmhouse itself rose over the top of a hill, illuminated by spotlights so that it seemed to float above the dark hillside. I parked and crunched up the gravel drive toward the metal slab door.

I pulled the antiquated key out of my pocket and then saw

that there was no visible lock. For a second I panicked. Why would Bethany give me a key that didn't work? Then a green light flashed in the door crack, and an answering light blinked in the seams of the leather key fob. I'd gotten it backward. The real key was electronic; the rusty piece of metal was only a key chain.

With a soft swish, the door swung gently inward on hidden hinges.

The room was a dark glass cave sliced through at odd angles by the outdoor spotlights, the refractions and doubled shadows leaving deep pockets of blackness in unexpected places. I couldn't see any light switches; they must be concealed or perhaps operated by remote control. As my eyes adjusted, I made out the edges of reflective surfaces in the kitchen: a glimmer along the corner of the deep tin sink basin, a puddle of shine in the unscarred center of the chopping block. It seemed like ages ago we had all bustled around the kitchen making a spaghetti dinner like old friends, steaming up the walls with hot food and laughter, certain we were on the right side of the glass.

The floating staircase was a stack of shadows. I climbed carefully, rising slowly past the deconstructed farm machines on the wall, fractured combines and plow parts jutting off the gray wood in the dark like the jaws of giant prehistoric fish.

The loft itself was smaller than I'd expected, a clean white cave with high clerestory windows and just enough room for a bed and an industrial metal desk. I could see what Rocky had meant about there being plenty of privacy up here. The sight lines were carefully managed, the wooden display wall extending up into a railed pony wall that hid the low-line bed from the fishbowl of the first floor. Here at last, tucked away, was something I recognized as a working office: a single-board bookshelf for the project of the moment, a printer, and a banker's lamp, which I switched on with relief.

The desk drawers held little but the draft pages of Bethany's new book. The briefest glance was enough to show me it would be as incomprehensible to me as the last.

I had an hour, but the clock was ticking. I looked around the tiny space. Where would Bethany keep her secrets? It had to be somewhere in the loft, the only sheltered spot inside a glass house. But there were no hiding places that I could see, no cabinets or furniture large enough to conceal a crawl space.

There was only the bed.

It seemed too easy, where a teenager would hide a diary. But then again, as Tess had once pointed out, Bethany's behavior sometimes verged on the adolescent. I dropped to my knees and looked under the bed. Sure enough, shoved into the corner was a fat brown accordion file wrapped with string.

I fished out the folder and started rifling through it. In one pocket I found two deeds to the farmhouse: a grant of sale to Robert Joyner from a holding company, dated 1989, and a quitclaim deed signing the title over to Bethany Ladd in 2001, the same year Bethany Ladd had been hired at his alma mater. The contracts from the Munich architecture firm were in the same pocket, and I had no doubt that if I investigated, I would find that they, too, were on Joyner's payroll. Joyner had paid off Bethany handsomely.

The reason why was in another of the pockets: a thick sheaf of faxes between Joyner and Peter Armstrong, curled with age and, judging from the fringe along one side, rescued from the shredder. Bethany had proof that Joyner knew about the rotten hedge fund.

No wonder she held so much "influence" with the Joyner Fellowship committee. It wasn't a thank-you for her ex-husband's loyalty. She had been blackmailing Joyner for years.

It fell into place. When Bethany had first arrived at DHU, Emerging Studies only existed as an interdisciplinary degree, not a full department. But within a few years of her arrival, the Joyner Foundation came into existence, offering a fellowship so extravagant for the humanities that the academic community sat up and took notice. The university had acquired its reputation in those early years, as rising superstar Bethany Ladd's students won the award year after year, forging connections between DHU and prominent European institutions that reinforced the department's cachet.

Bethany Ladd had done more than put the Program on the map. She had built it from the ground up, her very own house of cards. An intellectual pyramid scheme.

If only I could find something that linked Bethany directly to the foundation, not just to Joyner. I kept digging. But before I could get through it all, headlights slid along the wall. A quick glance confirmed that Bethany's car had pulled up outside.

Panicked, I looked at my phone. She must have left the reception early. I cursed myself for having stopped to look instead of just grabbing the documents. I emptied them into my bag and slid the empty folder back under the bed. Maybe I could still get out with them, if I could fool her into believing I was there for her. I shed my coat and sat on the bed, trying to look as if I'd been waiting, while the door opened below.

"Bethany?" I called into the darkness after a moment of silence. "Is that you?"

She appeared at the top of the stairs.

"Hello, Beauty Queen."

I made an effort to smile, painfully aware that Bethany had always been able to see right through me. "I used the key. I was going to surprise you."

"It's certainly a surprise," she said mildly.

"I—I wanted to apologize." I put on a serious expression. "I didn't mean to bail on you last Friday. I was just overwhelmed by the news about Bird and I needed some time to process." Was my voice shaking? I forced myself to stand up and close the distance between us by a few steps.

She regarded me coldly. "I saw you at the service earlier."

I stopped in my tracks.

"I was disappointed that you didn't come to the reception afterward," she went on. "That's why, when I got an alert that someone was in the farmhouse, I hurried up here. I was so hoping it would be you."

"Alert?"

She held up her phone. "My trusty security app."

Of course. The electronic key, the light system.

"This place is so isolated. I like to keep track of comings and goings. I would hate to come out here to write on some lonely night and surprise a thief."

My face went hot. She was not fooled for a second. "I was just about to message you to come join me," I said lamely.

"You were taking your sweet time about it."

I stammered. "I thought you might be mad after the other night. I—I was thinking of ways to make it up to you. I'll be your research assistant. Anything you need." I tried to add a note of flirtation, but the effect sounded desperate even to my ears.

"What's that sticking out of your bag?" She gestured to a

corner of paper and said in a mocking tone, "Don't tell me you brought your proposal to work on at last."

The mention of the Joyner, intended to humiliate me, gave me a backbone instead.

"As a matter of fact, I finished it. All I had to do was get away from you."

As if she hadn't even heard the second part, she dropped the smirk and said, with genuine excitement, "Mac, that's wonderful! Let's take a look."

She stretched out her hand, but I stepped in front of my bag.

"Why bother? You don't need to see it. I've seen your letter for Gwen. You pick who you want. 'The best fit.'" I laughed. "The Joyner isn't really the Joyner at all, is it? It's the Bethany Ladd. Or, to be more accurate, the *Elizabeth Armstrong.*"

The lines at the corners of her mouth deepened by perhaps a fraction of a millimeter. After a brief pause, she said, "Can you expand on that remark?"

"You would know more than I would about the details. All I know is you're blackmailing Joyner, and screwing the rest of us."

Her lips folded tight, she gave me a long look, as if she were reading me, gauging my readiness for something. Nothing I ever said or did seemed to surprise her. It enraged me.

"Don't you have anything to say?" I spat. "This game you've been playing—jerking me around, making a show of being scared you'd lose to Rocky, pitting me against Gwen and then turning around and handing the Joyner to her. What was it all for, Bethany? Does the power turn you on?"

She heaved a deep, weary sigh. "You really should have come to me with that letter, Mac. I could have given you the answers you're looking for."

"I don't want answers, Bethany. The only thing I want from you—the only thing I've *ever* wanted—is the Joyner."

"That's really all?" She looked a little sad.

"And if I don't get it, I'll go to the department, the press, and the police with what I know."

She walked past me and set her laptop bag on the desk as if it had suddenly become unbearably heavy. "Nice to see you back in the game, Mac."

I ignored her. "What I can't understand is, why the elaborate system? Why not just take the payoff for yourself?"

She shook her head. "Of course, you don't understand. You think everything is about money. There are other things."

"I've heard that one before," I said. "So, tell me what's so much more important to you than money. It's not justice, obviously, or else you'd have turned in the evidence against Joyner instead of keeping it for your own personal use."

"Is safety a good enough reason for you?" she snapped. "I did my part for justice, Mac. I helped the Feds put my ex-husband away. He was out in less than two years—pissed off, no doubt, at his bitch of an ex-wife. Can you blame me for holding back a little something for myself, to safeguard against catastrophe? What would *you* do to guarantee no one could take away the life you earned for yourself?"

"I—"

"You think you're not ruthless? You're just a *hard worker?*" She threw it in my face like an insult. "Wait until you've really achieved something. Wait until you have something to lose. Then you'll see how ruthless you can be."

"You don't know what I'll do. You don't know anything about me."

"I know everything about you."

"Just because you read one essay—"

"I *was* you, Mac!" she exploded. "You think I came from money? I was a high school dropout from the Florida Panhandle when I met Peter. I flunked the temp agency test three times before they sent me to answer phones at Peter's rinky-dink real estate office in Tampa. Nobody'd ever called me smart or pretty before Peter." She cast me a sharp look. "How old were you, Mac, when you first learned you weren't worthless? Who told you?"

I looked away. Of course, she knew it was Gwen.

"Peter was no mastermind. He was lousy at everything, even real estate." She laughed. "What he really excelled at was the good life. Looking like he had it, and making other people want it. I was part of that, his perfect wife. He taught me how to dress, what to order at dinner, and how to say as little as possible to cover up the fact that I was still a stupid hick underneath."

I'd never seen Bethany like this. When she had opened up to me the night at the hotel, she had seemed in control. Now the memory seemed to be fighting its way out of her.

"He met Joyner on the Florida links, and when we moved to New York, he started working Joyner's connections, passing himself off as a real estate genius at a time when everyone was investing in real estate. But in a Ponzi scheme, you have to keep roping in more and more marks, and that means more chances for something to go wrong. You have to woo new investors, keep the old ones from pulling out their money, and act like you haven't got a care in the world. Golf all day, dinners and openings and parties all night. His concentration started to slip. He left me at home a lot. I got my GED. One day I surprised him with the news that I was going to CUNY. I thought he'd be pleased, his hayseed wife going to finishing school at last. That was the day I learned what Peter really was."

Sucked into her story, I had sat down on the bed without realizing it. "What . . . he was?"

"Peter's a sociopath," she said matter-of-factly. "With everything else spinning out of control, my growing independence must have flipped some kind of switch for him." She shuddered. "I think things might have gone very badly indeed if the fund hadn't collapsed. He ran away. Thank god."

She leaned back on her desk, playing idly with the lamp switch.

"I had no money—all of his assets were frozen—but I was *good* at something. I enrolled in CUNY under my maiden name and a variant on my first name. After that, Columbia. I was finishing my doctorate when the Feds tracked Peter down." She flipped the lamp off, then on. "The minute I testified, I knew it was a mistake. A five-year sentence commuted to two, minus time served, was the sum total of his debt to society. With good behavior, he was in prison a grand total of eighteen months before popping out, good and mad." She paused, as if weighing whether to say the next thing. "I was starting my first academic job by then at Penn. The night I found out, I slept with Rocky for the first time."

"He was your student."

She hopped off the desk. "He was old enough to make his own decisions. And it wasn't all take. I helped him get a job so he wouldn't have to go back to Ukraine." She looked exhausted suddenly. "I earned my life, Mac. I went to Robert Joyner to secure it for myself, forever. I didn't do it to hurt anyone."

I snorted. "You think you haven't hurt people?"

"There are always winners and losers. If we didn't game the system, do you think people like you and me would ever win? Or would it all go to the Gwens of the world?"

It was a thought I'd had a million times. Why did Gwen deserve the Joyner instead of me? Because she was perfect? I'd be perfect too, with her money. What was money if not just another word for gaming the system? Maybe that was what Bethany had meant by calling it a placeholder. Power, privilege, luck, even brains — if you had enough of one, you could do without the rest. But money was the universal.

Bethany stepped forward, and I stepped instinctively back.

"I'll give you the Joyner, dear, if it'll make you happy. You don't have to threaten me. And anyway" — she pointed to my bag — "you don't have enough in there to prove anything. Just a cozy relationship between the university and an alumnus-run nonprofit. Trust me, it's not the dirtiest money anyone's seen, not by a long shot. Everyone prefers not to look too closely into these things."

"What about Rocky?"

"Rocky was a mistake, made out of fear. I'm not scared anymore."

"Why not?"

"Because you came back." She put a hand on my cheek.

"I didn't come back for you." I tried to move away, but her eyes wouldn't let me.

"Even better." She pushed my hair back behind one ear, touching my earring. "We could be so good together, Mac — the academic power couple Rocky and I never were. All I was waiting for was that proposal. Now I know you're ready. You're right, I don't need to see it. I know it's brilliant." She leaned in and kissed me.

I could taste her breath, bitter and salty, like olives, and all I could feel was chosen. That vertigo. Her hands slid under my sweater, and I yanked at my jeans as we stumbled to the bed, Bethany pulling me closer, choosing me, devouring me. She made her way down my body, past my navel, to the darkest part of me, her tongue lapping like warm black waves until the abyss became unbearable and I came like one of those last-minute slips on the way to sleep, a deep underwater swallow. Then I pulled myself upright and pushed her down under me.

What felt like a long time later, we lay in our sweat, heads together and bodies splayed apart. One of my feet dangled over the side of the bed, and one of hers propped against the wall.

"My Beauty Queen." She sighed, and I could feel her head vibrate at the point where it touched mine, a single, hot point of contact the size of a dime.

"Why do you always call me that?"

Without looking, she reached a hand up and stroked my hair off my forehead dreamily. "Maybe I'm just jealous that you never had to feel ugly."

There was a pause while I processed this. Despite the swimminess of sex, my head felt clearer than it had for a long time.

"You changed Rocky's name, too, didn't you? It was the same as Peter's: Pyotr."

"A damn good reason, if you ask me."

"He said he got it playing soccer."

"Well, he could hardly say his adviser didn't like screaming out her ex-husband's name when they made love, could he?" She said it lightly but a bit testily.

"You named him Rocky, because you felt weak. Just like you

named me Beauty Queen, because you felt ugly." I felt curiously detached, as if I had solved a puzzle. "You have a pattern."

"So I do."

She didn't sound amused.

"And Bird."

She sat up abruptly. "What about him?"

"You named him that because you wanted to feel free." For the first time since I'd started the Program, I could see the outlines of things again, crisp and sharp. "Is that all it means, ethical negation? Taking what you need from people, so that they'll feel so empty inside, they'll always need you back?"

"Everyone feels empty inside, Mac. It doesn't make you special."

"It doesn't make me your plaything either." I stood up.

I knew I must be escaping her at last, because I could see the alarm on her face despite her efforts to compose it. "Besides, darling, *you* don't need me. It's what makes you different from Rocky or Bird or any of the others. When I push you out of the nest, you're going to soar."

"I think you just answered my question." I stood up and took a step away.

"Wait, Mac!" she said in a strangled voice. "There's something important I need to tell you."

Then the lights all came on at once.

"Hi, girls," said Rocky.

December 30, 2021, 2:59 a.m.
SkyLoft Hotel, Los Angeles

Stepping out onto the tar paper roof under the lidless night sky feels like slipping naked into dark, freezing water. A shock and a glory. I hear Gwen gasp softly behind me, and I know she feels it, too.

I notice a random brick lying nearby and use it to prop open the emergency exit door, the kind that locks when it swings shut. When I glance over at Gwen, I see her silhouetted against the stars, few and faint in the light pollution, but beautiful all the same.

Tears spring to my eyes in the stinging wind. It's not regret I feel, exactly. Because when I look back at all the things that led us to this moment, I can't honestly say that I'd do anything differently. At every step, I fought for what was mine. I'm still fighting for it now.

It's just that, in a way, every beautiful thing in my life—even this—is because of her. And somehow, despite everything, I know that's how she feels, too.

"What happened, Mac?" she says. "We used to be best friends."

"Yeah."

"Sometimes it felt like . . ."

"Like we were sisters?" It's the purest version of what I wanted, all those years ago.

"Like we were the same person."

She sounds so sad. I want to grab her hand and tell her it's okay. But it isn't. Because Gwen knows something about me that no one can know. She knows who I really am, and what I'm capable of. She knows about the cold, hard hollow at my center.

"But we weren't the same, were we?" I say. "It only felt like that because I wanted to be you."

"I wanted to be you, too." She turns toward me. "You had passion and ambition. You always knew exactly what you wanted. I envied that, I thrilled to it. You don't know what it's like, having too much."

"No, I don't," I say coldly.

"It can paralyze you," she says, ignoring my tone. "The things you need—every passing desire, however fleeting—it all materializes before you can really choose it. Things happen just because they can. You lose the habit of wanting things. It's like—" She gestures toward the starry void. "It's like you're floating in space. There's nothing to grab on to." Her voice becomes fervent. "Rocky was the first thing I'd wanted for so long."

"He wasn't worth it."

She grins ruefully. "Don't you think I know that? It's childish, but that's how I knew I wanted him for myself. Not for my parents, not for you—not even for Rocky. He didn't really approve of our relationship either. It made me less perfect." She pauses and presses her hands to her chest. "But I'm not perfect. I'm human."

I think of Mom and Lily, their needs pressing in on me so

tightly that I sometimes don't even feel fully human in their presence, more like some sentient vending machine. How hard I have fought to escape that feeling without abandoning them, as if there were really any difference. "Maybe you wanted to be me, Gwen, but you didn't want my life."

She bows her head. "I didn't want mine either."

"Fuck you," I say. "How *dare* you not want your life. I clawed and scratched my way to every one of those things that came so easily to you. How *dare* you act like they're not worth it."

"Are they, Mac?" She turns to me. "Are they worth everything you did to get them?"

We're coming closer to the end of this. A bottle of wine shattering on a cold stone floor, the glitter of Gwen's engagement ring in my pocket, the icy crust of the far-flung stars: they all merge in my peripheral vision, shrapnel from some distant explosion that happened in the past. The lights on a spinning carousel, a mirrored baton twirling in the sun.

"What do you mean?" I say softly. "'Everything I did'?"

But Gwen is looking down at her feet. "You've always made me feel so guilty about what I have," she says slowly. "I wonder, is that because it helps you justify the way you treat people? The way you use them?"

"What people?" I take a step closer, but she doesn't notice.

"Connor. Me." She looks up and lets out an ugly little laugh. "Look at us, all of us who were in the Program together. Who came out on top? That night at the farmhouse, I lost my career, my lover, and my best friend. All in one night. At the time, I couldn't make sense of it. But after tonight, I'm finally starting to see."

She wraps her sweater tightly around herself and starts to walk back. "Leave the ring at the front desk. Tell them I didn't answer the door. Tell them anything, I don't care. I don't ever want to see you again."

I can't let her leave.

I step in front of her, blocking her exit. "It's not over until you tell me what you're talking about."

"You know. You all but told me earlier tonight, in the bar." Her voice sounds weary, but a thread of rage trembles beneath.

"What? What did I say?" Panic makes me reckless.

"You really don't remember?"

I shook my head.

"You sobbed on my shoulder. Apologized, said everything was your fault. Wallowed in self-pity. Said you were scared you weren't capable of love. And I actually felt *sorry* for you." She laughed, but it was raw. "How could I be so blind, not to realize what it all meant."

"What?" She turns away, and I grab her shoulder. "Out with it. You've been hinting around at something all night. What are you accusing me of, Gwen?"

She looks at me as if I'm beneath contempt. The way I've always felt, but never had to see reflected in her eyes before. She spits out a single word. "Murder."

15

Well, well." Rocky held up a vodka bottle, sloshing it a little to show that it was half-empty. "If I'd known this was a party, I'd have brought enough to share."

I stumbled backward onto the bed and covered myself with the rumpled sheets, eyes darting instinctively to Bethany. Her face was a rigid mask of calm, but I could see her knuckles whiten for a moment as she gripped the back of the chair behind her. Then she sat down, crossed her legs, and threw one arm over the chairback. "Hello, darling."

"Working late, Beth?"

"I might ask the same of you. You're up past your bedtime, dear."

They had snapped into character immediately—her amused disdain, his buffoonery—but there was a crackle of danger in the air.

Rocky shrugged. "You said you were going back to the apartment. I was in the mood for privacy, so I thought I'd come out here and see what you find so appealing about this place." He looked at me. "Now, of course, I understand quite well."

"Of course, darling. It's your farmhouse too, and you can have your friends over any time you want," Bethany purred. "Are we expecting Gwen? I'll put on some tea." She started to rise.

"Sit down," he growled.

Bethany sank into her seat slowly, as if appeasing a snarling dog. "It is still Gwen, isn't it? You haven't moved on to the next one?"

"I think I'll ask the questions," Rocky said, resuming his pleasant affect. "Since I'm the one wearing the clothes."

He took a few steps toward me, and I flinched, instinctively clutching the sheet to my chest.

"Mac." He nodded a greeting. "Gwen always told me what a hard worker you were, but I had no idea . . . !"

"Is she really coming?" The thought that Gwen might walk in any minute was enough to break my silence.

"Any minute now."

I started to reach for my clothes on the floor, and then snatched my hand back at his glare.

"What's the rush? We're all friends here. Practically related, now that you've fucked my wife." I opened my mouth, but he waved a hand to cut me off, his face losing a little of its edge. "Don't worry about it. Trust me, I know how it is. First comes the flattery. 'You're a brilliant writer, Mac.' No, no, that's not it. Let me think." He gave me a calculating glance. "'You're so strong.'"

I flushed.

"Ah, bull's-eye! And then came the sex. Obviously." He eyed me, the hardened look descending again like a veil. "Next, she showed you the cracks in her armor. She hinted at a tragic secret in her past. An abusive ex, perhaps?" Rocky smiled bitterly. "Or was it me she warned you about? Did she tell you about my temper? My fits of jealousy? *This?*" He held the bottle at arm's length and sloshed it back and forth. "Perhaps she told you about the little things I did when I was a boy, for my uncle in Kiev. He was not a nice man and they were not nice things, not at all. But I assure you, I had to do them. You understand, don't you, Mac?"

For the first time I felt his full animal force, a coiled tension that could unleash itself in my direction at any moment. But even as he lurched toward me, looming over the bed, I sensed that it was all a performance for Bethany. He stared at me, but he was seeing her, threatening her, hating her. It made the situation feel more volatile, not less.

"Bethany is *fascinated* by violence," he went on. "The more I hated my brutish past, the more she loved it. Right, darling?"

He smashed the vodka bottle to the floor at his feet. I screamed in terror, but he only laughed.

"I wonder what it is that fascinates her about you, Mac?"

With an expression of sudden boredom, Bethany stood up. Without hurrying, she pulled a paisley silk robe from a hook on the wall, threw it on, belted it, and dipped into the pocket for a pack of cigarettes and a lighter. When the lit cigarette was crackling in her hand, she leaned against the desk and gestured toward me. "Be a gentleman, darling. Mac will catch a chill." She crossed her arms languidly in front of her chest and took a drag.

Rocky bowed mockingly to me and turned his back.

My hands shook as I wriggled into my clothes. When I stood up, relieved to be dressed again, the loft seemed to shrink around me. It was built for two, not three, and every nerve in my body screamed that we were too close. I had to get out of here before Gwen came. The thought of her tangled up in this sordid mess nauseated me.

Before I could make a move, Rocky blocked the stairs. Bethany touched his arm, and he angrily threw her off.

"Rocky, darling, be sensible. This is the first time I've crossed a line—since you, of course," she added affectionately, reaching out to caress his cheek. Rocky jerked away and she took a step back. "Besides, I've never given you a moment's trouble about your little infatuations."

"My 'little infatuations,' as you call them, are what I get for being such a good boy," Rocky said. "Always falling in line. Wasn't that the deal?"

"The deal is that you don't come after my students," she snapped. "And you certainly don't fall in love with them."

"Gwen was never your student," he said with scorn. "That makes you crazy, doesn't it? You're supposed to get the ones with promise, and I get the rest. You were always greedy, but losing Gwen has made you rapacious."

She rolled her eyes. "Go on, dear. I don't think Mac knows yet just how much you hate powerful women."

"And that has made you careless," he continued. "Or else you would never have made a mistake like *that*."

It took me a second to realize he was talking about me.

"What do you care? Aren't you going to ride off into the sunset with Gwen the Good?" She bit off the words slowly. "You ingrate. I've done everything for you."

"Oh, yes. You plucked me out of the waste bin and married me so I could stay in the country and fuck you. You even built me a fabulous career, the better to reflect your glory. Only I've been such a dreadful disappointment, haven't I? My god, I should have stood up to you years ago." His face twisted with a strained conviction. "Gwen believes I can be a good man. She loves the best in me, not the worst. And she'll succeed on her own. The Joyner belongs to her, and there's nothing you can do about it."

I had been listening with mounting disbelief, and now the words flew out of me. *"Rocky doesn't know?"*

They both turned to me.

"Mac!" Bethany cried sharply.

But I couldn't stop myself. A moment ago Rocky had jeered at me for falling for Bethany's bullshit, but I'd only been under her spell a few months. He had known her ten years. I started laughing helplessly. "I'm sorry. I was just so sure he was in on it. But he was your first mark, wasn't he? Not the Robert Joyner at all. The Elizabeth Armstrong."

He didn't even recognize the name. Poor Rocky. "What is this about, Bethany?"

"Mac, stop. You don't know what you're talking about." Bethany looked frightened.

Rocky's face went a dark, ugly red. He stepped toward me again, shaking, and said quietly, "Tell me, Mac. Tell me what I don't know."

"Haven't you ever wondered how Bethany got so big, so fast? She's blackmailing Joyner. She can give the fellowship to anyone she wants. The farmhouse, both of your jobs, and of course all her wins—it's graft. Don't feel bad." I was still hiccupping with laughter, but it was no longer a relief. I just couldn't stop. "She learned from the best. Her ex-husband was a con man."

Rocky turned slowly back to Bethany.

"She's lying, Rocky." She started talking quickly. "She wants to come between us. She hates you for not picking her. She's always been jealous of Gwen."

Something was unraveling in Rocky, and hearing Gwen's name snapped another thread. I couldn't bear the tension in the tiny, airless loft and felt overcome by the urge to smash it. "I bet she wouldn't tell you his name. He was too *dangerous,* right?"

"You know nothing, Mac," she whispered.

"Bethany's ex-husband was Joyner's old business partner, Peter Armstrong."

Bethany looked down.

Rocky stared at her, contempt plainly written on his face. "So you're a fraud. And I'm just another misfit toy for your collection."

Bethany cast him a scathing glance. "And what do your protégés all have in common, Rocky? They always drop out before I can get a good look at them."

"Better they get out early, before they turn into us," Rocky said bitterly.

She guffawed. "I couldn't care less whose career you ruin. I've never been one to interfere. But let's not pretend you're doing them any favors. You fuck them right out the door." She stubbed out her cigarette on the aluminum desk.

"At least mine tend to stay alive."

She flinched as if she'd been struck. When she looked back up at him, her face was blanched white with hate. "Gwen makes you feel like quite the man, doesn't she? Not like me. And she's clever enough to keep you feeling that way. You'll enter your distinguished phase the way real men are supposed to: with a full head of hair and a beautiful young wife devoted to your career. Does she want babies, Rocky? The way I never did?" She nodded shrewdly at his reaction. "Yes, I thought so. And she'll take a long leave of absence to look after them, won't she? Perhaps never to return. And everything will be right with the world at last."

Rocky stepped toward Bethany, his eyes alight with a dangerous glow.

But she kept talking, her chin jutting out defiantly. "Or maybe it won't. You're not strong, Rocky. You're weak, weak, weak." She shook her head, disgusted. I'd never seen her so angry. "When you don't have me to blame for your failures, how long will it be before you start taking it out on the nearest woman?"

"Gwen loves me. She doesn't believe I'm like that."

"You are like that. You're a wild dog. You should thank me for keeping you on a leash all these years."

He clenched his fist, and she sauntered up closer, so that he towered over her.

"Let's get one thing straight," she said. "You have benefited from our relationship every day of your career, every day of your miserable existence since I first called on you in that seminar where you were, let's face it, humiliating yourself."

I recognized her tone, her body language, from the job talk. She was moving in for the kill. She took a step forward so that she was looking almost straight up at him.

"With your Levi's and your Eastern Bloc haircut and your *eagerness,* and your face still frozen at the moment you became past saving."

"Bethany—" Now he was the one turning his face away.

"Rocky worked for his uncle's protection racket in post-Soviet Ukraine, Mac." She didn't take her eyes off him when she said my name. "He was seventeen when he saw his uncle kill someone for the first time. He never talks about why he decided to emigrate to the States—not while he's awake, anyway. But I have my theories."

"Shut up, Bethany."

"Gwen may think she picked you because she fell in love

with you. But she picked you because you're a coward. I think she needs someone to control as much as I do."

"Stop it, stop talking." He put his hands over his ears.

"Even if you push her out—and she won't fight you—you'll still be you, and it'll never be enough. She's perfect. And you're *nothing*."

Rocky hands went around her throat as mechanically as if he were not connected to them. He began to squeeze.

I had been frozen in place, but now I instinctively ran and grabbed Rocky's arm to pull him off. He didn't even seem to notice I was there. Bethany's face was turning red, her eyes watering. I looked around. A large piece of the broken vodka bottle lay near me on the floor. I picked it up and slashed wildly at his wrists and forearms.

He roared and whirled. A second before I felt it, my head snapped backward and I saw the blackout lightning of a punch to the nose. Then the pain exploded everywhere. When my vision cleared, I was on the floor, my face in vodka fumes, the smell of impact in my crushed nose. Bethany was gasping and coughing at the base of the wall, one hand around her neck, the other clutching the balcony railing.

Rocky faced me, blood dripping from his clenched fists, shoulders hunched like a boxer as he advanced, panting. His face was unlike anything I'd ever seen. Shattered into a million pieces, rearranged into an animal snarl. He looked at me like I was an object he was going to smash. I put my hands over my head. He raised his fists.

Then a flash of light swept through the plate glass, and all three of us froze. Outside, a car door opened and shut, and the car drove off. The moment that followed felt so slow, so almost languid, that I had time to think about how much the cab must have cost.

"Gwen?" The wild animal was gone from Rocky's face, and he looked lost. He loosened his fists and stared down at his blood-dripping hands as if they belonged to someone else. Then he stepped toward the balcony. With a pathetically boyish gesture, he ran a hand through his hair, leaving a bloody streak. As the massive steel door beeped green, he leaned out over the railing and opened his mouth to call her name out loud and, I thought, ask for either forgiveness or help.

I never found out which, because while Rocky stood frozen at the balcony, I rose to my feet and hurled the entire weight of my body at his back.

He went further than I'd expected; the blow took him by surprise, and his reflexes were dulled from drinking half a bottle of vodka. The other half of the bottle was lying on the floor, and we both slipped in it at the same time, me reeling back onto the floor from the impact and him flopping forward onto the railing. One of his feet flew up off the floor, and I quickly slid myself under his legs on my hands and knees in the puddle of vodka that, for reasons unclear to me, was starting to turn pink. Then I saw the broken glass everywhere and my hands started to sting.

Bethany had come back to life. She screamed Rocky's name, or tried to—it came out a hoarse, strangled yelp—and rushed over to throw her arms around him. When I delivered the final shove, bracing my hands against the wall and heaving his weight upward with my shoulders, I thought they might both go over the edge together, clutching and clawing at each other in midair. But Bethany, like me, was a survivor. As Rocky's center of balance tipped out over the edge for the last time, and the railing seemed to suddenly release him, she sensed it and let go.

The twenty-foot drop headfirst onto concrete might have killed him on its own, but as it happens, it was an antique plow-share that did the job. On the way down, grabbing for something to stop his fall, he knocked it loose from the wall, and they fell together. The rusty blade sank into his abdomen to the sound of explosively shattering glass.

Gwen had stopped on her way to the farmhouse for a bottle of champagne.

December 30, 2021, 3:07 a.m.
SkyLoft Hotel, Los Angeles

I t was an accident."

It comes out easily enough, a sentence I've repeated to myself many times over the years. But adrenaline strobes through me as the word *murder* hangs in the air between Gwen and me.

"That's what the coroner's inquest ruled. That's what I thought at the time. Now, I'm not so sure." Even angry, Gwen trembles a little at her own words.

"You didn't see the struggle."

"I saw something."

"Yes, Bethany at the railing, trying to pull him back." I have never lied about that, never even been tempted. But that doesn't mean I am unaware of how it looked from the doorway: Bethany leaning out over the balcony with her arms around Rocky's waist, letting him fall to his death, while I crouched behind the pony wall, invisible.

Gwen shakes her head. "No. Before that. Through the window, when I was walking up to the house, I saw Rocky standing at the balcony. Not struggling, not fighting. He looked like he was alone. Waiting for me. I even thought I saw him say my name."

I wait for her to go on, but she doesn't. "Well?"

"The door blocked my view for a second. And then I saw him fall."

She says it bravely. Well, she can afford to be brave.

"I can't imagine how awful that must have been for you." I lace my sympathy with just a touch of pity, hinting that she can't possibly expect herself to remember all the details.

But she continues as if she hasn't heard me. "People don't just go flying over balconies when they're perfectly still. Someone was behind him. Someone pushed him. I always knew— someone pushed him."

"Gwen, I know you loved Rocky," I say in my most reasonable voice. "But you didn't see how drunk he was that night."

"Of course, I thought it was Bethany. It made sense for it to be Bethany. And with those marks on her throat—" She shudders. "I understood. I forgave. I didn't think she deserved to go to prison for defending her life. What I couldn't figure out was why you'd lie for her."

"Nobody lied for anybody," I say, more firmly this time. "Bethany asked for my help since Connor had quit. When Rocky showed up and saw Bethany, he went berserk. He was furious with her for approaching you, and they started fighting and—" I hold out my hands helplessly, as if I still can't understand the way things went after that. "Look, it's clear from what you've said tonight that you've held on to some romantic notions about Rocky, despite everything. Fine. I don't begrudge you that, even though he nearly killed Bethany right in front of me. You obviously need this last noble vision of him standing on the balcony, calling your name, to ease your guilt. But don't—"

"Guilt?" Her eyes go wide.

"In my room earlier, you said you thought it was all your fault."

"Because I shouldn't have gone to grad school," she said. "Not because of that night. God, Mac." She looks me in the eye. "You ask why I left. When those emails came out, I was a pariah. The Other Woman, the bunny boiler. Because that's the simplest story to understand, isn't it? A jealous wife kills her cheating husband over the mistress?"

"I never said those things."

"No. But you were careful not to rule it out, weren't you? What was it you said at the inquest? You were on the floor, you couldn't see what happened. All you could verify was that Rocky was the aggressor, that he was violent. The marks on Bethany's throat, Rocky's history, your eyewitness testimony matching hers—it all backed you up. But it didn't really rule out the seedier story, did it? Nothing provable, just a stink of something criminal about her. Sometimes a rumor is more powerful than the truth. I always wondered why you wanted to protect her from the law. Until tonight at the bar, when you told me what you were to each other."

So, that's it. The blood rushes to my face. Tiny stinging droplets of freezing rain start to fall.

"I thought your relationship with Bethany explained everything. She still had a hold over you, somehow. But since our conversation at the bar, I've gotten, shall we say, some conflicting information. And all night long, I've been trying to figure out what to believe. *Who* to believe." She shakes her head. "I really wanted it to be you, Mac."

The revelation that I told her about Bethany temporarily blurs out my ability to hear or think about the rest. The unfairness of it, that I could excise someone from my life so thoroughly, rout her so completely, *win,* as I did in the loft, and still be in her thrall. I know I should be focusing on what Gwen said about not believing me, but instead I hear myself making the feeblest of denials. "The thing with Bethany felt like a big deal at the time," I say. "But I've moved on."

"No, you haven't." She laughs incredulously. "You should see yourself, Mac. She messed with your head, and you're out there paying it forward every chance you get. All your conquests—Harvard—'Love's just not in the cards for me.' It's sad, really."

"Spare me your sympathy."

"I thought you were protecting her with the story you told the police, but it's the opposite. You're holding something over her, but you didn't want to use it. You wanted the power over her instead." She shakes her head. "But when you let someone define who you are, they have the power. Always. And you let her make you a murderer."

I stand silently. Yes. I am a murderer. Over the years I have justified it to myself as self-defense, and of course if I'd been accused that would have been my story. Rocky might even have killed me, if Gwen hadn't come in just when she did. But perfect Gwen had come at the perfect moment to save my life, and still I had killed him. He was a reprehensible man, possibly a killer, and certainly a violent abuser, in the moment at least. Although I believed Bethany when she testified, one eye painted red with broken capillaries, bruises efflorescent on her neck, that he had never harmed her before, it didn't exonerate him. On top of that, he used his female students abominably, including Gwen, whom he had made into an ordinary, even boring cliché. That alone could have driven me to murder.

But in the moment, if I'm being honest, I had no feelings

at all. The same part of me that first took over when my mom left Lily and me to fend for ourselves took over in the loft that night. It was as if my humanity disappeared, and I became pure unadulterated self-interest, a kind of hyperrational psychosis. Probably I became a murderer long ago, even though I didn't push Rocky until ten years later, when a cold, rational voice in my head said, *This is how you get rid of them both at once. Quickly, you only have a second.* I had audio of Bethany saying she wanted to kill Gwen and Rocky, Bethany advising me to "get rid of" anyone who knew too much about my past, Bethany threatening Bird. To be sure, there were things on those recordings I'd rather not make public. But I would survive them. Bethany, the voice told me, wouldn't.

I hedged my testimony at the inquest carefully, so that if I ever wanted to change or add to it later, claiming I had been intimidated into silence by Bethany, I couldn't be accused of having directly perjured myself. The recordings on their own would not be enough to convict her, probably, but with no other witnesses, and with a time-stamped journal I wrote alluding to how frightened I was of Bethany, they would make a difference. The beauty of not using them right away, in fact, was that it gave the rumor mill time to do its work for me, setting the stage for the later reveal, should I ever choose to push the button.

But all that has changed.

Because now I know there was another eyewitness.

Gwen has gone pale. "You did it for the Joyner, didn't you?" Furious, she laughs and cries at the same time. "You didn't have to kill Rocky for that. I was going to tell him I was dropping out. That was my 'ultimatum.' I wasn't forcing him to choose between me and her. I was choosing him over the Program." She makes a wild noise in her throat. "You killed him for nothing."

"Careful, Gwen," I say.

But she won't be silenced now. "Imagine killing someone not because you have to—not even because you want to—but just to get power over someone else." She curls her upper lip like she's smelling something disgusting. "It makes sense to me now, the new name. You wouldn't want to live with that person. Someone who did *that*."

What I had to do to win was strictly my business. But it is true that it has haunted me every day since. It's not remorse I feel, exactly. It's disappointment. That there's nothing on the other side of the very last door. No colors. No beauty. No transcendence. Just one generation teaching the next the brutal lessons of self-loathing until each, in their turn, becomes obsolete.

"I think I must have always known it, deep down," she says. "That night at the police station, you looked distraught. But also something else."

"Ruthless?" I say softly.

"Triumphant. Like you'd *won*." She shudders. "I wouldn't have you at my wedding even if you really were my best friend. Not even if you were my sister. It's true, I was in denial about Rocky—just like I've always been about you. But at least he was trying to be a better man."

It infuriates me. As if anyone knows more than I do about trying.

"Virtue is a luxury good," I snarl. "And if you can't admit that, you're in denial about yourself, just as much as you ever were about Rocky." I pull the ring out of my pocket and turn it in the light. "Real diamonds. You can afford to be pure, can't you? I went down on my back for Bethany because I couldn't afford not to. I worked for it, just like I've had to work for everything. But you're too good for sex—so you get love, the big prize. Well, I took it away once. I can take it away again."

"We're done here," she snaps. "Give me my ring."

As she reaches for the ring, her hand white against the night sky, I am reminded of the day we met in homeroom, when she stretched out her hand to grab *La Règle du jeu* out of my backpack. How easily she identified and claimed the very best thing that had come into my life.

"Fetch," I say.

The ring seems to fly out of my hand on its own. It arcs high over Gwen's head, and we both hear the tiny clink as it lands on the raised ledge, bounces, and rolls, coming to rest an inch away from the edge of the building.

Gwen lunges for it, and I lunge after her. Six feet from the edge, the spongy tiles give way to metal flashing, now slickened by the rain. I catch up to her and tackle, my knee slamming to the ground, ripping my leather pants. Her chin thuds on the metal. She elbows me in the stomach and scrambles to her feet, but I'm up in time to keep her hemmed close to the edge of the roof. I feint toward her, and she steps back instinctively, her ankles hitting the foot-high ridge that holds the gutter. Black buildings rear up behind her against the starry, smoggy sky.

Her voice shakes. "Are you going to push me, Mac? Like you pushed Rocky?"

Am I? It takes less than a nudge to send some people tumbling over the edge. Others, you can throw your whole weight against, and you're the one who winds up taking the fall. Which kind of person is Gwen? There's only one way to find out.

I take a step closer.

"Because before you do, you should know that Bethany sends her love."

I stop in my tracks.

Gwen laughs, her eyes still wide with fright, but now slightly manic, too. "Why did you think I came to this hotel? For Bethany, of course. I went from our drink at the bar straight to her room."

"You're lying." But in my mind's eye, I see the key card lying on the floor, right in the entryway. As if someone slid it under the door.

I feel dizzy. The world spins, flecks of freezing rain swirling in the void between us and the nearest rooftop. A gust of wind hits my back like a raging current, shoving me closer to the edge, and I can feel the whole building sway under my feet.

"Believe what you want, Mac. I don't care what you think of me anymore."

I raise a hand, but she grabs it and shoves me easily to one side, pushing past me so that I slip on the metal and fall to my knees, ripping the other pants leg. I get a glimpse over the edge, and my stomach lurches as the possibility enters my body that gravity will simply release its hold on me, the world will turn upside down, and I will float downward like the pinpricks of rain on the wind. I throw myself back away from the ledge and hug the rooftop, shaking.

Gwen stands over me, just out of reach.

"It's been so nice catching up," she says, as if we're still at the bar, air-kissing one last time before we part ways. "I'm going to my room for a long hot bath. Then I'll go straight to my private charter jet. I'll sleep on the plane — it's so comfortable, you really should try it sometime. I'll wake up in Rome, where I'll join my rich, handsome, talented fiancé as he does a job you never had the courage or the means to try. And after that I'll head to Tuscany for a gorgeous wedding, like something in a magazine, only better, because it's mine. And after that—well, who knows? I have the rest of my life to learn what I want. I don't have to explain myself—not to you, anyway. Because I'll never see you again." She leans down, puts her hands on her knees. "Tomorrow when you're grubbing around with your academic pals, and then boarding a flight back to your school in the sticks, and your knees hit the back of the seat and you pay extra for your luggage and then lug it out to the taxi stand because you can't afford a valet service—just think of the infinite beauty that infinite wealth can buy, and how easy and sweet my life will always be because of it."

"I don't care," I croak.

Ignoring me, she walks over to the ledge.

"You know, diamonds aren't really my thing." She looks me in the eye, lifts her foot, and gives the ring a nudge. I gasp a little as eight carats drop over the edge and vanish into the night.

"Andreas won't mind. We'll replace it with something more to my taste." She walks over to the propped-open door and yanks it open. "You want to be on top, *Claire*? Fine. Enjoy."

I cry out as she lets the door slam shut, locking me on the roof.

I lie in a heap on the roof tiles, my cheek pressing into the pebbled wet surface. My hand rests on something I thought was gravel, but which I now realize is a pile of broken glass. I'm lying in the remnants of someone's late-night conversation, some hotel worker or construction crew, or maybe a pair of lovers. Who knows why people go as far up as they can? My palm stings. I raise my hand and shake loose a couple of blood-grimed shards. I don't have the energy to sit up. Instead, I roll onto my back and look at the stars.

It's a funny thing about stars, how they seem to run away from you. There's always a thicker, brighter cluster in the far corner of the sky, but when you look directly, the stars there dwindle to insubstantial pinpricks.

Bethany sends her love.

I pull out the hotel room key and read the green Sharpie on the sleeve again:

PH-12.

The penthouse.

16

The scandal at Dwight Handler University was delightfully sordid stuff, fodder for moralizing op-eds and impolite jokes at dinner parties. Rocky's predatory philandering and Bethany's willingness to trade academic favors offended everyone and shocked no one. Everybody knew of similar rumors in their own departments. It was the indignity, more than the tragedy, that was unforgivable.

Gwen, being Gwen, told the police everything at once. After turning over her email account for evidence, she immediately disappeared to Cape Cod or St. Moritz or wherever people like her go to lick their wounds. That was just as well, because soon afterward the emails were leaked to a reporter, and for a time she was painted in a rather unflattering light by the press. Then Soo-jeong came forward, followed by three more former DHU students who had dropped out after a sexual relationship with Rocky, and the conversation changed. Rocky's family connection to a Ukrainian mob boss was mentioned in the stories, but only sparingly, to spice the lede. I suppose they couldn't find anything definitive. I myself occasionally wondered if he'd embellished his dark past to get women in the sack. But then I remembered the way his soul seemed to leave his body when his hands went around Bethany's neck.

Reporters quickly dug up Bethany's past marriage to Peter as well, but since she had cooperated with prosecutors, all that came of it was a general air of unsavoriness. More damaging were the whispers that she had killed Rocky over Gwen, which, despite my protestations, I confess I did not do much to dispel. Bethany had made a lot of enemies, not just in the Program but all over academia, and there were plenty of people ready to proclaim, after a few too many glasses of shiraz at dinner, that they "wouldn't put it past her." However, the official reason the university gave for terminating her contract was the quid pro quo she had offered Gwen. That sort of thing is taken very seriously in the academic world.

The IRS also took it seriously. Bethany's promise to Gwen and the provenance of her farmhouse triggered a self-dealing investigation into the Joyner Foundation, but thanks to Joyner's legion of lawyers, the foundation dealings were all found to be aboveboard, and Bethany's claims of influence looked like empty talk. Nevertheless, the committee announced with deep regret that, due to the distressing allegations of misconduct at DHU, including the resignations in disgrace of Margaret Moss-Jones and Dean Cadwallader, the fellowship would be discontinued after this year.

Tess settled her discrimination suit against DHU out of court, for an undisclosed sum that I hope and pray was astronomical. Grady Herschel took over as chair, to the tune of a great deal of closed-door murmurings about what a relief it was to have a man running the department again.

Not that there was much to run, anymore. In the wake of

the accident, the department hemorrhaged students. Gwen, Connor, Letty, Arjun, and Morgan all left. Tess and Soo-jeong were already gone. Three more left within a year. After that, Aggressively Bland Matt and I were the only ones left from our original cohort. The Program was a ghost town.

The very last Joyner Fellowship went to me on the strength of my *Viridiana* project. Thanks to Lorraine, Margaret's recommendation letter had already been drafted, signed, and sent; Grady, with his typical keen sense for the way the wind was blowing, wrote the second. Given the sudden demise of one of my professors and firing of the other, the committee waived the third recommendation requirement.

I did not list, under "additional materials," stolen faxes implicating the head of the foundation in a decades-old conspiracy to defraud investors. Nevertheless, I assume they helped in some way. Not that I made contact with Joyner personally—I never did meet him, and in fact he died a few years later—but anyone who knew about the papers could take an educated guess as to where they were now. Bethany clearly didn't have them, Gwen would have turned them over to the police, and Rocky was dead. I was the only other person in the loft that night.

The reasons I gave for my presence there were never challenged—certainly not by Bethany, who corroborated my story in a state of shock, knowing I could turn on her at any minute. Connor had quit his research assistantship in front of dozens of witnesses, and everyone knew I had been gunning for the job. Probably the only person who was surprised I took it was Connor, though he never spoke to me again, so I don't know for sure. Nobody seemed to find it at all out of the ordinary that Bethany would call me out to the isolated farmhouse after dark to help her go through her manuscript, or that she had received me in her bathrobe, or that she and Rocky would come to blows in front of a student. Everyone who'd worked with her knew what Bethany was like, and those who hadn't, had their own Bethanys and Rockys to deal with.

Bethany, it was rumored, took a job at a small liberal arts college in rural Florida, only to leave after a year for parts unknown. Perhaps she was ashamed of her fall from academic glory and had gone into hiding to plot her next step. Or else she had become a born-again Christian and gotten a job on an alligator farm. I didn't know and I didn't care. I kept my recordings, those reckless words from her office hours, in a safe deposit box, along with the evidence that she was blackmailing Joyner. Only an idiot keeps that sort of thing under the bed.

I was out from under Bethany's thumb for good. And with Gwen gone, there was nothing to impede my rise to the top.

From time to time, I missed them both.

I did my two years at Lyon, which was every bit as beautiful as promised, but I didn't see much of it. I was too busy writing. I finished the Program at breakneck speed, landed my current job, and revised my Joyner project into a well-received manuscript that achieved a minor crossover success. I was written up in the *London Review of Books*. The Very Important University came calling.

All good things. But nothing came close to the feeling of depositing that first Joyner check and registering Lily for twice-weekly therapy sessions at the Healing Power of Horses Ranch. Maybe nothing ever will. By living frugally, I managed to pay for weekly housecleaning for my mom and Lily, along with a meal delivery service and regular maintenance to the house. I still avoided visits home, and they halted altogether for the two

years I was in Lyon. But as long as the checks kept coming, my
mom never complained.

Besides, Lily and I video-chatted regularly now. The horses
relaxed her, and although she still avoided eye contact, she'd
grown much more talkative. She spent all her extra time volun-
teering at the ranch and wanted to get a real job working with
horses someday. I told her we couldn't afford to upset the Social Security situation again right now by giving her an income,
but once my situation stabilized a little more, we could think
about it.

About the Social Security fraud: we never learned who did it,
though the police investigator blamed the online horse forums
Lily had been active on for years. I had trouble believing Lily
would be so careless with her personal information online, but
it didn't matter in the long run because there were no further
problems with the account and no fraudulent charges to dis-
pute. Eventually my fear of phone calls from angry creditors
abated, the fraud report went through, and the Social Security
payments started up again.

As far as I ever found out, my mother had been clean the
whole time. We avoided each other when I was home, but she
did not harass me further about my snobby friends or my books,
and she never brought up my father again. She knew that whatever I had done in that mysterious Program, it had worked.

And it kept working for ten years.

December 29, 2021, 3:45 a.m.
SkyLoft Hotel, Los Angeles

I stand up.

It occurs to me, briefly, to get down the way the ring did, but curiosity gets the better of me before I can make any rash decisions. There's more than one way to get down from a rooftop. Gwen's not perfect, but she's not — well, me.

It doesn't take long to find the ladder that leads to the fire escape, but the descent is not a pleasant prospect. Even for a nearly hundred-year-old structure, the zigzag of steeply tilted ladders and minuscule landings seems precarious.

The first metal rung, slippery and freezing cold in the fine, driving rain, sends a blaze of pain through my cut palm. I squeeze harder and concentrate on moving one foot after the next. Foot, foot, hand, hand. I look at each limb before I move it, terrified I'm going to miss. That means looking down. The swimming pool is a tiny lit-up rectangle of turquoise surrounded by palm trees the size and shape of starfish. I make out the spikes of a black wrought-iron fence poking up from a bed of cacti a hundred feet below. At some point, dead vines scratch at my ankles, and I try to remember how far up the side of the building they grow. Five stories, maybe four.

Slowly but surely, Los Angeles rises to meet me. When I step off the ladder onto the ground, my legs are shaking.

I walk into the empty lobby and limp past the startled night concierge to the elevators, leaving puddles on the shiny black floor. There's never just a button for the real penthouse. You have to use a key. I slide mine into the slot next to PH-12, and the elevator ascends rapidly, releasing me into the hallway with a ding. I follow the scarlet strip of carpet to the door at the end of the hall. Unlocking it, I turn the door handle and push it open.

"Hello, Mac," says Bethany. "You look awful."

I step inside and let the heavy door close behind me.

"So do I, of course," she says as I continue to stand in the entry. "But it wouldn't be polite of you to say so."

Bethany sits on one of three sofas arranged around the square sides of a large glass coffee table with an orchid center-piece. She wears loose layers of mauve silk, a gypsyish scarf tied around her head, and plain black rubber-soled flats. She looks completely different than the Bethany I knew. She looks twenty years older instead of ten. She looks every bit as beautiful as when I saw her last.

"Bethany." In a dream, I walk to the closest sofa and sit across the glass table from her, noting with detachment that the orchids in her room are real. My eyes travel to a cane leaning against the sofa: industrial-strength aluminum with a four-point base and rubber feet.

She sees me looking. "Ugly, isn't it? I like it that way. You have no idea how long it took me to find one without a snazzy pattern or a red chrome finish." Peering down at the cane curiously, she rolls it back and forth a few times on its feet, making the dimples in the aluminum wink. "People are frightfully occluded about death, aren't they?"

"Not everybody with a cane is going to die," I say carefully.

"I beg to differ."

Let her chuckle at her grim joke. I don't need to hear the word *cancer*. With my family history, I can spot used Fentanyl patches in a trash can from twenty yards. I play up my impatience to hide the instinctive surge of fear and pity.

"You slid a key under my door, so I assume you have something to say to me."

She stands the cane upright and rests her hand on the crook, like a seated monarch with a scepter. "I'm so proud of you, Mac."

I roll my eyes. "Cut it, Bethany."

"Why should I? You've done so well for yourself. I've been watching your progress. Research I, tenure track. So young for a keynote. *Brava*."

"Thank you," I say stiffly.

"Up for tenure soon, aren't you? How's that second book coming along?"

"Fine, thanks."

"It's the important one, you know. Easy to make a splash your first time out, but people are watching now. You have to stick the landing."

"Thanks for your concern," I say drily. "I'm finding it much easier than the first."

"Good, good," she says approvingly, skipping over my implication. "I'm not surprised, after tonight. You were magnificent down there. Confident, authoritative. I found myself believing every word."

I stare in disbelief. "You were at my keynote?"

"Of course!" She smiles. "I wouldn't have missed it."

I rack my brain trying to re-create the scene, but the talk at the beginning of the night feels like it happened a million years ago: all that comes through is a packed ballroom, my nerves jangling, eyes darting from the paper in front of me to the hiring committee in the back row. I can't imagine having missed Bethany Ladd in the audience.

She raises an eyebrow. "It's no wonder you already have groupies."

Groupies. Harvard.

"We held the elevator door for you," I say.

"Your friend held the door," she says, in a tone of gleeful reproach. "You walked right past me."

It's true. That moment in the elevator, unlike the talk, is perfectly intact in my memory and as minutely detailed as a diorama: Harvard's finger on the hold button in my peripheral vision, Gwen sitting at the bar across the lobby, and between them, crossing the polished black floor toward me, a mother and son, two professors, and, yes, Bethany. Head-scarfed, with a cane.

A crystal-clear memory from well before the blackout. Yet the most important detail completely escaped me.

What else am I missing?

She watches me carefully. "Don't take it so hard. I'm an old woman now, with the gift of invisibility. It's wonderful how the moment you turn sixty you cease to exist." She hoists her cane. "Add the barest hint of mortality, and people will cross the street to avoid looking at you."

"I was distracted by—"

"Gwen, I know." She rearranges her dress over her knees.

"She didn't recognize me either. Too busy chatting up that Rocky type at the bar." She laughs mirthlessly. "Now men, they don't disappear with age. They become silver foxes. If they live."

I flinch, but she only heaves a sigh and goes on.

"She's an odd girl. Do you know she came all the way out here just to forgive me for killing my husband and apologize to me for screwing him? Or not screwing him. Which probably screwed him, and me, even worse." She laughs again, bitterly this time. "She went on and on about closing the chapter, learning to trust herself again, being worthy of her fiancé. Blah, blah, blah. Gwen stuff."

Being worthy. I can hear Gwen saying it, believing it, *needing* to believe it. So, that's why she kept taking off her ring—not to hide her upcoming marriage, but because it reminded her of the part she had played in destroying someone else's.

"You told Gwen I killed Rocky."

"Didn't you?"

I don't say anything, just look at her.

"Your silence speaks volumes, dear. Anyway, I only did it to wipe the noble expression off her face. How was I to know she'd believe me?" She snorts. "Maybe I was feeling the smallest bit peevish toward *Claire*, as you call yourself these days. What a pathetic farce. How cowardly you've become, Beauty Queen."

She's right. Standing here in my ripped, sodden clothes, I can admit to myself that Claire Woods is a fiction, a veneer of taste and privilege over a bottomless pit of yearning. Claire buys her scarves at museum shops and her tote bags at independent bookstores. She owns a co-op apartment with age-softened hardwood floors, the rough spots covered with Berber rugs, and nods sympathetically when her colleagues at the state school agonize over whether to hang on to their Manhattan studios while they're stuck in this backwater town. Claire knows how to spend money so that it shows, but it doesn't *show* that it shows, and what she can't afford, she politely appreciates in others.

But shake Claire, and you can hear Mac rattling around inside her like a dirty penny.

Bethany is still staring at me amusedly, waiting for me to recover. I think of what Gwen said on the roof. *She messed with your head.* "Don't call me that."

She pretends to be wounded. "Not even once, for old times' sake?"

"You were my mentor, my adviser." The betrayal feels fresh, after tonight. "You let me try so hard."

She grins wickedly. "Don't tell me you didn't like it."

Hot tears of humiliation burn my eyes. "Of course, I liked it. Do you understand what you were to us?" I see Harvard heading up a parade of students I've toyed with, psychologically if not always sexually. I see myself emailing them late at night to rave over their papers, initiating flirty exchanges, trying to get into their heads. I hear myself making vague promises of recommendations, jobs, fellowships, over drinks and dinner. Testing my power over them, running hot and cold. We're all so cozy with each other's insides, it's easy to get access to someone's dreams —both the ones that academia squashes and the ones that it deforms into grandiose delusions. And once you have access to someone's dreams, controlling them is easy. "Yes, I liked it. But you should have stopped it."

"Why?"

"Because you were in a position to hurt me more than I could hurt you."

Bethany bursts out laughing. "Do you really think so?" She holds up her cane and gives it a savage shake.

"You're not blaming me for that, are you?"

"You would be surprised just how much I can blame you for, Mac. You took away my job—which, by the way, came with health insurance—and ruined my reputation. But most of all, you took Rocky."

"He tried to kill you. You should thank me."

"It wasn't your choice!" Her eyes go harsh. "I don't expect you to understand this, but afterward, it all came back. The fear. The panic. I used to wish he would haunt me, just so I would be less alone. I woke up every night shivering, fear gnawing my guts. Who's to say my stomach cancer didn't start there?"

I feel myself shrinking under her stare, unable to look away.

After a long moment, she recedes with a chuckle. "Then again, it got my mother, too. It's probably genetic. Still, it would've been goddamn nice to have someone to tuck me in at night."

I stiffen. "I hope you're not here looking for volunteers."

With surprising fondness, she says, "No, dear. Of course, I'm happy to see you. You'll always be the one that got away." Then she shifts to a businesslike tone. "But it's Peter I came here to meet."

The name takes half a beat to register, it's so out of context. "Peter, your ex-husband?"

She just looks at me, waiting for me to figure something out. Evidently this whole conversation has been a distraction, and she has something else in store for me entirely, some revelation waiting in the wings. For the first time it occurs to me to wonder whether the real purpose of those incomprehensible lectures in her office was to spin me in circles, throw me off-balance, make me vulnerable.

It worked then. It's working now. *She learned from the best,* says a voice in my head. I should listen to it, not to Bethany. But I can't stop myself from asking all the wrong questions. "You're not scared of him anymore?"

"Maybe a little," she admits. "But not as much as I am of dying penniless and in pain. I came to ask him for money."

"I thought money was just a placeholder."

"It's a placeholder I fucking well need, thanks to you," she snaps. "I'm unemployable. I can't afford my insurance premiums, I can't afford my treatments. I'm running out of meds. With Joyner dead, Peter's the richest person I know. He has a couple million stashed away somewhere, payoffs from Joyner for not flipping on him. I threw myself on his mercy. Unpleasant as that was." She shrugs. "He wasn't pleased to see me. I'm afraid he took it as a nasty surprise."

"You did put him in a federal prison."

"Barely!" she scoffs. "People like that never experience real consequences for their behavior."

Neither do you, I think at her, with all the hate in my hateful little heart. Something is needling me again, a piece still missing. Everyone at the same hotel, Gwen here to see Bethany, Bethany here to see Peter. It reminds me of our grim little quartet in the Program—Rocky and Gwen and Bethany and me. But Rocky's gone now. Who's the missing piece?

"But if it was a surprise, that means he was here to see someone else," I say slowly. "Who was Peter here to see?"

"Haven't you guessed?"

I see another snapshot from the hotel lobby, before the blackout. Gwen's admirer, or so I thought. The silver fox.

"You always were a little slow."

I was, wasn't I? Always catching up with the car that drove away when I was a child. *You don't know the first goddam thing about your father.* The missing piece, cut out of family pictures, erased from our lives, leaving nothing real behind—not the earrings, not even his name. My memories of him, all from under the age of eight, and all wrong, so wrong that I've stared straight at actual photographs without recognizing him. Just like in grad school, I've been looking in the wrong place my whole life, missing the big argument, hung up on irrelevant details.

"No."

She nods.

"It's not true."

"It is true."

I put my face in my hands.

"Peter Armstrong is your father."

After he left, my mother never spoke of him again. I remembered him the way I wanted to: calling me princess. Saying, *You don't belong here any more than I do. We were made for better things. Remember that.*

But if I was made for better things, why didn't he take me with him?

It's the right question at last. The tears well up out of the hollow place inside me, pour out of me.

Bethany sits there, watching in fascination. Savoring.

"How did you—?" No. Wrong question. I swallow hard. "*When* did you know?"

She flashes me a death's-head grin, and I know before she says it. I feel sick.

"'I was born Mackenzie Claire Woods in Wheatsville, Illinois,'" she quotes.

"My impersonal essay."

"Woods is a common enough name, it didn't ring any bells for me. But Wheatsville did. The suburb where Peter buried himself for nine years with his new wife after he fled New York, the perfect hiding place. The Peter I knew wouldn't have been caught dead there. Sometimes imagining him living the life of a midwestern schoolteacher, slogging away in a boring small town with a family to support, almost made up for the nothing prison sentence. You don't forget the little things that get you through the night. But to tell you the truth, I had never really thought about the family." She casts me a meaningful glance. "Just so you know, when he drove away that day, he only got as far as Milwaukee."

I wonder how she can keep looking at me when I'm not there anymore. Not a person. Nothing.

"Don't you want to know how I found him again?" she says brightly. "It's actually quite a funny story. I'm still on the Joyner Foundation mailing list. Apparently, no one ever gets around to scrubbing the database of blackmailers and suspected murderers. Every once in a while, a holiday card or an annual appeal finds me. So, a few years after Joyner died, I'm tossing out one of their newsletters and I see Peter on the arm of Robert Joyner's widow, Ina, at a fundraiser. Isn't that a scream? In the *newsletter,* Mac."

I can't even focus on what she's crowing about. One thought eclipses everything. "You knew—when we—" I break off, disgusted. "And you didn't tell me."

"What was there to say? I knew your father a long time ago, before you were even born. We're not related, Mac. I'm not your wicked stepmother." She cackles. "Don't make such a big deal out of it."

"Don't make such a—" It's no use. I look at Bethany and see, for the first time, how little she believes in anyone's humanity besides her own. *Peter Armstrong is a sociopath,* she once told me, but who is she? Even now, dying of cancer, she cares nothing about the fact that she stole ten years of my life, kept from me a secret about myself that might have made me feel closer to whole. And then, when I was on the cusp of feeling good enough at last, she threw it in my face, just to watch me crumble.

"I wish you hadn't told me. I would have been happier not knowing."

"Happiness isn't the point of ethical negation," she says smugly. "Anyway, I thought you'd be pleased. He saw your keynote. He's been following your career from afar, as have I. He seems to read the fellowship alumni bulletin as avidly as I do." She smiles beneficently. "He's proud of you, Mac."

In a sense, it's what I've been waiting to hear my entire life. That my father still loves to see me win.

A sickening feeling scrapes the bottom of my stomach: hope.

"If he came here to see me, then—?"

"He came here to *watch* you," she says regretfully, like she's declining a dinner date on his behalf. "He's already gone."

And just like that, I'm left all over again. I go dumb with grief.

Bethany straightens. "Well, now that we're all caught up, let's talk business."

I'm almost relieved. I've been waiting for this moment since I walked in the door. "You're blackmailing me over Rocky's murder." She waits a beat, and I look around. "And you're recording this, aren't you?"

"I learned from the best," she says with a grin. "Now, don't think I want to put you under undue financial strain, dear. I know what an assistant professor makes, and I think we can do better. So, here's what I propose. You're going to find an excuse to go to Venice, where your father is holing up with Ina in her pied-à-terre, engineer a tearful father-daughter reunion, and then milk as much money as you can out of that offshore savings account. The whole two million, if possible. Don't worry about how. We'll be in constant contact. I will direct you. And I'll even give you a cut. I'm not a monster." She chuckles, pleased with herself. "You should have seen the look on your face just now when you realized I was going to blackmail you for the same crime you've been blackmailing *me* for, all these years."

My head is meant to be spinning again, but it's already been spun too many times tonight. Now that we're finally talking about money, the ground feels firm beneath my feet. I've always been good with money. And this money sounds familiar.

Offshore savings account. Two million dollars.

The laugh catches in Bethany's throat, and she starts coughing and can't stop. Her face goes red, and each percussive bark grows louder and more rasping until she doubles over, clutching at her stomach and leaning heavily on her cane.

Gradually, I allow my expression to register concern, then alarm. "Can I get you some water?" Not waiting for her to reply, I take an empty glass on the nightstand to the sink in the kitchenette and refill it. I hold the glass while she takes a small grateful sip, her face still contorted with pain.

I point to a pill bottle I brought in from the kitchen with me and loosen the cap. "Is this right? How many?"

She eyes the bottle, apprehensive even in her anguish. She clearly doesn't trust me, and I don't blame her. I open the safety cap for her and hand the bottle over, so she can see for herself that they're her pills and administer the correct dosage. Her hand trembles badly, and the pills spill everywhere, but she manages to pinch her fingers around two of them and get them up to her mouth. After she swallows, she folds her lips together and mashes her teeth down, sending explosive breaths through her flaring nostrils. I help her drink more water, and some of it dribbles out of her nose. I lean over to dab at the spill on the carpet and pick up the dropped pills. When I come up, she gestures weakly toward the kitchen.

"Tea," she wheezes softly, pointing.

"Of course." Despite myself, my heart contracts. She would never travel anywhere without her special tea. "Can I help you lie down first?"

She nods, completely changed. Her face is flushed, the eyes rheumy behind thick, weary eyelids. Giant blue veins stand out on her temples and forehead, and her head scarf has slipped, revealing her bald skull. She looks fifty years older, a hundred. She looks like a death's head. She looks beautiful, still.

I bend my arm supportively around her back and half lift her by the armpits, feeling her leaf-light body under all those layers. We hobble over to the king-size bed. Then I cup her body gently in my arms and arrange the pillows in an arc around her back. Once in position, she closes her eyes with a sigh.

Satisfied that she's comfortable, I go to the kitchen and find the wooden tea chest in a drawer. I pick up one of the little pouches and tear open the cellophane wrapping. It is really excellent tea. Close up, I am filled with admiration for the clever little drawstring bag, the tiny shriveled blossoms and twigs.

By the time I come back with it a few minutes later, Bethany is barely awake, her breath whistling softly through cracked lips. I stand beside her, hesitant.

"Bethany."

"Hmmm."

I swirl the spoon in the steaming tea, agitating the honey at the bottom of the mug and absentmindedly compressing the tea bag against the side to hurry the steeping.

"Why did you write that letter for Gwen?"

"Hmmm, Mac. Are you still thinking about that?"

"Yes, Bethany." I keep stirring the tea. "I am."

She looks like a puppet, strings cut, lying motionless in a heap. I hand her the mug, and she begins slurping at the rim.

"Careful, it's hot."

She takes a slower sip, sighs. Her eyelids flutter, her speech slurs. "You think I sold you out for Rocky."

"Didn't you?"

She drains the rest of the mug, and I take it before she drops it on the bedspread.

"You have to know everything, don't you?" She smiles at me weakly, her eyes already starting to fade. "You think everything's going to be better if you just know a little bit more. But it won't. It really won't."

"Tell me."

She lifts herself as high up on her elbows as she can and leans over to whisper in my ear. "You didn't need the Joyner, Mac. Gwen . . . was perfect. But you . . ."

She opens her mouth to say more, but falls back to the pillow with a grunt. I don't need to hear what she thinks of me. She's told me before. But I lean as close as I can anyway. Her breathing is already so weak I can barely feel her words, much less hear them.

". . . you were magnificent."

She falls asleep. Soon she will be unwakeable.

It's time for me to go.

I place Bethany's room key in its sleeve next to the empty

mug on the nightstand and arrange her arms on the bed-spread.

Then I reach under the bed for the laptop I saw when I bent down to pocket the pills after Bethany spilled them. The dictation app is open, the bar undulating with every rustle. I close the app and delete the file. Then I place the laptop on her bed next to her and carefully wipe it clean with the edge of the sheet. I pick up her hand and, using her finger, type a single word.

Goodbye.

The Fentanyl patches take some finding, but that just gives me a chance to scrub every surface I've touched in the past hour with a towel. In the bathroom, I find an unopened box of five patches. I peel them open and apply them, one by one, to her bare arms.

Probably no one will find her until tomorrow. Most of the broken pills in the drawstring tea bag will have dissolved among the chamomile blossoms, but the patches and the note will point police in the right direction. It won't be hard for anyone to believe a woman who once wrote that the only ethical way to live is not to live at all had negated herself at last.

I'll be on a plane to Italy by then. I have a wedding to attend, a father to hunt down, and $2 million to claim. It's Lily's money, really, since my father stole her identity to hide it, and I'll make sure she gets good use out of it. I'll buy land upstate and start a school for equine therapy where Lily can live and work — Mom, too, if she wants. I know of a wonderful property that should be coming up for sale soon. It's a working farm, with horses. All very American.

But right now, I have to get back to my room, shower, and change. I have a job interview in a few hours. I'm underpre-pared, but I think I'll do just fine.

Acknowledgments

Happy books are all alike, but every unhappy book is hard to finish in its own way. Thanks to all who believed I'd finish this one, starting with my amazing agent, Sharon Pelletier, whose vision, values, and intelligence make the industry, and thus the world around her, a better place. It's such a privilege to work with you, Sharon. Tremendous thanks to my editor, Jaime Levine, for lending this book her ferocious energy, empathy, and brainpower just when it needed it most, and for great conversations even before we worked together. (Is there a more auspicious way to meet one's future editor than at a bar in St. Petersburg, bonding over a shared love of Sara Gran?) To the brilliant Helen Atsma, whose enthusiastic support early on made this book possible, thank you for urging me to take the time I needed to get it right. Lauren Abramo at DG&B continues to work miracles with my foreign and audio rights, and Michelle Triant at HMH is a goddess among us. Erin DeWitt helped me untangle a thoroughly knotted timeline. The cicadas thank you.

Many thanks to the talented members of my writing group —Alissa Jones Zachary, Linden Kueck, Dan Solomon, Paul

Stinson, and Victoria Rossi—and to the wonderful Mary Helen Specht, who's always up for coffee and commiseration. Zack Budryk and Lubna Najar swooped in with character help at the eleventh hour. Thanks, too, to Laura Trice and Shirin Kaleel for life support via group texts about babies who somehow became toddlers while I wrote this book.

Long ago, I survived my own grad school journey with help from Art and Lyn Gentry, Alissa Zachary, Nina Cartier Bradley, Lubna Najar, Michelle Yacht, Jett McAlister, Margaret Wardlaw, and so many more that the full list is twice as long as this book. Special thanks to Debbie Nelson for asking me if I was depressed (I was!), and to everyone working on behalf of grad students and contingent faculty.

Last and best thanks to Curtis, whose formidable brain no less than his unflagging love and support makes everything feel possible. In writing and in life, you inspire me to do and be better.